THE FIND

THE FIND

Sheryl,
Enjoy the read!
Marilyn Jax
September 4,
2008

MARILYN JAX

Beaver's Pond Press, Inc.
Edina, Minnesota

This book is a work of fiction. Names, characters, places, and incidents either are products of the author's imagination or are used fictitiously. Any resemblance to actual events or locales or persons, living or dead, is entirely coincidental.

ISBN 13: 978-1-59298-160-1

ISBN 10: 1-59298-160-7

Library of Congress Catalog Number: 2006935464

Book design and typesetting: Mori Studio, Inc.

Author photo: Patrick Broderick

Printed in the United States of America

First Printing: January 2007

11 10 09 08 07 5 4 3 2 1

Beaver's Pond Press, Inc.

7104 Ohms Lane, Suite 216
Edina, MN 55439
(952) 829-8818
www.BeaversPondPress.com

To order, visit www.BookHouseFulfillment.com or call 1-800-901-3480. Reseller and special sales discounts available.

Dedicated to my father, my pillar of strength, my inspiration and role model of the highest ethics, morals, and integrity.

I miss you.

Acknowledgments

I would like to thank Daniel for his steadfast love and support throughout the writing of this novel, and my many friends and relatives for their constant encouragement.

I would also like to thank my editor, Catherine Friend, for her wise guidance and nudging.

Prologue

Thursday afternoon
Miami Shores, Florida

UNRELENTING MIAMI HEAT raged. Workers doused with sweat performed duties mechanically, counting the minutes until break time.

"Shut the backhoe down! Now! Stop the digging!"

The persistent clamor of the apparatus drowned out the pleas of the on-site consultant, so the equipment operator continued to lower the bucket into the ground and hoist up more backfill, oblivious to the urgent situation that had developed.

Sprinting to the opposite side of the hole, the consultant frantically waved his arms in the air, continuing to holler. "Shut it off! Shut it off!" His flailing arms finally caught the attention of the driver, who, within seconds, pulled the bucket from the ground and brought the machinery to a screeching halt.

"What the hell's going on?" the driver called out, hostility raging in his growling voice, nostrils flaring wildly. "I've got a job to finish *today*."

"We've got a problem," the consultant said. "A big problem. There will be no more digging here today." Looking into the hole, he grabbed his cell phone and rapidly punched in a number. "Miami-Dade Police Department. I've got an emergency."

The operator jumped from his cab and walked to the edge of the opening to peer in. That's when he saw it, and his eyes and mouth opened wide. With his left hand, he removed his hard hat and tossed it to the ground, as he dropped to one knee. To ward away evil and fear, with his right hand, he touched his forehead, his breastbone, his left shoulder, and then his right shoulder, eyes glued to the unearthing.

Like an invisible net, an eerie silence fell upon the assemblage as one by one the other workers made their way to the cavity and caught sight of *the find*.

1

Thursday afternoon
Cayman Islands, British West Indies

THE SHORT FLIGHT from Miami delivered Claire Caswell and Guy Lombard to the tropical island of Grand Cayman. Surrounded by the crystal turquoise waters of the Caribbean Sea, it beckoned when they needed a break from the hurly-burly activity of their perpetually scheduled lives. Stepping from the comfort of the plane's air-conditioned cabin, they walked into the sizzling and humid atmosphere of the British West Indies. A colorful, lively, three-piece reggae band played welcoming local music as they entered the immigration and customs building fifty feet from the aircraft, at once setting the mood for their vacation in paradise.

After months of tireless work with no time off, this getaway seemed especially well deserved and Claire had dreamed about it for weeks. Feeling grateful for the opportunity to jump off the merry-go-round and unwind in the secluded and peaceful setting of the tropics, she paused briefly to take it all in. A sense of extraordinary and undeniable happiness surrounded her at the thought of spending ten quality days alone with Guy on an island—totally removed in every way from the stresses of daily life.

However, she'd watched his face lately and just knew he planned to ask her to marry him on this trip. If he proposed marriage, he would ruin the time away, not to mention their perfectly fine relationship. After all, matrimony itself had emerged as the catalyst for several of her friends' break-ups and she did not want the same to happen to her. Please, she begged silently, don't ask me. Not yet.

Claire Caswell, a fraud investigator for the State of Florida, had earned the reputation of being exceedingly competent—tracking cases like a virtual bloodhound. After fifteen years on the job, her qualities and characteristics defined the quintessential successful investigator: patience, focus, discipline, curiosity, quick reasoning, tremendously uncommon common sense, intuition, ability to resolve complex issues without becoming fixated on irrelevant data, and a good listener with an open mind—hearing what people did *not* say as well as what they *did* say. She also kept a cool head, exercised appropriate judgment, was resourceful, possessed an inquiring mind, had an in-check ego, demonstrated an incredibly good memory, and displayed well-honed verbal, non-verbal, and written communication skills. To top it off, she had personal integrity and tact. Combined, these traits qualified her as an investigator par excellence.

Complex and multi-issue cases were routinely assigned to her for investigation, and on each and every file it seemed as if she used a magnifying glass to see clearly and examine thoroughly the small and fine aspects and details of each matter. Driven by her inner determination to resolve each complaint in a constructive manner, utilizing her well-balanced mode of operation—one she had developed over the years—she would first gather all relevant facts using a high degree of sensitivity and discretion; next, meticulously organize the data collected; and, finally, take the time required to analyze the information obtained, thoroughly and completely, before forming any conclusions.

Knowing full well *the devil is in the details*—that the individual facts painting the big picture could be the most problematic aspects of any probe—she prided herself on being detail-oriented, painstakingly documenting every component along the way in her methodical and conscientious investigations. In the end, her grammatically correct, accurate, and timely memoranda created a picture in words that could easily be understood by anyone reading them. For Claire Caswell, facts alone led to conclusions. She was a perfectionist, and a workaholic, helping to make the world a better place by righting wrongs and seeking justice.

Currently, she had several troubling files in her caseload relating to the government financial assistance program offering reimbursement to owners and operators—*responsible parties*—of underground and above-ground storage tanks where the release of a petroleum product had occurred. Qualifying costs included only those *reasonable* and *necessary* to protect public health, welfare and the environment. Clean-ups could be expensive propositions, and the program defrayed costs for those responsible parties, volunteers, and others who took the corrective action.

The *troubling* cases involved property owners, and sometimes the consultants or contractors hired to do the work, submitting fraudulent requests for reimbursement of work never completed, or out-and-out illegal padding of actual expenses incurred. These applications required utmost examination, the sites often remaining open for endless months, while the process of pulling old petroleum tanks from the ground and cleaning up the areas of pollution they caused—both in the ground and to near-by water sources—progressed. As leaks from petroleum storage tanks constitute one of the nation's leading causes of groundwater pollution, this was an important State-assisted program, but it was ripe with opportunities for fraudsters to take advantage, so Claire had to be ever vigilant. She needed this time out—more than ever.

The thought of being away from all of it for ten delectable days delighted her inner being. Lately, there had been an overwhelming number of characters to watch in the clean-up industry and the job drained her. Sometimes she yearned for an exciting new twist in her career path—work that would present her with fresh and out of the ordinary challenges.

Walking across the parking lot to Coconut Car Rentals, she and Guy Lombard signed for the Jeep Guy had reserved. They drove to a nearby store to pick up groceries, and in no time at all pulled into a parking spot adjacent to the condo Claire had booked on the island's west side—*Seven Mile Beach*—a modest and immaculately tidy one-bedroom unit located near the water. It was there that they would spend long and glorious days away from the pressures of the workday.

An arresting woman of thirty-six, Claire Olivia Caswell had a slender frame and a look of Nordic ancestry—having mainly Swedish roots, with a lesser and interesting mix of English, Scottish, Welch, Irish and French in her gene pool. Her captivating and sparkly green eyes radiated a unique combination of warmth and intensity, and her perfectly formed full lips, complimented by a particular shade of coral lipstick that had become her trademark, emphasized a smile that could brighten any day. An aquiline nose and pleasantly defined eyebrows added to her alluring face, and blunt cut strawberry-blond hair fell just below her jaw line—with bangs trimmed to perfection. Tastefully applied make-up completed her classic look, and a medley of animated facial expressions added to her buoyant personality.

She wore tailored and well-cut clothing—most days dressing in a black, brown, or navy suit, accented by an unadorned silk or cotton tee, and simple jewelry of solid character that included understated diamond stud earrings, a stainless-steel Cartier Tank Française watch, and a dazzling-with-luster princess-cut diamond band that Guy had given her on the fifth anniversary of their relationship.

The love of Claire's life, Gaston Jasper Lombard, hated his birth name. And because of that intense dislike, he used his given name only when signing legal documents or conducting official business. To his family and friends, he insisted on simply being called *Guy*.

As a lead Miami-Dade State Attorney in charge of the prosecution of major felony level cases throughout that County, including all of Miami and its suburbs, Guy Lombard had been at the job for nearly two decades. He, in essence, ran the show, assigning incoming files to various attorneys within his office and personally handling the most difficult ones. A seasoned pro and an ace prosecutor, with the decisive advantage of being highly intelligent and able to think on his feet even in the toughest of situations, defined him. Keenly aware of his own talents, everyone who worked with or against him in a court of law quickly recognized the unique genius of Mr. Lombard, as well. The reputation he built for himself, case by case throughout his note-worthy career, remained without blemish. In fact, he had never lost a case. He felt rage at injustice, and did his part to keep serious law-breakers behind bars.

Entering the rental condo, Claire heard the telephone ringing. She ran to answer it, but the dial tone sounded just as she picked up.

"I'm sure whoever it was will call back," she said. "That is, if it's important enough." She looked at Guy, gave a contented little smile, and threw her arms around him. "We're finally here," she said. "Ten wonderful days. And I have you all to myself. No cases to think about. No emergencies. No late night calls. Nothing to interrupt our blissful relaxation. It's strange, but I don't know if I even know how to relax anymore."

The following day, New Year's Eve, meant going out for a romantic dinner and who knew what that may possess Guy to do? She would have to steer the conversation in other directions—if it became too serious.

Guy pulled Claire close and kissed her. She meant everything to him and he could not imagine his life without her. "I think we'll fall into it without too much trouble. Like learning to ride a bike, you never forget how to relax." He kissed her again, this time with more pronounced passion. "I think we're going to have a killer time here."

"Let's hit all the tourist spots between doing absolutely positively nothing at all. For example, we could…." She stopped mid-sentence. Guy was looking at her and smiling strangely. That same smile. The one she'd been seeing lately. Something clearly occupied his thoughts, and she was so certain what it was.

Single-handedly, Guy had successfully prosecuted many of the murderers, rapists, child-molesters, pimps, and various other slippery varieties of con men acting within the County of Miami-Dade, and several of them had threatened to put him six-feet under upon their release from prison. But he never let the threats of bodily harm get to him. He had a job to do—to protect the unsuspecting public from disgusting predators operating in the Miami area—and he did it well, making it his focus at all times.

An elegant man of forty-six, he had a stocky build—a physique he kept nicely toned by working out an hour each morning, beginning at six a.m., four days a week or sometimes five, whichever his schedule would allow. The majority of his thick, once-black hair had turned an icy shade of white and he combed it straight back. Penetrating dark-brown eyes that took in everything, thin lips, and substantial black eyebrows gave him a most distinguished look. His olive skin tanned easily, and he preferred having the look of a Florida tan whenever possible.

Grabbing Guy by the hand, Claire led him to the back door and outside into the balmy, humid air. Kicking off their shoes they strolled down to the beach, in no hurry at all, feeling the sugar-fine white sand oozing up between their toes. They rolled up their jeans and together walked into the warm Caribbean Sea until it covered their ankles. Claire reached down, cupped her hands to fill them with the luxurious saltwater, and splashed it in Guy's direction. "Ah. This is heavenly," she said. "Let's go swimming."

"I thought you'd never ask." He looked at her intently, and smiled mysteriously, cocking his head to one side. "I love you, my angel."

What *was* he up to? "Love you, too." She turned and ran back to the condo, Guy following closely behind. Just as she stepped inside, she again heard the ringing telephone. Moving with a decisive and bounding stride, she raced across the room and grabbed it, but heard only the dial tone when she answered. "Somebody's trying to reach us, that's for sure. Not many people have our number here."

But Guy seemed wholly unconcerned. Thinking other thoughts, he grinned like a Cheshire cat. "Let's try out the bed before we go swimming."

"How about we go swimming *first*?" Her eyes were bright with merriment and she looked as alluring as the first time he had ever laid eyes on her. The adoration she felt for him could not be contained in her facial expression, and he marveled at the fact that she loved him. Often seeming childlike in her exuberance toward life, it was a quality Guy found irresistible, for she forced him to laugh often and not take things too seriously, bringing equilibrium to his life in a way no one had before. And that did not go unnoticed.

The thought of life without Guy disturbed her and she quickly dismissed that scenario from her mind. She pondered whether she'd lose him if she did not accept his proposal of marriage—should it come. After all, they had dated for seven years and most relationships either led to marriage or a break-up by then. And people were always asking when she planned to tie the knot—marriage somehow being the end-all cure-all for everything—and she wished they'd stop asking that question.

"Whatever you prefer, my princess," he said. "I am your willing slave of love."

Okay, that was it. He was acting way too mushy, and so out of character. She no longer doubted what he was up to. Rolling her eyes, she chuckled. Being the significant other of the prestigious, hard-core and somewhat pompous prosecutor, who loved her in the way that he did, was special and she felt blessed by the devoted relationship they shared. But the thought of marriage—that would be a profound and complicated step. Wouldn't it?

They quickly changed into swimming attire and went for a leisurely swim in what felt like bath water. Afterwards, they stretched out on cushy lounge chairs on the screened porch attached to the condo, lazing comfortably in the welcoming heat and humidity of the island's salt air. Heavy sleep fell upon them and before they knew it two hours passed. Awaking feeling groggy, they showered and changed into casual clothes before deciding to drive to a nearby restaurant for some local fare.

An overly dramatic youthful waiter, with a distinctively Scottish accent, heartily recommended the daily house special—*the catch of the day*—broiled grouper with vegetables and rice, and they followed his suggestion. Afterwards, under the light of the moon, they took a slow-paced walk around the grounds surrounding their rental unit. The island's still-warm air was infused with the sweet perfume of night-blooming jasmine, and the setting was fairy-tale perfect. Before long, feeling pleasantly content, they went to bed, not particularly interested in sleeping.

The following morning, Claire awoke with a start. Already past nine, Guy still slept soundly. She slipped out of bed, showered, and made her way to the living room, where she opened the buff-colored wooden blinds covering the oceanfront windows and peered outside for the length of time it took to assess the situation. Although the island's amazing weather—usually predictably sunny, clear and hot—could be counted on, this particular morning the skies held a heavy cloud cover, promising to burst forth any moment with a torrential downpour. When this kind of front hit the island, it could last for several days, or longer. Not a pretty picture, on vacation.

She gave a grimace of disappointment. Spending long hours inside the condo would never do. She'd have to start thinking about other creative ways to occupy their days, and fast. Too much time for Guy to think about their relationship could present a problem. It might encourage him to ask the dreaded question.

Today, New Year's Eve, Claire thought about the restaurateurs feverishly preparing for the expected crowds set to arrive that evening to bring in the New Year. Since most eating establishments had outdoor seating, rain would certainly create a difficult situation for the diners and servers alike, and put the kibosh on the elaborately planned fireworks displays—scheduled to go off precisely at midnight at several points around the island.

Chaise lounges dotted the beach in either direction, holding determined tanners, who, despite the weather, preferred being outdoors and near the water's edge to being inside their rental condominiums or hotel rooms. Tourists were spending good money to come to this resort spot—to enter into the mystical ambiance so exotically portrayed in the advertisements and on the travel agency brochures—and planned to enjoy the beaches one way or another, come rain or come shine.

Deciding to make the best of it, Claire returned to the bedroom and gently woke Guy from his sleep. Plying him with kisses, she quickly convinced him that exploring the south side of the island would be an interesting way to spend the day, since a good beach day it was not. Engaging tales of pirate treasures hidden throughout the Caribbean had always intrigued them both—tales that indicated incredible spoils had never been located, so, today, they'd be treasure-seekers.

While Guy showered, Claire threw together a picnic lunch. As she worked, images of wooden chests bulging with rare gold and silver coins, and priceless gemstones and jewelry, danced across her thoughts. Finding pirate plunder intrigued Claire more than she cared to admit.

The ringing telephone grabbed her from her daydream, and quickly returned her to reality. "Hello?" she said. "How are we enjoying our vacation? Well, it's really just beginning. I'm surprised to hear from you. Is everything okay?"

She listened intently as Gary LuVasse, her supervisor at work, informed her that a *situation* had developed on one of her files, and then made an unexpected demand.

2

COMFORTABLY SETTLED IN the passenger seat, Claire studied Guy as he drove the white Jeep along the coastline toward the island's south side. Driving on the left-hand side of the road took a bit of getting used to, but within a short time he had adjusted just fine and seemed to actually prefer driving in that manner.

Appearing to be of Italian or Greek ancestry, Guy's family had, in point of fact, come to the United States from Hungary, three generations earlier, at which time his great-grandfather had changed the family surname to Lombard—a name he had recalled from learning the history of early Hungary (*Lombards* being a ruling tribe in the land now known as Hungary—after the fall of Rome and subsequent to the rule of Attila the Hun).

Guy usually dressed in a single- or double-breasted dark suit, a crisp and heavily starched white cotton shirt, and a power tie—his commanding appearance and manner intimidating to say the least. It was a demeanor that worked well for him in legal settings. Today, however, dressed so casually in Bermuda shorts and a flowered print shirt, he looked regular, harmless, and even approachable.

Seeing the great and powerful attorney Gaston Lombard in typical tourist clothes amused Claire to no end. While the attire somehow didn't seem to fit the man, he certainly appeared to be enjoying wearing it, along with the drastic change in his daily routine, and that brought a smile to her face. Despite the weather, his mood seemed upbeat.

"What are you thinking about, my beauty?" he asked, shooting a pensive glance in her direction.

"Oh, nothing, really. Just how nice it is to be away. We really should do this more often." She turned the corners of her mouth upward and expressed sudden interest in the breathtaking flowers they were passing along the way. She'd decided not to tell Guy about the phone call from her supervisor. Not yet. She would wait until after New Year's Day. At least they'd have until then, and she didn't want to ruin it. On Sunday morning she'd fill him in on the bad news. After the startling call from LuVasse, she had called Cayman Airways immediately to change their return flight, but unfortunately, or fortunately, they could not fly out until Sunday afternoon. So the weekend belonged to them and no one could take that away.

"You seem a million miles away," Guy said. "What's going on inside that pretty head of yours?"

"What?"

"You seem wrapped up in your thoughts, honey. You'd tell me if something's bothering you, right?"

"Of course I would. I couldn't be happier being here on this beautiful island with you. Nothing could be better than this."

He smiled at her, but she had not convinced him.

Claire's eyes fell to the platinum Rolex watch sitting proudly on Guy's wrist. Since the time his father had presented him with the pleasing-to-the-eye timepiece, on the day he graduated from the University of Miami Law School, it had become an inseparable part of him. He felt strange if he was not wearing it, like something was missing. His father had set a wise example of living a principled life, and the watch was a constant and faithful reminder of Mitchell Lombard's never ending sagacity.

She couldn't get over how different Guy looked driving a Jeep, instead of his usual black, late-model BMW, and decided on the spot that she fancied the relaxed version of the prominent attorney—in unfussy clothes, driving a less distinguished vehicle—for a change.

Usually likable on a personal basis, Guy could easily become an insufferable pain-in-the-neck in the courtroom. His professional reputation preceded him, and opposing counsel almost never wanted to take him on—even the arrogant types with oversized egos. But those who did rise to the challenge, either reluctantly or with eagerness to go into the ring against the champion who had defeated all previous opponents, usually ended up exiting the courtroom deflated, feeling nauseous, and wanting to give up practicing law. Early in his career, Gaston Lombard had reached for the brass ring and grabbed it. And he had held on tightly throughout his distinguished *métier.* Being a superstar meant everything to him, and he was painfully aware of how quickly another lawyer could snatch the crown from his grasp if he as much as loosened his grip.

But with Claire he acted like a pussycat, most of the time. He loved this woman with his whole heart, and at times even resented the hold she had on him—how he lost his innate sense of self-protection whenever he was around her, becoming weak in the knees, uncannily agreeable, non-threatening, so profoundly tender. What was it about her that simply melted him? Deep and impassioned karmic love was the only plausible explanation that made any sense.

They'd met while working on a case her office had referred to his for criminal prosecution, and had started dating almost immediately. Their eyes had connected, and if there is such a thing as *love at first sight*, it had happened with them. A handsome and polished couple, they lived a love affair envied by all who knew them. After a year of dating, they'd moved into a three-bedroom condominium on the eighteenth floor of a high rise, located on the intra-coastal waterway in North Miami Beach, to share a home and their lives. So far everything seemed to be going well, and Claire did not want to upset the apple cart by doing something silly, like exchanging *I Do's*. Yet she fought the nagging voice within her saying marriage might not be such a terrible thing—especially with Guy Lombard.

Soaking up the splendor and energy encompassing them as they drove along the roadway that morning, Claire began to feel rejuvenated. Despite the overcast weather, the island package presented a wonderful retreat—a private place away from everything and everyone, except each other—a sanctuary, a calming secret garden, in essence, that seemed to re-vitalize their spirits and soothe their very souls. She breathed in the healing air deeply, and exhaled.

The majestic palm trees, verdant fichus hedges, bright fuchsia bougainvillea, vivid orange and pink flowering hibiscus, usually endless blue skies, glorious sunshine, and warm, humid tropical breezes, so typical of this island, together created an undeniably intoxicating amalgamation. Here, the rest of the world simply faded away. For Claire, the addictive ambiance of the surroundings allowed her to put the not-yet-revealed revelation awaiting her at work out of her mind, at least temporarily.

"I remember sitting in my college history class and learning about the valuable items found by the sailors coming from Spain, the *Old World*, to the newly-discovered lands of Mexico and the northern parts of South America, the *New World*," Guy said.

"They found the new lands rich beyond their imaginations in gold, silver, and gems. The sailors set up mints to turn the precious metals into coins, making them easier to load onto their sailing vessels, together with the other valuables they found, or took, however you want to look at it. They brought the treasures back on their ships to the King and Queen of Spain who had sponsored their journeys to the New World. They passed *these very waters* returning home."

Guy considered himself a history buff, and his vast knowledge of the past often showed. He could never seem to quench his thirst for knowledge of world history, and all accounts of the past fueled his insatiable curiosity, providing insightful mappings of human behavior he found beneficial in his profession.

"Some of the vessels ended up shipwrecked on the voyage home and the coins and other cargo fell to the bottom of these waters, together with the ships and sailors, sometimes all being lost forever," he said.

Reliving the pages of history as Guy prattled on, Claire's mind drifted in wonderment as she daydreamed of treasures remaining buried on the island or in the surrounding waters. "Hmm…," she said. "Interesting."

Manning the wheel, Guy hummed along to the reggae music emanating from the radio. Claire smiled to herself, thinking how much she was enjoying the day and their lives together. Guy reached over, grabbed her hand, and pulled it to his thigh. He liked driving that way. They continued along the road for close to an hour in comfortable silence, often passing quite primitive land, infrequently meeting a car traveling in the opposite direction. But it seemed no other cars were heading south that day.

"Look!" Claire said suddenly, pointing to a road sign. "*Iguana Crossing*."

"Wonder how big *those* things get?"

"They come in many sizes, some quite large."

Once they reached their destination, Guy found a suitable place to park along the roadside. He grabbed his backpack and the lunch Claire had prepared from the backseat, and off they went to spend the day exploring.

"Those clouds look menacing," Claire commented, looking upward. "Very dark. Hope we don't get caught in a bad rainstorm. They can be brutal here."

"Well, if we do, we'll count it part of our great adventure today, right?" Guy said, looking convinced that he'd take on whatever came their way that day.

After nearly two hours of hiking and exploring, it began to sprinkle. And before long, Claire and Guy found themselves in a veritable downpour, accompanied by mighty and driving winds. Desperate for shelter, their eyes searched the area as their legs sprinted so fast their feet barely touched the ground, looking anywhere and everywhere for something to shield them. They could find nothing. Drenched and half-blinded by the hard rain, Claire at last thought she spotted ahead what looked to be a large hole in the rocky hillside bordering the ever-increasingly choppy waters. She would easily have missed the gap but for the enormous gale-force winds blowing the thick foliage that covered the opening into a position almost horizontal to the ground. She motioned to Guy. Clutching each other's hand, they raced over the wet and jagged rocks, slipping occasionally but not falling, until, at last, they reached the aperture and stepped inside. Relief came instantaneously.

To their surprise, they found themselves in a rather large, cool, dry cave, offering the sanctuary they so desperately craved to escape the elements. Outside light provided minimal, but welcomed, illumination within the cavern. It felt good being out of the storm, but dripping wet clothing caused Claire to start shivering, uncontrollably.

Guy pulled a thin blanket from his backpack and wrapped it around her quivering frame. Relieved to find the blanket mostly dry, he held her close, sharing his perpetual warmth with the woman of his dreams. He placed a prolonged kiss on her forehead, and then moved down to her trembling lips, where it continued. The momentary passion helped erase the cold.

"Things *could* be worse," he said. Her look told him she wasn't buying it. "Well, we are getting the unplanned escapade we've always wanted. And we are out of the rain. You must admit those are good things."

"Right," she said, her voice lacking the same vigor. Claire hated being cold. Oh, how she abhorred it. Hard to warm up after getting so chilled, she found herself in a situation she did not like one bit. Daydreaming about submerging deeply into a warm bathtub—to raise her body temperature—became a pleasant thought that helped her dodge the moment.

Guy gave it his best try—desperate to make a miserable predicament more palatable. He held Claire in his arms for another twenty minutes, nuzzling her affectionately, kissing every inch of her face and neck and whispering sweet nothings into her ear to distract her from the reality of the situation, until warmth, at last, found its way back into her awaiting body and the shaking subsided.

Claire's eyes had now adjusted to the semi-darkness in which she found herself, and she decided to take a look around, reluctantly breaking away from the comforting arms of the man she adored. Taking a few steps farther into the cave, into the unknown, the stone floor appeared to drop off severely into the darkness. Approaching to take a closer look, the periphery gave way and she plummeted into the dim and murky obscurity. She screamed as she fell, and then silence filled the air.

3

Friday
Miami, Florida

A HANDFUL OF die-hard employees in Claire's office worked diligently, playing catch-up on a day without ringing telephones—the New Year's holiday. Whispering launched among them as one by one they became acutely aware of something big and secretive going on in the office of Gary LuVasse. While in the closed-door meeting with Miami-Dade Police Sergeant Jack Massey, news reporters and cameramen hunkered down in the lobby—waiting to interview the two men at a press conference scheduled to take place momentarily. Highly unusual any time, but especially on a holiday.

"Have you reached this Claire Caswell dame, yet?" Sergeant Massey asked.

"Yes, I've reached Ms. Caswell. She and Gaston Lombard will be returning on Sunday—back in the office bright and early Monday morning," LuVasse said. "I hated to call her back, but I had no choice. I want *her* on this case. There will be time for vacation later." He pulled a yellow legal pad closer to him, and reached for a pen. "Now, I want every detail, Sergeant. Leave nothing out."

"Okay. Okay. I'll tell you all I know. I received a call at the precinct, yesterday afternoon, from an environmental consultant out at a clean-up site in Miami Shores—the old, abandoned Whitney property on a dead-end road. According to the environmental consultant, they were conducting a tank pull when he noticed the equipment was unearthing something other than top fill, a few feet down. He called an abrupt halt to the digging, of course."

"That's one of Claire Caswell's sites. Go on."

"Well, the equipment operator jumped from his machine and peered into the hole. He saw it, too. Turned out to be human remains some five feet down—an unclothed skeleton. A partially unearthed mass of bones, appearing to be mostly intact; the apparent framework of a human being."

"Four words. I get the picture. Please continue."

"Apparently all the workers began to gather around the hole, and it started quite a commotion. The consultant sent them away until further notice, and agreed to stay at the scene to wait until I arrived with my team. Twenty minutes later, I had a crew out there. Me, three uniformed officers, two homicide detectives, a specialist crime scene investigator, and the Assistant Medical Examiner-Coroner. After a glimpse of the collection of bones, the men moved quickly, at my direction, treating the dig site as a potential crime scene."

"So you took control, Sergeant. Then what?"

"We secured the area, and took a number of photographs of the skeleton—both from an up-close position within the hole and from ground level looking downward. Then, with the help of two officers, wearing evidence-handling gloves, we freed the remains from the surrounding dirt and transferred the body of bones onto the Medical Examiner's stretcher, but only after applying painstaking care to first slide a straight wooden board under the conglomeration, making certain not to disturb any detail of it. We covered it with a sheet of heavy black canvas and loaded it into the Medical Examiner's panel truck. No decomposition odor was detected. Too far gone."

"Sounds like you did everything right."

"Hell, yeah. I told my men to remove the skeleton in one piece, and they did. If an officer fails to follow a directive from me to a tee, he will pay the price later. My men obey me, LuVasse." The Sergeant cracked his knuckles on both hands, as he had done nearly every three minutes throughout the interview. It annoyed LuVasse greatly.

"I'm sure they do, Sergeant. Never before has our Department had a situation like this on our hands, but we will handle it. Caswell is the best I've got and I plan to have her involved in every aspect of the investigation. If anyone can determine how the skeleton got there and give it an identity, she can. I'm assuming you'll involve the State Attorney's office immediately, as well."

"Slow down, LuVasse. Not so fast. First, we need to confirm that we even have a homicide on our hands. We can assume nothing, you know, until we have the facts."

"Of course. I realize that."

"And if, and I repeat, *if* foul play can be determined, then we will refer the matter to the State Attorney's Office for criminal investigation and prosecution."

Sergeant Massey's gruff manner was wearing thin on LuVasse. He eyed the man carefully, and noticed the Sergeant's beady and darting eyes did not appear to ever blink. The Sergeant, a tall, barrel-chested, humped over man, weighed over three hundred pounds. A bulbous nose took up most of his face. At first glance, he reminded LuVasse of an ogre right out of *Grimm's Fairy Tales.* Hardened by years of tough and thankless work on the streets of Miami, the Sergeant put up with flak from no one, least of all his underlings. The feral look in his slightly crossed eyes told people not to mess with his head—that he could be capable of just about anything—something his vulgar, crude, and usually offensive language seemed to bear out. Today, he controlled his tongue more than usual.

In his world, everything boiled down to a matter of black or white. No shades of gray existed. Those under his command followed his orders precisely, and flawlessly, or they could look for employment elsewhere. He reminded them of this fact often, and he meant it. There were no exceptions. Rules had to be followed to the letter. Period. One bark of an order, and it must be executed quickly, without questioning, and with absolute efficiency and no mistakes. In this business, mistakes were not allowed.

Due to a long history with the department and its intricate workings, politics and all, and because of his photographic memory, allowing him instant recall of the most salient details concerning past investigations, his superiors gave him broad latitude. Therefore, his inappropriate use of foul language and cantankerous manners were usually overlooked for the good of the Department. He was an asset the force could not afford to lose, as he alone knew the streets of Miami and its suburbs like the back of his hand, and this knowledge provided license for his crassness and crudity.

He silently believed a man should be doing the job of this Claire Caswell lady—that she had taken away an employment opportunity a man could have used to support his family. But he would not mention his view to LuVasse, as he did not seem like someone who would share his views. Admittedly old-fashioned, the Sergeant kept those feelings to himself most of the time, unless he was in all-male company at the biker establishment he frequented every Friday afternoon, after each long week on the job. After downing a few beers, he often became offensively verbal regarding his true feelings on equal rights and the feminists.

And while the thought of a potential murder victim buried and rotting away on someone's property should have sickened him to his core, it did not. For the unlawful premeditated killing of one human being by another no longer carried the same sting it once had, when he was a rookie police officer, as he had seen too much of it over the many years on the job, and was hardened to the violence.

Sergeant Massey cursed under his breath, thinking silently that the last thing he needed to add to his Department's already bulging caseload would most assuredly be the impossible and time-consuming investigation of some aged skeleton that had probably been in the ground for decades on end. Yet at some level, deep within, one he would not publicly admit to, he realized the potentially chilling nature of the discovery. And he wondered if an identity were to somehow be attached to the skeletal remains, might it be a name he or others would recognize?

"I called the Office of the County Coroner's Chief Medical Examiner yesterday and spoke to Michael McKay, the chief Medical Examiner. I asked him to personally be involved on this one, after I explained the unusual circumstances. Told him we would need the usual—approximate date of death, gender, approximate height, weight, and age at time of death, and an educated guess on how many years this thing lay buried in the ground. And most important, I told him we need to know if we're looking at a homicide," Sergeant Massey said.

"Anything else?" LuVasse asked.

"I told him the specific cause of death would be of great help to us, too, and also any other information he could garner on this John or Jane Doe. He's busy, but I insisted he make this a priority. Told him I don't want excuses...excuses are for candy-asses. Oh, yeah, and one more thing. Something was dangling from the skeleton's neck—a necklace, or chain of some sort. Guess that's what reflected in the sun and caught the attention of the site consultant. That's how they noticed the bones. I told him to check that out, too—to take some photos of it, dust it for prints, and bag it as evidence."

"My concern at this moment is that the reporters are going to have a heyday with this one, and I assume it'll be on the news as a feature story," LuVasse said. "There's an eerie element to the likes of this discovery, and in a minute or two we'll have to face that crowd of reporters and photographers and answer questions."

"It's impossible to keep the press away from a story like this," Sergeant Massey said.

Unbeknownst to LuVasse, the Sergeant himself had placed an anonymous call to a local news channel tip-line to report the skeletal find—making certain to amply disguise his voice. Publicity was always good for his Department; however, coming directly from him it might not appear proper.

"A simple tank pull has turned into a potential crime investigation. That in mind, I would suggest we treat this as an open investigation and tell the press very little," LuVasse said. "We'll be barraged with questions, but let's agree to state only that it's a confidential matter at this time, while it remains an open investigation."

"Of course," Sergeant Massey agreed. "What else would we do?"

Members of the press followed the receptionist to a meeting room down the hall to set up, and both LuVasse and Sergeant Massey entered shortly thereafter. Microphones and cameras, from all vantage points, simultaneously emerged in front of their faces, and reporters yelled out one question on top of another. The situation rapidly became chaotic.

"Let's have some order here or we'll call this press conference off," LuVasse shouted. The room quieted. He pointed to one reporter. "You, first."

"Are we looking at a homicide investigation?" the young, bright-eyed lady asked.

"Not at this time. We have not made that determination, yet," LuVasse said. "You, next." He pointed to another.

"Do you consider the skeleton a murder victim? Any idea on the identity, yet?"

"*Again*, we do not know at this point if the skeleton met with foul play. And of course, we do not have an identity at this time. Next?" LuVasse asked, pointing to another in the crowd.

"Who will be working on the investigation?" an eager male reporter yelled out.

"We are not at liberty to name investigators," LuVasse said.

"Claire Caswell," Sergeant Massey boomed, simultaneously.

Reporters frantically scratched her name on notepads.

"That's the end of this press conference," LuVasse said. "We will provide you with further public information as it becomes available."

When the room cleared, LuVasse cornered the Sergeant and glared at him. "Why on earth did you feed them Claire Caswell's name? Now her name's out there. Not smart. She'll surely be hounded."

"No big deal, LuVasse. Cool down. We had to throw them a bone."

LuVasse continued to scowl at him, disheartened by the tasteless man.

"Okay. Okay. So I slipped up. What are you going to do? Shoot me?" He smiled at LuVasse, clearly not taking the matter too seriously.

Turning on his heels, LuVasse walked from the room without shaking the hand of the insolent Sergeant Massey. He wondered how anyone put up with him. And he hoped Massey had not put Claire Caswell in jeopardy.

4

Friday
Grand Cayman

"CLAIRE! CLAIRE! ARE you hurt?" Guy yelled frantically. "Claire? Answer me!"

Suddenly he remembered the small yellow flashlight in his backpack. Ripping it from the bag, he turned it on, and crawled on his stomach toward the opening, being careful not to disrupt any more of the crumbling circumference. Aiming the paltry light directly into the vertical drop, he peered in. There, in a heap at the bottom, he saw Claire. When the light beam hit her face, she responded by moving slightly. Then she opened her eyes.

"Guy? Help me."

"Honey, I'm coming to you. Don't move. Are you okay?"

"Yeah, I think so. It must be a ten-foot drop down here. The fall stunned me, but I'm all right. Really. I landed on soft ground and nothing seems to be broken. I've been told I have strong bones, and now I believe it. Wait a minute. Keep that flashlight pointed down here, will you?" Something had grabbed her attention.

"Thank goodness you're not hurt. What are you looking at?"

"Looks like steps, about every two feet or so, all the way down. But they're very narrow and zigzagged on the wall. Use them, but come down slowly," she pleaded. "Be careful."

Guy made his way down with a fair degree of ease, losing his footing only once but managing to hold on and avoid a fall. Reaching the bottom, he scooped Claire into his arms and held her. When he looked her over with his flashlight, he noticed several slight tears in her clothing and minor abrasions on one leg and one arm, presumably caused from scraping the wall on her way down.

"You'll live," he pronounced. "Nothing too serious. But don't try that move again. Don't want to lose you now." He grinned at her until she laughed. Pulling a small tube of antibiotic cream and some bandages from his backpack, he treated her wounds in no time, relieved it had not been worse.

"Let's explore," Claire said, pulling herself together. "Nothing hurts."

"Sure you're up to it?"

"Absolutely. Where's your sense of adventure? When did you last find yourself in a hidden cave? We must seize the opportunity."

"Point taken. And it's still storming outside, so we wouldn't be leaving any time soon anyway. I'm game if you are."

With the aid of the light, they realized they were in a spacious area that led to a curious tunnel of some kind. Holding their misgivings at bay, they daringly stepped into the passageway. After walking a short distance, they saw to their surprise that outside light was filtering in, sporadically, providing enough illumination for them to trudge along with very little difficulty. Guy returned the flashlight to his backpack to conserve the batteries. The path was wide enough to walk side by side, with sufficient headroom to stand fully upright, and it felt warmer in the tunnel.

"We've stumbled upon some elaborate kind of cave and tunnel system. It's incredible," Claire said, awed by what she saw.

"I'd say you literally *fell* into it."

"Look, up ahead. It's another open area similar to the one I tumbled into."

This space replicated the other, and had the appearance of a small room with a rather flat floor and ceiling. Much daylight streamed in from a fracture in the overhead rock, making it the brightest spot so far along the track.

"I'm starved," Guy announced. "Let's eat."

"Me, too," she admitted.

Guy removed the blanket from his pack and spread it on the hard stone floor. They sat down, and voraciously devoured every morsel of food Claire had packed—thankful to have it.

"I'm less hungry now," Guy said. "And I'm glad I remembered to bring water."

"Yeah, so am I. That lunch hit the spot."

"I don't know about you, but I'm exhausted," Guy said. "Actually, I'm *overwhelmed* by exhaustion. I have to lie down."

Reclining on the blanket, he fell asleep immediately. Claire nestled next to him and nodded off into peaceful slumber, her head on his chest—feeling snug, well fed, and free from danger.

A little over an hour had elapsed when Claire awakened abruptly to Guy's loud shouting. Still lying flat, with one eye open, he pointed to a prehistoric-looking, five-foot-long lizard slowly making its way through the cavern, inches from his feet. The creature appeared to be looking straight ahead, not at them, and seemed totally unaware of the humans that had invaded its territory.

"Look at those thick, chubby legs, Guy. It's in no particular hurry to go anywhere fast, wouldn't you agree? And look at that crest of spines from its neck to its tail. It's really quite beautiful. And blue. I've never seen a *blue* one." Claire's cheeks were flushed with excitement.

Guy's eyes revealed sheer apprehension. Once it disappeared from sight, he seemed to breathe easier and could finally explain how the *monster* had treaded across his ankle and jarred him from his restful sleep—nearly scaring him to death.

Obviously looking for a little sympathy after such a dreadful experience, Claire chuckled softly and smiled warmly. She gave him an extended and reassuring hug. "Oh, you poor, poor thing. You've been through such an ordeal," she said.

"How did I know it wouldn't take a bite out of me?" Guy asked.

"Oh, come on now. What happened to your zest for adventure? It would never have hurt you, honey. It's only an iguana—a kindly creature. They're really innocuous, you know. But I will admit, they look a whole lot scarier than they are, and that's certainly the largest one I've ever seen—even in textbooks. In fact, I think that's as big as they come."

"Comforting, Claire. I, too, know all about them. It's just, when one awakens you by crossing over your body, it's a little unnerving. Anyway, I just wanted some consoling from you," he said, winking and pulling her close. "That thing—the creature—would not be my idea of a perfect wake-up call, if you know what I mean."

Although he wanted her to think he had recovered fully, she knew him all too well. Watching him out of the corner of her eye, she realized that anxiety still had a hold on him and kept him somewhat shaken.

"Where to next?" Guy asked, acting brave.

Looking around, her attention went to the split in the grotto near the ceiling, the one allowing light to pour into the room. "Give me a minute, will you? I want to check something out." She climbed up several side wall rocks, until she could peer out through the fracture and glean a glimpse of the sky. The rain had all but stopped for the moment, and the sun, strategically placed between clusters of the remaining thick clouds hanging without movement in the afternoon sky, attempted to show its cheerful face.

Carefully clambering back down the way she'd gone up, she turned her full attention to Guy. "Let's walk deeper into the tunnels and find some hidden treasures taken by the Conquistadors," she said, boldly.

Guy laughed. "Some of the things I love about you, Claire, are your sense of adventure, your *vivid* imagination, and your ultimate persistence. Those lips aren't bad, either."

His playfulness had returned, and that was a good thing. It showed the trauma of the unforeseen encounter had started to wane.

"I'll follow you," he said. "Let's go for it. Unless you think we should be starting back, of course." While some indefinable part of Guy secretly wished Claire might agree to call it a day—thinking it would probably be a wiser decision to retreat than go on—he knew better. And truth be told, the secret world intrigued him equally as much as it did her.

"We've got plenty of time, Guy. Let's see where this leads."

Together they ventured deeper and deeper into the unpredictable underground system of connected tunnels and caves, amazed at the extent of the hidden labyrinth, taking in everything, trying to determine how the layout may have formed—ultimately agreeing it had probably created itself over years and years of time as a result of volcanic eruption. The only real problem they encountered along the way involved walking atop intermittent patches of jagged and pointy rock formations on the tunnel floor. But while those stretches slowed their momentum, by requiring careful, deliberate placement of each and every footstep, they did not discourage the two of them from marching onward. At this point, nothing would.

"What do you suppose those hollowed-out areas in the side walls are?" Claire asked. "We keep seeing them."

"They seem spacious enough for one or two people to sleep in, don't they? Or, maybe to store provisions?"

"Look, over there, at the stream of crystal-clear water cascading down the rocks." She pointed. "It's pooling into a basin."

"I see it."

"And Guy, look at that large, bowl-shaped area in the floor. The perimeter's a perfect circle. It's easy to imagine fires aglow in that pit—for heat or to cook food. Or both." Her fascination with the surroundings went without saying and her imagination was on full throttle.

"Well, I'd say we're concluding that human occupants lived here at one time, and we're probably correct," he said.

"My thoughts exactly." Claire let her mind drift and easily envisioned a time when pirates dwelled where she was standing, using the tunnels to travel back and forth between ships moored on the Caribbean waters and the hidden caves. As she embellished the scenario in her mind's eye, the fantasy sent chills down her spine. A rare glimpse into history had ensnared them as they'd happened upon this secret world. And she couldn't help but wonder just how long it had been since other humans walked the paths of the incredible underground maze.

Out of the blue, something streaked past Claire on the tunnel floor. "Whoa! What was *that*?" she asked.

"I don't know. A large rat, perhaps? Let's keep moving."

Claire shuddered at the thought of sharing space with a possibly diseased rodent. "Eeew!"

Advancing forward, along the craggy and scabrous underground, became hypnotic, and intrigue diminished perspective on how far into the foreboding territory they were trekking.

"Look. Up ahead," Guy said.

Claire saw it, too.

As they approached the ultimate brightness, the tunnel filled with brilliant and radiant light, and soon they found themselves in the midst of another cavern, this one amazingly well illuminated. Inside the space, they felt as if they were standing in broad daylight—due to a powerful ray of the sun bursting forth through a miniscule opening in the overhead rock, a bolt of sunlight so forceful that it created a steady and laser-like beam channeled directly into the chamber's darkness, seeming to focus with exact precision on a fixed location.

"Looks like a marker to me," she said, keenly eyeing the beacon of light. "As though someone intentionally created the hole up there to channel the strong rays of the afternoon sun down here—to this exact spot on the rock. Even today, with the sun's limited rays, the strength of the beam is incredible."

"Strange," Guy said, taking it all in. "But it does seem that way."

"I wonder why?" Claire asked. Digesting her words, she attentively examined the oval, gray-speckled stone—the seeming target of the laser. Dissimilar to the surrounding rock, it appeared smoother in texture, lighter in color, and larger. And the longer she looked at it, the more it appeared strangely out of place. She touched it, and to her bafflement it shifted easily in place. When she put both hands on it, it seemed loose.

Guy's curiosity piqued sharply. He kept a close eye on Claire as she wrapped her arms around the stone and lifted it effortlessly.

In unison, their eyes fell upon the object the hollowed-out stone had concealed so completely.

5

"WHAT ON EARTH…?" Claire asked, unable to withdraw her eyes from it. As the beam of sunlight now settled directly on the object, goose bumps rose all over her flesh. Guy backed up a step. They gawked without speaking at what the stone had hidden so thoroughly only moments before.

Finally able to summon words, Guy spoke. "What the hell is it?"

"I have no idea," Claire said.

Eyes riveted on the amazing discovery, neither Claire nor Guy seemed to feel the outpouring of cold air suddenly encircling them like a shot. Looking fixedly at the piece for several long minutes, they were unable to make a move, as if frozen in place.

"It's some kind of statue," Claire said at last. "A carved statue. It's breathtaking."

Kneeling side-by-side, afraid to touch it, they eyeballed the extraordinary sculpture—from top to bottom and bottom to top, powerless to look away.

"The detail, Claire. It's flawless. A masterpiece. Crafted with the greatest of expertise. I'm not sure if it's pottery? Or stone? Dipped in gold? Maybe solid gold?"

"And the headdress, Guy. It's gorgeous. It's the most ornate and elaborate thing I've ever seen. Looks like it's inlayed with colored gemstones. And that face. The gaze is nothing short of menacing. Terrifying, actually. It has the look of a warrior charging into battle." She locked in on the eyes of the imposing face. Their stunning and radiant green color absolutely glowed with mystical and magical qualities that bewitched the onlooker.

"I'd say it's either Aztec or Mayan in origin," Guy said. "I'm quite sure of it. In either case, we're looking at an *extremely* old relic, with a charisma and allure I've never seen the likes of. Its eyes are haunting and captivating at the same time. Almost eerie."

"*What have we found?*" Claire asked.

Unable to shift his gaze from the piece, he did not respond.

Minutes passed in quiet stillness.

All of a sudden, he spoke. "When I studied for my advanced scuba instruction for wreck-diving, I read about treasures buried in island caves and lost at sea in the Caribbean waters. Some of my instructors even lectured on old coins and other artifacts lost forever in pirate shipwrecks, but in all honesty I never believed such treasures really existed. But now...we stumble upon *this*. Both civilizations are ancient, and if I remember my history correctly, the Aztec Empire controlled much of Central and south Mexico—*before* the Spanish conquest in 1521, I believe; and the Mayas lived throughout Mexico, Guatemala, Honduras, and Belize, much earlier—from about 300 B.C.E. to A.D. 900—if my dates are right. They built a major pre-Columbian civilization that included magnificent pyramids, hieroglyphic writings, and amazing sculptures. Both empires existed geographically close to this very island. This ancient relic is definitely a significant piece of history, I can assure you."

Claire was numbed in the moment—mesmerized by the uncovering and Guy's detailed elucidation. Unexpectedly, an icy jolt riveted her body and she shivered from the awareness that a profoundly striking chill had entered the air. "Come on, Guy. Grab that thing and let's get out of here. The sun will be setting soon, and it's freezing in here."

Immediately, Guy felt it, too—the bone-chilling air hovering all around them. Recognizing a look of unmistakable apprehension on her face, even raw fear in her eyes, it hit him like a ton of bricks. Soon it would be dark and become extremely difficult to retrace their steps out, for they had ambled deep into the forbidden underground. Exercising extreme caution, he pulled the artifact from its hiding place, wrapped it in his blanket, and carefully wedged it into his backpack.

"What about *these*?" Claire asked. She scooped up a handful of old coins, sitting in the dished area where the relic had stood.

"Throw 'em in my backpack. We need to get out of here. Now."

Following his request quickly, she also replaced the speckled stone to its original position, and together they began the lengthy hike back to the outside world.

Moving with the speed of gazelles, never stopping to talk, they followed the familiar pathway that had brought them in, retracing their steps through the seemingly endless maze of tunnels and caverns, bending low when necessary, depending on the flashlight in an ever-increasing way, astonished at how far into the mysterious labyrinth they had wandered. Thoughts of being trapped in the frigid air and total darkness of the secret passageway terrified them both. The temperature seemed to be dropping even further as the evening rapidly descended upon them, and a myriad of strange moaning sounds sporadically emanated throughout the tunnels. Adrenaline kicked in, pushing them forward like never before.

Tripping and stumbling to the ground, Claire picked herself up before Guy even realized she had fallen. She ignored her bleeding knee. One thing and one thing only was on her mind—finding the place where they'd stepped into this ghastly adventure and stepping out. Was it getting harder to breathe or had sheer panic taken hold, compressing her lungs? She wondered why it seemed so much farther out, than in.

In the blink of an eye, pitch-blackness fell hard upon them, and the hair-raising and unnatural sounds became louder. Horrified, they now relied completely on Guy's flashlight—with its negligible and inadequate provision of light—to guide them. Claire wondered whether even that light seemed to be dimming with each passing moment, or could her imagination be playing tricks on her? Wanting acquittal in the worst way, she couldn't take much more. Claustrophobia appeared from nowhere and seized her by the arm, holding on with a tight grip, pulling mightily to hold her back and keep her captive in the stifling atmosphere. She fought the demon of darkness with all her will, and surged forward. She was not about to give in to the dark force.

"How are you holding up?" Guy yelled.

"Okay," she said, not convincingly. "Probably as good as you are."

Their pace picked up. Fatigue attacked them like a swarm of locusts, but they rebelled and fought it off. Blood streamed from Claire's knee, but she ignored it. Her legs felt heavy, but she maintained her stride, robotically and mechanically, reaching into the core of her soul for strength, desperately searching for the way out.

The flashlight's noble beam was diminishing. There was no longer any doubt about it. And it was becoming increasingly more difficult to see. Then, all of a sudden, it blinked on and off, erratically, and went out altogether, leaving them in pure and unmitigated darkness. They stopped cold in their tracks. Claire held back tears. She couldn't breathe. Fight, she told herself. Fight. Weary, fearful, and wholly uncomfortable in the murky and threatening maze, she held her head high. She was a strong woman, and would be gallant. Forcing herself to take one breath, and then another, she pushed onward—survival commanding absolute control and directing her legs to keep moving. Progress slowed, as together they felt their way along the passageway. At last, the place they'd started to think would never appear confronted them abruptly—the rock wall Claire had fallen down at the beginning of the unexpected escapade. The two of them exhaled a simultaneous sigh of relief.

With Guy close at her heels, Claire scurried up the welcomed site with a renewed vigor, grabbing each next step her hands could find to hoist her higher and closer to the top, seemingly unaffected by the steepness of the tall, vertical panel. But when they reached the summit, they found to their horror no opening to the outside world. Only a flat plateau. They had made a wrong turn along the way and ended up finding a wall with steps, but the wrong wall.

A torrent of thoughts of never getting out saturated Claire's mind, and she had trouble catching her breath. "Are we going to die in here?" she asked.

"No. We'll get out. Stay with me," Guy commanded. He held her close. He abhorred being swept into a situation he could not control, and now found himself in precisely such a predicament. "Maybe we should have turned *left*, when we turned *right*, a hundred or so yards back. We'll have to retrace our steps. Come on. We have no other choice. We must hurry."

Cautiously climbing down the footholds, he grabbed her hand at the bottom. Operating on raw instinct alone, and in silence, they vigilantly made their way back to the fork in the passage, trekking through the darkness like soldiers, blocking out the ubiquitous groaning sounds that now predominated the system, at last reaching their destination, and then proceeding along the other leg in the path. After what seemed to be an interminable amount of walking, another wall with steps presented itself.

"You wait here," Guy said. "I'll go up and take a look. That way, you won't have to waste your energy, if you don't have to." Nobly, and with amazing agility, he ascended the foot supports to check things out at the top. A short delay followed. "There's an opening to the outside up here, Claire," he yelled. "Not the same one we entered through, but we can get out this way. I'm coming down for you."

But Claire had already scampered nearly to the top. She could wait no longer to step out of the suffocating underground world. She desperately needed to breathe fresh air.

Within minutes, they pushed through the thick bush covering secreting the entrance so completely from the outside world and stepped outside, into freedom. They inhaled and exhaled deeply the welcoming evening air. Claire grabbed Guy and hugged him in delight.

It was eight o'clock; time to race home and get ready to bring in the New Year. Like childbirth, the pain of the experience nearly disappeared as they left it behind.

"Boy, am I happy to be out of there!" Claire exclaimed. "You have no idea."

"Oh, I think I do. And just imagine, we discovered not one, but two, covered entrances to the hidden labyrinth—and this one's even closer to where we parked."

"Yeah. It's hard for me to get too excited about it, Guy. You couldn't pay me enough to go back into that maze…ever again."

"At this point, I agree with you."

The luminescent moon sat contentedly wedged between the thickset clouds that remained in the nighttime sky, lighting their way back to the Jeep. The grueling day had exhausted them thoroughly, but neither was willing to give up the plan to celebrate New Year's Eve together on the tropical island; after all, they'd planned their vacation at the end of December for that very reason.

Safely inside the vehicle, traveling back, Claire glanced at Guy. "I noticed you kept looking over your shoulder after we left the cave. What was that about?" she asked, curious what his answer would be.

"You do notice everything, don't you, my beauty? Not sure. I had the strangest feeling someone was shadowing us back to the Jeep. It was probably nothing. I saw no one. I bet you're thinking that it's now *my* turn for a vivid imagination, huh?" He chuckled, but Claire did not.

"No," she said. "I trust your instincts, as you do mine. Maybe someone *did* follow us. Perhaps someone saw us go into, or leave, that cave, and wanted to know what we were doing there." Claire had suppressed a strong sense of foreboding blanketing her on the walk back to the Jeep, and now, for sure, she wouldn't share it with Guy, as she knew it would ruin their special evening, for he had come to highly respect the internal nudging so much a part of her—extra-sensory perception, a sixth sense—something she had inherited from her grandmother, the accuracy of which could not be ignored. It would be best to keep silent on the issue, especially in view of his suspicions. Nothing would ruin this night.

Retrieving the ointment and a bandage from Guy's backpack, Claire tended to the cut on her knee as he sped home. It had bled a lot for such a little cut.

"You certainly got banged up today," he said.

"Everything's minor. I can't wait to examine the artifact closer when we get back to the condo."

"You're reading my mind."

BACK INSIDE their rental unit, Guy secured the doors and closed the blinds, and Claire loaded an Andrea Bocelli CD into the disc player. She closed her eyes, briefly, to appreciate the sensational, classical, operatic singing of the Italian tenor superstar. Guy slowly pulled the relic from his backpack, and they sat side by side on the couch. Ever so carefully, he peeled away the blanket. Rotating the ancient statue in his hands, the two of them gaped in wonderment at the astounding remnant of history. Hearts pounding, they re-examined it inch by inch.

"The longer I look at this, the more convinced I am that we've found something of monumental value, historically and monetarily," he said.

"I can't seem to get past its eyes," Claire said. "They seem alive to me. I'm captivated." *Those eyes*, she thought, *those lovely green eyes.* She could not stop looking at them.

"The eyes are exquisite," Guy said. "Oh, shit!"

Claire looked up to see blood spurting wildly from his hand.

6

MERRIMENT WAS UNDERWAY when Claire and Guy arrived at the restaurant shortly before eleven o'clock. They would still have time to enjoy a sumptuous dinner before watching the fireworks and ringing in the New Year.

Bunches of brightly colored balloons had been tied to outdoor lightposts and to the trunks of surrounding royal palm trees that had first been painstakingly wrapped, from top to bottom, with strings of tiny white or green holiday lights. The majority of the tables had been placed outside on the waterfront patio, with the remaining few set-ups indoors, just off the entrance.

As requested, the maître d' showed them to a pleasing table for two very near the water. Pulling the chair out for Claire, he threw a pensive glance upward, commenting that he was "keeping his fingers crossed" the weather would hold out until after the fireworks. He wished them an enjoyable evening and rushed away to tend to other patrons.

"How's the thumb?" Claire asked. She looked at Guy with deep tenderness in her eyes. "And are you sore from the tetanus shot?"

"Actually, I'm feeling very little pain right now." He looked at her adoringly, and flashed that strange smile she had been seeing lately.

"That was a nasty slice," she said. "Thank goodness it wasn't on your right hand."

He looked at her for some time without responding, that same smile conspicuously remaining on his face. "Don't you think it strange that the artifact has a razor-sharp piece of metal protruding from its bottom?" Guy asked. "You wouldn't even notice it—unless you were specifically looking for it. It was cleverly placed, that's for sure. And the amount of blood it drew was frightening, not to mention the excruciating pain and damage it caused me."

"I think running the cold water over it immediately and applying pressure with the towel helped curtail the bleeding," she said. "Guy, you wailed."

"I don't remember that. All I remember is sickening pain."

"When the doctor was stitching you up I got a good look at the wound. It's a wicked injury, honey."

Claire looked up and observed the large patches of cottony rain clouds still hanging so perfectly in the sapphire sky. As if the island needed more rain. Dazzling stars, twinkling with the brilliance of white diamonds, appeared almost within reach in the cloud-free spots that dotted the heavens, and the majestic palms swayed ever so gently in the warm and humid tropical breezes of the evening. The setting was unforgettable, despite the threat of more precipitation.

Hunger gripped them. Claire ordered lobster bisque and veal piccata, and Guy ordered fried calamari and a filet mignon with béarnaise sauce. Warm, freshly baked rolls and Caesar salads accompanied the dinners, and for dessert everyone received an on-the-house coconut sorbet—creatively served in the half-shell of a real coconut. The meal was delectable, the evening memorable.

The waiter poured Tattinger champagne into their glasses, and they reminisced about the past year, about many of the things they had been through together—the good and the bad—and they laughed. For the most part, life seemed really good. Guy, being cautiously aware of mixing alcohol with pain medication, allowed himself only a sip or two of the sparkling beverage.

"Our cave experience just seems like a bad dream now. I can think of nothing but your lovely face, Claire, and how ravishing you look tonight in that knockout orange dress."

"How about you, counselor? You look dashing in that white silk shirt, especially considering the color of your hair."

"We are very fortunate to have each other. That I know," Guy said. "We have a mighty romance, and we're best friends. Can't ask for more than that."

"I'm so aware of that, my darling. I could never picture my life without you."

The conversation definitely seemed to be on a specific track. Claire could feel what was coming next. She took a sip of the chilled bubbly. How *was* she going to answer?

Mercifully, just then, it started to sprinkle, within seconds turning into the second downpour of the day. They had no choice but to run inside, to a place quickly becoming standing-room-only, as all those seated outdoors had the same idea. The diners verbalized loudly their fear that rain would bring a halt to the much-awaited fireworks event—due to start sharply at midnight—only minutes away.

However, Guy appeared more concerned about a tall and lean balding fellow with a thick and dark handlebar mustache, a man who was staring fixedly in their direction from across the room. And to Guy's puzzlement, when he leaned over to whisper in Claire's ear, to alert her to the stranger looking squarely at them with too much interest, the man seemed to vanish into thin air.

"I'm sure nothing will come of it, Claire," he said. "Kind of odd, though." As Guy reassured her, he had little or no doubt in his own mind that they were the target of the man's intense gaze. But he didn't know why. He'd keep his eyes open for this interesting fellow.

As fate would have it, the rain stopped almost as quickly as it started, and, within minutes, servers were back outdoors, running around frantically, wiping down the furniture and changing table linens and place settings. All in record time. Hastily and eagerly, patrons returned to their tables.

The rain had made the air that evening even more humid, if possible, leaving the atmosphere quite uncomfortable. Dinner had been a great respite and allowed them the luxury of forgetting about the artifact and the injured thumb for the time being, but now the evening was winding down rapidly.

Guy glanced at his wristwatch. In exactly two minutes, the clock would strike midnight. Servers hectically ran from table to table, handing out noisemakers, streamers, and party hats, while at the same time chaotically filling each glass of champagne on every table to the rim.

At the stroke of twelve, patrons clicked glasses and grabbed one another to hug, kiss, and dance in place, all shouting "Happy New Year!"

Claire and Guy stood together, his arm around her shoulders, as they toasted in the New Year—as always, starting it with an impassioned kiss and a mutual promise to make this year even better than the last.

"Happy New Year, my love," he said. His eyes locked on hers.

"Happy New Year back to you." Her eyes exuded unwavering ardor.

"I love you very much," Guy said. His demeanor became extremely serious.

"And I love you, my handsome guy." Her gaze shifted to the sky.

Guy fingered the ring in his pocket and licked his dry lips. The moment to ask her had presented itself. Hadn't it? But despite Claire's New Year's Eve merriment, something seemed to be on her mind. What if she was too distracted to give him the answer that he wanted, that he needed? He thought fast and hard. With a heavy sigh, he left the ring in his pocket. He would wait until the perfect moment.

Just then, as promised, the much-awaited fireworks exhibition burst forth with tremendously loud bangs, drawing every eye upward to the stunning explosions of colors—one after another—in the nighttime sky. The overhead universe was wondrous and entrancing and for that short time everyone was a child again, as magic and enchantment took over the upper atmosphere.

"I'm exhausted," Guy said. "Let's go home." The painkiller the doctor had given him earlier was starting to wear off, and his thumb began to throb in exquisite agony.

"I'm with you. It's been a day of memories, hasn't it? And one I wouldn't want to repeat anytime soon," Claire said. She was relieved he hadn't proposed.

Arriving home, Guy unlocked the door and stepped aside to let Claire enter ahead of him. When she flipped on the switch to illuminate the entryway, she bellowed, "No!"

Their world had been torn apart.

7

GUY SET A foot down in front of Claire. "Stand back! Wait here!" he ordered.

Ripping an umbrella from the front closet, he clutched it in his fist and made his way through each and every room, making certain the intruder had left the premises. After satisfying himself beyond a doubt, he signaled Claire to enter. Then, without delay, he dialed the police emergency number and reported the burglary. The dispatcher assured him an officer would be there shortly to write-up a report, and encouraged Mr. Lombard to make a list of the items stolen.

"What next?" Claire asked. "This day has already seemed like a week, and now *this*?"

Working with each other, they looked around at the disgusting mess the trespasser had left behind and tried to assess the damages. Rapidly developing a ferocious headache, the last thing in the world Guy wanted or needed to deal with stared him directly in the face. All-out exhaustion had kicked in, and his thumb pulsed with shooting pain. In the worst way, he wanted to take a pain pill and fall asleep, to simply dream pleasant dreams, and deal with this intrusion in the morning. He let out a deep inarticulate sound of despair.

"My thoughts exactly," Claire said, dismayed at the amount of work it would take to bring the unit back to order. "Someone thoroughly trashed this place. They say bad things happen in threes, you know. Today, a horrific storm caught and trapped us in the caves; you received that terrible gash on your thumb; and now this. So nothing else bad can happen. Let's agree on that. At least we're starting a new year, and hopefully the worst is behind us. I'm optimistic." It sounded good, but she did not believe her own words, as it seemed *too* many dreadful things were happening.

They looked through every room, searching to figure out what the burglar had taken.

"Funny. Nothing is unaccounted for," Claire said.

"My take, too."

Remembering at the same moment, each shot a horrified glance in the other's direction.

"The artifact!" Guy shouted.

Claire ran to the master bedroom and looked up at the A/C access panel on the ceiling, relieved to see that it appeared intact.

Guy retrieved the stepladder and a Phillips screwdriver from the laundry room and met her in the bedroom. Hastily, he climbed the ladder, loosened the screws, removed the panel, and peered inside. "It's here. It's okay." A heavy sigh of relief came from his depths. "We did a good job hiding it."

Just then, a loud rapping sounded at the door, and Claire went to answer it. Wasting no time, Guy secured the access cover, returned the ladder and screwdriver to their usual spots, and walked to the kitchen to gulp another pain pill with some water.

"Yes?" Claire called out.

"Police Officer Robbins. Reginald Robbins. May I come in?"

Opening the door, she greeted the officer. "Yes. Please, come in."

Officer Robbins was a tall, young man, who dressed in a uniform appearing much too large for his lean frame. At first glance, he looked like a youngster playing dress-up in his father's clothing. But his serious demeanor, apparent when he began to speak, at once signaled that he meant business. Looking around at the state of the place, he twisted his face into an ugly expression. Then he righted a chair and sat down. Wanting to obtain a detailed report, he first recorded basic background information about Claire and Guy, and then began the important questioning. He jotted notes continually throughout the interview.

"Items taken?" he asked. He did not glance up from his clipboard.

"That's the funny thing, officer. Between us, we can't come up with a single thing that's missing," said Claire.

Officer Robbins looked up and stared at her with cautious distrust. "Excuse me? I asked you what items are missing from the burglary. Cash...Jewelry...What?"

"Not a thing," she said.

"*Nothing*?" Officer Robbins asked.

"Nothing," Guy said. "Zip. Nada. Zilch."

"Strange. Most peculiar," the officer said. He gaped at the two of them. "What was the burglar searching for?"

"Now how would *we* know that?" Guy asked.

"One would think the intruder rummaged around for something specific, based upon the disorder left behind," Officer Robbins persisted.

"That may be, but how would we know what that was?" Guy asked.

"Look. I'm not here to play games with you. It's New Year's Eve, and we're busy," Officer Robbins said. "You need to level with me." He turned his attention to Claire. In his experience, women tended to speak more freely then men when it came to situations like this. "Look, ma'am, I'm only able to help you if you'll let me."

Biting her bottom lip, she felt Guy's piercing eyes penetrating hers. For a fleeting second, she contemplated telling the policeman about the artifact, but quickly thought better of it. It seemed too early to discuss it with anyone—even the police. "I don't know, officer, what the burglar may have been after. The money we left in the dresser drawer is still there, along with the jewelry I did not wear this evening. What else can I tell you?"

Guy winked at Claire, unbeknownst to the patrolman, signaling his approval of her answer.

"Did you lock all doors before you left?" Officer Robbins asked.

"Yes, all of them—except the screen door leading outside from the patio. We noticed that lock didn't work yesterday, after we arrived," Claire said. "But the sliding door accessing the unit from inside the patio, we locked that one for sure."

The officer again gave each of them a prolonged look. Obviously, he did not believe their story, but he also could not force them to talk and he knew it. He got up and physically examined the premises, determining the intruder had entered through the screened porch area, and then probably used a jimmy to pry open the sliding glass door. Positioned on the side of the unit, tall flowering hedges surrounded the porch. In the dark, the odds remained high that no one had witnessed the person or persons slip in or out of the condo. But he agreed to interview the neighbors in the morning, just the same. He turned his attention back to Claire and Guy. "Did either of you see anyone suspicious hanging around here today?"

"Actually, we spent a good part of the day hiking around the island's south side. And then we went out for dinner tonight to celebrate the holiday, sir," Claire said.

"Any dubious sorts hanging around the restaurant?" the officer asked.

"Now that you mention it, I did see a man who caught my attention at the restaurant tonight," Guy said. "I caught him glaring at us in a conspicuous manner, and then, just like that, he disappeared. I did not see him again."

"Describe him for me," said Officer Robbins.

"Well, I'd put his age in the mid-to-late forties, and his height at about six feet. He had a slender build, muscular arms, tan complexion, dark eyes, and a mostly balding head—with a scant remnant of dark hair. He had a thick, dark mustache, too—the *handlebar* type."

Officer Robbins looked up and studied Guy. "*Very* thorough description, Mr. Lombard. Remarkably detailed, in fact. Do you happen to recall the clothes he was wearing?"

"As a matter of fact, I do. He wore a short-sleeved tan shirt, dark trousers, and an expensive belt with silver hardware. He dressed nicely."

In an odd sort of way, the officer did not seem at all concerned with this new information, and it almost seemed to Claire as if he covered a snicker while Guy painted the vivid portrait of the stranger.

"Why is it that you recall so clearly the description of this man—when you saw him for so brief a time, Mr. Lombard? Your specificity intrigues me."

"I'm trained to notice such things, sir. I'm a criminal prosecuting attorney in Miami."

Officer Robbins was not impressed—at least that he let on. He completed his report, asked them both to read and sign it, and reminded them to have the sliding door lock repaired as soon as possible. "I imagine you'll be just fine here tonight. This island has little or no crime. Most folks here don't even lock their doors." But at Claire's insistence, he agreed, as a precautionary measure, to arrange for a squad car to drive by the condominium every hour or so until morning. After promising to let them know if anything further developed on the case, he bid them goodnight.

Both Claire and Guy knew they would never hear from him again—that his report would simply be filed away as a random ransacking with no items stolen. No big deal to the police—especially on an island with virtually no crime.

Tired out, Guy and Claire righted the remaining tipped furniture and agreed to deal with the rest of the jumble in the morning. After preparing for bed in record time, they pulled back the lightweight floral coverlet, and fell in between the white cotton sheets on the oh-so-inviting queen bed. The trying day needed to end, and they desperately craved the escape that only sleep could deliver.

"Do you still believe we're on the perfect holiday, Claire?" Already dozing off, Guy's speech slurred from exhaustion.

"Pleasant dreams, my love," she said, rolling on her side toward him. "You don't suppose all these bad things are happening because we disturbed that ancient artifact, do you?"

8

Friday evening
Miami, Florida

ALL LOCAL MIAMI news channels carried the story of the skeletal find as the premier story of the day.

Each report began with similar dialogue. "We begin tonight's news broadcast with a mysterious breaking story. Yesterday, while in the process of hoisting a gasoline tank from the ground in our very own Miami Shores, a human skeleton surfaced. The local police are working diligently to determine if murder led to the demise of this individual. We will be following this puzzling story closely."

Two channels interviewed the nervous property owner, John Lawden, about the skeleton turning up on his land. With the help of his on-site consultant, Lawden explained that contractors had begun hoisting dirt from the ground, to access the last of three tanks buried on his property, when the gruesome discovery came to light. Lawden swallowed hard, frequently, and talked too fast. Using few words, he clarified that he had purchased the land in question several years earlier, and indicated a gasoline station had stood on the property far back in its history.

The tanks had been abandoned, together with the real estate, long ago, and now that Lawden wanted to construct a house on the land, he had to first comply with federal and state laws. Those laws required him to replace, upgrade, or remove all underground buried petroleum tanks on the property, and to clean up soil or water contamination caused by corroding tanks leaking petroleum into the environment. Lawden expressed his utmost surprise and revulsion at the unearthing of the human remains on his property.

Both channels also interviewed Gary LuVasse, and Sergeant Massey. LuVasse cautioned, repeatedly, that no conclusions could be drawn at this early date regarding the identity of the skeleton, nor could one venture a guess as to whether he or she had met with foul play. When questioned further by the eager network reporters on how he intended to proceed at this juncture, LuVasse would only indicate that investigative techniques and findings would be kept confidential for the time being. But he promised to provide updates to the public, as the law would permit, secretly hoping the public's curiosity would wane rapidly when another story of interest hit the news.

Sergeant Massey did his best to swing the story around to him and his men, elaborating on the efforts of his department to carefully remove the skeleton in an effort to preserve any forensic evidence that may be present at the scene. When asked whom the case would be assigned to for investigation, he again blurted out State Investigator Claire Caswell's name, quickly volunteering that Gaston Lombard of the State Attorney's Office would most likely be involved, as well—probably as the primary investigator.

LuVasse jumped in to clarify, as he had in the earlier press conference, that investigators would not be named, adding that assignments would take place early the following week, if justified. Knowing full well the press already assumed the matter would turn into an official homicide investigation the minute Sergeant Massey mentioned Gaston Lombard's name, LuVasse repeated his previous statement that they had no confirmation at this time to indicate the person had met with foul play.

The Sergeant's loose lips profoundly perturbed LuVasse. Naming investigators could well put them in jeopardy, and the Sergeant knew that—especially if a criminal element were involved. LuVasse asked the press to stay away from the investigators assigned to the case if the matter turned criminal—to give them a chance to investigate without being hounded to answer questions. Again, he promised to release any public details as they became available.

LuVasse played by the rules, and he resented the way Sergeant Massey seemed to make up his own. He would warn Claire about the Sergeant when he filled her in on the case and gave her tapes of the broadcasts to review.

The news concluded with the broadcaster making a promise. "We will keep you informed of any new developments in this macabre, breaking story."

Oh how LuVasse and his staff hated the way the media embellished the facts to feed the public frenzy. And he wondered who had tipped them off to this one.

Saturday morning
Grand Cayman

GUY AWOKE to a persistent pounding in his thumb. He walked straight to the kitchen and downed a pain pill with some orange juice. He filled the coffee pot with cold water and poured it into the coffeemaker. Then he added ground coffee beans to the permanent filter, and turned it on. Seconds later, an eye-opening, rich aroma filled the air. He filled another glass with juice, opened the front door, and poked his head out to observe the weather conditions. The nightlong rain had fortunately stopped, leaving behind a clearing sky and the promise of a sunny day. Returning to the bedroom, he found Claire struggling to open her eyes, stretching with effort. "Morning, my sexy queen," he said. "I come bearing juice, My Lady." He bowed, handed her the glass, and opened the Venetian blinds halfway.

She chuckled. "Good morning, handsome prince. How long have *you* been in my court?" She conspicuously looked him up and down, oohing and aahing. "My thanks to you for the compliment, and the juice, my worthy courtier. Your fawning and honeyed words will get you everywhere." She showed him a teasing smile. "What time is it, anyway?" She took a sip of the sweet beverage.

"Time to *carpe diem*—seize the day. And I do mean *seize*. He pulled out an imaginary sword and pretended to be dueling. After he had won his make-believe contest with his nonexistent deadly weapon—in order to please *Her Majesty*, and settle a point of honor—he became Guy again and turned his undivided attention to Claire.

"You are one silly thing," she said. "But you do make me laugh."

"Always willing to please," he said. "And unlike yesterday, today will be a perfect day—a day beyond compare. I'll do everything within my power to make that happen."

"I concur. Honey, that statue haunted my dreams throughout the night. I kept thinking we shouldn't have removed it…that maybe because we did, bad things have happened. But I don't know…."

Guy looked at her in disbelief. "I can't believe you just said that. I had those dreams, too—actually, *nightmares*—about the very same thing. In my nightmares, punishment came to us from some greater force for disturbing the artifact's peace. That's how the lore goes, you know. When the instructors in my scuba training lectured about the hidden treasures, they told us the islanders believe just that—that it's bad karma to find and disturb, or steal, one of these vestiges of history."

"Ooh. Frightening…if you believe it. Personally, the more I think about it, the more the myth sounds like poppycock," Claire said. "What's come to pass since we found that statue can only be called happenstance. I'm sure of it." She sipped more juice, happy being on the island with Guy, but anxious to get to work on the case waiting for her in Florida—curiously fascinated by the daunting prospect of a new and intriguing investigation.

"Well, I hope you're right. Let's talk about how we should spend the day," Guy said. He thought it best to change the subject. "It's New Year's Day and I'll bet only restaurants will be open—probably none of the shops. And my dear, you'll be happy to know it's cleared up outside, so I propose we make it a beach day, and maybe go have some lunch a little later on. How does that sound?"

The word *propose* hit Claire squarely between the eyes. "What did you say?" she asked. Oddly, though, it hadn't scared her as much as she had expected it would.

"Not quite awake yet, eh?" he said, and repeated the question.

"Sounds like fun."

He crawled in next to Claire and took her in his arms. "First though, I want to start this year out right." Without hurrying, he brushed his lips past and around hers, slowly and seductively, until they landed fully on her awaiting mouth. She could feel his heat and smell the scent of his skin as they French-kissed with passion and became mutually aroused. With one hand, he pulled her peach silk negligee up and over her head, tossing it to the floor. Aroused by desire, he made his way down her voluptuous, velvety body, until he had gorged himself on her smooth and sweet-smelling skin. They made love with acute sensitivity, until satisfaction encompassed both of their souls.

Afterward they rested in each other's arms, feeling peaceful and fulfilled, until, without warning, Guy leaped from the bed. "Close your eyes, honey. Don't move." Three minutes later, he returned to the bed clutching the artifact in his hands. They sat quietly, considering the stunning piece with renewed inquisitiveness and spirit. Tipping the relic on end, they examined it in full daylight. The razor-sharp, saw-toothed insert, appearing to be made of copper, stuck out ever so slightly on the bottom of the statue and was barely visible to the naked eye.

"Clearly, the creator of this piece carefully designed it with the ability to lacerate for a reason. There is no doubt the placement is deliberate," Guy said. "Maybe to discourage thieves from taking it. Maybe it played on the lore we talked about—that stealing a piece like this would trigger the punishment of the gods—and certainly a hidden jagged edge, like this one, almost guaranteed serious injury to anyone who tried to take it. It would have seemed like retribution from a higher source. Or possibly poison poignantly positioned with precision on the piece of protruding metal would have proven physically perilous to anyone who nabbed it. I wonder. Who knows for sure?"

Now he was being silly again. Being away from work certainly had an impact on the prestigious Mr. Lombard. He had dramatically overemphasized the "p" in every "p" word he had uttered, obviously quite amused by his own clever usage of the intricacies of the English language. Claire rolled her eyes.

"I know. I know," he said, laughing. "*The Shadow* knows," he concluded, in a low and mystical voice. He set the artifact on the bed, and wafted his arms in the air, wiggling his fingers in Claire's face.

Seeing him in such rare form triggered an onslaught of laughter until her stomach hurt and her eyes watered. Finally, when she could laugh no more, she pursed her lips and shook her head while staring at the tough and arrogant Gaston Lombard. If others could only see him now—the man she knew behind closed doors, the man so different from his public persona—they wouldn't believe it, she thought. "Enough already, my prolific pontificator," said Claire.

Both in an imbecilic mood now, they rolled around on the bed, frolicking in each other's arms like children, careful not to get too near the ancient artifact.

All at once, sunlight, streaming in from between the Venetian blinds, lit up the artifact's eyes with an amazing green glow, recreating the cavern scenario of the day before. It was as though the statue had been electrified. Claire moved onto her hands and knees, and gazed closely into its face. The nearly translucent green eyes looked to be precious or semi-precious gemstones. There was simply no other explanation. They were dazzling, and overflowed with élan and vitality, transmitting a disquieting brightness. She thought for a moment and an idea struck her. "Let's bring it back to Miami. We can have it appraised by Robert Holden—the antiques dealer my family knows so well. You've met him. He's been in the business forever, and he'll certainly be able to tell us the real story—where it came from, where it belongs, what it's worth. He'll know all of those answers, and more. What do you think?"

"I think it's a bad idea." His tone became serious. "It's really not ours to take, is it? And what about U.S. Customs? If they figure out what we have, the agents will surely confiscate it. And I certainly don't want us being caught surreptitiously trying to bring an ancient artifact we found in the Cayman Islands back with us to the U.S. That would never do. We could wind up in jail."

"You're right. That would be bad."

"I'm *not* doing it," Guy said. "Forget about it."

"Let's give it more thought," Claire said. "There must be a way."

"I don't need to give it more thought. *What if we get caught*? What if someone turns us in? No. I will *not* be involved in this. We'll have to turn it over to the police before we leave. I see no other option."

"We'll figure something out."

"I'm done talking about it, Claire. I mean it. Leave it alone. End of discussion. It's all done. Finito." He stormed from the room.

There has to be a way, Claire thought to herself. She hated the angry side of Guy. He could be so dismissive and controlling at times—a real jerk. Luckily it was a side she didn't see often, but when she did, she didn't like it one bit. After dressing for a day at the beach, without speaking further to him, she started the process of cleaning up the mess the intruder had left behind. She wanted to do the bulk of it before going outdoors.

Darting a glance in her direction, every now and then, Guy's mind flooded with thoughts of how much he loved her. She looked breathtaking in her chartreuse bikini and matching sandals. He hated himself when anger got the best of him, and he hated himself for lashing out at Claire. She didn't deserve his wrath.

Continuing to ignore him, she filled a giant beach bag with a tall bottle of Evian, some magazines, and sunblock.

"I just reached the property manager about the sliding door lock," Guy announced. "She said her brother will fix it today—even though it's a holiday." He walked over to her, and stood directly behind her. "When I explained to her what happened, she apologized, over and over, and said she hoped it wouldn't ruin our vacation. She told us not to worry about cleaning and straightening the place. Under the circumstances, she agreed to arrange for a maid to come in this afternoon—to do it all. So that's good, right? Oh, and we can use the office safe until the lock gets fixed, if we need to."

Claire did not respond, nor turn around, still feeling hurt and disrespected.

"It's almost noon, honey," Guy said. "Let's please go have a nice lunch together somewhere on the beach. We are on vacation, aren't we? And I did promise you a perfect day today. Can we begin again?"

Still, she did not answer.

He slid his bulky arms around her slender body, from behind, and pulled her close. "I'm sorry, my beauty. Will you accept my apology?"

9

"WHAT CAN I get y'all this afternoon?" Miss Marilynn asked.

The menu at the beachfront restaurant offered a variety of tantalizing dishes, including turtle stew, conch chowder, spiny lobster salad, and broiled mahi mahi—as the fish of the day.

"I'll have the famous house specialty—the grilled chicken breast sandwich." Claire said.

"Ooh. You'll like that," Miss Marilynn said. "Comes with barbeque sauce, melted Swiss, lettuce, tomato, and a lightly-seasoned mayo. Fries and coleslaw, too."

"Sounds delish," Claire said. "And I'll have a mango iced tea, please."

"For you, sir?"

"Same as the lady, including the iced tea."

"Easy enough. I'll bring your drinks right out."

Violet tablecloths, and vibrant yellow napkins, added cheeriness to the tables; rattan chairs with tangerine cushions provided comfy seating; and turquoise, hand-painted walls, portraying lush tropical scenes, created a welcoming island atmosphere—together singling out the establishment as an unforgettable Caribbean experience. Packed to capacity with tourists and islanders alike, it seemed that everyone was taking advantage of the beach day holiday.

Miss Marilynn promptly delivered the beverages, and served the food about fifteen minutes later, refilling the teas. "Enjoy now. I know you will," she said. She smiled from ear to ear, revealing a missing front tooth.

The marvelous sandwiches lived up to the billing—tender, and spiced just right, with a combination of flavors overwhelmingly satisfying even to a sophisticated palate.

Guy's eyes met Claire's. "Listen. I'm glad we're talking again, Claire. I can't stand it when we fight. It tears me up inside."

"You need to get your anger under control, Guy. I won't be around it. But I did swallow mine and accept your apology. I want to enjoy our time here." Claire looked at him. She still hadn't told him they would be flying home tomorrow, and she struggled internally with her decision. She watched him pop a pain pill with his tea.

Miss Marilynn returned. "Would you care to try the homemade pineapple ice cream for dessert? Or the coconut cream pie? They're both *really* good!"

"Why not," Guy said. "Bring us one of each, will you please?"

While enjoying the refreshing desserts, Claire overheard several islanders conversing behind her, at a table in close proximity to where they sat. The discussion centered around the caves on the island, and her curiosity was piqued at once. She turned in her chair to face them. "Excuse me," she said. "I couldn't help but overhear you talking about caves, here on the island. I'd like to know more about them."

They looked at her, then at each other, and shrugged their collective shoulders. Not a one responded.

Claire cleared her throat. "Could you *please* tell me about the caves?"

Again, no one said a word. It was as if the *speech thief* had entered the room without detection and taken away their ability to express themselves using articulate sounds.

She turned back to Guy. "Must be a big secret."

While Guy paid the tab, Claire walked to the ladies' room—down a flight of stairs and at the end of a long and dimly lit corridor. On her way back, unexpectedly, and out of nowhere, a figure rammed her from behind, forcibly pushing her into a wall, and nearly knocking her wind out. Simultaneously, the attacker slammed up tightly against her and reached around to cover her mouth with a large, right hand, affording her little leeway for breathing. She could not scream or struggle free, and felt like a straight jacket secured her. The raspy voice of a man whispered in her ear, and she could feel his hot breath on her skin and smell a putrid odor on his clothing—the distinct aroma of dead fish, she thought. It made her nauseous, and she struggled to not throw up.

"Hey lady, you wannna know about the caves, do ya? If you ain't seen 'em, you ain't seen the island. But don't ask nobody about 'em. Nobody's gonna tell you nothin' about 'em. Git it?" He loosened his hand enough to allow her muffled speech.

"What? What does *that* mean?" She spoke so boldly that it surprised even her. Refusing to reveal the intense fear she was feeling, she acted with unflinching courage. "Let me go!"

"Listen carefully, wench. Stay away from 'em. Drop it." His voice was deep and annoying, and forbidding.

"I *said*, let me go!" she demanded again.

Suddenly she heard footsteps on the stairway, and realized, with relief, that another person was heading down to the rest room. That meant help was on the way. With a rough and wrenching yank, the assailant released his hold on her, and sprinted up the stairs—thrashing past the descending patron. Claire swung around and ran to get a look at him, only to see the flash of a silver blade in his left hand as he raced upward.

Shaken and struggling to gain composure, Claire ascended the staircase in a slow and steady momentum, leaving the incident mostly behind, and deciding she would not tell Guy because it would only upset him and ruin their *ideal* day. Most of the islanders she had met were delightful and charming individuals. Why did she have to run into this contemptibly obnoxious man?

"What took you so long?" Guy asked, seeing her at last in the entryway. "I thought about sending down a search party." He grinned.

"Wish you would have," she said under her breath.

"Pardon?"

"Oh, nothing. Let's go lie on the beach for a while. I'd like to relax for the rest of the day." In the worst way, she wanted to expel any and all remaining thoughts of the creepy encounter from her mind.

"I'm with you," he said.

Back at the condo, the sliding door lock repaired, and the entire place cleaned up and put back together, not a single remnant remained to remind them of the malicious ransacking. Claire slung the tote over her shoulder, and grabbed large beach towels from the closet, and Guy picked up two collapsible lounge chairs from the porch. Side by side, they walked on the glorious white sands to the seashore.

The sun was bright, and the temperature: Cayman hot. But a heavenly breeze made the intensity of the heat tolerable. Yesterday's thick cloud cover had all but disappeared—leaving behind endless stretches of blissful blue sky. Reaching the water's edge, they set up in positions that would afford them optimal advantage of the beautiful sunshine, and applied plenty of sunscreen. Stretching out on the loungers—each covered with a long towel—felt incredible, and provided the precise relaxation they so craved. Claire would not allow herself further thoughts about the restaurant assault, other than to realize it could easily have turned into a worse situation. She was thankful it had not. This last day of vacation, she'd enjoy the sun's tanning rays, no matter what.

Exhaling deeply, her body began to relax in the amazing salt air of the unmatched Caribbean. Behind dark sunglasses, she closed her eyes. She needed time to think. Tomorrow they would fly back to Miami, and Monday morning Gary LuVasse would fill her in on the mysterious happening involving one of her files. The *Lawden* file, he had mentioned. He'd actually told her very little over the phone, and she could not imagine what could be so important as to mandate cutting her vacation short—especially since she had not taken one in a long time. On the other hand, LuVasse would not call her back to a situation less than serious, so she waited in anticipation—eager to learn more.

Claire opened her eyes. Several other tanners had positioned chairs nearby, and walkers and joggers, in all shapes and sizes, dotted the irregular coastline for as far as she could see in both directions—those in the far distance resembling a string of tiny, marching ants. Parasails floated peacefully in the sky, and sailboards, kayaks, snorkel and dive boats, and several other varieties of water toys peppered the nearby waters.

Guy had turned on his side, facing her, and placed a towel over his head. But she could still see his face. Sound asleep, he looked so peaceful. The events of yesterday, including the severe wound to his thumb, had taken a toll on him, she knew. At lunch, he had finally confessed that the pain still overwhelmed him at times—whenever the pills wore off. The doctor had stressed it would be a couple of days until it felt any better, and she had seen him taking pain relievers every few hours since it happened. Right now, he needed rest and relaxation. And sunshine. Healing sunshine. She hoped the soreness would subside soon.

Both strong-willed people, they often did not see eye-to-eye on things, and they fought sometimes; yet, neither could imagine life without the other. The deep love they shared surpassed this lifetime, she was sure.

Strong nectars emanated from nearby flowering shrubs and mixed with the humid and briny tropical air, producing an overpowering desire to sleep. Before long, Claire too succumbed to its temptation and fell into hypnotic slumber. When she awakened, a good hour later, she reached into the tote for the bottle of Evian and took a long drink.

"Have a nice snooze, my darling?" Guy asked. He looked up from his money management magazine and turned his attention to her.

"I think we *both* did, didn't we? There's something about this air. It seems to work like a sleeping pill."

"I know what you mean. Mind if I have a taste of that water?" he asked. Claire passed him the bottle, and he chugged a good portion of it. "This is one hot day," he said. "I like it."

Just then, Claire's eyes were drawn to an elderly man wearing tropical print Tommy Bahama swim trunks, walking along the beach in their direction. His frame was trim, and his head was covered with thick, wavy, chalk-white hair—a near match to the pale color of his delicate skin. She guessed him to be in his mid-seventies, or so, and thought he looked very fit for his age. The man entered the sea, and quickly moved into deeper waters, where he began to swim laps, back and forth, horizontal to the coastline, about thirty feet from shore. Nearly forty-five minutes later, he emerged, and continued his walk near the coastline, ultimately passing right by their chairs.

Noticing that Claire was looking at him, he smiled warmly.

"You're quite the swimmer, sir," she said. "I watched you."

He walked near to her, and extended a hand. "Thank you. The name's Nathan Lund. Pleased to meet you." He shook her hand, vigorously. "But my friends call me Nate."

"Claire Caswell," she said, returning the shake with a firm grip. "And meet Gaston Lombard—but please, call him Guy."

The two men greeted each other and seemed to have instant rapport. Nate had a fatherly quality about him, and Claire liked him right away.

"I've been a swimmer most of my life, so I figure, why stop now? It's what keeps me young and slim," he said, patting his flat stomach and making an amusing face. "The secret to growing old gracefully, you see, is to keep moving. Once you stop being active, it all goes downhill rapidly."

"Well, since you've put in your exercise time for today, would you like to sit down awhile and keep us company?" Guy asked, motioning for Nathan to sit on the end of his chair. Guy, a great conversationalist, could engage in meaningful dialogue with just about anyone, on any subject, at any time. He enjoyed meeting people and listening to life stories.

"Don't mind if I do," Nathan said.

Conversation ensued easily, and in no time at all they learned a lot about Nathan. He, too, resided in Miami Beach. He owned a condo on the island, and had spent the majority of his last twenty winters there. He'd witnessed, first-hand, the many changes that had occurred on the island over the last two decades—the construction of the numerous condominiums and hotels along the beach, the large increase in the number of automobiles on the limited roadways, and the commercialization. Yet to him, it remained the best place on earth to be, and far superior to the filled-to-capacity metropolis of Miami Beach.

"It'd be nice if they could stop the island's growth here and now, but there is really no way to curtail progress. Can't be done. It's as natural as life itself," Nathan said. "There are too many cars here now, so the traffic has become greater than ever before. The roads simply cannot handle the number of vehicles on them, and it takes too long to drive anywhere at certain times of the day—but I work around it. I try to go out and run my errands when it's not so busy. And they're building a new road—to relieve the main road some—so, we'll see what happens. I know I'd never go anywhere else."

He spoke of being a widower for twenty-five years, and while he'd gone on with his life, without his beloved wife, Caroline, he'd never remarried. His children and grandchildren visited him on the island every winter.

"Nate, what do you know about the caves and tunnels on this island?" Claire asked.

"What an interesting question, Claire Caswell. Why do you ask?"

She gave Guy a momentary glance and in that split second decided not to tell Nathan about their experience or the artifact. It was too early to tell anyone about the relic—even a new friend. "Because I can't get anyone to tell me about them," she said.

10

"VERY WELL." NATHAN sat on the sand, between their chairs, and leaned back. "It's a subject no islander will discuss with you for a reason," he said. "I, on the other hand, have done a lot of research in the area, and consider myself a bit of a self-proclaimed expert—both on the caves and tunnels and the pirates who terrorized this area long, long, ago."

"*Pirates*?" Claire asked. Her enthusiasm hit a high note as she realized he could be an excellent source of information regarding the history of the island.

"Yes. Pirates. You see there's a castle near the edge of the water on the south side of this island. Legend has it, although *inaccurate*, that the infamous pirate, Blackbeard—one of the most notorious pirates in all of history—used the castle as his lookout and hideaway.

"It's rumored that Blackbeard lured ships to the island by placing a lantern on top of the castle, and ships carrying all sorts of treasures sailed toward the island, believing the glowing light to be a lighthouse—*a safe harbor*—but in reality, the vessels would run onto jagged coral reefs, tearing out their bottoms and sinking almost immediately.

In truth, Blackbeard probably did erect a beacon of some sort to attract ships toward this island and onto the treacherous reefs. And then, when the few hands surviving the wrecks swam to shore, Blackbeard and his men did capture and put the sailors into stocks, torturing them endlessly—until death relieved them of their agony. The pirates would seize the ships' treasures by free diving each time into the waters to retrieve the sunken booty.

"But he did not hole up inside the castle, because it had not been constructed at the time Blackbeard ruled these waters. What we do know, though, is that Blackbeard sailed around this area, and he most assuredly spent time on the island's south side, in the vicinity where the castle now stands, and the rumors that he stored the stolen riches in secret hiding places in and around the nearby cliffs and grounds near the castle location are, most likely, very true—probably within the underground caves and tunnels.

At the mention of *stolen riches, hidden in underground caves and tunnels*, visions of the ancient artifact with the dazzling green eyes pranced through Claire's mind.

"Later inhabitants of the island believed dead pirates haunted the caves—those who had voluntarily stayed behind to guard the riches—and tradition foretold a brutal end for anyone who dared to snatch the loot."

Claire shuddered imperceptibly.

"Blackbeard was despicable, wicked, and corrupt. He wore a broad-rimmed hat, and always had several pistols dangling in holsters from his wide belt. He ranted and raved with unbelievable passion, and proclaimed his powers of evil and ability to inflict injury on others—at times even calling himself a "Son of Satan." Ugly inside and out, even as a boy he had a hideous face—eyes that glared with anger and violence, and the smile of a devil. As an adult, masses of jet-black hair covered his head and face, and he had a beard that reached to his waistline, it is told. This formidable pirate was a terrorist. He had a sinister plan and feared no man. His repulsive appearance seemed to work to his advantage as he partook in dastardly deeds, like killing, stealing, raping, fighting, and general plundering and ravaging. In his day, ship after ship fell at his hands, many surrendering at the mere sight of the fearsome and grotesque pirate without even putting up a fight."

"The lore fascinates me, Nate. But why do the islanders refuse to talk about the hidden caves? Why all the secretiveness?" Claire asked. The memory of the restaurant incident flashed before her eyes.

He gave her a long and contemplative look. "They won't discuss it with you, Claire, because you're a foreigner. Many of them still believe that pirate treasures remain hidden in the surrounding waters and caves, and they have confidence and believe with all their hearts that any treasures found in this area rightfully belong to *them—to the island*—and not to mere visitors, or treasure seekers, who might stumble upon the valuables and take them away for their own purposes. That's why they'll not discuss their existence with non-islanders. In fact, they'll do anything to steer tourists away from searching for the hidden caves. *Anything!*

"You see, there are those among them who have made it a lifelong mission to locate the lost treasures, and still actively search for them on a daily basis. And on rare occasions, old coins still wash ashore, onto the beaches of certain properties owned by the islanders. A few of these coins hold *high* value—monetarily and historically. In fact, some of the treasures—coins or otherwise—would be highly sought after by museums of the world...and the black market, of course."

"Fascinating," Guy said.

"It could be *extremely dangerous* to find any of these secreted spoils and attempt to remove them from the island, especially if someone knew you had found something," Nathan said.

Claire swallowed hard. It almost seemed as if Nathan knew *they* had found something, and was warning *them*. But how could that be?

"You could get your throat slit," he added.

CLAIRE AND Guy walked back to the condo without talking, absorbing all they'd heard.

"Nathan really has the knack for storytelling, doesn't he?" Claire asked.

Guy returned her gaze, gave her a gentle kiss on both cheeks, and said nothing. He did this when he wanted to make a point. Okay, she understood. Maybe it wasn't just a *story*. Sinking deeply into a living room chair, she closed her eyes. Guy clearly had concerns. He had clarified that without speaking. But so did she.

For dinner that evening, Claire spread a large towel on the beach. They'd picked up takeout Chinese food for dinner and planned to watch the spectacular sunset in total relaxation.

"It's funny, Guy. Of *all* people, *we* find a hidden treasure—without even looking for it, not really. And I'm going to bet no one has walked through the tunnels we found, not since the time of the pirates…or at least in a very long time. It's strange how things work sometimes, isn't it?"

"Yeah. You can say that again."

"Think about it," she said. We've heard more about pirates in the last day and a half than most people hear in a lifetime. Personally, I haven't even had a passing thought about them since watching *Peter Pan* as a child. And now, suddenly, we're thrown into this incredible lore. You have to wonder why. They say there's no such thing as coincidence…that everything happens for a reason…."

"That's what they say—whoever they are." Guy said. He was a dyed-in-the-wool doubting Thomas and it showed.

Chopsticks in hand, they ate the yummy Chicken Almond Ding and Mongolian Beef out of the cartons, and drank white wine from plastic glasses. Afterwards, Claire stretched out fully and laid her head on Guy's lap. Casually dressed in loose-fitting shorts and tee shirts, it became easy to unwind and embrace the tranquility of the serene surroundings. Before they knew it, thoughts of anything else wafted into nothingness. Living in the moment, Claire smiled to herself. How could that simple dinner have been one of the most romantic they'd ever shared—not the most fancy, but definitely the most romantic?

She felt a powerful connection with her lover that spanned time and space. It was a sensation she experienced frequently.

"How's the thumb?" she asked.

"Not sure. I haven't felt the throbbing for a while now, and I've stopped taking the pills, so I think it's doing fine. I tend to heal pretty fast, you know."

"Good. I can't stand it when you're hurting."

Appearing as a glorious and radiant ball of orange in the tranquil heavens, the sun hovered majestically over the waters. Soon it would be setting, and they'd witness firsthand the magnificence of a Caribbean sunset. Once it started its descent, it would happen rapidly.

"Watch closely, Guy. And don't blink, or you'll miss it."

"Aye, aye, captain."

With humidity just right, and no clouds appearing on the horizon, everything was lined up perfectly for it to occur.

"Are you looking? It's going to happen," Claire said. "Don't blink, or you'll miss it," she repeated.

Eyes affixed to the large glowing sphere, they watched eagerly as the sun began its movement downward—until it vanished from sight into the apparent line of demarcation between the waters and the sky.

"There it was! Did you see it?" Claire asked. Sheer exuberance bubbled from her being. At the moment the sun disappeared into the waters, a brilliant *flash of green* appeared for a split second.

"Afraid not. And I *was* looking," he said. Disappointment was evident in his voice and on his face.

"Oh, honey, I'm sorry. Maybe next time?" She kissed him with tenderness.

After the sunset, the no-see-ums came out in hordes—the biting insects so small they are virtually invisible to the human eye. They gathered up the blanket and empty containers in haste and sprinted back to the condo.

Early Sunday morning

AFTER A hot morning shower, and a fresh cup of steaming coffee, Claire prepared a light breakfast and set it up out on the screened porch. Outside, birds chirped merrily, children played nearby, and a neighbor busily trimmed palm fronds and ferns overhanging onto his sidewalks and mowed patches of visible lawn. A small lime green lizard ran up and down the screening. She woke Guy, and together they enjoyed a plate of fresh tropical fruits and cinnamon toast. Afterwards, they grabbed beach shoes and took an unhurried walk along the white and sandy shoreline. The warm water splashed their feet and ankles with each step, and the cool, damp sand felt refreshing. Each footprint they left behind quickly disappeared, as the gentle Caribbean waters lapped ashore.

"We never looked at the coins we found with the artifact," Claire said.

"I totally forgot about them." Guy looked at her in astonishment. "Wonder what they are? Especially after listening to Nathan yesterday."

"Honey, there's something I need to tell you," Claire said. "Can we stop for a minute?"

"Sure. What is it? Talk to me." He turned toward her and grabbed both her hands. "What's on your mind?"

"I don't know how to tell you this, other than to just tell you. We have to fly home this afternoon."

"*What*? *Why*? *How*?"

"Gary LuVasse called the morning after we arrived. You had just jumped into the shower, and didn't hear the phone ring. There's an emergency situation involving one of my files, and I must get back to work. I couldn't book us on a return flight home 'til today. I didn't want to ruin the couple of days we had here, so I didn't tell you until now. We leave this afternoon. But think of the bright side. At least we had a nice New Year's together."

"I'm shocked. Why did you keep me in the dark?" He picked up a piece of coral that had washed ashore and lobbed it into the water. Then he kicked at the sand, obviously venting his anger.

"So you wouldn't have to think about it—so it wouldn't spoil the short time we had here. I wanted our time away to be special."

"Next time, tell me. We're partners. And I'm a big boy. Next time, let me know when something's going on, will you?"

"Yes, of course. I apologize."

He picked up another chunk of coral and hurled in into the air over the water.

"I mean it, Claire. Either we're in this together, or we're not. You've got to trust me with this stuff." He pulled her close and wrapped his arms around her. Melting into his embrace, she thought about how he had handled the situation with such dignified decorum. She knew, more and more, how much she loved him. "We've got a bigger problem facing us now, as I see it," he said. "What are we going to do with the artifact?"

"I've given that serious thought. I have a plan, and I think it will work."

They continued on their stroll, his hand locked around hers.

"I hate to leave, Claire. Seems like we only just arrived."

"Me, too. We'll come back."

"Promise?"

"Promise!"

Returning to the condo, they changed into swimwear, grabbed towels, and ran down to the sandy edge of the welcoming turquoise waters for one last swim.

11

"ARE WE READY to pack the artifact?" Claire asked.

The ongoing ethical debate about how to handle the precious relic and coins had been the source of heated discussion and disagreement. Claire had found a shipping crate and packing materials the day before when she ran out to pick up a newspaper, and now stood ready to set her plan into motion. But she felt another argument brewing.

"Dammit, Claire. What do you think you're doing? You're going to get us into a lot of trouble. I don't think we should do this. But you won't listen to me."

"We have to, Guy. We have no other choice. It'll be fine. You'll have to trust me. No duty applies to art or antiques, and the relic is certainly an *antique*, if not *art*, wouldn't you agree? So there may be no questions whatsoever."

"That's a stretch, Claire, and you know it. Obviously, the law was not written to include *ancient antiquities* stashed away by *pirates*. The law clearly is referring to antiques or art one would *purchase* at an antiques or art store."

"Yes, that is technically true, but there is no other way to get the relic home and have it appraised by an expert to determine what it is. If we turn it in here, we'll never know anything about it or what happens to it. And besides, the question remains to whom it actually does belong. I could argue it's the person, or persons, who found it. At least until we determine where it belongs, I think we should keep it with us. Aren't you curious to find out where it came from, what it's made of, and who hid it? I know I am. And knowing you the way I do, I'd bet you want answers to those questions, too. You can't deny it."

"Finished?"

"I am."

Guy stormed from the room, and walked outside to smoke a Cuban cigar—to cool off in the heat. After he had had ample time to think things over, he went back inside.

"Now it's my turn," he said. "I know I'm going to surprise you, but you convinced me. We *should* take it back with us. And we *will* figure out where it belongs, and put it back in the hands of the legal owner. I'll agree to those terms. That's the best thing we can do, and, after all, our actions are selfless. Our purpose is not to line our pockets, but to do the right thing. I'm not worried about the coins, because they sell old coins in many of the shops here, and most of them have only nominal value anyway." He smiled a broad and apologetic smile. "Let's get to it, Claire, and get that thing packed up."

She nodded and smiled back at him, surprised but thankful for his change of heart.

Painstakingly they wrapped the relic in layer upon layer of bubble wrap, and then wedged it tightly into the container. If questioned by customs officials, they would honestly answer that the piece was an antique. Hopefully they would not be pressed further or be asked for a receipt. Clearly understanding their mission, they held ethical concerns at bay for the time being—focusing only on the big picture. After all, who would fault them for trying to return the piece to its proper owner?

Arriving at the airport with time to spare, they checked their luggage and the crate at the ticket counter, relieved that no one questioned them. They boarded the plane and flew to Miami.

Miami, Florida

THE U.S. Customs agent at the Miami International Airport became seriously interested in the crate and its contents, and the questioning began.

"Passport please." The agent opened Claire's official document issued by the U.S. government, authenticating her identity and right to travel to and return from other countries, scanned it, and looked at her with probing eyes.

"Where did you go when you left the U.S., Ms. Caswell?" he asked.

"Grand Cayman, sir. The British West Indies."

"How long were you out of the country?"

"We flew down last Thursday and today is Sunday, so about three days, or four, depending on how you look at it."

"Purpose of your trip?"

"Vacation. A pleasure trip."

"What do you have in the crate, Ms. Caswell?" he asked.

She smiled at him. "They have a wonderful antiques shop on Grand Cayman, sir—in downtown Georgetown. We are bringing back a souvenir from the island."

Okay, so far so good. She had told no lies. There is a nice antiques shop on the island, *and* they did bring back a souvenir—in the form of a famous Tortuga Cayman Island Rum Cake. Both true statements, independently.

"What's in the container, Ms. Caswell?" he persisted.

"What's art to one may be an antique to another. Whichever, there's no duty on either one, right?" she asked.

"Who's asking the questions here—you or me?" he boomed.

"Well, you are, of course," she said, politely.

"Your receipt for the item?"

Claire hesitated momentarily.

Just then the agent noticed Guy standing behind her, and his demeanor changed suddenly, without explanation.

"*Your* passport, sir."

Guy handed it to him, and the agent scanned it through his machine and looked it over quickly. "As I suspected. Why didn't you say so? I'd recognize the famous criminal prosecutor anywhere. I've seen your picture in the *Miami Herald* more times than I can count. Did you enjoy your vacation on the island, sir? I see you picked up a present for the little lady." He winked at Guy. "You're both free to go. Welcome back to the United States." The agent smiled at Guy. "Keep up the good work!"

Guy returned the smile, and nodded. They walked away briskly, Guy pushing the cart.

"Clearly too close for comfort," he said.

"Tell me about it," Claire said. "He questioned me, not you."

"And you did a superb job dodging bullets, my dear. Masterful, in fact!"

"Thank you, counselor. I'll take that as a compliment. And you made that stoic agent smile. Bet he hasn't done that in a while."

Hailing a taxi, they loaded the suitcase into the trunk and placed the crate onto the front passenger seat. Together they huddled in the back seat, holding hands, thankful that Customs had not presented a more serious problem.

WALKING INTO their home, after being away, always triggered feelings of serenity—no matter how short a time they'd been gone.

"Take a walk with me, Guy," Claire said. "We can unpack later."

Strolling along the flower-filled sidewalks of their neighborhood, they saw others—walkers and joggers alike—who had the same idea on such a beautiful day. It felt fabulous to stretch their legs.

"Tomorrow promises to be interesting," Claire said. "I can't wait to find out what's going on with this file of mine."

"It had better be good. Or I'll be mad as hell we had to cut our vacation short," Guy said.

Claire stared at him, uncertain whether his anger centered on ending their vacation early or the fact that his plan to ask her to marry him had not materialized. She couldn't ask.

"I mean it. I'll have words with LuVasse if it's not a real emergency," he thundered.

The unmistakable harshness in his voice took her aback, as it always did, and put her on the defensive. Lately he seemed angrier than usual, or maybe just more frustrated. She gave him the benefit of the doubt. "Excuse me? First of all, you'll do no such thing," she said. "And secondly, he would not have called me back unless it was absolutely necessary. This, I know. It's something big, I can assure you."

"You don't *know* for sure. You and LuVasse had better be right."

Claire walked in silence. She'd better be right, or what? Continuing the banter seemed pointless when he got into a mood like this, and his comments made her angry. Holding her feelings inside, she decided nothing would be resolved if she threw a card in and continued the exchange game.

Guy wanted to apologize to Claire in the worst way for speaking harshly, but he could not. Sometimes he just talked that way. He didn't mean to offend her. After all, he argued for a living and it came naturally to him. He could argue with anyone, at anytime, about anything, and enjoy it thoroughly. He grabbed her by the hand, and they walked without talking. Guy did not see talking as the end-all cure-all to rectify all disputes. Why did Claire seem so hypersensitive? More often than not, all women seemed overly thin-skinned to him. What *was* that? He didn't understand. Just the presence of Claire was all he needed. This notion of perpetually talking things out seemed highly overrated. He squeezed her hand as a sign that he loved her.

Back at the condo, Claire undressed and climbed into bed to take a nap. She settled in, under the cozy and lightweight down comforter, on her side, adjusting the jumbo down pillow under her head until it felt just right. Before she nodded off, she felt Guy slide in beside her, pull her close, and repeatedly kiss her back with purposeful tenderness. As rest came, anger melted away.

Monday morning

THE BUZZING alarm clock jolted Claire from sound sleep. She got up, showered, dressed for the business day, and drove to work.

Gary LuVasse sat in his office, drinking his morning coffee, going over year-end enforcement statistics, and waiting for her. "Morning, Claire," he said, seeing her walk past his office. "Thanks for coming back early from your vacation. Grab your Lawden file and a cup of java and come back in here. I have a lot to tell you."

In short order, she filled a large cup with black coffee, grabbed her file and a notebook and pen, and returned to his office. Burning with curiosity, needing to know why Gary had summoned her back, she couldn't wait another minute. "The suspense is killing me," she said. "What's going on?"

"Claire, when the process began to remove the third tank from the ground out at the Lawden property, an unpleasant discovery was made," Gary LuVasse began. He furrowed his brows in a way she had not seen before.

12

THE PROPERTY OWNER, John Lawden, hurled his coffee mug into the wall. In the worst way, he wanted this clean-up to be over and to receive the reimbursement monies due him from the State. But he knew the routine all too well. Having previously cleaned up two other parcels that he owned, he was well aware of his legal responsibilities, and this would be his final obligation.

He was determined to push the envelope to the hilt on this final job—to walk away from it a rich man. If no soil contamination turned up on his land, the State would not reimburse his expenses, and that would never do. So he had concocted a plan to ensure that petroleum would be found in the hole left behind by the third tank. And on that very day, when the workers had taken a break, he had planned to make his move.

But then this cursed skeleton had shown up on his property, forcing him to postpone his carefully thought out scheme—maybe even permanently if he didn't act cleverly enough. He thought long and hard about his dilemma, and concluded he would proceed with his brilliant plan. He went to the kitchen and made a sandwich. Conniving took energy.

The anxiety in his psyche needled him relentlessly. To proceed at this juncture would increase the risk of detection, especially with this Claire Caswell investigator snooping around; yet, he had no choice but to proceed—with extreme caution, of course. The golden opportunity for wealth would not be available forever. And if he thought she asked too many questions before the find, she certainly would be asking more now. If she saw him milling around the excavation site secured with yellow *Police Line Do Not Cross* tape, or spotted him holding a gasoline can, or worse yet witnessed him dumping petroleum into the hole, he could wind up sitting in a prison cell on a serious fraud conviction. That would never do. He'd have to figure out a way to keep this crime buster, Claire Caswell, from catching him. He picked up the phone to make a call—then slammed it down. Why was this consuming him? Sitting pensively, he ate the sandwich.

Damn! He thought to himself. *Damn!* This incredibly untimely discovery of the hunk of bones on his property really threw a wrench into things. Now there would be insurmountable delays in the cleanup process, with the reimbursement payments, and ultimately in the construction of his new house, for the entire project would be scrutinized far too closely. Luck had not taken his side. He had counted on this money. But now, because of this blasted skeleton, he'd have to be really smart, to devise a new strategy…or at least wait for another prime opportunity.

"WHAT? WHAT was discovered at the site?" Claire asked. "What was it?"

"A human skeleton," LuVasse said. "Fully intact, according to Sergeant Massey of the Miami-Dade Police Department, although I haven't seen it for myself."

"A *skeleton*? On the Lawden property? That's a bombshell."

"Yeah. The remains of a person—just bones."

"Who found it, a contractor?"

"Apparently when the backhoe operator was scooping out top fill to access and pull the third tank, the on-site consultant spotted it. I guess the sun flashed on something in the hole and caught his attention. "

"Flashed on what in the hole?"

"According to Sergeant Massey, a necklace, or neck chain of some kind, that was around the skeleton's neck. He's instructed the Medical Examiner to photograph it, dust it for prints, and bag it as evidence. It should be available for you to look at soon."

"How curious, Gary. This is a strange one. Is Lawden a suspect?"

"Claire, at this point we don't know if we're looking at a murder or whether the person died of natural causes and simply ended up being buried there. We're waiting for a report from the Medical Examiner, and hopefully we'll know a lot more once we get it. If homicide is established as the cause of death, the State Attorney's Office will be called in to prosecute the matter. And then, you can bet your bottom dollar that your Gaston Lombard will be assigned to it. That's another reason I want you to stay on the case. The two of you work well together, and if this turns into a criminal investigation, I think you are the ones to work it up."

"A *criminal* investigation? You want *me* on a *criminal* investigation, Gary?"

"I do. Your sleuthing skills are admirable, Claire. We all know it. And this is no doubt going to require some tough and creative work to put together. I have the greatest admiration for your investigative talents. If it's solvable, you and Gaston are the two who will do it."

"Thanks for your vote of confidence, Gary. I'm honored. Truly. And I've always wanted to work up a criminal felony case."

"You're ready to do it, Claire. Have been for a long time. I know you won't let me down. Now, while we're waiting for the Medical Examiner's report, why don't you start by interviewing Lawden, and the consultant overseeing his clean-up. Remember, the consultant was the first to spot the skeleton—for whatever that's worth. Take a look around the site. And review the tapes I left on your desk, along with these newspaper clippings." He handed her a stack of articles. "You'll be brought up to speed quickly on all the details we know so far."

"Consider it done."

"Talk to Sergeant Massey, too. Look at the photos taken of the skeleton at close range and from the top of the dig site. He has those. They may give you a clue to follow. And don't forget about the necklace. Find out the particulars on that thing. Use those well-honed investigator skills of yours and see what you can come up with. It'll be good to get a jump on these things—in case this goes the way we think it will."

"I agree. I'll get right on it, Gary. The whole thing is a bit unnerving, I'll admit, but I'm intrigued nevertheless. What about my other case files?" she asked.

"Everything's under control. I'm ahead of you on that. They've already been split up and reassigned to other investigators—all but the Lawden file, I should clarify. You stay on that one. We don't know, yet, if Lawden and the skeleton are connected in any way. Actually, at this point, no one knows which way this case may turn."

"I assumed you had taken care of my other files when I didn't see them in my office this morning. It felt strangely empty in there."

"Claire, this investigation may dead-end right away, or not. If it takes off, it may go fast. You are on your own. Work at home, if you'd prefer, or split your time between here and home. Do what you need to do. But I will ask that you keep me posted on your progress as time allows," LuVasse said. "We may hear from the Medical Examiner yet today, or tomorrow for certain. He's been asked to put a rush on his findings. Then you'll have more to go on. Now get out of here and prove me right. Use your best fact-finding skills, and give that skeleton a name."

"I'll do my best."

"Oh, one more thing. I don't want to poison the well, so to speak, but this Sergeant Massey is a character. He's a little rough around the edges. Don't let him get to you."

"Not a chance, Gary."

"And apologize to Gaston for interrupting his vacation, too, will you? I certainly don't want him on my bad side."

"Yes, I will, and no, you don't." She chuckled.

Returning to her office, she decided to look through the stack of mail dropped on her desk during the briefing with Gary LuVasse. But first, she noticed several pink message slips indicating Gaston Lombard had called, each requesting she call him back *ASAP*. Picking up the phone, she dialed his number.

"Honey? It's me," Claire said. "I just got out of a meeting with Gary LuVasse and you won't believe what he told me."

"That a skeleton turned up in Miami Shores at one of your clean-up sites, perhaps?"

"How did you know?"

"It's all the scuttlebutt at my office, Claire. Everyone's talking about it. Most are assuming it's a homicide victim and that my office will be involved shortly."

"Yeah. We should find out soon, Guy. And you'll be surprised to hear that LuVasse wants *me* to investigate the matter from this end. So, perhaps, we may be working together to solve a murder, if your office does get involved."

"Good for you, darling. It's about time you started investigating the big stuff. We both know you're more than capable. Bravo, my beauty! And I hope we do get to work together on it. I can think of nothing I'd rather do than investigate a case with you. I mean, it, Claire. With your natural abilities and track record, we would make an unbeatable team, don't you think?"

"I think, at best, we'll have our work cut out for us on this one. But listen to me. I'm assuming too much too soon."

"I'll take that thought as an omen—knowing you the way I do. Let's hope the Medical Examiner doesn't keep us waiting long for his findings. Bye for now."

Claire hung up, grabbed her stack of mail, and started a pile for correspondence relating to the reassigned files; that way LuVasse could disburse the letters to the appropriate investigators in her office. Reaching the middle of the stack, she noticed an envelope addressed to her marked "Confidential." Examining it closer, she became conscious of several factors. It was still sealed, and contained no return address. Also, the sender had incorrectly spelled her last name, and inaccurately indicated her job title. Further, she noted what seemed to be oily stains, or discoloration of some sort, on the envelope's backside. Grabbing a letter opener from her top drawer, she sliced it open and pulled out the single sheet.

Computer generated words set forth the simple one-line message: "*Stay clear of the skeleton investigation if you know what's good for you.*"

It was not the first time she'd been threatened over the course of her career, and if the author of this letter thought it would make her jump out of her skin, or make her hair stand on end, he or she thought wrong. It did not frighten the daylights out of her, or spook her, or unnerve and intimidate her, or even shake her. But it did inform her that someone did not want *her* investigating the find for a reason. Why? What did the despicable person not want her to discover? Claire resolved to dig her heels in firmly. She would not be dissuaded from giving the investigation her all.

High odds existed that no good fingerprints would be lifted from the letter or envelope, as most people sending menacing letters wore gloves. And additionally, several people had already handled the mail before it made its way to her desk. She pondered the situation. Contemplatively, she folded the sheet of paper and returned it to the envelope. Then she opened a bottom desk drawer and dropped the correspondence far to the back. She would not tell LuVasse or Guy about it and risk being pulled from the case, for it was too important to her reputation and career. LuVasse counted on her to solve this mystery and she would not let him down. And besides, in her heart of hearts, she had always yearned to investigate felony cases. This was her chance—her foot in the door. She'd handle it her way.

Claire spent the remainder of the morning going through the rest of her mail, reading the newspaper articles relating to the discovery, and watching the broadcast tapes in a conference room, taking detailed notes of everything she read and viewed.

Lawden and his consultant had agreed to meet her at the dig site that afternoon for an interview. Meeting at the property would give her an opportunity to look around the excavated hole and examine the precise area where the skeleton surfaced, just in case the team of professionals Sergeant Massey had assembled had missed anything. She glanced at her watch. She was more than anxious to interview the men and observe the demeanor of both. After eating a quick bite, she drove out to the clean-up locale.

Arriving earlier than the scheduled meeting, she allowed herself ample time to assess the surroundings before talking to the interviewees. Walking over to the dig location, she ducked under the yellow police tape and moved with difficulty down into the cavity, to the exact spot where the skeleton had rested. The imprint of the panoply of bones remained clearly and eerily visible in the soil layers of clay, sand, and limestone—an aggregate that had probably played a key role in preserving the bones for later examination—the clay element being instrumental in keeping the skeleton intact, and the sand portion being resistant to retaining water. Using the gardening tool she had thoughtfully picked up on the way, she dug ever so carefully around the impression, looking for any overlooked clue. But her search of the surrounding area turned up nothing.

Climbing back to ground level proved to be somewhat of a challenge, but with extra effort Claire made it to the top. She decided to take a fast look inside a small and dilapidated shed, situated on the back property line—a structure she'd noticed when she arrived that afternoon. The edifice's gray barn-wood door barely hung on by its rusty hinges, and heat had warped it making it difficult to open, but she tugged at it until ever-so-slowly it popped open far enough to allow her slender body to squeeze through. Inside, daylight streamed in from the narrow spaces created by the irregular slats of wood nailed up in a horizontal fashion to form the building's four primitive walls. Darting her eyes in every direction, she observed piles of old boards in various sizes and shapes, numerous coils of rusty barbed wire stacked near the center on the moisture-distended floor boards, and old and worn tin gas station signs leaning against one side wall.

Turning to leave, she noticed a filthy, oil-stained towel covering something in a front corner of the simple structure. Pulling the towel away, she saw a shiny, red, five-gallon gasoline can—and it felt close to full when she lifted it. Using the towel, she unscrewed the cap and smelled the contents, satisfying herself that it was, indeed, gasoline. She recapped the container, threw the covering back over it, and exited the shed the way she had entered. Stepping outside, her eyes flitted to a mature oak tree not fifty yards away. Was it her imagination, or did she just see the face of a man dart behind it?

13

TEN MINUTES LATER, Lawden and his consultant drove up to the property in a late model, red Lincoln Navigator, parked curbside, and walked toward Claire, standing near the location of the skeletal find. She made a mental note that the consultant was the driver of the vehicle.

"Sure hope we didn't keep you waiting long, Ms. Caswell," the consultant said.

"Actually, you're right on time, Mr. McDonald."

"Please, Ms. Caswell, call me, Joe."

The three of them stood as Claire conducted the interview. The consultant had little, or nothing, to add to the discussion, other than to relay how the *glint* in the hole, caused by some kind of metal catching the blazing rays of the sun that day, caught his attention. He attributed the preservation of the skeleton to his noticing the *flash*—stating that a moment later, the backhoe would have done serious damage to the framework of bones.

Claire turned her attention to Lawden. "Mr. Lawden, this is your third clean-up. You and I have worked together on your previous two, and Mr. McDonald has acted as your environmental consultant on all three of these. On the first two projects, surprisingly, the tests performed on soil samples taken from the surrounding basins revealed extremely high levels of contamination. I say, *surprisingly*, because none of those tanks had badly corroded, sir. Yet both sites required an extreme amount of cleaning up—according to your consultant here, Mr. McDonald—or Joe, that is, and we received, and paid, your requests for exorbitant amounts of reimbursement in each case."

"What are you implying?" Lawden growled.

"Just stating the facts, sir. Did I say anything not correct?"

"Well, it seemed...." Lawden stopped short, and leered at Claire.

"Now, let's talk about *this* site, Mr. Lawden. You had a total of three underground tanks that needed hoisting from the ground on this property—to comply with federal and state laws. Soil tests relating to the first two pulled show no contamination whatsoever in the basins surrounding those tanks. I'm going to guess the third basin's tests will show similar results, once the police give the go-ahead to continue with the tank pull, that is. Wouldn't you suspect the same?"

"No, I wouldn't. One never knows until the test results come back, right Joe?" Lawden looked to his consultant seeking confirmation.

"Why, yes, I would have to agree with Mr. Lawden on that one, Ms. Caswell. No one can predict what soil samples will show. Often we, too, are startled by the results."

"I'm sure you are, Joe," Claire said. "But we can both agree that it's usually the old buried tanks, the ones constructed of non-galvanized steel, those installed fifty, sixty, or even seventy years earlier, the ones corroded to the point that they actually break apart when they're hoisted from the ground, those are the tanks that cause the big problems, sir." She shifted her questioning back to Lawden. "What are you planning to do with this property once your clean-up is completed?"

"What I do, or don't do, with my property is really none of your business. Why do you ask?"

"Just curious, sir." She eyed Lawden. The man made her skin crawl, and the disconcerting smirk on his face displeased her greatly.

Thoughts of the can of gasoline sped through her mind. He had plans, she wagered. Lawden and his consultant needed careful watching. And while McDonald appeared to be more polished and professional than Lawden, especially since he spoke with the unctuous politeness of Eddie Haskell, her instincts warned her not to be fooled. She guessed him to be in cahoots with Lawden up to his eyeballs, sharing visions of exploiting the system and splitting exaggerated profits yet another time. But she needed proof. "Mr. Lawden, do you have any idea on the identity of the skeleton?" Claire asked.

"Now how the *hell* would I know that?"

"It did turn up on *your* property, didn't it?" She looked him straight in the eyes.

"Yeah. Big deal. So what? That means nothing. Have you talked to previous owners? Or are you just badgering *me*?"

Ignoring the question, she turned to Joe. "How about you? Any thought on the skeleton's identity?"

"Ditto for me, Ms. Caswell. How would I know? I just work here. But I can appreciate your interest." He smiled a forced and insincere smile.

"Right. Of course. Well, if either of you come up with a possibility, or recollect anything that may be of help in this matter, be sure to let me know. And Mr. Lawden, and Joe, I'd be very surprised to see contaminated soil samples from this third tank basin, since no contamination has showed up so far out here, and I'm sure you would be, too. Looks like this may turn out to be a non-reimbursable clean-up. We'll see." She shook hands with each of them. "Thank you for your time, gentlemen."

As Claire walked to her car, the eyes of the two men bore into her back.

"She's trouble," Lawden said. "Big trouble."

"I told you I'd take care of everything," McDonald said.

CLAIRE RETURNED to her office and made detailed notes of both interviews, and the site findings, and placed a flag in the file regarding the full gasoline can she'd found in the shed. Lawden and McDonald required close monitoring. Next she picked up her phone and scheduled a meeting with Sergeant Massey for the following day.

WHEN CLAIRE arrived at Sergeant Massey's headquarters at ten the next morning, a receptionist offered her a cup of coffee and brought her to his office. Sergeant Massey stood and extended his hand, looking downward. "Pleasure to meet you, Ms. Caswell. I hear you're a crack investigator."

"Thank you, sir. Good to meet you, as well."

"Have a seat. Please." He started shuffling through papers on his desk.

She sat, and pulled a legal pad and pen from her briefcase.

"Now, what can I do for you, Ms. Caswell?" He cracked his knuckles.

"Well, for starters, I'd like to go over everything you told Gary LuVasse about the skeletal find, in case I've missed anything. I'd also like to see the photos your officers took at the site on the day of the discovery."

"I've got those right here for you to look at. In fact, take them with you. We don't need them right now and, quite frankly, if criminal wrongdoing is confirmed, I will be referring the matter to the State Attorney's Office. And I understand you'll be working with that office—if it goes in that direction. Just sign this release and they're yours to take."

Claire signed, and quickly perused the glossy photographs. "Gruesome, isn't it? Oh, and that neck chain I heard about. I see it here on the skeleton. Did you figure out what's hanging from it?" she asked.

"No. The Medical Examiner's office has that in its possession. You'll have to ask them about it."

Never looking up from his desk, the Sergeant filled Claire in on all the facts he was aware of, to date, regarding the bizarre surfacing. She jotted meticulous notes as he spoke. It became clear to Claire that

Sergeant Massey felt acute discomfort talking with her, but she didn't have a clue why. Sitting on the edge of his seat, he cracked his knuckles repeatedly. He seemed uptight, tense, and incomprehensibly nervous, avoiding nearly all eye contact with her. His next question startled her.

"You're an attractive woman, Ms. Caswell. How did you end up working as a government investigator?" Still, he did not look up, and kept his eyes riveted to the paperwork in front of him.

His demeanor, and now this question, rubbed her the wrong way. "Why would the way I look have anything to do with my career choice?" she asked.

Sergeant Massey did not answer. Claire would be about the same age as his daughter, Pammy. In his divorce proceedings, the courts had believed him to be an abusive father, based upon vindictive testimony from his ex-wife and that of her siblings, and wrongly denied him visitation rights. When Pammy came of legal age, and he'd called her, she'd made it crystal clear that she wanted nothing to do with her "absentee and neglectful excuse for a father." And while he had attempted to make contact with her again later on—two or three times—to explain what had really happened, her attitude had remained the same, so the opportunity never presented itself, and the truth remained buried forever. Silently, he resented this Claire Caswell dame for reviving the agony he kept so well contained, just beneath his hardened surface.

When Claire extended her hand, and the two exchanged firm handshakes, he allowed himself a fleeting glimpse into her eyes for the first time—eyes that portrayed strength and intelligence, yet at the same time, innocence, just like he remembered Pammy's.

"Thank you, Sergeant, for the information on the skeletal find. You've been most helpful," Claire said. She was formal and businesslike.

He watched her leave his office. If only he had hired a skillful attorney to represent his interests in the fight to participate in his child's life at the time the divorce settlement terms became permanent. If only. At the time, it had seemed easier to drink his way into oblivion than to fight the forces of his ex and her family. In truth and in fact, he had always treated his little daughter like a princess, and never, under any circumstances, had he been abusive to her. His head fell into his hands, and he could not hold back tears. In a flash of his mind's eye, he pictured his little girl as a baby, and remembered how he'd carried her around on a pillow. She had been his world. He adored her. But his ex-wife, furious with a career that demanded long hours away from her, and enraged at the long list of other women he kept company with at the watering holes he'd visit after long days on the job, had taken her away. She'd wanted to punish him eternally, and she had. If only he'd been more attentive to his wife. If only. He had loved her, too, once upon a time, more than he cared to admit.

He brushed the tears away, and sat erect. The past had ended, and he'd moved on with his life to the best of his ability. Why open old wounds? What was the point? Feeling powerless and deflated, and vulnerable and weak, he retreated to his self-created emotional cocoon—a safe place where emotions were not allowed. He took a deep breath and dismissed all thoughts of Pammy from his mind. For a brief time, he'd let himself feel the piercing pain he had kept so well suppressed for what seemed like a lifetime, and the resulting anguish, once it surfaced, still stung like alcohol on a fresh wound.

Reaching into a desk drawer, he pulled out a small flask of clear liquid, and took a prolonged swig. Then another. He returned his concentration to work, to his papers, and felt strong again. The sight of Claire Caswell had resurrected excruciating and heartbreaking memories of Pammy, his only child—the offspring he would never know. He hated this Caswell lady.

14

GUY SAT AT his work desk, absorbed in minutia, when the phone rang.

"Mr. Lombard, it's Michael McKay, the County Coroner's Office Chief Medical Examiner calling. Sergeant Massey asked me to give you a ring after I hung up from him. I'd like to meet with you and Claire Caswell in my office—this afternoon. Are you available?"

"Certainly. Might I assume you determined the cause of death to be homicide?"

"Most definitely murder, Mr. Lombard, murder most foul. I'll fill you both in on the details this afternoon. Say 2:30? Call Ms. Caswell, and set it up with her as well, will you?"

"We'll be there. I look forward to hearing what you've come up with."

"Oh, and call the Sergeant also, will you Mr. Lombard? He'd like to speak with you directly."

Guy hung up, dialed Sergeant Massey, and engaged in a short conversation with him. The Sergeant officially transferred the case of the unidentified skeleton to Guy's office, requesting a criminal workup be done. As predicted, Guy personally took the file assignment on behalf of his office, and phoned Claire to give her the news, and to inform her of the upcoming meeting.

Poking her head into LuVasse's office, Claire told him of the Medical Examiner's determination, and also of their plan to meet with McKay that very afternoon. "It's what we suspected," Claire said.

"Well, see what the two of you can come up with, the sooner the better, of course. We don't have endless resources to spend on this investigation, so try and wrap it up in a couple of weeks, if possible. Keep me posted—phone or e-mail. I expect Sergeant Massey will stay on me to get a quick resolution. Most folks are probably placing wagers that this case cannot be solved. Prove them wrong, Claire."

"I hope it's not as tall an order as it sounds. Oh, and before I forget, I found a full five-gallon container of gasoline in a shed on the Lawden property. We need to put that clean-up under a microscope, and keep it there until the job is completed. I don't trust either Lawden or his consultant, Joe McDonald. Both men are on our watch-list—due to past clean-ups where we've suspected they've intentionally contaminated sites, and then submitted false or padded billings to fraudulently obtain monies. My guess? They've done that in the past, and on this last clean-up involving Lawden, they'll attempt to continue the scam. We can't let this one slip through the cracks. I smell something brewing out there. These guys are crooked. Stay on it for me if I'm not available, will you?"

"You got it. I'll *personally* stay awake on this one, and see it to conclusion if need be. You have my word on it," LuVasse said. "Oh, and before it slips my mind, I'm sure you're now aware that Sergeant Massey gave the reporters your name as an investigator on this case—in our press conference and during his television interviews. Be careful, Claire. I mean it. And I can't stress it enough. Be careful!"

"I will, Gary. I realize we don't know who or what we're dealing with here. Not yet, anyway."

At 2:30, Claire and Guy walked into the Office of the Medical Examiner. Michael McKay came out to greet them, and handed them each a full copy of his report, complete with diagrams. "Please, follow me back to my office," he said. "I'll fill you in on the facts concerning your John Doe."

They trailed behind him and sat down on straight-backed chairs across from his desk. Claire pulled out her pad and pen.

"Your skeleton is that of a male," McKay said. "We're able to tell that from the elbow angle, and the thicker and longer arm and leg bones."

Guy pulled a small pad from his shirt pocket to scribble notes.

"And we're looking at murder. I listed a substantial fracture of the skull as the cause of death. Probably caused by multiple severe blows to the back of the head. Pretty brutal, as you may well imagine—blows severe enough to *crack* the skull. The victim may never have known what hit him."

"Wicked," Guy said.

"Must be a low moisture content in the soil where he ended up—maybe part clay," McKay continued, "because the bones are preserved extremely well—all 206 of them. That helps us a great deal, of course."

"Amazing," Claire said. "I noticed the soil in that dig hole was a clay mixture."

"We have some pretty sophisticated, newly-developed DNA testing available when all you have to work with comes down to bones," McKay went on. "We extracted a sample of the victim's DNA from his bones. Please understand, in decades-old bones the only surviving DNA is located within the mitochondria—the components of the cells of the bone that produce energy. We snipped a segment of the DNA out of the mitochondria and thoroughly analyzed it. That might help us tremendously in a case like this, to provide additional information. But you'll need to locate a maternal relative of the victim before those tests can be run."

"A *maternal* relative? I'd say the prospect of that is extremely doubtful, McKay. Do you have an approximate date of death?" Guy asked.

"I do. Best guess? He's been dead some thirty-five to forty years, give or take a couple of years either way."

"That's helpful," Claire said. "Other conclusions?"

"My staff and I have calculated that the victim's approximate height, at time of death, would have been five-foot-eight; his weight we're putting at around one-hundred-sixty pounds."

"Anything else, Mr. McKay?" Claire asked.

"Yes. We're estimating his age at time of death between late thirties and late forties—probably closer to the middle or higher end of that range."

"Good job, McKay," Guy said.

"You have your work cut out for you though, I must say, Ms. Caswell and Mr. Lombard. Not a lot to go on. But I do have one more thing that may be the most helpful of all."

Claire and Guy pricked up their ears.

"As you'll see on the report I gave you, the victim probably exhibited an abnormal walking pattern—due to a left leg at least two inches shorter than his right. Could've been born that way, or a childhood or later disease of some kind might have caused it. With that difference, he most likely wore a corrective shoe, I'd guess."

"That's the single best fact you've given us today, McKay," Guy said.

"I agree," Claire said. "Is that it?"

"I'm afraid it is," McKay said. "But now I'd like to explain briefly the DNA fingerprinting process, so you'll understand more clearly."

Claire and Guy listened attentively.

"The mitochondrial DNA's always inherited from the mother. So if we can extract DNA from blood samples provided by *maternal* relatives of the victim—mother, grandmother, aunt, uncle, you get the picture—the relative's DNA sample sequence could then be compared to the DNA sequence taken from the victim's bones, and we would be able to confirm, with almost absolute certainty, if they are from the same family or gene pool. What are the odds of finding a living maternal relative of the victim in this instance?"

"At this juncture, I'd wager about slim to none," Guy said.

"Oh, one more question before I forget," Claire said. "What about the chain found around the skeleton's neck?"

"I almost forgot, Ms. Caswell. Glad you brought that up," McKay said. "You'll have to take a look at that. Maybe you can figure it out."

15

THE SUCCEEDING MORNING Guy summoned a junior attorney to his office, and reviewed with him the criteria McKay had assigned to the skeleton—including age at time of death, height, weight, gender, and approximate date of death. He requested the young lawyer run a local, state, and national missing persons query entering those specific variables. And he asked the newly hired member of the bar—so eager to please—to plug the same variables into a similar query of unsolved murder cases. Guy demanded the information *yesterday*, stressing the importance of a speedy turn-around. The subordinate acted jittery, obviously feeling the crunch of the order, agreeing to get Guy what he wanted, and quickly. It was time to perform, and perform he would.

Next Guy picked up the phone and called Claire at her office. "The case printouts are in the works as we speak. We should have them soon."

"Great. How many missing persons are we talking about?" Claire asked.

"Well, I suspect there are close to 100,000 missing persons in the country today. Using our variables, we should eliminate about half of those right off the top because they're female. Strangely, it's always about a 50-50 mix on gender. Then, out of the remaining entries, a good percentage will probably hit on many of the criteria guidelines entered. So it's hard to say for sure. Rest assured, we'll need to review a substantial number of them."

"In the meantime, while we're waiting for those reports, what about doing some research on the necklace today? Why don't we meet at home around noon, examine the piece closely, and go from there?" Claire asked.

"You read my mind."

The Medical Examiner had turned the chain over to Guy at the conclusion of yesterday's meeting, after Guy signed the required evidence release form, and he had placed it in his briefcase. The police had unsuccessfully dusted it for prints at the tank pull site, so they could touch it and examine it freely. The possibility was strong that the jewelry could provide a substantial clue, and it warranted in-depth examination.

Arriving home, Claire grabbed her jeweler's loupe from a dresser drawer in the master bedroom and met Guy in the den. Settling into an ergonomically correct leather desk chair, she pulled open the sealed, heavy-plastic evidence bag, and lifted the necklace from it. Holding the special magnifying glass snugly to her right eye, using her right hand, she brought the piece in close with her left, holding it just under the loupe. This allowed her to view the chain with magnificent magnification—ten times that of the real size—and all details, flaws, and surface blemishes became instantly apparent.

"It's quite a nice piece," Claire said.

Guy sat at her side, ready to take notes.

Pulling the desk lamp nearer to her, she manipulated the chain until she had it in the ideal position and lighting to allow for the closest of scrutiny. Years in the earth had dulled and even darkened the chain slightly, but not enough to curtail her inspection.

"This chain is heavy. Expensive," she said. A short delay followed. "Here it is. The marking I was looking for. It's stamped 75 on the clasp, indicating 18-carat gold. That's a marking common in Europe." Next she moved the attached pendant under the loupe's magnification, and studied it for a time. "You won't believe this. It's a *coin*, Guy. But not a U.S. coin. It's a *very* old, *very* worn, *foreign* coin of some kind."

"An *alien coin*? Okay. Interesting."

"Yeah. I second that. And it's turned green from age, so I'm going to assume that it's copper."

"Could be a serious clue."

"We won't know for sure until we find out more about it, but I tend to agree with you," she said. "We need to figure out just what kind of coin we're looking at, and where it came from originally."

"Mind if I take a look at it with the loupe?" Guy asked. "Maybe my *Coins of the World* book will shed some light on this piece of stamped metal for us. It's worth a try, isn't it?"

He looked at the coin, briefly, and then got up and pulled a thick book from a nearby bookcase. Thumbing through it, page-by-page, and cover-to-cover, they searched earnestly for the coin but could not find a match. Feeling noticeable frustration, they drove to the county library, taking the necklace and pendant with them, determined to identify the coin, and spent the remainder of the afternoon there looking though book after book dealing with coins of antiquity. Yet despite their best efforts that day, they did not learn much about it, other than to find a similar-looking coin that had been minted in ancient Greece. Their efforts had not produced the results they needed.

"Let's bring the coin to a numismatist tomorrow," Claire suggested, "and ask for a professional appraisal, and see what he or she comes up with."

"Roger," Guy said. "Your request has been received and understood." He smiled a goofy smile. Adding humor to a humorless situation often helped him through the lull. If truth be told, this whole coin identification thing was taking much too much time. He did not have the patience for it. He wanted answers, and he wanted them now. There was a murder to be solved.

"We really don't have much to go on yet," Claire said. "We do know for certain the body emerged in the ground *above* the buried tank. So we can also deduce it was placed there sometime *after* the tank had been buried. This morning I looked at the property records on that site in my file, and it looks like those tanks went into the ground about fifty years ago—at the time a gas station opened on the property. So we know, absolutely, the body has not been in the ground longer than fifty years. That jibes with what the Medical Examiner said—that he estimated the murder occurred thirty-five to forty years ago. It's just a double confirmation of the time period of the death, I guess."

"Actually, it gives us a definite time frame to consider, but a broad one," Guy said.

"And I've been thinking. If the body had not been put in the ground above a buried tank, and if the law did not require old tanks to be hoisted from the ground, the skeleton would probably never have been found. That's a terrible thought."

They arrived home, put the neck chain in a safe place, and decided to go out to a neighborhood café for a hamburger and a Coke. On their way out, the telephone rang.

"I'll get it," Claire said. "Go start the car. I'll lock up and be right out."

"Hello?" she answered.

A muffled voice uttered chilling words slowly. "*Time's running out, bitch. Better watch your back.*"

"What? Who is this?" she asked.

The sound of the dial tone echoed in her ear.

Claire looked at the Caller ID. It displayed: "Private Caller." She swallowed hard. Now a second threat directed at her. And this one came in on their unlisted home phone number. Only family, close friends, and certain co-workers had it. The sufficiently hushed and enigmatic voice made it impossible to tell whether the caller was even male or female. Without a doubt, someone didn't want her snooping around on this case. Why? Not knowing the answer to that question troubled her deeply. She locked up and walked to the car, preoccupied with her thoughts. These threats would not dissuade her. No way.

"Who called?" Guy asked.

"Wrong number, I guess. Just some faint speech."

"Weird. We don't get many of those on that line."

"No, we don't."

Over dinner, they reviewed the facts of the case that McKay had gleaned, in a relatively short period of time, concerning the strange find of the skeleton found buried in the ground on the Lawden property. Interesting particulars, but where would they lead? They had more information than they'd had only a short time ago, which was certainly encouraging, and tomorrow, with any luck, they'd find out more about the mysterious coin. The more Claire thought about it, the more she believed that learning the specifics concerning the coin might break the case wide open.

BRIGHT AND early the next morning, after jotting down names and addresses of many coin shops and numismatists from the Yellow Pages, they drove to downtown Miami. Anxious to get some answers, they pulled into the parking lot adjacent to the first on their list and entered the shop.

"How may I help the two of you, today?" the owner asked.

"We'd like to have a coin appraised," Claire said.

"That's what I do. Now, let me have a look at it."

Guy handed him the chain with the attached coin.

After several short seconds of examination, turning the coin over and over from back to front, viewing each side several times, he looked up at them. "I've been in this business a long time, but I've never seen a coin exactly like this one. But then, I don't specialize in exotic coins. I don't know where to suggest you take this. Maybe a numismatist with knowledge of ancient coins may have some idea. I'd try some others. Sorry I couldn't be of some help."

They thanked him and left. The words *exotic* and *ancient* rolled around in Claire's mind. What on earth was this coin, and where did it come from?

Morning passed, and the afternoon was rapidly waning. After driving to and visiting several other coin shops in different areas of the downtown area, they found that no one could identify the strange coin. Not getting answers frustrated Claire, and exasperated Guy to no end. In the late afternoon, they stopped at the second to the last shop on their list. A buzzer sounded as they walked across the threshold into the business.

A pleasant-appearing woman in her sixties appeared. "How may I assist you?" she asked.

"Do you deal in foreign or ancient coins?" Guy asked.

"Why yes, it's my specialty. What are you looking for?"

"Actually, nothing," he replied. "We're wondering if you can help us identify a coin." Maybe, at last, they had found someone who could shed some light on the unfamiliar coin. Guy explained that they needed an appraisal, and handed it to her, along with the chain.

After giving it a pithy look over, she responded without hesitation. "Why, this is an ancient lepton," she said. "A rather worthless old copper lepton."

"Did you say *lepton*?" Claire asked. "As in l-e-p-t-o-n?"

"That's right," the woman said.

"Where did it come from?" Claire asked.

"A lepton like this would be from ancient Greece," she replied.

"What else do you know about leptons?" Guy asked.

"The plural is *lepta*. Well, let me see. Lepta were also made of bronze—copper or bronze. Many of these small coins made their way to ancient Israel, from ancient Greece, and they were used in trading. The coin has only nominal value, even to a collector, I'm afraid. It's really nothing to get too excited about."

"Is that it?" Claire asked. "It's important."

"The only other thing would be that any lepton found in the U.S. must have made its way over from Europe or the Middle East. I don't know if that's helpful, or not. It's really all the information I have for you." She handed it back to them. "That will be twenty dollars—for the appraisal. Do you need it in writing?" she asked.

"We do," Guy said, handing her an Andrew Jackson.

She grabbed it from his hands, and prepared a handwritten assessment in no time flat. For value, she indicated, "nominal." "I'm not commenting on the chain, you realize—just the coin," she added. "That neck chain would be a different story altogether."

"We understand. Thank you," Claire said.

"Don't know why someone would hang a low-grade coin like that from a fancy chain in the first place," the woman said. "Oh well. Do you have anything else for me to appraise today? Any other business for me?" Suddenly she seemed displeased that they had bothered her with such apparent nonsense.

"No, I'm afraid that's it," Guy said. "Thank you for your time and the information, madam." He thought about mentioning that she was assisting them in a murder investigation, but he did not. Her attitude bothered him.

Their next stop was a reputable jeweler. They drove to one they had personally done business with in the past—a trustworthy enterprise possessing a sterling reputation, also located in downtown Miami. It was time to ascertain the value of the necklace itself.

The owner greeted them fondly, and upon examination of the chain, he reported that the 18-carat gold necklace was "a handsome piece," and provided them a gratis written estimate placing a retail value on it at $2000, conservatively. Afterward, he suggested they return to do some personal shopping, as their schedules would allow. They thanked him and departed.

On the way home, Guy looked over at Claire. "Sorry to interrupt your pensive mood, but care to share those thoughts with me?"

She glanced his way. "We can now add more facts to what we know about the victim. The coin he wore around his neck is a lepton—a worthless copper coin of ancient Greek origin, a coin used in trading, a coin that may have turned up in Israel. Also, it would have made its way to the U.S. from Europe or the Middle East. Very interesting stuff, wouldn't you agree?"

They absorbed the new information in silence. When they arrived home, Claire turned to Guy. "I've figured out the motive for the murder."

16

Friday and the weekend

UPON RETURNING FROM the Caribbean, a virtual whirlwind had hit their world. The deep mystery of the unearthed skeleton had swallowed up Claire and Guy. In the worst way, they wanted to identify the victim of this atrocious crime, and bring the perpetrator to justice—but for different reasons. Guy had his perfect track record to preserve and protect; Claire wanted to prove to herself, LuVasse, and Guy that she could work up and solve a criminal felony case. She believed, too, that if she could bring this hopelessly impossible assignment to a positive end, the career change she wanted so badly might even materialize. Unbeknownst to either of them, colleagues in both offices had laid wagers that the age-old case would never be solved. Behind their backs, cohorts laughed, and thought they were on an obscure and senseless track that could never reach a satisfactory conclusion. They viewed the case as a waste of time and energy.

Guy had another motivation for solving the case, too. Twice, since returning from the Cayman Islands, he had almost proposed to Claire. Yesterday he'd come close, but unfamiliar terror had gripped him. What if she said no? His question, and her answer, would ruin everything. No, he would wait a little longer. He wondered whether the supposed curse—attached to finding and removing the artifact—had anything to do with the strange sense of dread plaguing him about asking the woman he loved to marry him.

They spent Friday doing additional research on the coin, mapping out a strategy for investigating the case, and interviewing Lawden's neighbors in the Miami Shores neighborhood to determine if anyone knew anything about the identity of the murdered man. Although their efforts produced no worthwhile leads to follow, they had to do the spadework.

EARLY SATURDAY morning, Claire ran out to shop for groceries. While waiting in line to check out, she heard the loud voice of a man calling out to her.

"Claire Caswell? Is that you?"

She turned her head to see Harry Hartmann, the business partner of Robert Holden. Robert Holden had been a dear friend of the Caswell family since long before her birth, and he really considered himself a member of the Caswell household—even though technically he could not appear on the Caswell family tree. Together, Robert Holden and Harry Hartmann had started a business dealing in antiques and rare antiquities, five decades earlier: *Hartmann and Holden Rare Antiques and Collectibles*—a name that had become highly respected within the industry—a name earning them the well-deserved reputation as one of the top retailers of upscale and rare antiques in the Miami area, and for that matter in the world.

Claire had not seen Harry in a couple of years, not since she and Guy attended an elaborate holiday party at his swanky condominium on Collins Avenue in Miami Beach. She still remembered the priceless antiques peppering his showy apartment. He always appeared so decadent to her, while Robert seemed such a simple man. In many ways it was an odd pairing, but in the business world the enduring partnership had worked remarkably well and stood the test of time.

"Harry? Harry Hartmann?"

"How have you been, Claire?" he asked. "Haven't seen you in a long time." He extended a limp handshake.

"Good. You?"

"Oh, fine. Say, I heard your name mentioned on the news the other night. If my memory serves me correctly, it had to do with a body they found buried at some dig site in Miami Shores. You must be climbing up in the world, Claire, assigned to investigate a case of that caliber."

"Well, I'm not sure why they mentioned my name. That should be confidential, you know. It's an open investigation. I'm afraid I can't talk about it, Harry. But before I forget, how's Robert? I haven't spoken to him in a while."

"Always fine, too. A pillar of the community, that man. They broke the mold when they made him. I don't know another person like him in all the world, and I don't know what I would have done without him as my business partner all these years. I couldn't have asked for a better one."

"I'm sure. He's special, there's no doubt. Tell him to expect a call from me in the near future, will you?"

"Okay. Should I tell him what it's about?"

"Not necessary. Just let him know I'll be contacting him." She smiled a polite smile at Harry, and Harry smiled a polite smile back at her. She liked Harry, but always thought it strange he could never maintain direct eye contact for more than a second or two. He made her nervous. Robert had once said Harry fell into the shy category, she recalled. Funny, he never acted shy.

Seeing Harry triggered thoughts of the artifact as she drove back to the condo. They had had little time to give it as much as a fleeting thought since arriving back in the U.S. Maybe Robert would have a chance to look at it in the next couple of days? The longer she thought about it, the more eager she became to hear Robert's assessment. She decided to contact him straightaway. Arriving home, she told Guy about running into Harry, and how the encounter had revived thoughts of the relic.

"Claire, it's like we've forgotten all about it," he said.

"I know. Maybe Robert will have time to look at it soon. I promise I'll call him this weekend."

"Hey, while I still remember, I sent an e-mail to Roman this morning. I'm on tenterhooks waiting to see if he'll be able to find out more about ancient lepta for us," Guy said. "Let's hope for the best."

"Smart move. I will."

Working on an undergraduate degree in Archeological Studies at The Hebrew University of Jerusalem, Roman, Guy's son from an early marriage, had recently turned twenty-two. A fiercely-independent young man, he could come across as aloof, or even arrogant, due to his reserved nature. Highly intelligent and clever, Roman was also conspicuously handsome. He had golden-brown eyes, thick and wavy sandy-colored hair, and deep facial dimples that appeared whenever he smiled—a look that together created a very enviable face. Predictably an honor student in college, school had always come easy for Roman. Although relatives expected him to select medicine as his field of endeavor, as he had talked in his youth about becoming a brain surgeon one day, he had surprised everyone when he'd announced during his first year of college that Archeology would be his major, voicing his insatiable interest in Hebrew studies.

Already having completed three digs in Israel over summers and interim college breaks, excitement pulsed through his veins as he anticipated graduation this year and the possibility of leading digs on his own throughout the Middle East. He was too absorbed in studying to be seriously involved with any special someone at this time in his life; yet his status as a very eligible bachelor—a reputation that secretly brought a smile (and dimples) to his face, and knowledge that when the time proved right, he'd marry the person of his dreams—preceded him wherever he went.

Claire flashed back in time to a year when Roman was a teenager, to a day when she had performed a magnificent magic trick for him. Only a single other person in the world knew how to execute the trick, as it had been passed along to her by a substitute teacher-magician when she attended high school—and he had told her just that. He'd made her promise to one day, at the appropriate time, pass it along to a single other person. And she had. She'd entrusted Roman with the secret to performing the incredible feat of magic. Now he held the torch, and the responsibility to pass it on—to one other—when the perfect opportunity presented itself. The memory of this special time warmed her heart.

Of course Roman would be the obvious person to ask about the lepton. In the midst of intellectuals at the University, someone may well know much about the ancient coin. Her hopes soared. She had total confidence they would soon find out more.

A haunting feeling perplexed Claire—a feeling that she had seen a lepton somewhere before. But she certainly had not even known what a lepton coin looked like—until just a day ago. Yet as hard as she tried, she could not shake the persistent internal nudging.

Guy wrapped Claire in his strong arms, held her tightly, and kissed her.

"You smell good," she said, inhaling deeply the John Varvatos cologne penetrating his neck.

"Let's enjoy the weekend, my beauty," he said. "Monday will be here soon enough, and I'll have all the data I requested. The new attorney I assigned to the project insisted on working throughout the weekend to pull it together. Once we get the printouts, they will entomb us. So let's enjoy today."

"Okay. You've convinced me. But first, let me try to reach Robert. He's the only one to ask about the artifact. Maybe, just maybe, he'll have time to come over tomorrow and take a look at it. You'd enjoy that, wouldn't you?"

"You know I would."

She looked up his number and dialed. "Robert? It's Claire Caswell. How are you?"

"Good, child. How are *you*? It's been far too long since we've talked."

Child—the name he had always called her, as far back as she could remember—had become a term of endearment reserved only for his use.

"I'm good, too, Robert. Really busy. But I'm wondering if you could stop by our home tomorrow, say, one o'clock, for lunch? We have something we'd like to show you."

"Sure. I believe I'm free at that time. Mae plans to attend a church function tomorrow afternoon, so I'll make a point of it. What do you want me to see?" he asked.

"I'd like to hold off on telling you that, until tomorrow."

"So much intrigue. Very well, then, I look forward to seeing you and Guy tomorrow. Bye for now, child."

Guy and Claire went to a movie to escape into fantasy and enjoy the evening together. But as hard as they tried to remove images of the artifact from their thoughts, they could not. While the murder investigation clearly took precedence, seeing Robert and learning more about the ancient relic also ranked high on their list of important things to do. After all, Robert could provide some long-awaited answers. He alone could be trusted with this. Never before had waiting been so difficult. In anticipation of what they would soon learn, they sat on pins and needles, as the drama played out before them.

ROBERT ARRIVED as scheduled on Sunday, looking his usual dapper self—his fine and thinning soft gray hair parted down the middle, combed neatly into place. His conservative attire included: a navy suit, white oxford button-down shirt, and pale-yellow club tie. Over an appetizing lunch, they enjoyed catching up with each other.

Robert never seemed to age. His pale steel blue eyes and perfect features made him a distinguished looking man, although today Claire had to admit he looked a little pasty and somewhat under the weather. He had a softness about him, and a maturity and wisdom she'd always admired. After growing up as childhood friends, and serving together in the Navy during WWII in the Pacific arena, Robert and her father had remained connected throughout the years.

"How are you feeling these days, Robert?" Claire asked.

"Same as ever, child. Thanks for asking." He quickly changed the subject. "Your cooking is as marvelous as ever. I really enjoyed the lunch."

"Glad you liked it. We love having you visit."

Small talk continued for a brief time, until, finally, she could hold back no longer.

"Robert, we have something to show you. And it must be kept in the strictest of confidence at this time. You'll understand why when you see it."

"What could it be, child?" His brows furrowed and he appeared in distress.

"You'll see in a minute."

Guy left the room, and returned almost immediately, proudly carrying the artifact in a soft flannel pillowcase. Carefully removing the covering, he passed the statue to Robert—but only after first giving him a stern warning about the bottom's hazardous protrusion.

Holding it in his hands, Robert stared at the piece in quiet awe for several minutes, looking it over methodically. The air was thick with anticipation.

"In all my years in the business…I've only seen pictures of an artifact like this. But I've never held the real thing in my hands. It's simply extraordinary."

"Yes, isn't it?" Claire asked.

Then something changed. "Where did *you* get this?" His eyes snapped with anger.

Robert's sudden reaction took Claire aback. But before she could respond, he apologized for the outburst.

"It's just that this…this is an *ancient* piece…of museum quality," he said. "And I can't for the likes of me understand how the two of you got your hands on it." He attempted to smile.

Between them, they relayed the entire story, step by step, making certain not to skip any part of it. Robert listened, paying close attention, and seemed to show particular interest when Claire mentioned where they'd found the relic. When they finished their account, Robert stated, with some certainty, that he believed the artifact was an idol carving of some kind, more than likely a figure of idol worship, created during the time of the Aztec or perhaps even Mayan civilization. Then, just as suddenly as before, his tone changed again. "Or, it may turn out to simply be a good replica of an Aztec or Mayan image of worship. These things sometimes fool you."

Shocked by yet another unexpected turn-a-round on the part of Robert, Guy and Claire shot quick glances in each other's direction. *What* was going on?

"With all due respect, Robert, do you really believe that something of this obvious quality could be a mere replica?" Guy asked.

"Yes, I do. It's quite possible, actually." Cheeks blushing, he avoided Guy's piercing eyes, and turned his attention to Claire. "Have you showed this to *anyone* else?" he demanded.

"No, we haven't. We wanted to show you first." She stared at him, confused by his strange behavior, and a bit suspicious.

"Good. Good. I'll have to take it with me for a short time, with your permission of course, to do some research on it."

They agreed, reluctantly—not feeling at all comfortable that the precious piece of history would be gone from their sight, even temporarily. A strange sense of foreboding forcibly seized Claire, but she didn't understand it. Why would she have to fear Robert? She held a long breath, as she stared deeply into Robert's eyes.

"Don't worry, child. I'll take good care of it," Robert said, sensing her apprehension. "I assure you, you'll have it back before you miss it." He seemed pleasant again.

"I want you to know, you're the only person on the face of this earth we would allow to take this artifact from us—even for a short time," Guy said.

"You know I'm trustworthy. But I wouldn't get too excited over this. Not yet. When all is said and done, it may not turn out as you expect.

And even if it does end up being an original, it may be a very common piece after all, with no historical or monetary value to speak of. We'll have to wait and see what I come up with. I'll get back to you as soon as possible. That, I promise. I don't want to keep you waiting in suspense."

Without explanation, his original excitement had clearly waned. Claire continued to eye Robert, vigilantly, as he returned the piece to the pillowcase, exercising extreme care. He stood, graciously thanked them for the pleasant luncheon, and departed. He was gone, and so was the artifact. As she watched him drive off, Claire acknowledged to Guy that she felt weighty disappointment with his reaction. He'd started out clearly thrilled, and then his enthusiasm had changed so suddenly, and without warning. It puzzled her thoroughly, and something seemed terribly wrong. But Robert—not them—had earned, over the many decades, the recognition of being a world-class expert in the field of rare antiquities, and they would certainly get the real story from him, on that they had to rely. They had no other choice.

"What *was* up with him today?" Guy asked. "It was kind of creepy."

"I have no idea. He had little color today, and he certainly seemed on edge. I've *never* seen him act like this before."

17

Monday morning

GUY WALKED INTO his office and observed his desk laden with piles of printouts. The newly hired lawyer had come through with flying colors. A note on his desk indicated the colossal compilation of data, entered by the FBI and police precincts around the country, constituted all appropriate Missing Persons/Unsolved Murder Cases data. Guy made a mental note to thank the rookie attorney for his efficient and professional work—a task that must have taken him a generous piece of his weekend to complete. The information, available upon request to all law enforcement officials, included statistics on missing persons, fugitives, and unsolved murders.

His eyes scanned the top portion of one entry. He noticed a "Disclaimer" section, and a "Search Variables" section—indicating all factors considered prior to running the query. Everything appeared to be in order. All variables accurately encompassed the information provided by McKay, as well as allowing for a reasonable margin of error. Guy noted the "Date/Year Reported Missing" category that allowed for the thirty-five to forty year span the Medical Examiner indicated the homicide victim had been deceased, and also the fifty-year period Claire had determined the tank had been in the ground—knowing the victim was placed in the ground after the tank was buried. The printouts provided multiple thousands of possibilities within the search parameters.

He picked up the phone to call Claire. She sat at home, reviewing the information they had obtained to date, waiting to hear from him.

"Claire, I've got the data. I'm coming home. We'll work better there."

It took several trips to carry in all of the stacks of information. That day, the tedious task of weeding through the bulky piles began. Claire grabbed a chunky bundle, energized to commence the search—knowing full well it may lead nowhere. Guy, likewise, selected a mound to initiate the undertaking. They discussed the need for careful review of the pages, not knowing exactly what they were searching for, but hopeful one of them would recognize it when, and if, it surfaced.

For two full days they meticulously combed through the compilation of data, until late the second evening when Claire made a startling comment. "Why are we limiting the search to only local, state, and national missing persons and unsolved murders in the U.S.? Based upon the information we received on the lepton and the chain, wouldn't it make more sense to also be looking at *internationally* reported missing persons and unsolved murders? Despite the fact the body was discovered here, there is a very definite international connection. I don't think we can put limitations on our search."

Guy thought about it. "Brilliant, Claire. You just might be on to something. Of course we have to consider all possibilities."

"Well, think about it," she said. "We know the skeletal find emerged in Miami, but the neck chain is definitely European, and the lepton minted in Greece. We learned from a reliable source the coin may have made its way to the U.S. from Greece or Israel—Europe or the Middle East—so there's certainly a strong possibility the victim may have been wearing the lepton while visiting this country, or even that he moved here from another country."

"Say no more. You've convinced me. The search *must* be international, as well."

Unexpectedly, howling gusts of wind blew up from nowhere, and rattled the condo's sliding glass door leading out to the balcony, creating banging sounds so loud that they almost believed the gales had fingers of their own and the ability to grab the handle and shake the glass from its frame. A chill ran through Guy's body, and he knew Claire was right. Then, just as suddenly as the wind had appeared, it disappeared, only adding to the eeriness of the moment.

"Okay, that was ghostly," Guy said. "I'll ask the junior attorney first thing in the morning to get the international entries to us ASAP. Until then, we have no choice but to continue raking through these."

"My thoughts exactly. It's a painstaking process picking through all of these, entry by entry, isn't it? And we must be so careful not to miss anything important."

"I'd describe this more like a pain in the—"

"Hon," Claire interrupted. "It *has* to be done."

"I don't have the patience for this, I'm telling you. It's burning me out."

"A huge part of investigations involve nose-to-the-grindstone work. You know that."

"Yeah, well, I'm not cut out for that part. I prefer to do my work in a courtroom."

"You're doing fine, Guy. Really. Look at the progress we've made in a mere two days. Maybe we'll be able to actually finish reviewing all of these by the time we receive the international query results—if we keep at it. So far, nothing has jumped out at me. Our skeleton seems to fit squarely into most of these."

"That's the problem."

"Well, when we see it, we'll know. Something will pull itself off the pages and leap into the air," Claire said. "That's how it works."

The hours and the progress moved slowly. Onward they pressed, working late into the evening hours. It would take clever detective work to pull this together. More than a cold case, this was a *frozen* case, and they'd been assigned to thaw it out and see what was under the ice. Like a submerged submarine that eventually must surface, they yearned for a clue, long ago hidden away, to break through the torrent of paperwork and show itself.

That night, holding each other, their minds preoccupied by the case, sleep came quickly.

Wednesday morning

AFTER A quick glass of orange juice, a call to his office, and shower, Guy walked into the den to check his computer. A wide grin appeared on his face when he saw that Roman had replied to his e-mail, but it disappeared just as quickly when he read the response.

> Hello!
>
> Good to hear from you guys! I've been ridiculously busy with school and dig activities lately, but I've spent some time looking into lepta for you. I did some research on my own and also talked to several of the professors of Archeology and other historians here at the University and also at Bar-Ilan. I have a little information for you, but I'm going to guess it'll be nothing you don't already know. Here goes. Lepta originated in ancient Greece and there are very few of the ancient ones still around today. Some were brought to ancient Israel and used in trading and commerce between the two civilizations. The old lepta, common coins in their day, had little worth, and they continue to hold modest to no value today. The Greeks struck this small coin from copper and bronze, and neither medium is more valuable than the other.
>
> It seems no one knows much more about this simple coin and it apparently had no significant bearing in the annals of history. Hopefully, this will be of help to you. It isn't much, I'm afraid, and I'm sorry I couldn't find out more. Keep me posted on this case. Sounds interesting! Give me a call or I'll call you soon and I hope to see you both in the very near future. (I'm trying to arrange a trip home for a few days as we speak.)
>
> Roman

Guy absorbed the contents of Roman's e-mail as he headed to the kitchen to find Claire.

Awaiting receipt of the international printouts became the carrot that kept Claire motivated as she returned to reviewing data at the kitchen table that morning. She was hard at work when Guy walked in and interrupted her.

"Roman e-mailed us back, Claire," he said, holding the printed response in his hand.

She perked up. "What does he have for us?"

"Unfortunately, nothing new. There's not much to know about ancient lepta, apparently. They were, and are, unremarkable coins."

"Speaking of coins, grab the ones we found in the Caribbean cave, will you?" she asked. "We need to look at them."

Returning to the room in no time, he spread the handful of coins out onto the table. Claire looked them over intently, and finally picked one up. It looked familiar in a strange sort of way. Then she understood why. "Guy, look at this coin. What do you see?"

He looked at it, turned it over in his palm, and then walked over to a lamp and held it under the light to get a better look. "Is it another lepton? Unbelievable! Looks like a different coin altogether, until you look closely. This one's in better shape."

"*Much* better shape—like it's had very little use. I knew I had seen a coin like the one around the skeleton's neck somewhere before, but I couldn't remember where until just now. They look so amazingly different, yet they're one and the same. If these coins are so rare, it seems peculiar we found one in an underground cave in Grand Cayman, and another surfaced around the neck of the skeleton here in Miami Shores. What are the odds? Are we to be following the bread crumbs? Is this the universe nudging us and telling us to keep our eyes on the lepton? Does one connect to the other in some weird way?"

"How could they be connected?" Guy asked. "No way. That would be stranger than the howling of the wind at our balcony door."

"I've been thinking, too, about the motive of the murderer," Claire said. "Do you agree it's safe to assume the motive for the murder could not have been robbery—since the neck chain would indisputably have been taken if that were the case? And if it wasn't robbery, then it must have been *personal.* It seems someone targeted this victim for a specific reason other than robbery. That gives us another piece to the puzzle."

"It does, Miss Investigator," Guy said. "You are very good at this."

"Thanks."

"I'm going to run the lepton—the one in evidence—over to our lab. I'd like to see what Benjamin Kern has to say about it," Guy said.

"Good idea. You know where I'll be."

Guy kissed Claire before he left. "I'll be home before you know it. Let's hope he'll be of help."

THE LAB, located about a mile north of Guy's office building, had always been helpful to Gaston Lombard in prosecuting criminal cases, and he expected, without hesitation, it would come through for him again. Arriving without delay, he asked for Benjamin Kern—the most senior of the technicians, and, without a doubt, the most intelligent. Appearing in the lobby within five minutes, Benjamin greeted Guy cordially. Guy explained what he needed, stressing the high-priority nature of the case, and requested Benjamin to place the coin under a high-intensity microscope, or do whatever he needed to do, to get a better look at it. "I want you to handle this personally, Benjamin," Guy said, "as it may well end up being some weighty evidence for us in an interesting case."

"I'll look at it right now, Mr. Lombard. While you wait. Follow me back to the lab if you'd like."

Benjamin seemed energetic and eager to please, as always. Leading Guy to his station, he gestured for him to sit in a side chair, and went to work. First, he inserted the coin onto the high-intensity microscope stage; next, he turned the apparatus light to the "on" position; and finally, he began to focus in on the object by dialing and playing with the adjusting screws. "Let's see what this will do for us," he said. He turned the knobs back and forth, looking at the coin through the instrument's eyepiece for three or four long minutes before he spoke. "Wow. You'll have to see this for yourself, Mr. Lombard."

18

GUY STOOD AND peered through the eyepiece. “What in the heck are you seeing?” he asked.

“Let me take another look, will you, Mr. Lombard?” Benjamin asked. He returned to his inspection of the coin, while Guy watched—overtaken by curiosity.

About forty-five, Benjamin Kern was a brawny, thickset man, who had worked in the lab for twenty-five or more years. He wore perfectly round tortoise-framed glasses, which at the same time defined his alert and beady eyes and called attention to his ruddy and pockmarked complexion. Greasy auburn hair, tied back in a ponytail, showed off the diminutive diamond stud he wore in one ear. A photo of the pride and joy of his life—a red and white, fully restored, 1958 Panhead Harley-Davidson, complete with original saddlebags and the 50’s style horn—adorned a simple picture frame sitting at his workstation desk. Unmarried, with no children, his career and motorcycle comprised the totality of an existence devoid of friendly companionship.

Benjamin’s co-workers viewed him as particularly cautious—maybe overly so—and thought him to be a slow and steady plodder, scrupulously too fussy with detail. He was the only technician who examined carefully, from every angle, before drawing his nearly always accurate conclusions, and clients, more often than not, asked for him by name. Performing his job exceedingly well, he alone had provided invaluable assistance to Gaston Lombard over the years in numerous high-profile murder and rape cases, and because of that Gaston Lombard insisted that all lab work required on his files be conducted by Benjamin Kern.

Being the tech in the workplace that provided exclusive services to the distinguished Mr. Lombard gave Benjamin clout, and teeth to sway the lab in any direction he wanted to take it. That situation made his colleagues jealous. They ostracized him, even called out names, like fag and queer, when they passed him in the hallways. In reply, he would simply turn up the corners of his mouth, and tell them to have a nice day, adding, "Jesus loves you." It had the effect of heaping coals of fire on their heads.

CLAIRE SAT at home, faithfully making her way through the printouts. At times, data on the pages blurred from the indistinct vision of her tired eyes, and she often found herself blinking to bring words back into clarity. Drained by the task, she would not relent.

The telephone rang, and she answered, thankful for the break.

"Child, it's Robert Holden. I'm calling about your relic. But before we discuss it, I want to thank you again for the lovely lunch. It was so good to visit with you and Guy."

"You're most welcome. We consider you family. Come see us anytime. Now, what do you have to tell me about the artifact?" Her cheeks reddened and became hot in anticipation of what he would reveal to her.

"Before we get into that, child, I understand from my partner, Harry, that you're involved in a murder investigation and working alongside the State Attorney's Office. Is this true? Why on earth would *you* be working on a murder investigation? Does it involve an environmental clean-up that went bad? What is it, child?" he asked, chuckling.

Claire thought it odd that he seemed so inquisitive, and almost sarcastic, about her involvement in a criminal homicide investigation, and his laughter bothered her. It was inappropriate. Why was he so concerned about her job? "Well Robert, since it's an open investigation, I'm afraid I can't discuss the facts of the case with you at this time. Although, if formal charges are brought, those will become public, and then you'll probably hear all about it on headline news."

"Really? Sounds gripping, child. Be careful out there. Now, about your relic."

"THIS COIN has been subjected to extreme wear and tear, Mr. Lombard. I'm not a hundred percent sure, but I believe there is some kind of engraving on one side."

"Engraving? As in, someone carved something onto its surface? *What*?"

"Give me another minute, will you? I'm trying to make it out, but it's not easy. The coin is small to start with, and the space for engraving extremely limited, not to mention the brown patina that has settled on it from oxidization as a result of its age." After several more minutes of examination, he gave up. "Let me try something else here. I'll take a photo of it, download it to my computer, and enlarge it on the screen. Maybe that will show us what we're looking at."

After positioning the lepton just so on a sheet of plain white paper, he photographed the side with the engraving on it using a digital camera. Guy failed to notice exactly how Benjamin did it, but before long an image of the coin appeared in full color on the computer screen.

"Impressive," Guy said. "I own a camera with that capability, too. Bought it awhile back, but I have to admit, I don't know how to use the darn thing yet. Suppose I'll have to read the manual one of these days, when I have the time. You know what they say, if all else fails—consult the manual."

"Yeah, you should. Comes in real handy when you need it."

As Benjamin tapped away on the keyboard, the coin image began to enlarge, until it had increased dramatically in size. Zeroing in on the engraving, he exaggerated that portion of the image. Then he adjusted the focus to bring it into crystal-clear definition.

Guy watched in amazement at the computer technology that often baffled him.

"This equipment makes things a lot easier for us, Mr. Lombard," Benjamin said. "Now take a close look with me. What do you see?"

"WHAT ABOUT it, Robert? Tell me everything," Claire said, enthusiasm evident in her voice. "I need to know. What is it? What did we find?"

"Okay, child. Okay. After considerable research, it appears that what you and Guy found can be described as an object having only marginal value, both historically and monetarily, although I'm a bit surprised by it myself. In fact, I'm taken aback. It seems there are several dozen *originals* of that very piece—displayed proudly in museums around the world. And archeologists continue to dig them up throughout Mexico on a fairly regular basis. Your particular statue, as it turns out, is classified as a *replica* of an authentic Aztec idol—albeit an excellent copy in mint condition, in my opinion."

Reeling from the pronouncement, Claire fell silent.

"Are you there, child?" Robert asked.

"Yeah. I'm here. I just can't believe what you said. It doesn't sound right."

"It's a reproduction of a common and sacred warrior idol, an object-of-worship within the Aztec empire. They placed pieces like these in palaces and temples, and workshops and homes—to keep evil spirits away. Quite frankly, your piece probably has more value to you and Guy—as a remembrance of quite an adventure—than to anyone else. I'm very sorry to disappoint you, child. I know you both thought you had discovered a priceless piece of antiquity, and quite honestly, so did I for a time."

Before Claire could respond, beeps alerted her that another caller was attempting to ring through. "I have to take another call, Robert. I'm not going to hide the fact that I'm stunned. Thank you. I'll send Guy over to your shop to pick up the artifact. Do we owe you anything?"

"Absolutely not. Stay in touch, child. Again, I'm sorry for the bad news."

She touched the flash button to pick up the next call. "Hello?"

"*You don't listen, do you? Stay away from this investigation…or die.*"

The horrifying words of warning resonated from the same unnerving and muffled voice she'd heard one other time. "Who is this? And how did you get my number?" she demanded. Claire continued to hold the phone to her ear as the dial tone echoed in offensive mockery.

Staying with the investigation had clearly triggered yet another threat. It made someone mightily malcontent that she was still working on the case. Was the killer within easy reach? Feeling threatened or squeezed? She resented the threats—a letter and now two phone calls. But still, she would never abandon her assignment.

The phone rang again, and Claire froze. She did not want to answer it. What if the chilling and menacing voice harassed her again? As the answering machine clicked on, Roman began to leave a message. Relieved to hear a friendly voice, she picked up the phone and talked excessively fast. "Roman? I'm so glad it's you. So delighted you called. So happy…."

"Claire, are you all right? You sound a little shaken."

Crestfallen by Robert's findings, and disturbed by yet another ominous call, she struggled to pull herself together. "Yes, I'm fine. How are you?"

"Good. Busy all the time, but what else is new, right? Hey, how would you guys like a house guest for a few days?"

"WE ARE definitely looking at initials of some kind, Mr. Lombard. I'm sure of it," Benjamin said. "But they're so worn down that even with this highly developed view, it will be difficult, if not impossible, to make them out. Almost looks as if each initial is engraved on one of three ears of barley issuing from between two leaves."

He enlarged the screen projection a final time—to the maximum view allowed without distorting the image—bringing the initials into instant clarity. But even then, after more and thoughtful consideration, it was not an easy call.

Guy shook his head. "I can't make out a single initial, Benjamin. Now what? Where do we go from here?"

"Well, Mr. Lombard, I can make an educated guess on two of the three. I have a Master's in Linguistics, and speak several languages fluently, so letters and words come fairly easily to me."

"I had no idea. I always thought you were a bright bulb, I just didn't know how bright. Why didn't you continue in the field?"

"Actually, I taught at the college level for six months, but didn't like it much, and there wasn't anything else I could do with the degree at the time, so I ended up here, in this lab. I've enjoyed the work over the years, so I stayed. It challenges me, I guess. But who knows, one day I might try something else. We'll see."

"Interesting. So tell me, smart Benjamin, what *are* we looking at here?"

"Well, now that's the tricky part." Guy's flattering comment made him feel self-conscious, and caused his face to turn red. He eyed the computer screen intently, so he didn't have to look at Mr. Lombard and give his embarrassment away.

"Give me your best guess, will you?" Guy persisted, oblivious to Benjamin's distress.

"Okay. Sure. I would say the first could perhaps be a "d"; the second possibly an "o," or a "c"; and the third initial is really too abraded to even wager a guess. I'm sorry I can't be of more help to you on this, Mr. Lombard. You're dealing with a very old piece of evidence here. I'm afraid it's the best I can do."

Guy scribbled down the information he had just received on a small pad. "As always, you've been a real help to me, Benjamin. *Merci beaucoup*."

Benjamin chuckled. "*De rien*!" They shook hands heartily, and Benjamin's face turned pink, again unbeknownst to Guy.

"And if you ever decide to change vocations and need a job reference, you know where to find me. But for my sake, I hope you don't," Guy said.

"I appreciate your vote of confidence, sir, but I think the time for changing my line of work has long since passed by—at least in this lifetime."

It always pleased Benjamin when he could assist, in any way, the celebrated Mr. Gaston Lombard. When Mr. Lombard singled him out from the other technicians, it made him feel special, and brightened his day. He would never let him down. Benjamin believed that Mr. Lombard, by leaps and bounds, excelled as the best and most highly skilled prosecutor in the Miami-Dade State Attorney's Office. And besides, he'd had a secret crush on the commanding Gaston Lombard for some time now—one that would remain just that, a secret.

When Guy arrived home, he yelled out to Claire.

There was no answer.

The telephone rang.

"Hello?" Guy said.

The caller hung up.

19

JUST THEN GUY noticed a note Claire had left behind. The written message informed him that she had driven to her office to check in with LuVasse, and to see how things were progressing with the Lawden clean-up. She also wrote that Robert had called with disappointing news on the artifact, promising to fill him in on the details when she arrived home. She asked him to swing by *Hartmann and Holden Rare Antiques and Collectibles* to pick up the precious piece.

Grabbing his car keys, Guy jumped into his BMW and drove to Robert's place of business to retrieve the mysterious relic. Sleep would come easier that night knowing it was back in his (and Claire's) possession. Along the way, he wondered how the news could be disappointing on the statue. Not possible, he told himself. Not possible.

Even though Robert had been winding down his business over the last couple of years or so, he still enjoyed dabbling in rare antiques and collectibles—although now admittedly on a smaller scale than years past. He claimed it was the client contact that he so enjoyed, and the thought of giving the business up completely devastated him. Nowadays, he went to the shop only two or three days a week, and occasionally on weekends, and for just a few hours on any given day. This reduced schedule allowed him more quality time to spend at home with his wife of a lifetime, Mae.

As Guy stepped into the plush entrance of Robert's elegant shop, a buzzer sounded and Harry Hartmann appeared in the lobby to greet him. Harry, too, had scaled down his side of the business over the last two years, and now also worked on a very part-time basis—scattering his hours on an as-needed basis. Closing the doors of the long-time business in the not too distant future was the ultimate goal of the partners, despite the fact that neither of them really desired full retirement. But the time would never be more ripe. Robert and Harry had entered the golden years. Thoughts of things they'd never taken the time to do—like pleasure traveling, or merely relaxing—tugged at them with a powerful and persistent force, seeming more appealing than ever before. The time was soon, or never.

So, at best, irregular business hours had become the norm, and more and more these days they dealt with customers on an appointment-only basis. Yet it didn't seem to hurt their enterprise in the slightest, and they continued to sell pricey pieces to well-known antiques brokers and dealers, and individuals who had been loyal *habitués* from day one. And in truthfulness, regular clientele didn't believe for one minute that Robert and Harry would ever really shut their doors permanently.

"Mr. Lombard, welcome to our humble business," Harry said. "It's not every day that a man of your stature graces our presence."

"Hello, Mr. Hartmann. You greatly embellish my importance." *Humble* was not a word that came into Guy's mind to describe a place packed to the gills with elaborate and costly objects of antiquity. Harry certainly seemed to have the knack for understating, and overstating.

"Robert's not here today, if you're looking for him. Actually, I'd just thought about closing up for the day myself. You caught me in the nick of time."

Propped in one corner of the entrance cove sat a strange-looking item that immediately attracted Guy's attention. "What's that... thing?" he asked.

Harry laughed heartily. "That *thing* is a one-of-a-kind, unbelievably rare, grass basket that once contained the remains of a mummy—probably Central or South American in origin. We purchased it from another dealer a couple of years back, and it's taken up that space ever since. May I interest you in purchasing it? I'd be willing to deal."

"Thank you, Harry, but not today. Will you actually *find* a buyer for something like that?"

"Well, I'd say, yes, or perhaps. There's usually a buyer for everything—eventually. But sometimes we wait an awfully long time to find that buyer, or for that buyer to find us." Again he laughed out loud. "You've heard the saying, '*One man's junk is another man's treasure*,' haven't you, counselor? Well, based upon my wealth of experience, that certainly appears to be the case."

"Actually, I'm here today to pick up a piece Robert appraised for us," Guy said. "I understand it's ready."

"Oh, yes...your artifact, of sorts. Give me a minute and I'll retrieve it for you." Harry disappeared into the back room and reappeared shortly, toting the flannel pillowcase containing the relic. Guy thanked Harry and asked if he could pay for the appraisal.

"Heavens no. It's *gratis*, according to Robert, Mr. Lombard. It is our pleasure, indeed, I can assure you."

"Good day, Mr. Hartmann."

"Good day, Mr. Lombard. Delightful to see you today. Enjoyed our conversation immensely. And say hello to that gorgeous lady of yours, will you? Oh, and by the way, if you ever become interested in purchasing that lovely mummy basket, please give me a ring. You know where to find me."

"Afraid I'm really not interested in that. But now, if you ever find a *daddy* basket, I may change my mind," Guy teased, winking at Harry.

Both chuckled vigorously, and Guy shook Harry's hand and departed. Driving home, he picked up his cell phone and called Claire at her office. "Anything new on the Lawden matter?"

"No, but he's being watched closely. They're on it."

"Good to hear. Hey, I stopped off and picked up the artifact at Robert's business. He wasn't in, but Harry Hartmann was there. I feel better now, having it back in our hands. Anyway, what did Robert come up with?"

"I'm getting ready to leave here right now to drive home. I'll see you there in half an hour. I'm anxious to hear what you found out at the lab, and I'll fill you in on everything Robert told me then. You won't be happy."

"I gathered that. Okay. See you soon. Drive carefully, my beauty."

Claire's mind wandered as she drove home. Thoughts of how much she enjoyed working with Guy on this murder case engulfed her. She liked that he seemed respectful of her, and of her thoughts and ideas on the investigative process. Both of them had been in unsuccessful relationships in the past, but this time they had vowed it would be different. They knew what they wanted, and they'd found it in each other. Commitment to making this one work acted as a highly-motivating factor, and they liked and loved each other enough to overcome any obstacle thrown in their paths. Most of all, in each other, they had found the love of a lifetime. Claire felt herself smiling, and then breaking into a full-scale grin. Maybe, just maybe, marriage wouldn't be such a bad thing after all.

She enjoyed her daydream until, suddenly, thoughts of the lepton and the skeleton darted into her mind—pushing aside the surprising elation she was experiencing at the thought of marital bliss, and jerking her back to reality. Thoughts returned to the case. The coin intrigued her no end, and she needed to know more about it. What significance did wearing a worthless coin around his neck play in the murder of the victim, if any? Perhaps it held sentimental importance to him? Had someone special given it to him? She could not shake the feeling that the lepton held indisputable importance in this mysterious case.

A nagging internal voice reminded her that murders—discovered this long after the fact—usually remained hopelessly and enigmatically unsolved forever. But this fact did not discourage her—rather, it seemed to spur her forward and encourage her to do the impossible. She longed to notify any remaining relatives that their long-lost kin had, at last, been found.

What kind of person had the victim been? What had he done for a living? Why had he been so brutally murdered? Could he have been involved in illegal activities? Or was he merely at the wrong place at the wrong time, and saw something he shouldn't have? Did he have a wife or children, or friends or relatives, who searched for him when he disappeared? So many questions without answers.

She thought about how the persistent and pouncing newshounds so far had left them alone; how the plea of Gary LuVasse during the press conference had been respectfully honored—to date. And she hoped the reporters would continue to keep their distance until the matter came to some conclusion or resolution. Sergeant Massey had informed her that he would field all media questions while they worked up the case, and, thankfully, he had held true to his word. He had even gone so far as to notify the press that anyone interfering with the assigned investigators could face charges of interfering with a criminal investigation, if brought to his attention.

Claire had total confidence that if it was possible to do, she and Guy would place a name on the skeletal remains. After all, she was a trained investigator. A detective, of sorts. A sleuth. An inquisitor, examiner, analyst, and questioner. She thought and moved like an investigator. She breathed like an investigator. She analyzed facts like an investigator. Once turned on to a particular case, she could not turn off, until she solved it. And this case would be no different. She would not let this victim down. Together, she and Guy would not only identify the victim, but also find the perpetrator and bring him or her to justice.

As she rounded the bend approaching the condo, without warning a dark sedan shot out of nowhere, screeching past her at what seemed like a hundred miles an hour, nearly sideswiping her car, and then peeling off. She stepped on the brakes and pulled over to the side of the road to catch her breath. It had happened so fast that she didn't get a good look at the car, or memorize the license plate. Her hands started to shake. That was close. Way too close. Now she had to tell Guy about the threats. She could no longer keep them to herself. For it was clear that the threats were serious. Someone wanted her dead.

Walking into the condo, minutes later, she wore her fear on her face. "Hold me," she said.

Taking her in his arms, Guy felt her involuntary trembling. "Claire? Talk to me. What happened?"

"Let's sit."

They sank into the couch and turned to face one another. Guy held her shoulders with his hands.

"I need to tell you something," Claire said.

"You're scaring me."

"Some things have happened that I haven't told you about."

"*What*? What kind of things?" Guy persisted.

"I've received some threats since I began working on this case."

"*Threats*? What kind of threats?"

"It started with a letter sent to my office. And then phone calls. And just now, a car almost ran me off the road."

"Why haven't you told me before now?" he boomed. "Why?"

"Because I didn't want you to fear for my safety and pull me off this case."

"You're off now."

"You can't do that. I choose to remain on it."

"I'm telling you, you're off. I'll finish working it up myself."

"You'll do no such thing. This is exactly why I hesitated telling you earlier about the intimidation tactics attempted on me. The person behind them wants me off the case, too."

"I'm mad as hell you didn't let me in on it, Claire. I mean it. Mad as hell. I could have protected you had I only known."

"How? I have to live my life, don't I?"

"I want to know every detail about each and every threat, right now," he demanded.

Remaining seated, she filled him in on the particulars of the letter, both calls, and the near-collision.

"You need to remove yourself from this case, immediately. I mean it," he said. "If you won't, I will. This is nothing to take lightly."

"That's not going to happen, Guy. I don't take the threats lightly, but I'm in this investigation for the long haul. Obviously, we're hitting a nerve with this person, and that tells me we're on the right track. I will not give the person what he or she wants—to get me out of the picture. It's not going to happen."

Realizing he could not persuade Claire to back away from the case, he picked up the phone, dialed Sergeant Massey, and filled him in on everything he had just learned. The Sergeant agreed to go to Claire's office and pick up the letter—after Guy identified its location in her desk drawer—to dust it for prints. He instructed Guy to keep a closer eye on her, promised to put a tap on their home phone until the case was resolved in one way or the other, and ordered Guy to call him, without delay, if any other threats were made. "Sounds to me like the murderer may be alive and well," the Sergeant said. Then, before hanging up, he added a final comment. "Be careful."

Guy pulled Claire close to him. "My life would end if I lost you. Don't you understand that? I want you within my sight at all times until this case is over, Claire. *Comprende*? I love you."

"I love you, too, my darling. I'll be fine. And we'll watch over each other."

"From now on, we hide *nothing*. Agreed?"

She nodded. "Yes, I promise." As she wrapped her arms around Guy, she realized he no longer had that look in his eyes—the one that had made her so sure he was about to propose. What if they hadn't cut their vacation short? What if they weren't embroiled in such a complicated case? Claire closed her eyes briefly, so unsure of what she wanted.

Over cups of hot black tea, they took turns informing each other about the day's events. Guy let Claire in on all he had learned from Benjamin Kern at the lab; Claire told Guy about Roman's call and upcoming visit, and brought him up to speed on Robert's findings regarding the artifact.

"I don't buy it, Claire. It smells like dead fish."

She studied him. He was right, of course. She felt it, too.

Returning to the stacks of printouts, they worked in silence.

Thursday afternoon

THE TELEPHONE rang. It was the doorman, Chad, calling to notify Guy that an attorney from his firm had just dropped off several weighty packages for him. He agreed to bring them up promptly.

When the buzzer sounded, Guy opened the door to see Chad standing next to a metal cart brimming with a number of bulky parcels.

"Shall I bring them in, Mr. Lombard?"

"Yes. Please. Set them on the dining room table, will you?"

"My pleasure, sir. These are heavy bundles."

Guy thanked Chad and tipped him.

20

THE INTERNATIONAL PRINTOUTS easily exceeded the volume of the local/state/national ones, and upon closer analysis appeared more exhaustive in detail—providing greater specifics with respect to the Scars/Distinguishing Marks category and other pertinent data. Guy exhaled deeply.

Working non-stop, they would finish their review of the original documents that evening. Then they could turn their full attention to the international listings the following morning. It was a game plan they agreed on. Noses to the grindstone, they toiled until midnight, eager to finish the task that lay before them, stopping only to eat a light dinner. Disappointingly, no lead worthy of follow-up materialized.

Falling into bed, exhausted, they slept in perfect comfort—lying close together, sideways, his front to her back, knees bent, fitting together like spoons.

ALL TOO soon, an annoying buzzer signaled morning—time to rise and shine. Still dog-tired, they forced themselves to get up and shower. After eating a quick breakfast, Claire placed two cups of strong black coffee on the kitchen table, and Guy hauled the new stacks over.

Dividing the piles between them, they once again began the mind-numbing exercise of plowing through them—analyzing one entry after another, page by page. Guy loathed and resented the laboriousness of the task—a job that redefined tedium to his way of thinking. He was close to reaching the limit of his endurance. But for now, he had no choice but to muddle through.

In stillness they toiled, as time ticked away—second-by-second, minute-by-minute, and hour-by-long-hour. Knowing full well the task was akin to looking for the proverbial needle in a haystack, they pressed onward because, at the moment, it seemed the only haystack they had. Lumbering on, one heavy step at a time, noon arrived, and hunger overtook them.

After a short break to eat lunch, they returned to the monotonous activity. Guy had not been exercising since this case had landed squarely in their laps, and he could feel the stiffness that had set into his not-as-flexible-as-usual body. He yearned for his personal trainer to make him perform the dreaded and repetitious sets of exercises that hurt so good. This case was beginning to take its toll, and it seemed, despite the information they had gathered so far, that progress was in no hurry to go anywhere fast.

"I need a clue. Give me a clue!" Guy shouted, breaking the peace and quiet.

"Believe me, I'd like to find one as much as you would," Claire said.

So much time had elapsed since the murder, and Claire was desperately aware that solving a murder that had gone this cold would mimic putting together an intricate jigsaw puzzle—a mosaic of sorts; only in this case, trying to assemble the conundrum without having all the pieces. All the pieces could never fall into place on a case of this age, but they needed enough of them to figure out the puzzle. With kismet, reason, and clever detective work on their side, they stood a remote chance.

Reviewing entries as she spoke, Claire recited aloud the information they now had. The victim was: male, murdered by severe blows to the back of the head that crushed his skull, killed 35-40 or so years ago, approximately 5'8" and 160 pounds, and in his late thirties to late forties at the time of his demise. He had a left leg shorter than his right—most likely causing a pronounced limp. And he wore an expensive, gold, European neck chain with a worthless ancient lepton coin—from Greece or Israel—hanging from it. The coin contained three engraved initials—a "d," an "o" or "c," and a third unreadable letter. Robbery could be ruled out as motive, and an assumption could be made that the motive for the crime was personal. Lastly, the skeletal remains had been found buried in Miami Shores, Florida, strangely intact, on a now-vacant lot where a gasoline station once stood.

They looked for anything to link an entry to those specifics—a Greek or Israeli or European or lepton connection, a leg problem—anything that would pop out as a worthy clue to follow. Gliding through the inexhaustible mounds, they searched hopelessly for a lead. More elongated hours passed. And more. The day dragged out.

Guy threw his pages down on the table. "I can't do this anymore! I'm losing my freaking mind, and finding nothing. Nothing at all. What a royal waste of time. *None of these*, and *all of them*, fit squarely with our variables. It's like looking for a piece of *hay* in a haystack. A needle would be easy!" he thundered.

"Take a break. This *is* horrible—but we have to do it," Claire said.

Guy went out on the balcony to light up a cigar. At the end of the second week of investigating this case, internal pressure to get the matter resolved—or at least to make significant headway—pummeled his psyche. Utterly frustrated and full of anger, he pounded his fists on the railing, and sighed heavily. The case possessed him. He let his mind drift.

Someone knew to whom that skeleton belonged; someone somewhere wondered what had become of a missing family member. The victim had a mother and father, maybe a spouse or siblings—someone who knew him and in all probability noticed him missing all those many years ago. And someone, at some time, in some place, knew the meaning of the lepton, too. He and Claire had the obligation to find that person—if he or she still breathed the breath of life. After all, they owed it to the victim. His murderer must be brought to task for this horrific crime—regardless of the passage of time. The accountability for justice in this matter weighed heavily on the infallible prosecuting attorney.

He continued to drift in his own world—alone to dodge the demons that launched more and more pressure his way with each passing hour the murder remained unsolved. He could actually feel the immeasurable burden on his shoulders. And he felt ashamed for succumbing to his inclination to light up a cigar whenever he felt overwhelmed by work, or life. During non-stressful times he never smoked, and he saw the habit as a hideous crutch for weak-minded people, but when he found himself in a pressure-cooker situation, he found that it forced him to slow down and step off the merry-go-round, if only for a fleeting minute, or thirty.

Hopelessly lost in thought, he pondered finding another way to calm down, to deal with his anger. Claire was always suggesting he take an anger management class. Maybe instruction on how to vent his rage in healthy and non-stressful ways would be helpful. Perhaps he'd sign up one day soon.

Claire left him alone, knowing he had to compose himself in his own way, and in his own time. Meanwhile, she kept working.

Half an hour later, Guy returned, noticeably less agitated after his respite. He walked over to Claire and kissed her on the cheek. "Better now," he said. "I'll get back to it." He continued on, numbed by the project, setting himself on automatic pilot.

Claire could sense the great pensiveness that surrounded him, and knew that solving the murder haunted him in a profound way. Concerned by the enormity of the prospect, he didn't know where to turn next. What if they never found a clue? Their professional reputations were on the line. She knew many out there who would like nothing better than to see the two of them fail—competitors, vultures, those preying on the downfall of others. Those who would enjoy, in particular, seeing the notorious Gaston Lombard knocked down a notch or two—opposing lawyers he'd made mincemeat of during very public trials, to name a few. And now, with this impossible homicide case unloaded on them, and with no new clues to follow, the pressure cooker was heating up. How do you solve a case with no leads to follow?

As he read, Guy held at bay the self-imposed drive to perform perfectly that was mounting within him like a volcano ready to erupt. Could their inability to find a clue be the result of disturbing the ancient artifact? No, it couldn't be. Or could it?

After nearly two weeks and uncountable hours of work behind them, and with no inkling or significant clue surfacing, Claire, too, felt hope slipping into oblivion. And she did not understand the instinctive nudging of urgency that had been annoying her to no end. Time was running out, but she didn't know why. What was she not seeing?

Claire and Guy collapsed in bed that night—mentally spent.

The weekend

SATURDAY CAME and they spent the entire day searching through the data. Mercifully, Sunday proved to be more fruitful in the investigative process, but not before completing an additional six hours of trudging through more burdensome stacks. Guy found nothing of real interest, although, admittedly, some of the entries came closer to being in range than the earlier ones. But each time, some factor or another would rule each one out.

When Claire finally struck gold, she stared at the entry for some time, in disbelief, before uttering a word. The potential major clue to date—the proverbial *smoking gun*—had risen up to break through the oceans of printed material heaped on the table before them, and it jumped out at her, hitting her directly in the face, when she least expected it. She'd just about told herself that maybe Guy had been right all along—that their hours and days of searching the bloody-long printouts could end up being nothing more than a grandiose waste of time, that the two of them might end up suffocated by the thick mounds of collective data, unable to find any puzzle piece whatsoever that would fit into the bigger picture.

What all investigators hope against hope for in a case of this nature, here, near the end of her portion, poked its head up to get noticed—an entry seeming to fit all of the victim's known variables, each and every one of them, plus more. And she'd nearly missed it, as her mind had blurred from the paralyzing task—each entry starting to meld into a plethora of meaningless words that started to look like the last, and the next. But undeniably and unbelievably, a plum had emerged. *The coveted plum. The frosting on the cake*. The words *Polio Victim/Limp*, under the category of Scars/Distinguishing Marks, seized her, suddenly and out-of-the-blue, forcefully pulling her back into acute awareness. Then her eyes scanned each of the other variables listed, one by one, in rapid succession, and, amazingly each of them lined up perfectly, falling neatly into place, and appearing to be right on target.

After silently reading and reviewing the words to make sure she saw them correctly, she blurted them out to Guy, who in turn grabbed the document from her hands to read them again. "This could be it!" he bellowed. "It could be it!" Adrenaline pumping, he jumped to his feet, and grabbed Claire around the waist, lifting her high into the air.

Experiencing the same feeling that came upon him each time a jury reached a conclusion and he was summoned back to the courtroom for the reading of the verdict, he fought back the internal voices that seemed ever present, reminding him, over and over again, that he may not prevail. Because, in trial, no matter how strong a case appeared to be, he could never predict what a jury might do. Too many times, he had heard of *airtight* cases being lost on a technicality, or because the jury did not understand its precise role in the process, or because key evidence ended up being tossed out due to a typo on a search warrant.

Then and now, he was keenly aware of the rapid, heavy pounding of his heart—the organ keeping him alive, reminding him of his mortality with each and every beat—the repetitive thumping so clear, so strong, so loud, that at this very moment he wondered if Claire could hear it. With all his might, he fought back the nagging voices of doubt stirring within him.

"Finally, something solid to follow. *Finally!* Each variable hits our John Doe exactly on target, and, surprisingly, it's the only report we've seen in this monstrous morass of paperwork that does," Guy said, speaking loudly, embarrassed to let Claire in on his personal struggle.

"I agree," she said. "Even the first initial of his first and middle name—the 'd' and 'c'—jibe with what Benjamin Kern told you." Flabbergasted by the unanticipated and startling apparent match, she sat calmly. "But we'll need to get an update on this missing person, before we put a feather in our cap. As good as it appears, you never know. Maybe this missing person has already been located, and they've simply neglected to update the posting. We can't be certain until we reach the contact person." She knew from past investigations that hot leads often went nowhere, and significant-appearing clues many times led down dead-end roads.

This particular missing person report came in from London, England, and read as follows:

==

Entered by:	Scotland Yard
Location:	London, England
Case number:	Y6601129-507
Name:	David Crawford Post
Gender:	Male
Height:	5' 8"
Weight:	163 lbs
Date missing:	November 29, 1966
Age:	44
d/o/b:	March 29, 1922
Scars/distinguishing marks:	Polio Victim/Limp
Employment:	Chauffeur/Mechanic
Evidence of foul play:	None found
Status:	Body not recovered/ Foul play suspected/ Presumed dead
Disposition:	Case closed – December 1967
Contact Person:	Detective Sergeant Edmond Penwright

==

It seemed close to dead on, allowing for only a slight margin of error from the estimated variables McKay had given them. Could it be the break they desperately needed to focus the investigation, to continue on their linear track to solving the case? At least it seemed to be a clear and strong lead—just when they'd thought there might not be one.

"Claire, nice work," Guy said. "I mean it."

Quickly reviewing the remaining entries in each pile, they concurred that it appeared, indeed, the sole clue worthy of immediate pursuit at this time. Other *maybes* could be looked at more closely later, if need be, but none matched the magnitude of this one.

Tomorrow would be Monday. As it was six hours later in London than Miami, Guy would place a call to Scotland Yard at 2:00 a.m. Monday morning in an attempt to reach the contact person noted on the report. It would be 8:00 a.m. London time.

With providence on their side, the Detective Sergeant would shed some light on the person who mysteriously went missing in London so long ago, and maybe, just maybe, that missing person would turn out by some strange quirk of fate to be the skeleton found in Miami Shores. Although it seemed farfetched, stranger things had happened, and truth often proved stranger than fiction.

Anticipation ran high that this lead would yield high dividends. At the same time, a wave of foreboding still preoccupied Claire—one she could not shake off. *Time was running out!*

21

Monday morning

PERSISTENT BUZZING OF the alarm clock—signaling 2:00 a.m.—jolted Guy from sound sleep. Time to call London.

Claire opened her eyes and pulled herself into a sitting position. "D-day," she said, yawning.

The call to Detective Sergeant Edmond Penwright at Scotland Yard was crucially important. This fact could not be underscored enough. It would either take the case in a certain direction, or not. And quite frankly, they both believed that if it did not take the case forward, the chances of identifying the victim and nailing the murderer were about nil to none. The work day had just begun in London, and, tired as he was, Guy snapped into instant clarity as the magnitude of the moment hit him.

He dialed the local operator and asked to be connected to London information. Then, with deep furrows in his brow, against a background of trepidation, he dialed the number provided for Scotland Yard, hoping strongly the outcome would be good. His mind darted in many different directions. What if the Detective Sergeant no longer worked with the force, or had retired by now? Or, worse yet, what if he was deceased? They may never get the answers they needed. But on the other hand, there would be records of some kind, maybe even an investigative file, and Guy trusted that someone at the agency, if not the Detective Sergeant himself, would be able to dig through the archives and provide them additional information on the missing man.

After two rings, a pleasant female voice answered the phone. "Scotland Yard. Please hold."

Waiting a full minute, one that seemed much longer, beads of sweat collected on Guy's forehead and ran down his cheeks and neck, and he noticed his hands shaking slightly.

The genial voice returned. "Thank you for waiting. How may I help you?"

Guy stated his name and identified himself as a criminal prosecuting attorney for the Miami-Dade State Attorney's Office. Then he indicated he needed further information regarding a missing person's report filed by Scotland Yard's London office in 1966. He provided the case number indicated on the entry, the victim's name, and the contact name.

The woman on the other end sighed a deep sigh. "That is an extremely old case, sir. I apologize, but I will have to ask you to hold again while I do some checking."

This time Guy could hear the rapid tapping of computer keys on the other end of the line. He had a long wait. Swallowing hard, he became keenly aware of the acute dryness in his mouth, and suddenly he could hear himself breathing.

"Mr. Lombard?" Thank you for holding, sir. Detective Sergeant Edmond Penwright did handle that case, but he's been retired for a number of years now. It looks like we may still have a file on the matter—at least I'm seeing an indication that we do on my computer screen. I would be happy to connect you to Detective Chief Inspector Mollitt, if you'd like. He supervised Detective Sergeant Penwright for a time. That would be Detective Chief Inspector *Oliver* Mollitt. He currently supervises all of the detective sergeants in the office, and would be the one to assist you. Oh, wait a moment. I'm afraid he just walked into a staff meeting. It may be a while. May I ask him to call you back?"

"Yes. It's a matter of *utmost* importance, so please have him call me as soon as he's out of the meeting. You've been exceedingly helpful." He provided her with his contact information. People like her made his job a lot easier.

"You are most welcome, sir. I'm always happy to assist anyone in law enforcement, and I hope our Detective Chief Inspector Mollitt will provide you with the information you need. I'll see that he returns your call as soon as possible."

Playing the waiting game never appealed to Guy. While some would call his lack of patience a character flaw, it did tend to move things along in his line of work. Whenever possible, he demanded his requests be given top priority—even when the requests of others were clearly ahead of his own. A go-getter and a take-charge kind of person, he would step on anyone's toes, professionally speaking, to get the job done, when necessary. But this situation was different, and there was no way he could manipulate a quicker response. Not being in control wore on him. Waiting was the dealer in today's game, and he had no choice but to sit patiently until he was dealt a hand. He went back to sleep, nestled comfortably against Claire.

When the telephone rang at 4:00 a.m., Guy and Claire sat up straight in bed.

"Mr. Gaston Lombard? It's Detective Chief Inspector Mollitt, Scotland Yard London Office, at your service. It's early over there—must be 4:00 in the morning. I apologize for calling at such a dreadful hour, but our receptionist told me it's a matter of urgency. I understand you need some information on an old, archived file of ours?"

"Thank you for returning my call, Detective Chief Inspector. Yes, we're interested in any and all information you have in your file concerning the missing Mr. David Crawford Post." Guy placed the call on speaker phone, and Claire introduced herself. She pulled a pad of paper and pen from her bedside table and watched Guy do the same on his side.

"The receptionist had the file pulled from archives while I was in my meeting, so I have it in front of me as we speak. Why do you need this information, Mr. Lombard?"

Guy summarized the situation and explained how the investigative trail led them to Scotland Yard.

"Quite a story, Mr. Lombard. I'll help you in any way I'm able."

"For starters, did the case ever get solved?" Guy asked.

"No. Let me clarify. I've reviewed everything we have on that missing person, and according to the file and our computer records, no. I also have a vague personal recollection of this matter and my memory also tells me, no."

"Please tell us everything your file indicates about this Mr. Post," Guy said.

"Of course. Due to the age of the case, however, I'm afraid we have very little, aside from the case summation. Actually, our files are typically purged completely after seven years, unless a plea or prosecution results, but in the case of an unsolved missing person, we try to keep a skeletal summary of the case on file indefinitely—in case anything ever turns up, even years down the road."

Skeletal summary, Claire thought. Interesting word choice.

"It's a slim file, but it does contain a detailed typewritten summary of the investigation—several pages in length—more information than we usually find," he continued.

"So there's quite a bit you can tell us about this Mr. Post, then?" Guy asked.

"Well, yes. I'd say so. I've read through the comprehensive report a couple of times, so it would be no problem to summarize it over the phone, and then fax a copy to you for your records."

"We'd appreciate that," Guy said.

"Very well. Not a problem. It seems our missing Mr. Post worked here in London for a quite wealthy Lord Dobson—Lord Frank Dobson, now deceased. The lord's family had its fingers in nearly all aspects of the import-export business—coffee, silk, steel, coal, and everything and anything where money could be made. A collector of fine seventeenth-century Chinese antiques, I understand his estate was something to behold. Mr. Post became employed as his private chauffeur and stayed with him for many years—from 1946 to1966, according to the memo. He became a trusted friend and confidant of Lord Dobson over those decades, and, according to the report, the lord mentored him in the field of high value antiques, Mr. Post being a quick study."

"Interesting," Claire said, scribbling notes. "Please go on. Any information about the actual disappearance?"

"Yes, there is. According to the case summary, the lord was the one who reported Mr. Post missing. One morning in late November of 1966, Mr. Post apparently did not show up to drive the lord to an appointment, and a check of his room at the carriage house, located on the premises, showed the place had been madly overturned. No one saw or heard from Mr. Post again."

"Now that's a peculiar story, isn't it? His body was never found? Does your file discuss *any* clues to the disappearance that surfaced during the investigation?" Claire asked.

"That's the strangest part, Ms. Caswell. His body was *not* found, and absolutely no clues whatsoever came to light in this case. It was a mystery then and it remains a mystery to this day to our Scotland Yard detectives. A theory ultimately came about that Mr. Post most likely met with foul play, as he had a habit of going out to London pubs late at night—to down a few pale ales—oftentimes returning home in the wee morning hours. And he didn't always go to the best sections of town, if you know what I mean."

"I think I do," Guy said. "Please continue."

"Robberies were commonplace at that time. The only scenario that appeared to hold any merit whatsoever involved someone following him home late one night from a pub, with the intention of knocking him out and robbing him, and while the thief ransacked his place, Mr. Post started to regain consciousness, at which point the thief panicked and tried to subdue him—intentionally or unintentionally killing him, and then dragging his body out and dumping him into the river.

It was a method of operation that had happened to several other victims around that same time period, although we did find a body in each of the other cases. Anyway, like I said, the body of Mr. Post never surfaced. And please understand, this became merely a plausible explanation—a paltry *guess* on our part—to explain the eerie disappearance of a man who seemed to vanish into thin air."

"Understood. Anything else in your file?" Claire asked.

"Hold on. Let me take a look. Yes. Mr. Post had no living relatives, according to the lord, and led an extremely private, almost secretive life. After a full and routine investigation, we closed the file about a year later, and there's been absolutely no activity on it since that time."

Guy had listened intently, jotting notes furiously. "Is there more?" he asked.

"We have something here, but I don't know if this will be helpful, or not, at this juncture. There's a mention in the summary that Mr. Post survived polio. It indicates he had a decided limp and wore an expensive, specially-made, platform shoe to accommodate his one leg being inches shorter than the other."

"Excuse me, Detective Chief Inspector, but does the summation happen to mention *which* leg was shorter?" Claire asked.

"Well, let me look. Yes, it does. The *left*. As a result of the disease, he had a shorter left leg. And that's about it, other than the vital statistics you already have from the missing person's report."

"Thank you very much, sir. You don't know how helpful you've been," Claire said.

"Do you really think you may have located the remains of our Mr. Post, in the U.S.?"

"The unearthed skeleton appears to fit your description of the missing Mr. Post to a tee," Guy said, "including the shorter left leg. Any idea on how the body of your Mr. Post may have ended up here in Miami, Florida, Detective Chief Inspector?"

"Certainly not, sir. None whatsoever. That would be a true mystery now, wouldn't it? There's no indication in the file notes that we ever considered the possibility that Mr. Post either voluntarily left the country, or absconded for any reason, or even that he had the resources available to do so. On the contrary, all evidence we had at the time seemed to indicate he'd met with foul play—the turned-over living quarters and all. You may want to contact our former Detective Sergeant Edmond Penwright who originally worked up the case. He's retired now and close to eighty, with a serious heart condition, but his mind remains exceedingly clear and his memory is impeccable. He puts us all to shame that way. He may be able to recollect other facts that would be helpful to you. I seem to recall he had extreme interest in this case." He gave them Mr. Penwright's home phone number.

"Oh, Detective Chief Inspector, one more thing," Claire said. "You don't happen to have dental records on Mr. Post in that file of yours, do you?"

"As a matter of fact we do, but it would appear they are very limited partial records—not at all complete. I'm sure the rest of them somehow got separated from the file over these many years. You can have them if you would like."

"Please. They might be useful to our Medical Examiner," she said.

"Then I will send them to you immediately, along with the report, via DHL. You should have them without delay. I guess I wrongly assumed that after this length of time, the partials would not be of any help at all."

"Well, we'll see," Claire said. "You might be right, but this skeleton showed up in surprisingly good condition after being in the ground for so many years. It's almost as if *somebody up there* knew it would be unearthed one day and used to prosecute the murderer. The soil grave, surprisingly, did not allow for much moisture penetration, and the bones were preserved amazingly well."

"What a thought!" the Detective Chief Inspector said.

"We appreciate you sending us those dental records and a copy of the report, sir," Guy said. "And thank you. Scotland Yard and your bobbies on the beat certainly deserve the sterling reputation you've earned." He left delivery information for the report with the Detective

Chief Inspector, and the Medical Examiner's business address for the dental records, together with all contact phone numbers, and, before hanging up, promised to keep him appraised of the situation.

Next he telephoned Mr. Penwright—anxious to talk with him about the inexplicable disappearance of Mr. Post. As the phone rang, Guy made a mental note to call Michael McKay and let him know the partial dentals were on their way from London, and to request he perform comparison testing as soon as they arrive.

A deep and husky voice of a man answered. "Yes?"

Guy formally greeted the retired Detective Sergeant, introduced himself, and explained briefly the purpose of his call—making the point that he'd been referred to him by Detective Chief Inspector Oliver Mollitt.

A long pause followed with no response on the other end.

"Are you there?" Guy asked.

"Yes, I'm here. I've been waiting a long time for this call."

22

“DO YOU RECALL the case, Mr. Penwright?” Guy asked.

“Like it happened yesterday.”

“What do you remember?” Guy asked.

“Something did not seem right with that one when I conducted the investigation. I felt it in my gut. I did not think Lord Dobson told us everything he knew about the apparent evaporation of his long-time employee. I never believed his story. Not for a minute. But being a lord and all, back then higher-ups instructed us to watch how we questioned someone of his stature. They ordered us to tread carefully and not step on anyone’s toes.”

“I’d like Claire Caswell to join our conversation, Mr. Penwright,” Guy said. He touched the speakerphone function, and introduced the two. “You said you never believed the lord’s story,” Guy continued. “What did you think happened?”

“I guess I always thought the lord was keeping something secret—that for some unknown reason he did not level with me. My cop instincts told me he was covering for Mr. Post, but for the life of me I couldn’t figure out why, and with no real evidence to follow, the file eventually ended up closed. We had absolutely no solid leads to pursue, and I had no choice but to terminate the investigation. I kept the file open as long as I could, hoping some new evidence would crop up, but it never did."

When Mr. Penwright spoke, sporadic episodes of silence seemed to indicate he was turning back the hands of time—decades back—to the period when he'd investigated the bizarre vanishing of Mr. David Crawford Post.

"Well, are you sitting down, Mr. Penwright?" Guy asked. "Strange as this might seem, we *may* have found the remains of Mr. Post here in Miami Shores, Florida. We may, and I stress *may*, know as soon as we receive the dental records from Scotland Yard for comparison purposes, but we're not yet sure whether the partials will be sufficient for a positive identification match."

"Tell me more," Mr. Penwright pleaded.

"We discovered by chance the skeleton of a man, killed by severe blows to the back of the head, and now we're in the midst of a homicide investigation," Guy explained. "If we confirm the skeleton to be that of Mr. Post, our next job will be to find out who murdered him and why. And to seek appropriate justice. As you know, we have no statute of limitations on murder."

"Murdered? In Miami Shores, Florida? We never even checked to see if Mr. Post had a passport. We just assumed he did not have the means to leave the country, and suspected with certainty that foul play was the culprit. So certain we were. I'm literally stunned by your news. If there's anything I can do to help bring this matter to a final conclusion, anything at all, it would be my absolute pleasure to assist you. Please let me know. And keep me updated on any progress you're making. I'm very interested in this one, as you may well imagine."

"Thank you for your offer, sir. Do you remember anything that might not be contained in the memorandum on file?" Guy asked.

"Not really. It should all be in there."

"I have a question, Mr. Penwright," Clare said. "Did Mr. Post have any friends, relatives, or acquaintances that you came across during your investigation? Any persons you may have interviewed?"

Silence hung like a haze of smoke below a ceiling as he pondered the question.

"We located only one—a drinking buddy of his, I recall. But he would be an old man by now, if he's still alive. At the time I questioned him concerning the disappearance, he seemed almost afraid to talk to me. Claimed he knew nothing about the incident, and I couldn't get him to talk much."

"Do you recollect his name?" Claire asked.

"I do. First name, Joseph. Last name, Stone. Joseph Stone. I never forgot him."

"Would it be possible for you to find out if he's alive? And where he's living?" Claire asked. "That would be of great help to us."

"I certainly will attempt to uncover his whereabouts, and get back to you."

"Yes. Please. As soon as possible, if you could, sir," Claire said.

Guy left contact numbers, and instructed him to call collect, day or night, as soon as he had anything, and thanked Mr. Penwright for his help. Finding and being able to talk with the former Detective Sergeant was a gift that renewed their investigative spirits.

Now 5:30 a.m., Claire showered, put on a pot of strong coffee, cut up a plate of fresh fruit, and toasted whole wheat bread for breakfast, while Guy showered. It had not been a restful night and both Claire and Guy were ready to drop; yet, the new information they had gleaned somehow acted like high-octane fuel in their veins to drive them harder and faster. A glimmer of hope had arisen. It was a good day.

Claire waited until 8:00 a.m. to call LuVasse.

"How's the investigation coming along, Claire?" Gary asked.

"Well, we may have found the break we needed. It's huge. We'll know more soon. But I'll need a little more time to work on this."

"Quite frankly, Claire, I thought the two of you would have concluded by now that it's an impossible case to solve, so I'm heartened by your call. It's been a couple of weeks. I'll extend it another two, but no longer. Bring me results, will you?"

"I'll do my best, and keep you posted. Any news on the Lawden clean-up?"

"Police gave the go-ahead for the digging to resume, so they're working out there now—as we speak. You'll be happy to know I put on a hard hat every so often, and drive to the site to personally watch what's going on. They act nervous when they see me, and they never know when I may pop in next, so, for the time being at least, our pesky monitoring seems to be working. Don't worry about it, Claire. It's under control."

"Great. Sounds good. Don't forget about that gasoline can I found." The phone beeped, signaling an incoming call. "I should take that call, Gary. I'll stay in touch."

"Be careful. Sergeant Massey came for that letter in your desk. I don't like what's going on. Don't take chances. Be *overly* vigilant."

After saying quick goodbyes, Claire hit *flash* to receive the incoming call. "Hello?"

"Claire Caswell? Sergeant Massey here."

"Are your ears ringing?" she asked. "Gary LuVasse and I were just discussing the fact that you stopped by my office to pick up the threatening letter."

"I did. And we dusted it, only to find too many prints to get anything solid. Too many people have handled it. My guess is the anonymous author wore gloves, anyway. Usually do."

"That's what I thought you'd say, Sergeant. And I know the phone tap hasn't produced any results, because I haven't received another one of those sinister calls."

"You may not—not at home, anyway. The caller probably figures you've arranged for a tap by now. Ms. Caswell, you should be mighty careful. While many of these asshole callers, excuse my French, never follow through on their threats, some do. And quite frankly, I don't think either of us has an inkling who we're dealing with here. Far better to err on the side of over-caution. That's my unsolicited advice to you, and it's free of charge. You can take it or leave it, but I hope you take it."

"Thank you, Sergeant. I'll let you know if I receive another threat, of course."

"By the way, Ms. Caswell, how are the two of you coming on the identity phase of the investigation? Are you close to putting a name on that skeleton? I keep promising the press they'll get a big story when this thing is solved, but I don't know how much longer I can hold them off. They're like ravenous dogs trying to break out of a kennel, and soon they'll break the door down. Another bone to throw their way may keep them occupied in the meantime."

The phone beeped again.

"I hear you. We should know more shortly. Please keep the reporters away. I have to take this incoming call, Sergeant," Claire said. "We'll have something for you soon."

It was Mr. Penwright. She called Guy to the phone and hit the speaker function.

"We're both here, Mr. Penwright. What do you have for us?" Claire asked.

"That friend of Mr. Post—the one I told you about—Joseph Stone—I found him. But he's in pretty bad shape—worse than I imagined."

"Exactly how bad is he?" Guy asked.

"Well, he's in a hospice in the outskirts of London—hanging on by a thread—waiting to die. Apparently his liver is failing, and they've done everything possible for him. It's a matter of time now…days, or even hours. I have a phone number and an address for him, if you'd like."

Guy thought fast. "Mr. Penwright, would you be willing to interview Mr. Stone with us if we fly to London?"

"Of course, Mr. Lombard. I'm quite at your disposal. But you'd better hurry."

Guy and Claire agreed to book seats on a flight and get back to him within the hour.

"Claire, we can share a bag. We need to make the next flight," Guy said. "It will probably be cold and damp there."

Another wave of intuition owned Claire suddenly. Now she knew why she'd felt time was running out. It was. Near death, Mr. Stone might have the information they needed, and they had to see him. "Time is of the essence, Guy."

He saw the look on her face, and realized what they were up against. "What if…."

"What if what, Guy?"

"What if…." He stopped mid-sentence.

Clearing the travel with his office, he purchased two non-stop round-trip tickets to London on British Airways, set to depart that evening. Claire, likewise, informed her office of the freshly-perked plans. Then they called Mr. Penwright back to give him the flight information.

Interviewing Joseph Stone was of vital importance. It was now, or never. Guy held on to the feeble hope that Joseph Stone may know something important about Mr. Post, or his disappearance, to aid in the investigation. Claire, on the other hand, felt with undeniable certainty, from a place deep within her, that Joseph Stone would provide *major* information to help them solve the case. In fact, she knew he was the only person alive who could. He was holding on to life for a reason…but his hands were slipping, and his final days on earth were in a countdown. She sent a message to Joseph in her mind: *Hold on Joseph, we're on our way.* Throwing warm clothes, lined raincoats, gloves and an umbrella into a suitcase, they were ready to go.

THE FLIGHT dragged on, as Claire and Guy remained too keyed up to eat or sleep, despite crippling fatigue from shattered sleep the night before. As the clock ticked away, and the in-air hours passed, they both dreaded the very real possibility that they may already be too late.

London, England

LANDING AT Heathrow Airport, at last, they disembarked in haste from the giant plane, and collected their suitcase from the baggage area. Guy telephoned Mr. Penwright to announce their arrival and obtain detailed directions to his home—agreeing they'd be there within the hour.

The airport bustled, everyone seemingly in a hurry. Walking briskly toward the taxi station, Claire spotted a small fast-food restaurant. Now hungry, they stopped for moments to inhale a scone with marmalade and hot tea with milk, knowing that it may be some time before they'd eat again. The nourishment tasted good, sated them for the moment, and gave them an opportunity to discuss one last time the information they needed to obtain from Joseph Stone and how to approach the questioning.

It would take about an hour by taxi—or *black hackney* to the Londoners—to reach the residence of Mr. Penwright. Hailing a cab without much delay, the driver loaded their bag into the trunk, and off they sped. Multiple lanes of traffic—each resembling an endless series of railroad cars—congested for long stretches, as anticipated; yet, despite that situation, the vehicles moved along rather superbly and before long their taxi pulled up in front of Mr. Penwright's home.

A charming, brick, English cottage, located in a quaint, residential section of London, just outside the city limits, it was delightful to the eye. The well-maintained dwelling was surrounded by impeccably manicured shrubs, and blankets of color created by the many flower gardens appearing sporadically throughout the grounds. The entire setting reminded Claire of a Claude Monet painting.

Guy paid the fare and the driver pulled the suitcase from the trunk. They had started up the stone path leading to the home, when the front door swung open wide, and there stood Mr. Penwright, wearing an easy smile. A stocky man, with thick and wavy graying hair, and tiny, twinkly cerulean eyes, he had a handshake that could break a brick with ease, and a demeanor that could easily turn intimidating at the drop of a hat. Yet his face looked kindly and welcoming when he saw Claire and Guy. He lived an isolated existence at this point of his life—watching the years pass him by, no longer an active participant in the game, afraid of excitement, babying his fragile heart.

"I only wish your visit could be under better circumstances," Mr. Penwright said.

The interior of the cottage matched the exterior in neatness and orderliness. Decorated in soothing earth tones of green and chestnut, brick and straw, with heavily textured fabrics appearing everywhere, the setting exuded an immediate feeling of comfort—especially with the cozy and overstuffed living room furniture that encircled a giant stone fireplace. Claire could easily imagine a frosty winter's night in London, and the sanctuary the Penwright home would provide—shelter from the cold, and warmth from the blazing fireplace—the perfect milieu for sipping hot tea, and reading a good novel.

Tranquil gardening had become Mr. Penwright's only remaining pleasure and outlet for expenditure of energy. But he'd made a mindful decision to assist Guy and Claire when opportunity had come knocking on his door like an uninvited guest. The time had presented itself to once again jump onto the bandwagon of the living, to get involved, and help in any way he could to resolve this nagging and unsolved disappearance of Mr. Post, and he would rise to the challenge. After all, he'd been assigned to solve the case once upon a time, and, as it turned out, it became one of the few investigations in a lifetime career he'd been unable to bring to closure. But now, decades later, he'd do it. He had been given a second chance. Putting the strange disappearance of Mr. Post to rest, at last, would do his heart good. Life excitement erupted through his veins.

"I'm ready if you are," Mr. Penwright offered. "I called ahead to the hospice and they're expecting us any time. I also took the liberty of arranging a room for you at a B&B not far from here. It's a charming inn, run by an elderly English couple, and the rates are most reasonable—about seventy pounds a night, including a *fry-up* breakfast—more food than one might imagine, and good food, I must add."

Claire quickly calculated in her mind that seventy pounds would be less than the major hotels they'd looked into when booking flights earlier that day, including the one they had ultimately selected. She informed Guy.

"Let's load your bag into my car, and I'll drive you by the B&B to check in on the way. We need to hurry."

Guy thanked Mr. Penwright for making the arrangements, and used his cell phone to cancel the hotel reservation.

The B&B, a lovely and placid abode, had oak and mahogany wood predominating in the rooms, and corridors lined with works of art. Vases overflowing with fresh, multi-colored garden flowers appeared everywhere, providing a welcoming and homespun atmosphere—the goal of the elegantly enchanting, elderly couple who owned and ran the inn. After a speedy check-in, the pair promised to deliver the suitcase to a beautiful room—reserved especially "for the nice, American couple."

In the car, Claire and Guy reviewed the case in greater detail with Mr. Penwright, summarizing the information they had discovered so far about the skeleton.

"We'll be there in no time," Mr. Penwright said. "Let's hope he hangs on."

Just then, a loud boom penetrated their ears and the car lunged and came to a screeching halt.

23

"BLIMEY!" MR. PENWRIGHT shouted. He stepped from the car to assess the situation. "We have a punctured tire. The timing could not be worse. I have a spare in the boot, if you will allow me to fix it. I so apologize for this inconvenience."

"It's not your fault, Mr. Penwright. Let *me* do it. You can supervise," Guy said. He didn't want a man with a heart problem changing a tire.

The unexpected event delayed the momentum of the mission. Back on the road again, thirty minutes later, they drove to the hospice, parked and walked with quick steps up the winding sidewalk that led to the brown, nondescript building—set far back from the roadway. They entered through heavy, front double-doors, and moved with speed to the reception desk.

"How may I assist you?" a young man asked.

"Gaston Lombard, Claire Caswell, and Mr. Edmond Penwright, to see Mr. Joseph Stone. Official business," Guy said. He and Claire proffered business cards.

"Please have a seat in the lobby. We've been expecting you. The Hospice Administrator, Ms. Simpson, will be out to see you shortly.

And help yourselves," he said, gesturing toward a metal pushcart holding a large thermal pot, Styrofoam cups, a creamer and sugar, and a plate of small, hard cookies.

Thankful for the offer, Claire poured a cup of steaming hot tea for each of them. Waiting impatiently, they sat on stiff chairs—upholstered in a now-faded peach brocade, sipping the fragrant hot beverage. After close to fifteen minutes had passed, Ms. Hilda Simpson appeared in the lobby and introduced herself, shaking hands with each of them. A well-groomed and plump-around-the-middle lady in her early seventies, she had soft white hair pulled back into a loose chignon. A pale aqua boucle-knit suit complemented her naturally rosy cheeks, and pretty hazel eyes seemed to sparkle when she addressed them.

"I am very sorry to have kept you waiting, but I am afraid I cannot let you visit with Mr. Stone today."

"Why not? What's the matter?" Mr. Penwright asked.

"We rushed to get here," Claire said.

"He's taken a turn for the worse, and is extremely weak. We cannot allow you to question him today as the stress would very likely be too much for him. My apologies, again." Ms. Simpson turned away and began to walk from the room.

"That's it? But we've traveled from Miami to see him, Ms. Simpson. Our visit has to do with an extremely important murder investigation," Guy said.

Ms. Simpson hesitated, and responded without turning to face them. "I said, I apologize for the inconvenience, but that is my decision. Our job requires us to protect all patients at any cost, and to allow the dying process to be as peaceful as possible. He's simply not up to it today. Now, good day." She continued walking away.

"At least we should give Mr. Stone the option of seeing us, or not, wouldn't you agree? After all, it is *his* life and it should be *his* decision," Mr. Penwright said.

The powerful question and statement rang in all of their ears, and stopped Ms. Simpson cold in her tracks. After pausing for a moment, she turned around and looked Mr. Penwright squarely in the eyes. "You may be right, sir. I guess at this point, I can't argue with you. I will go and ask him. Please wait here a few extra minutes."

Brilliant! Claire thought. *Brilliant!*

After waiting for what seemed to be an exceedingly long "*few* extra minutes," Ms. Simpson reappeared in the lobby. "He will see you now, but you must not exhaust him. Follow me, please."

Trailing behind the administrator, down a low-lit hallway, a mélange of unidentifiable smells lingered in the air, and they could hear low-volume, soothing background music floating throughout the facility. Taken to a stark, but clean, small room at the far end of the corridor, they looked in to see a frail man lying on a bed of white sheets, multiple pillows stacked beneath his head for support, and a blanket pulled half-way up his spare frame. Three empty chairs sat alongside the bed.

"Please be gentle with him. He is an exceedingly sick man," she whispered. Ms. Simpson proceeded to maneuver Mr. Stone to a sitting position, propping several pillows behind him, and then, much to everyone's surprise, she leaned over and kissed him gently on the forehead before preparing to exit his room.

At once Claire sensed the depth of Ms. Simpson's feelings for the patient, and realized why she had tried so hard to protect him from anyone or anything that might disturb whatever time he had left. She smiled a knowing smile at Hilda Simpson, who nodded in response, smiled brusquely and quietly stepped from the room.

Mr. Stone, eighty-six years of age, had become a weak and slight shadow of a man. Drawn and chiseled features intensified his dark and deep-set eyes, which now appeared much too large for his emaciated face. His silver hair had thinned markedly, and serious etched lines—those that come only from years of living—competed for space on his troubled face. Yet despite his condition, he exuded a powerful sense of presence. At first glance, it was impossible to ascertain whether his agony stemmed purely from physical ailments, or if a deeper pain had taken up residence within him. But when he smiled, he exuded more warmth and gentleness than Claire had ever seen in a human being, and the years of aging seemed to melt away before her eyes.

It became immediately evident that his long life had been a difficult one. Many decades of drinking had caught up with him, and his liver had all but given out—wreaking havoc on his entire immune system, allowing cancer of the soft tissue to move in, and grow and multiply. His body had started the process of shutting down.

Two months in a hospice bed, Joseph now longed for the kiss of death. Ready to take the next step—a spiritual one—he yearned to leave this world behind, and soar into the next, free from the physical limitations of his now worn-out shell. In fact, he welcomed the thought. Living drained him, as never-ending fatigue had taken over his feeble body, and now merely staying alive seemed to require more energy than he had left. A tiredness, that sleep alone could never remedy, embraced him and continually tugged at him to pull him under. Slowly losing the battle, he somehow lingered on.

"Mr. Stone, I'm Gaston Lombard, a criminal prosecuting attorney from Miami, Florida. Claire Caswell and I flew over to meet with you and ask you some questions. It's a pleasure to meet you, sir."

"I'm Claire Caswell, an enforcement investigator with the State of Florida. Thank you for talking to us, Mr. Stone."

"And I'm Edmond Penwright. We met years back, Mr. Stone."

Joseph looked past Guy, and Claire, and zeroed in on Mr. Penwright. "I remember you…from long ago," he said. "Scotland Yard. You talked to me when Mr. Post disappeared. It seems like…only yesterday. You cared…."

"We would like to record our interview with you, Mr. Stone, if you have no objections," Guy said.

"Call me Joseph," he said, "my name. Mr. Stone sounds so formal."

"Okay, Joseph. Mind if we record our time with you?"

"I don't care. Tell me. You're here about Mr. Post, aren't you?"

"We are," Guy said.

"Is he dead? Did you find his body?"

"Joseph, human remains recently came to light during an environmental tank pull, at a site in Miami Shores, Florida. Our Medical Examiner gave us a pretty clear picture of what this man looked like at the time of his death. We scoured multiple thousands of missing person listings and found one entry that seemed like it may be the one we are looking for," Claire said. "That entry led us to Scotland Yard, then to Mr. Penwright, and now to you."

Joseph listened conscientiously to every word leaving Claire's mouth.

"There's a possibility the remains we found in Florida are that of your friend, David Post," Guy said.

Colossal tears pooled in Joseph's immense eyes, until, at last, they overflowed in a stream and ran down his hollow cheeks. He wept outright, until his broken body shuddered and his chin fell to his chest—his head now too heavy for his fragile body to hold upright for long. Clearly, he was devastated by the news.

A feeling of overwhelming sadness penetrated Claire. Even though she had met Joseph only minutes earlier, she felt as if she had known him always.

Silence filled the room for what seemed to be a very long time. Eyes closed, Joseph remembered. He held his gnarled fingers over his face as pain riveted through his feeble frame. Then words found a way out. "David Post…was my brother."

Again, silence predominated. Mr. Penwright's jaw dropped open, and Claire and Guy stared at each other, stunned beyond imagination by the unforeseen disclosure.

"We had no idea. None whatsoever. We are *truly* sorry," Claire said. "Should we leave you alone?"

"No. I have a story that must be told. I've waited too long, and time is short."

The boldness in his tone surprised them, and seemed to come out of nowhere.

Claire recognized a quality in Joseph that reminded her of her father—his unshakable strength of character and iron will, a trait both carried proudly.

"Joseph, do you have any knowledge of why, or how, your brother, David, may have ended up in the United States, specifically in the Miami, Florida area?" Guy asked.

Another period of stillness followed. Looking intently upward, toward the ceiling, Joseph's eyes remained wide open and darted from side to side, as if he were watching the years of his life pass before him. When he talked, his words came out sporadically, and slowly, with great difficulty—taking all the internal strength he could muster to formulate them. Bolts of intermittent and horrific pain coursed through his being, and even the large amounts of morphine—doled out to him on an hourly basis—did not absolve him from the agony of his misery. He winced, periodically, but continued on, a trooper to the end.

"I've lived in the darkness of a secret for many, many years…and I've prayed to the Almighty to be released from the hellish torment I have carried around for so long—before I leave this earth. Thank you…for finding me."

Claire, Guy, and Mr. Penwright each took a seat on the chairs provided, Claire sitting closest to Joseph. When Joseph folded his hands on his lap, Claire was the first to notice, in horror, the thick, two-inch long scars, running along the inside of both his wrists. She grimaced. Following her eyes, Guy and Mr. Penwright saw the marks, too.

"Please listen carefully to what I must tell you." Joseph said. A shooting pain riveted through him, and he winced. "I am a Jew…and a survivor of the Holocaust." He looked straight ahead as the words left his mouth, directing his gaze at no one in particular, as if wearing blinders.

"I was living in a small town in German-allied Slovakia with my parents and my younger brother, David, when, without warning, one night in the summer of 1942, we were rounded up, along with the other Jews living in that town, and transported by train to a Nazi extermination camp in a remote place close to the village of Sobibor—located near the present-day eastern border of Poland—then German-occupied."

Another sudden and piercing pain engaged his body. He alternated between holding his breath, and breathing in and out deeply several times in a row, trying desperately to manage the torment, waiting for a let-up.

"Soldiers, armed with rifles, rode on the top of the train cars, and would shoot anyone who managed to jump from the train in an attempt to get away. And while nearly everyone brought to Sobibor ended up being killed immediately, the Nazis kept a few hundred of us alive to help facilitate the killing process of the camp. You see, this happened when Hitler resolved to slaughter all the Jews of Europe. And Ukrainian Nationalists volunteered to collaborate with this evil government-sanctioned program and assist at the Sobibor death camp.

"David escaped this terrible fate only because of his hospitalization for polio. He was receiving physical therapy treatments at the time they hauled us away like animals.... I did not learn the fate of my younger brother until years later."

He stopped to catch his breath, and to rest, as talking demanded one hundred percent of his remaining energy. He gasped for air.

Just then Ms. Simpson rushed in. "You will have to leave now," she said. "This is clearly too much for him. He is completely worn out."

Due to the timing of her entrance, Claire realized Ms. Simpson had probably been hovering by the door, listening to the entire conversation—her curiosity getting the better of her.

They agreed to let Joseph rest, and informed Ms. Simpson they would call in the morning about returning to continue the interview tomorrow. She nodded as she pulled the blanket up and around Joseph's slight, shivering form. Filling a small eyedropper with liquid morphine, she squeezed it into his mouth, before escorting the others from his room. "He needs rest," she said, before whispering a faint goodbye. "We'll see about tomorrow, tomorrow."

24

DRIVING BACK TO the B&B, no one talked. It was as though silence slipped in and took all three hostage. Finding out that David Post's brother was alive seemed beyond the bounds of possibility, and far surpassed any expectations they might have had on the flight over. But the story Joseph had started to communicate carried with it the force of a crushing blow. And if more would come out...if only Joseph could remain persistent and determined in a more than difficult situation...if only he could hold out a little while longer...if the partial dental records came back a match—then they'd most probably have an identification on the skeleton, something they thought would never happen at the onset of the investigation. If only Joseph could finish his detailed account, then they would know how David Post ended up in the Miami area, and maybe even come away with clues as to who might have killed him. So much depended on Joseph, and so many *ifs* hung in the balance.

Claire sent a speechless message to Joseph. Don't give up! Hang on! Don't take the hand of the Angel of Death. Not yet.

Between general lack of satisfying sleep, jet lag, and the revelations of Joseph, Claire and Guy felt drained beyond measure. Rest was mandatory and could no longer be ignored. After Mr. Penwright dropped them at the inn, they climbed the seemingly interminable flights of marble stairs leading to their room, Guy's arm entwined with Claire's.

"I have the feeling we may never hear the whole story," Guy said.

"I have a feeling we will," Claire said.

A tiny rose-patterned chintz wallpaper, with matching draperies, accented the velveteen-covered furniture in the room. Tastefully decorated in calming shades of soft greens, mainly celadon, the space offered tranquil, undisturbed relief—just what the doctor ordered. The air exuded a mild scent of linden, and the bed looked comfortable and inviting. Shedding their clothing and crawling in between the sage, satin-edged linen sheets, they let their heads sink into the luxurious and oversized feather pillows, and, in no time at all, they fell into critically needed slumber.

Later that evening, after dinner, they headed back to the comfortable four-poster bed for a full night's sleep, anxious about what the next day would bring.

Wednesday morning

UP EXTRA early, Guy and Claire readied for the day, and went downstairs to eat. The fry-up breakfast Nathan had touted included: eggs, Irish bacon, bangers (English sausage), black pudding, grilled tomatoes, mushrooms, baked beans, brown sauce, fried bread with orange marmalade, and to drink, hot tea with milk. More like a farm-hand's breakfast, and so unlike the light meal they usually ate in the mornings, the heavy food did not appeal to them. But they did their best to sample many of the tasty morsels, not knowing what the day would bring, and when, or if, they'd have another chance to eat before evening.

Joseph was all that mattered. What he had to say was vital to the investigation.

After speaking briefly with the inn's owners, and praising them on their fine B&B, Guy placed a call to Ms. Simpson at the hospice center. The time was exactly 8:00 a.m.

"Good morning, Ms. Simpson. Gaston Lombard calling."

"Mr. Lombard, I'm glad you called early."

"How's Joseph feeling today?"

"He did not sleep well during the night. He had nightmares. Terrible nightmares."

"I'm so sorry to hear that. Maybe our meeting with him triggered his reliving things from the past."

"He has been calling out your names since the early morning hours. He wants to see all three of you. Can you return soon?"

"We'll be there as quickly as we can, Ms. Simpson. Let him know we're on our way."

"Please, I beg you. Hurry!"

Guy hung up, filled Claire in, and dialed Mr. Penwright, who agreed to pick them up in fifteen minutes. Waiting by the inn's front door, they jumped into Mr. Penwright's car as soon as he pulled up, and together they traveled to the hospice without delay. Again, very little conversation ensued en route, and the tension of the moment was palpable. Senseless chatter seemed silly at a time like this. Reaching their destination in record time, they walked through the double doors, and into the reception area to announce their arrival. Ms. Simpson entered the lobby before they had a chance to walk to the waiting area, and, without taking a moment to greet them, she led them to the room at the end of the hallway.

"I assured him you would be here soon," she said. "Go on in. He's waiting." She walked into the room with them. "Joseph, they're here. Mr. Lombard, Ms. Caswell, and Mr. Penwright. Just as I promised." She smiled a well-bred smile and left the room.

Sitting positioned on the bed, again propped up by pillows, seemingly in a world of his own, Joseph did not talk right away. The three sat down on the chairs from yesterday, waiting for the time Joseph would want to continue his story. Twenty minutes passed, and thirty, and finally he began speaking, slowly at first, but with great deliberation, staring straight ahead as if in a sightless fog. Fully preoccupied with his own thoughts, his words, after a time, began to tumble out.

"My brother's nurse protected him by bringing him to her home in the countryside, and explaining him away as a distant cousin who'd been displaced by the war to anyone who inquired."

Amazingly, he began exactly where he'd left off the day before, without skipping a beat.

"She saved his life by doing this. You see, only skilled prisoners, those strong and able, who could work hard, had a chance of surviving at this camp, and David, with his limp and polio complications, would, most certainly, have been killed without delay. Being a certified accountant, they kept me around to do their books.

"You need to understand that Sobibor was designated a *death* camp when it began to operate in May of 1942. Mass killings took place there. They killed our parents in that camp before my eyes, with me as the witness…." As his head dropped to his chest, uncontrollable tears began to well in his eyes and then roll down and over his protruding facial bones. As fast as they appeared, he brushed them away with one hand, or the other, determined that nothing would discourage him from what he needed to tell them. Minutes passed.

"In July of 1943, the camp began the process of changing to a *concentration* or *working* camp." He breathed in and out, deeply.

All in the room remained terribly concerned about Joseph's condition and did not want to add to his pronounced stress.

"David, a young man when they took us away, would now be close to eighty-three. I am three years older," Joseph said, contemplatively. "Eighty-six."

Pausing to sip water, he closed his eyes as he kept on, exhaustion and emotion getting the best of him despite his resolve to stave them off.

"Should we come back later? Maybe you need to take a break?" Claire asked.

"No. I'm very tired, but you cannot leave. I must keep at it." His stamina seemed at the same time extraordinary and impossible. He took a deep breath and exhaled slowly. "One day some Soviet Jews, with military knowledge—who had become German prisoners-of-war, and escaped from several prisons on the way to another death camp—were accidentally diverted to Sobibor. You see, I say, *accidentally*, because unforeseen problems caused the train diversion to our camp. Or maybe it was fate that intervened. For many of us had been planning an escape, and the Soviet prisoners-of-war heard about our plan and persuaded us to do it. They said our plan could work, and they gave us the encouragement we needed to carry it out."

Joseph took on a whitish pale—an almost ghostly appearance. But he continued to relate the story of his life, his eyes remaining closed, occasionally stopping for another swallow of liquid.

"We lived in quarters very close to the Nazis in Sobibor, and because of that we had neat and clean clothing and housing. You see, the Nazis couldn't stand being around dirt. So despite conditions too horrific to detail in other concentration camps—as I later learned—our camp was kept strangely in order." He paused, as if unable to go on, suffering the assaults of a body shutting down. Several long minutes elapsed, until again, unbelievably, he mustered the strength to speak. "Two-hundred-and-fifty-thousand Jews ended up being killed at Sobibor. *Two hundred and fifty thousand!* By some accounts, two-hundred-and-sixty-thousand or more. One day, the Nazis even held a party—to celebrate the number of us they had slaughtered. They all got drunk, and they didn't make us work that day.

"And they kept records of the killings…*detailed* records. They proudly documented everything."

It became too difficult to say if anger or his resolve to battle exhaustion became the greater force within him urging him onward.

"We knew we had to escape, to get the story out, or we would all be forgotten, forever, and no one would ever know what happened to us there. No matter what the cost, we decided it would be worth it to try to break out. So on October 14, 1943—a date I'll never forget—those of us at Sobibor who agreed to try the escape plan, liberated ourselves by starting a fire within the camp, and placing a stepladder up against the barbed-wire-fence that surrounded the area, and climbing up and over.

"The Nazis started shooting at us, and the bullets kept coming, but we continued climbing and running and we wouldn't stop. Many of us got shot, some in the head, but we went on, leaping over bodies and trying not to step on the land mines that surrounded the camp. And people panicked…we all panicked. The plan obviously did not go as we thought it would, and many ended up killed—trying to free themselves from the hideous captivity. Once over the fence, those of us who did survive ran through the woods and looked back over our shoulders to see the fire still burning."

Joseph started to breathe heavily again, and started to sweat profusely, as the warriors of death fought relentlessly to overtake his tenuous frame.

"Let's call it a day," Claire said. She could barely stand to watch his acute suffering any longer.

Unable to stop, he did not hear her. "We said our good-byes to each other the night before the planned escape." Joseph had resumed where he'd left off, and started to whimper, recalling each detail like it happened yesterday.

"Three hundred of us in the revolt initially escaped, others were shot trying to flee, and we killed SS supervisors and Ukrainian guards as we scaled the fence. Only about fifty to sixty of us survived to the end of the war. In ensuing days, all who stayed behind were murdered. They liquidated the camp site and disguised it as a farm, planting crops to cover the site of the horrors. And…the camp at Sobibor ended. That evil place of the devil was no more. And as we suspected, the only records of Sobibor are through those of us who escaped—as the Nazis erased all evidence of the camp's existence.

"My physical body gained liberation when I freed myself, but my soul remained forever imprisoned. I had watched them slaughter my parents. And as far as I knew, my brother, David, had also been killed. Thin and gaunt, I had no real desire to keep living…because sometimes it becomes more terrifying to live than to die."

He moaned.

"Once, I even tried to bring my miserable existence to an end, at my own hand, in the camp—but my attempt failed miserably when the soldiers found me and *saved* me. So that became my fate. To keep going. To keep on living, despite my longing not to."

Claire, Guy, and Mr. Penwright had remained onlookers making no sound as Joseph relayed his cathartic and liberating soliloquy. His head rolled heavily to his chest, and after minutes of heavy breathing, they realized he'd fallen into deep sleep, totally spent.

Ms. Simpson rushed in. "I'm afraid I must insist that you leave now. He's completely exhausted, again." Filling the eyedropper with liquid morphine, as they'd seen her do before, she steadily squeezed the rubber bulb, expelling the liquid narcotic into Joseph's mouth, until she had emptied the glass tube. Then she pulled an extra blanket up around his chilled body before leaving the room. "He needs to rest."

"Will you call us when he wants to talk again, Ms. Simpson? Or would you prefer we call you to check on him?" Mr. Penwright asked.

"Either way. But for now, sleep takes precedence."

A heavy mood of somberness accompanied them on the drive back to the B&B. Learning more of the grisly details of what Joseph had endured during his lifetime was almost too painful to take in. And he hadn't yet reached the part involving David's plight after he found himself separated from the family. They had to know more, but it was clear they could not rush Joseph. Assuming the skeleton ended up being David, how had he ended up in the U.S.? In Miami? Dead? Wearing a lepton coin around his neck? Joseph held the key. He alone could unlock the remaining mysteries surrounding David Post.

Mr. Penwright delivered Claire and Guy back to their quarters, and Guy promised to call him as soon as they knew anything further, thanking him for sticking with them on this difficult task.

"I would have it no other way," Mr. Penwright said. "I'll wait to hear from you."

Claire and Guy walked the familiar flights to their room and collapsed into overstuffed chairs. Deep in thought, Claire let her head drop back and closed her eyes. Guy looked over at the woman he loved beyond words, and scrutinized her assiduously. Pangs of guilt flooded him as he thought about the sterling life that they shared. Fate had certainly dealt them both a good hand. He realized it now more than ever, and he felt especially grateful, and humbled.

"I'm sick at heart about what Joseph told us today. And to think the skeleton may be the remains of his sibling. Those poor brothers," Claire said. Her eyes remained closed.

"We don't know for sure, yet. But hopefully we'll hear from McKay shortly. By the way, my beauty, have I told you lately exactly how much I adore you?"

She opened her eyes, and looked at him affectionately. "No, my love, I haven't heard that in quite a while." She got up, walked over to him, wrapped her arms around his neck, and kissed him passionately.

Soon the workday would be starting in the U.S. and they could make necessary calls to their offices—to check in and review voicemail messages. While Joseph rested, they'd spend time reviewing case notes accumulated thus far in the investigation, and grab a bite to eat.

Claire sent another voiceless message to Joseph. Hold on, just a little while longer. We want to hear your whole story, and we need to ask you crucial questions. Please Joseph, fight hard.

25

EARLY THE NEXT morning Guy telephoned Ms. Simpson. "Morning, Ms. Simpson. It's Mr. Lombard. How is Joseph?"

"He seems okay at the moment. I apologize again that you could not return yesterday after you left, but another visit would have done him in. He slept most of the day."

"And today?"

"I'd say you should come here early. Mornings seem better for him. He is asking for the three of you."

"Good. We'll be there soon."

Guy hung up, and called Mr. Penwright. Within a half hour, the three of them were on the road traveling back to the now familiar institution that provided care for the terminally ill.

Ms. Simpson greeted them as they walked in, and ushered them to Joseph's room without hesitation.

Joseph's eyes opened wide when he heard the trio come in. With the assistance of Ms. Simpson, and several pillows, he sat up in bed, anxious to proceed with what he had to tell them. "I've been waiting for you," he said. "I…."

As Claire looked into his eyes, she realized he was reaching far within himself to collect any remaining energy in his extremely exhausted being. She watched him with highly developed interest. Noticeably flushed, and entirely more haggard and feeble than the day before, today his face appeared to be quite swollen, and he seemed to struggle to get words out.

"Before we start today, Joseph, I have a question for you," Guy said. "I'm wondering if you will allow us to take a sample of your blood—for DNA testing, should we need it?"

"Of course…but it's not necessary."

"Why not?" Guy asked.

"I knew the skeleton you found belonged to my brother, David, when you first came here and told me about it—and I'll tell you why." Without justification he seemed to have renewed strength and tenacity.

"Hold on, Joseph," Guy said. "Give me a minute, please. I'll be right back." He left the room and returned with an on-site lab technician, who drew a blood sample from Joseph's lifeless arm. Guy asked the lab worker to prepare it properly for them to hand-carry back to the U.S., as shipping would be too risky. What if it got lost or broken during transport?

"Thank you, Joseph," Guy said. "I'm sorry for the delay. Now please, continue." Guy turned on his portable tape recorder, as he had each time.

"When I escaped, I started making my way back to my home town, on foot, traveling only at night, through the woods, hiding out during the day, eking out a meager existence, living on berries, and roots, and grass—anything I could find to stay alive. In the woods, I met up with a group of partisans who agreed to keep me hidden until the war finally ended, although it remained unclear to me if I even wanted to go on living.

"After the war ended, I made my way to the Jewish Relief Agency near my family's home, and it was there I learned that David had been saved from the camp and execution—that he'd lived with a nurse in the countryside, and had ultimately made his way to England to begin a new life. You see, David left a written note for me at the agency, not knowing whether it would ever reach me, saying he now went by the name of David Crawford Post, and would be taking a chauffeur's job, working for a wealthy Lord Dobson in London. His message said I should come and look for him when I got the information, and it begged me not to forget about him. Can you imagine?"

Joseph had now provided them with recorded testimony explaining that his brother went by the alias of David Crawford Post, Claire thought.

Joseph's mouth went dry, and he paused to ingest small sips of water. Drinking, and swallowing, were becoming ever more difficult for him. Angst now owned his body, and morphine no longer provided relief. He writhed as the cancer aggressively consumed his innards. Nothing mattered now except to finish his story. He had to keep on while he was able to do so, while ears could hear, while he had control of his mouth to speak. Someone had to hear the truth. *The truth!* His eyes watered.

"We both had only each other. I knew David's fate, but he did not know mine. Not yet. Neither of us had married before the war, so no wife or children enriched either of our lives. It was to become the two of us against the world. My little brother, David—the only fair-haired member of our family—had always relied on me to take care of him, to protect him, until they hauled me away, that is.

"Our last name was Posnick. My birth name was Joseph Posnick, and my brother's was David Posnick."

Claire politely interrupted him. "What *middle* name did your parents give your brother at the time of his birth?"

"Oved—David *Oved* Posnick. And mine was Jacob—Joseph Jacob Posnick."

Claire's mind raced to the initials engraved on the lepton. The "d" could have stood for "David," and the second initial—either "o," for "Oved," or "c," for "Crawford." If this fell into place like she thought it would, then Benjamin had been infinitely correct when he guessed at the first two initials on the coin. Would the third initial, had it not worn off, have been a "p" for "Posnick," or "Post?" Could this all be pure coincidence? Or could this be hard evidence that the remains found on the Lawden site, in fact, belonged to David Post, Joseph's brother? Claire assumed Guy was making the same connection at that moment.

"I followed my brother to London, after I'd learned of his whereabouts, also assuming a new identity—that of Joseph Stone, a name I thought sounded British. I found David without too much trouble, and our reunion was both emotional and gut-wrenching. I told him how our parents had been murdered, and it destroyed him to the core." Joseph cried, remembering.

"We agreed to remain living in London—where no one would know our true identities or be able to figure out our connection as brothers. He continued his work as the chauffeur for the wealthy lord, and I went to work on a cattle farm—just outside of the city, eventually supervising the hired hands and doing the books for the owner.

"David's polio did not impede his ability to drive a car with the use of his right foot, and the lord acted very caring of him—befriending him and paying him good wages. You see, David had endured extreme mental and physical pain, re-working and developing his crippled leg muscles, through a long series of treatments and exercises that ever-so-slowly restored his mobility, even though his left leg remained severely crippled by the disease. Mind you, after a brave and fierce battle with the illness, a limp, sporadic muscle cramping, difficulty breathing at times, and some physical activity limitations, were all that remained of the dreadful disease. Sheer stubbornness empowered my incredibly strong brother to conquer and cope, instead of succumbing to the permanent role of invalid."

Joseph stopped talking, to rest fleetingly, and sip more water, as his mouth was becoming so dry. Completing his life account seemed to act as the spur to urge him forward and force his tired life form to continue to speak.

"Eventually, he even confided in the lord, and told him about the camp his family had been taken to, from which he'd been spared, and the lord had great compassion for him."

All color had now drained from Joseph's face, and his eyes appeared glassy. He began to cough, but he refused to entertain Mr. Penwright's suggestion of taking a break. And Joseph started to insist that he no longer felt any discomfort whatsoever, and could continue on with no problem.

Claire realized he had started the final process of stepping away.

"David and I would meet at a little pub in London, several evenings a week, when our work days ended—staying late into the evening or early into the morning hours, talking over roast beef dinners, drinking pints of pale ale or jars of beer. He became my life blood, and only reason for living."

He broke to rest his eyes, as crushing fatigue was galloping through his body at an alarming speed, attempting to lasso him and pull him under—into oppressively heavy sleep. He fought it with everything he had left, and won a short victory.

"Are you sure you're up to this, Joseph?" Claire asked.

Staring in her direction, a benevolent look on his face, he did not seem to see her, as he now began falling into a semi-trance state.

"Thank you for coming here these days to listen," he said. "It has meant the world to me. Yes, there's more." He continued, robotically.

"A wonderful man with a heart of gold, David was a true *mensch*...a man of integrity, and honor. Despite the cards he'd been dealt in life, he never lost his kind-heartedness for others. I, on the other hand, surrendered my zest for living in the concentration camp. I released it to the winds, and never reclaimed it. We both kept very private, and dealt with an overwhelming amount of internal pain...and together we drank to numb the agony that ever so slowly and constantly ate away at us. We drank to forget. But in our sober moments, the pain always found its way back to us...and we'd...remember.

"Eventually, David forgave his enemies—those who tore our family apart and murdered our parents, those who oppressed us simply because of who we were—and some of his inner torment actually lifted. But I...I remained bitter and angry all throughout these long years, and my misery has never eased. I continued on, a tormented soul living with the element of shame—shame that I could not save the lives of my parents, shame that I stood back and watched them die. It has haunted my every day. I should have died trying to save them, but instead I acted cowardly....

"And then one night...another nightmare began." He closed his eyes. Silence covered the room like a heavy shroud, and he moaned in sorrow—gripped by rippling emotions too atrocious to bear.

"Joseph, what can I do for you?" Claire begged. "Please tell me."

Deafening silence screamed at them.

When he finally spoke, he looked at Claire, bewilderment evident in his huge and sad eyes. "Although they've systematically given me mega-doses of morphine for my physical pain, I have mental anguish that even the strongest of narcotics could never reach, dear Claire. Thank you for your concern. It will be the last tenderness I feel in this lifetime."

His voice and words melted her, and she began to whimper, tears flooding her lovely eyes. She moved her chair closer to Joseph and reached for his hand. He accepted it, gratefully, squeezing back as firmly as he could, and then hanging on loosely. Claire looked over at Guy and Mr. Penwright and saw that they, too, were overtaken by pure and raw emotion.

"I'm...so...tired," Joseph said. His head dropped back onto the pillows, and he fell asleep instantly, this time crushing fatigue being the victor.

Ms. Simpson hurried in. "That's it for now. You will have to come back later."

"We'll go to lunch, and let Joseph rest for awhile," Claire said. "Mind if we come back this afternoon? There's more he wants to tell us."

"Please call me first. I'll let you know then."

They showed themselves out, for they knew the way blindfolded. Mr. Penwright drove them to a crowded nearby pub, and they all ordered the special of the day—steak and kidney pie, with chips, mushy peas, and gravy. And to wash it down, a jar of beer for the men, and a Coca-Cola for Claire.

"It's a tough story to hear," Claire said. "My heart aches for that precious man."

"Yeah. It's devastating," Mr. Penwright said.

"What a life those brothers had. To think about what they endured," Guy said.

"The Nazis did atrocious and inexplicable things," Mr. Penwright said.

"And what's really hard to conceive is the mass appeal and following they had—why so many people, from all walks of life, and from so many countries, helped commit those atrocities or stood by and did nothing to stop them," Guy said. "But then, we must not forget the noble stories of the people who helped hide the Jews, either."

"We should thank God for the pillars of light in the world," Claire said. "Without them, it would be a pretty dark place."

The beverages arrived, as the three sat in stillness, reflecting.

"We haven't heard it all, yet," Claire said. "Let's hope we get the chance to go back this afternoon."

The savory food arrived after a substantial delay, and the threesome consumed it all—unaware of the level of hunger they had reached. When they had finished, the server brought them each a blueberry-pie-and-custard, included with the meal, and poured a cup of strong hot tea all around.

Guy excused himself, and went to find a quiet spot. Pulling his cell phone from his belt, he dialed Michael McKay's office. "McKay?" Guy asked.

"Mr. Lombard? I got your message."

"Then you know, we're still in London. Have you received the partial dentals from Scotland Yard?"

"Yes. They arrived just this morning. It's early here. Office just opened. I'm still reeling from the fact that you found dental records in a case of this age. What are you guessing the comparison testing will show?"

"It's too early to tell for sure, McKay, but I will tell you this. I won't be a bit surprised if you tell me they're a match."

"Let me get back to you. If everything goes without a hitch, within a few hours."

"Good. Call me on my cell as soon as you have something."

"Yes, sir."

"Thanks, McKay. I greatly appreciate it."

Returning to the table, Guy filled the others in on the conversation.

The server returned to refill the teas, and they sipped and relaxed, biding time, waiting to call Ms. Simpson.

An hour later, Guy telephoned Ms. Simpson from the table. Most of the other surrounding diners had departed by then, leaving behind an atmosphere of relative calm.

"Ms. Simpson, Mr. Lombard here. Did Joseph wake up?"

"Yes, and he's acting lively. He's rallied. I would suggest you drive here immediately."

26

"NOT A GOOD sign, I'm afraid," Claire said.

Mr. Penwright traveled along the roads as fast as law permitted.

"It's common for people to rally at the very end—sometimes a day or so, or even hours before, they pass away," Claire continued. "They seem more alert than they have in weeks, or months—at times *remarkably* alert—wanting to talk, or even asking for and eating a favorite meal when they haven't had an appetite in weeks. We must hurry, or we'll be too late."

Mr. Penwright pressed the pedal harder to the floor, and they made good time. Ms. Simpson greeted them at the front doors, and hurried them along the pathway to Joseph's room.

"Strangely, Joseph seems very on the ball since he woke up from his nap," Ms. Simpson said. "Better than I've seen him in a very long time, actually. He's been calling out each of your names with a renewed sense of urgency, and keeps repeating that he must finish his story. He's wanting to sit up on his own, and dangle his feet over the side of the bed—something he hasn't had the strength to do in weeks. And his energy level has spiked dramatically. I'm afraid this cannot be a good thing, folks. Many times we see this—just before the end comes."

Like sands through the hourglass, the days, and hours, of Joseph's life were rapidly coming to an end. Entering the room, they observed a revived Joseph breathing in and out deeply. When he saw that the three visitors had returned, he felt liberation from his burden was at hand. His skin looked doughy, and, oddly, he appeared thinner and much older than earlier in the day; yet, as Ms. Simpson had relayed to them, he definitely seemed to have gained a second, or third, wind.

"Joseph, we're here for you. Please tell us more of your story," Guy said. A tone of gentleness beyond measure emanated from Guy's voice as he spoke. He switched the recorder to the *on* position.

"I've been waiting," Joseph said. "Where did I leave off?"

"You had just mentioned another nightmare had begun," Mr. Penwright said.

"Yes. Thank you, Mr. Penwright. The second nightmare. I told you David and I would meet at a pub in London several nights each week to spend time together, and I had started to let myself verbalize the horrors of the camp…to talk about the fate of our parents…something I had been unable to do before then." He paused for a long drink of water, absorbed in thought.

"For many years we had blocked the memories of our parents, you see, because when something's too painful to recall, your mind has a way of helping you deal with the agony—by temporarily removing it from your intellect…but we had *started* to remember. Both of us had begun the process of opening up, going to the core of our pain, and talking candidly about feelings we had stuffed, and kept locked away, for so long." He sighed. "We relived the Nazis invading our hometown…."

Joseph began to meander into a world known only to him—in his mind's eye—and for some time he escaped fully into that private realm. Staring into the distance, as they'd seen him do so often before at times of recollection, now Joseph trembled convulsively, unable to focus. Alone in his secret sphere, he seemed to be fighting with death, bargaining with the Grim Reaper. Then, miraculously, clear visual definition seemed to return to him.

"I told you complications from polio had landed David in a local hospital just before word came that the Germans were coming. I tried to warn him, to get him out of the hospital, to hide him, but the doctors refused to release him, saying he required the treatments they were giving him to improve the quality of his life. I went, again, the next day to obtain his release, but found the facility deserted. David, and all the others, had disappeared.

"My family fled for our lives, without my brother…but they captured us, treated us like animals, and forced me and my parents onto the train bound for Sobibor. We did not know what had become of David, but we presumed he'd been killed. In reality, I tried to survive life in the camp, while he lived in the home of the nurse. And then, when things became too risky for her to continue to keep him, he'd moved on, traveling from one hiding place to another, living in cellars with a few other Jews in hiding, existing in one small room, with a bucket for a toilet, and nothing to eat but paltry amounts of hay and peas—and later, living in the woods with the resistance groups. Both of us tried desperately to survive, each in our own ways and under different circumstances, neither knowing what the other was facing or even whether the other had survived…both confronting death and holding it at bay, as I would later learn.

"By a miraculous twist of fate, the two of us did survive. We never knew why the shadow of death passed over the two of us at that time, yet fell upon so many others, or why the wheels of life turned the way they did for David and me. It would have been easier, and our preference, to die with our parents, of course…but destiny marked us for survival and hand-picked us to carry on."

He paused and took slow sips of water, a look of contemplation deeply embedded in his eyes.

"When the war at last ended, we each made our way to England, changing our names to blot out the past, to start anew. David seemed fanatical about it and destroyed everything he owned that had his name on it, anything that might reveal his true identity."

Based upon Joseph's words, Claire wondered if David had intentionally tried to mar the engravings on the lepton to hide his initials. Maybe age, after all, had not been the culprit—assuming, of course, the skeleton turned out to be the remains of David Post. *David Crawford Post* or *David Oved Posnick*—either way, two of the initials were a perfect match.

"Together, one night at the pub, we started to recall everything from our past. It seemed at long last the floodgates had broken open. And that's the night it began—the second nightmare."

He had been repeating himself somewhat, and they realized the heavy doses of medications may be causing a certain amount of confusion and short-term memory loss. But then, he started up again with a new part of his story.

"We said our usual goodbyes and agreed to meet back there two nights later. In the wee hours of the morning we parted, and on David's drive home he stopped to help what he thought to be a stranded driver. The man's car bonnet had been propped up and he was standing beside his apparently disabled vehicle, seemingly waiting for someone to stop and offer assistance. And along came David, the goodhearted, that fateful morning.

"He stopped and got out of his car to help the bloke, and soon realized what an irreversible mistake he'd made. But it was too late. He'd walked into a set-up, and the person he thought needed assistance pulled a knife on him and attempted to rob him. They struggled, and David fought the assailant for his life, gaining control of the blade and in self-defense stabbing the attacker, killing him.

"He panicked. No witnesses were present to corroborate David's story of self-defense, and he feared police involvement would lead to his arrest on a murder charge. Authorities would no doubt discover he was living under a false identity, and force him to relive the horrors of the Holocaust to explain why he had assumed a new name when he relocated to London. He wiped his fingerprints from the knife and fled the scene in his car.

"When he arrived home, he woke his employer, recounted the story, and begged for his help. Mercifully, the lord agreed to pull some strings—to arrange for a quick passport allowing my brother to travel to the United States, where the authorities would never think to look for him. And he gave David a supply of money to live on until he became gainfully employed. The lord arranged a hasty departure for David, leaving the very next day. You see, the lord knew David could only be telling the truth, so he agreed to help him vanish—in case the police came looking for him. Together, they overturned the furniture in David's room, making it appear that a fight had taken place. And the lord decided to wait a couple of days before reporting him missing to Scotland Yard, thereby giving my brother lead time to safely travel to, and arrive in, the United States.

"There would be a short investigation, and with no clues to follow, foul play would be suspected, and the matter would eventually be closed. Scotland Yard would never learn that the lord knew anything about the incident, and David would simply become another statistic—a missing person, presumed dead. They agreed that the plan would work and save David's future."

Joseph paused.

Mr. Penwright sat spellbound, hearing the true facts about the investigation he had been unable to solve all those years ago.

"David came to see me the next morning, bright and early, at my job, and I knew when I looked at him that something had gone horribly wrong. I took a break and we went into a small room with a door, where we could talk in private. It was there that he explained in vivid detail what had occurred the night before, and also what he planned to do about it. He saw no other alternative. He had to go away, in the event he became a suspect, in case the trail led his way. With no way to prove what had really happened in the dark of the night, he could not chance being sent to prison—not when he had acted in self-defense. He figured it would be only a matter of time until the police talked to the nearby pub owner and concluded that it was David who had left the establishment about the time of the murder, and also that he traveled home on that particular route.

"All I could think of as he told me his plan was that we'd be separated once again, and I realized on the spot that fate was out to destroy me. I felt as if I'd been kicked in the stomach by an otherworldly force and my wind had been knocked out. I couldn't catch my breath and felt faint. Severe pains shot through my chest like bolts of lightning, and I dropped to my knees. I could simply not believe, nor accept, the cruelty of this world. David helped me up, and made me swear to secrecy, agreeing I would never mention his plan to anyone. He promised to write as soon as he got settled—to let me know he'd made it safely to his new home. But he could never give me his address in the U.S., and I could never write back to him. This one-way communication was the only way to handle the situation that seemed foolproof. We cried, and hugged each other, and he walked away without looking back. I didn't realize then it would be the last time I would ever see him." Tears blurred Joseph's giant eyes.

Claire's body ached from his pain, and slow, steady, unstoppable tears rolled down her cheeks, as a time of deep silence ensued. At the outset, neither Claire nor Guy, or Mr. Penwright for that matter, could ever have imagined the depth of sympathetic pity and concern Joseph's life story would engender within them. The challenges of his life made Mr. Penwright conclude that evenhandedness in the world was a myth. It was the account of one man's life that would disarm the hardest of criminals, and certainly liquefy a block of ice.

"I've concluded it's during life's darkest times that we grow and learn the greatest lessons," Joseph said, when he finally spoke. "And I've learned, regardless of what happens to any of us, the wheels of life continue to turn. That's the pattern set down before us, and it will be the pattern long after we're gone. And none of us has any control to stop the tempo—or slow it down in any way, and certainly we cannot question it. Although, I believe fate, at times, has the power to intervene and steer things in a certain direction.

"Some of us are given short lives, others, long ones. Certain people are called upon to keep living despite incredible pain, while the life of others is cut short to end unbearable suffering. None of us can fully understand the complexities of life—but we must, as the saying goes, play the cards we're dealt. The only alternative would be to drop out of the game completely—and that's an option I now realize is always wrong.

"I waited to hear from David...I waited...and waited.... A couple of months passed, and although I worried about him, I somehow knew, at some level, that he was okay. Then one day, I received a letter from him saying he'd settled in Miami, Florida, and had obtained a government work authorization. He told me he'd performed odd jobs, at first, to survive, but recently he'd landed a real job working for a very successful art and antiques dealer, who let him handle the pick-ups and deliveries of priceless pieces of fine art and antiquities, and also do handyman work around the store. The knowledge of antiques that David had gleaned from the lord in London helped him secure that job, where the owner treated him well and paid him considerable wages. He felt thankful for work with regular hours that provided such a decent living, and he saved his money and planned to fly me to the United States to visit him one day, or even to live with him."

Claire made a mental note. They now had testimony that David Crawford Post lived in the Miami, Florida area. Another puzzle piece appeared to fall neatly into place.

"From that time on, he wrote me long letters—sometimes two or three or even four per week—for close to a year. But one day, I received a strange letter from him, telling me he'd overheard a phone conversation his employer had with another antiques dealer, and although David didn't know who was on the other end of the line, the discussion clearly centered around the importing or smuggling of *stolen* goods. Suddenly, David realized that his employer was engaging in illegal activities, and he feared being unwittingly involved. Well, he panicked. While trying to live a straight-and-narrow, honest life, destiny had once again interceded and brought trouble his way. The thought of guilt-by-association terrified him.

"He didn't know what to do. He dared not go to the police and risk their discovering he'd entered the United States illegally on a false passport, and then determining he used an alias, and potentially even putting two and two together and figuring out why he'd fled London in the first place. No, he could not risk that happening. Police involvement triggered extreme fear in him. How would he be able to convince enforcement authorities of his innocence when he worked for the man?

He wrote that he'd decided to confront his employer directly on the fraudulent activity, and then to walk away, to seek employment elsewhere, and anonymously report what he knew to the authorities....

"And that turned out to be the last letter I ever received from him."

Joseph had just handed them *motive*. Motive for the murder of David Post. By confronting his employer, David had sealed his own fate.

Just then, Guy's cell phone rang. "Excuse me, Joseph. I hope this is the call I've been waiting for."

27

"JOSEPH, I HAVE something to tell you," Guy said, walking back into the room and meeting Joseph's eyes dead on. "That call I just received was from our Medical Examiner back home, Michael McKay. We had Scotland Yard send him the partial dental records we told you about—from the missing persons file Mr. Penwright opened in 1966—so that he could compare them to those of the skeleton."

Guy's gaze shifted to Claire, then Mr. Penwright, and lastly returned to Joseph. Apprehension filled the room, and Claire held her breath. Joseph turned away from Guy's steady and intent look.

"I'm sorry to have to tell you this," Guy went on, "but we have a positive match—at least as far as our Medical Examiner is able to determine at this time. However, the records are not complete, and he'd prefer to have the full set for comparison purposes. But in his professional opinion, the skeleton found in Miami Shores appears to be that of your brother, David Post. Again, Joseph, I'm so sorry."

At first, Joseph did not say a word. Then he bent forward and let out a high-pitched cry of anger and grief. Claire, Guy and Mr. Penwright left the room to give Joseph the opportunity to mourn in private.

"Poor Joseph. Even though he told us he knew the truth, when you actually verified it, it was like a dagger stabbing through him," Claire said. "It's a dramatic revelation. Even the engravings on the lepton make sense now."

"Yeah. As amazing as it seems, the more we hear, the more things start to connect. McKay said he's willing to put his reputation on the line and testify that the dentals are a match. But if we can come up with some other corroborating evidence to prove the identification beyond the shadow of a doubt, he could then give us an airtight, locked up, definitive identification—one he'd feel more comfortable with."

"Like a fingernail belonging to David, or a strand of hair from a hair brush he used, right?" Claire asked. "Then McKay could compare the DNA fingerprint from one of those items to the DNA extracted from the skeletal bones in hopes of an irrefutable match. Fat chance of finding something like that at this point."

"And there's also Joseph's blood sample. I don't know what McKay can do with that," Guy said. "And I'm not certain that a brother qualifies as a maternal relative, anyway."

"Come back," Joseph called out. "Come back."

When they re-entered his room, he wiped his eyes. "I knew it was David's remains that you found—long before the dental confirmation. I knew when you told me a skeleton had surfaced in Miami. I thought I knew, anyway. But when you told me just now, the finality of the words…I guess I was not prepared to hear it."

"I'm sorry, Joseph, so sorry…," Claire said.

"It's dreadful, indeed," Mr. Penwright said.

"He never gave me his Miami address," Joseph said. "He didn't want Scotland Yard detectives finding him through me—in case they ever decided to track him in connection with the murder and discovered our family tie. He thought it better for him, and for me, if I didn't know his precise location. So I could never attempt to contact him after his last letter, to verify his safety or well-being, and I also could not notify the police for obvious reasons.

"He provided me no way to locate him. Miami covers an extensive area and I didn't know how or where to begin searching."

All of a sudden, Joseph stopped to catch his breath, and said he felt woozy and winded. For the first time since their return that day, Joseph admitted that all-out exhaustion had returned. Claire noticed an abrupt and marked decrease in his sense of awareness, as if a pin had burst his bubble. He fell back into a reclining position and lay very still. With one foot in this world and one in the next, he straddled between life and death.

Guy suggested they leave and come back in the morning. He, Claire, and Mr. Penwright walked to the head of the bed to say goodbye. Joseph didn't seem to focus on any of them, but he smiled dimly and called Claire's name, softly. His heavy eyelids started to close, involuntarily, as he muttered garbled words to her.

She leaned in closer to him, attempting to make sense of his utterances.

"Proper burial.... Give David...a proper...burial."

Claire kissed him gently on the forehead. "Shalom, dear Joseph," she said, softly, almost in a whisper. "And rest peacefully. Thank you for sharing your incredible life story with us." Turning back to look at him one last time before exiting the room, she spoke clearly. "We will be your witnesses." She thought she saw his mouth turn slightly upward at the corners.

Out in the hallway, Ms. Simpson was crying ever so quietly.

"Goodbye, Ms. Simpson," Claire said, looking at the administrator with compassion in her eyes. "Please give us a call if anything changes."

Ms. Simpson returned to Joseph's room—to cover him, and whisper "*I love you*," into his ear, like she had so many nights before.

Mr. Penwright drove Claire and Guy back to the inn and requested they call him in the morning if Joseph could be seen, and bid them good afternoon.

"All this seems like a lot of running for you, Mr. Penwright. I'm afraid we're wearing you out," Claire said.

"Rubbish! I'm bloody well fine. I wouldn't miss it for the world. And I wouldn't mind if you started calling me Edmond."

"Okay," Guy said. "We'll call you in the morning, either way, and let you know. And Edmond, thanks for everything."

Mr. Penwright smiled a tenderhearted smile and waved goodbye.

Many questions still remained to ask Joseph. Who had David been working for? Did David have friends? A partner? Why did he wear a lepton around his neck?

After a light meal at the B&B that evening, Claire and Guy walked to their room and crawled into bed—each adoring the other with the romantic affection that only lovers can know. Afterwards, they slept the sleep of the exhausted.

At exactly three in the morning, Claire jolted awake. Her heart raced and a feeling of panic overtook her.

SHE AWOKE to the sound of the alarm at seven-thirty and nudged Guy to wake him up. "We need to call the hospice," she said. "Right now."

Guy looked at the seriousness in her eyes and picked up his cell phone on the bedside table. But before he could dial, it rang.

"We lost him last night, Mr. Lombard," Ms. Simpson said. "Joseph passed away. I wanted to tell you and Claire."

"I'm sorry, Ms. Simpson. We lost a remarkable human being. We know you thought the world of him…and we're sorry for your loss. If there's anything we can do…anything at all…please do not hesitate to ask us." Guy struggled for words, as emotional situations were always so awkward for him.

"I sat next to him all night as he slept, sir, holding his hand. Just before three in the morning he awoke for a brief time and glanced upward, a look of glory on his face. He whispered that two magnificent angels, dressed in white, beckoned to him. He said he was ready to go—now that he'd told his story and released his demons. Then he thanked me for my kindness and closed his eyes. His last words, I'll never forget. He called out: *Hashem*, *Shaddai*, *Elohim*, as he left this world behind." Her words broke up as undisguised emotion took control. “He died with a serene look on his face, Mr. Lombard.” She began to sob outwardly, unable to maintain composure. “His passing has left a hole in my heart,” she blurted out.

Guy said nothing, but waited on the other end of the line for what seemed like a very long time. Frantically floundering for words of comfort, he attempted to speak—but overtaken by the emotion of Joseph’s passing, his lips would not move. He’d grown so fond of this man over the last few days. Looking over at Claire for support, he saw tears streaming down her face. He grabbed her hand and squeezed it. At that moment, he realized she had known when she awakened that morning.

Ms. Simpson spoke again. Fighting to sound calm and collected, she talked softly but with purpose. Guy could feel the strength of her will—something he imagined she would have to possess in her line of work.

“His belongings…Joseph’s belongings…. He left behind a full box of personal items—mainly letters, some photographs, and other miscellaneous things. He thought they may be of help to you, and before he died he made me promise I’d get them to you and Claire. I’ll leave the box at the front desk, if you wish, with your names on it. It’s here to pick up at your convenience and take with you—or, sit down and look through the container here, if you’d prefer.”

“Yes. Please. We’d like to look through the contents of the box. And thank you, Ms. Simpson, for all your help. He acted bravely, to the very end.”

“The bravest! I’ve seen many come through this facility in my day, but no one like him.”

Goodbyes were exchanged and the call ended. Claire grabbed Guy’s hands and closed her eyes. A sense of tranquility enveloped her being. “Shalom means cooperation, synthesis, harmony, and wholeness. I wish you all of these as you continue on your journey, dear Joseph. Go in peace. Shalom.”

“Shalom, Joseph,” Guy said. He pulled Claire into his arms, and, standing still, they stayed that way for a long time, sensing Joseph’s soul soaring freely, no longer contained by his earthly suit. "I loved that man," Guy said.

"Me, too," Claire said.

"We'd better let Edmond know, Claire. And go over and look through that box with him." Guy picked up the phone and dialed his number. "Edmond? It's Guy. Bad news."

On a first name basis now, after what they'd experienced together, they had bonded, and a friendship had blossomed between the three of them—one that would continue for years to come.

"We lost him. He died in his sleep last night," Guy said.

At first Mr. Penwright did not respond. Guy, too, remained silent, realizing Mr. Penwright was pausing in remembrance and reverence. Long minutes passed without an exchange of words.

"Joseph was a fine chap. He lived a long life…but one of such sorrow," Mr. Penwright said, eventually. "He made a lasting impression on each of us, and on Ms. Simpson, too, I'd say."

"Yes, I agree. It's hard for us to imagine the tormenting agony he carried around for most of his life—a weighty bundle for sure. You never know by looking at a person what's inside, do you?" Guy asked. "But now, at long last, he can rest in peace. It makes you feel fortunate for the life you've had, doesn't it? I know it makes me think about it."

"I've been doing nothing else."

"Ms. Simpson told me Joseph left his box of belongings for us to look through. Are you up for it this morning?"

"Absolutely. I'll get dressed and pick you up in half an hour."

Claire phoned the hospice receptionist and learned the facility had planned a small and private memorial service—to commemorate the life of Joseph Stone—to take place the following morning at nine. He invited the two of them, along with Mr. Penwright, to attend.

She called downstairs to the desk employee and obtained the name and number of a good, local florist. Placing a call to the shop, she ordered—in Joseph's memory—a spray of long-stemmed yellow roses for the memorial service, and for Ms. Simpson, an arrangement of pink and white roses. She requested a sympathy card to be attached to the flowers sent to Ms. Simpson, reading: "Dear Ms. Simpson, We know how much Joseph meant to you, and how deeply you cared for him. We share in your sorrow. Fondly, Claire, Guy, and Edmond." And she requested a blank card on the memorial spray, saying, "Dearest Joseph, Your life had great meaning. You taught us much in a short time. We will never forget you. Peace be with you. Your friends, Claire, Guy, and Edmond."

They drove to the hospice in quiet respect, mourning the loss of a great man.

THE 24 x 20 x 16-INCH covered, corrugated box sat at the front desk with their names on it, and the young attendant offered to carry it wherever they liked. "Are you taking this with you?" he asked.

"Actually, we'd like to look through it now if you have a room we could use," Mr. Penwright said.

"Certainly, follow me." He led them to a conference room across the way, and set the heavy container down on the table. "Take as much time as you need," he said. "And if you require photocopying, or anything else, please do not hesitate to ask. Shall I bring you hot tea?"

"We'd appreciate that. Thank you very much," Claire said.

In no time flat, the young man returned with a tray of hard biscuits and a large pot of tea. Claire and the men thanked him, and after he exited the room, Claire closed the door behind him so they could work in seclusion. Guy and Mr. Penwright sat very still as Claire lifted the lid from the cardboard container and peered inside.

28

PACKED TO THE brim, Joseph's box contained the many letters David had sent him from the U.S. And by the looks of it, Joseph had saved every one. Tied together with lengths of string, each of the thick bunches held twelve to fifteen of them, and Claire counted a dozen of those large bundles laying neatly cradled in the corrugated container. By quick calculation, that meant between a hundred and forty-four and a hundred and eighty letters took up the majority of the space inside the carton. Pulling one letter free from its binder and envelope, Claire counted seven hand-written sheets, filled on both sides with the most minuscule and meticulous script she'd ever seen. The perfectly precise penmanship astonished her. She passed it on, so Guy and Mr. Penwright could view the tidy and astonishing writing firsthand.

It would take great effort to read through them all—but they would do so, with the hopes of gleaning some clue as to the identity of the person who robbed David of his life. Operating under the assumption the victim was David Post (Posnick), all efforts would now turn to identifying his murderer. Motivation to solve the case had changed since assignments had first been made. Claire no longer saw it as a stepping stone to a new career, and Guy gave no further thought to maintaining his flawless record. For now, it had become personal to both of them. They would solve this murder for David…and for Joseph, and bring the perpetrator to justice.

Claire lifted all the packs from the box, and stacked them on the table in front of her. After removing the last of the collection, she noticed many black-and-white photographs protruding from a large envelope on the bottom of the carton. She lifted them out and together they took turns looking through them. Each of the pictures captured the same two boys—in various settings and at different stages of their youth—always with an arm around the other's shoulders, and mostly with gleeful expressions of exuberance or laughter on their faces. On the backside of several of the images appeared these handwritten words: "Joseph and David." One of the boys had light blonde hair (*the only fair-haired member of our family*) and the other dark, allowing them to easily spot David in each of the photos.

Providing them with their first glimpses ever of David Posnick, alias David Post—*the skeleton*—as a living and breathing human being, they realized what a handsome lad he'd been. And Joseph, too, so robust, eyes filled with joy and excitement at just being alive. At that stage in their lives, they could never have imagined what laid in store for them.

Other photographs—color shots—obviously had been taken in London, based upon the recognizable landmarks in the backgrounds: The Tower of London, Big Ben, Trafalgar Square, Scotland Yard, The Houses of Parliament, Buckingham Palace and The Changing of the Guard. These provided a different perspective altogether on the two brothers. When they turned the photos over, they observed that these pictures were dated between 1946 and 1965.

The trio spent time poring over the pictures of the Posnick brothers, anxious to study every last one. Somehow, David or Joseph had managed to save these photographs and they had ultimately ended up in Joseph's possession. How the years had safeguarded them—especially the youthful ones—they would never know, but without the precious photos David would have remained forever faceless. Even

Mr. Penwright had not seen a photograph of the missing Mr. Post at the time of his disappearance—back in 1966. Instead, only a description had been provided him by the lord.

Looking back and forth, intently, between the younger and older photographs, Claire could not help but notice the dramatic and touching changes in facial expressions of these two human beings. All zeal for life had, understandably, drained away as the years had progressed.

Next Claire lifted a small, hinged, claret box—covered with a now threadbare sateen fabric—from the container's bottom. She opened it slowly and with anticipation, almost afraid to look inside. What she removed caught the three by surprise. It was a lepton dangling from a heavy gold chain. And it looked like an identical match to the one found around the skeleton's neck—although this one appeared to be in much better condition. In fact, this lepton looked virtually new. She turned it over in her hands. There they were. The three initials—"*jjp*" for Joseph Jacob Posnick.

If any doubts remained that the skeleton belonged to David Post, they vanished quickly at that moment for Claire. The exact similarity of the chains and lepta—right down to the precise engraving style on each coin—left absolutely no hesitation whatsoever in her mind.

Then her eyes were drawn to a folded piece of paper tucked inside the modest box. Pulling it from its resting place, she carefully unfolded it. The tattered note, written in what appeared to be Hebrew, had in all probability been crammed inside the small space for many long decades. Upon further examination, it looked as if it had been opened and closed more times than she could envision, as the now-limp paper had yellowed with age and torn on some of the fold lines.

Guy carefully took it from her. "Stay put. I'll be right back," he said. He approached the lobby desk and the young gentleman manning it. "Excuse me. I'll need to photocopy this and fax it to someone. Can you assist me?"

"Certainly, sir. This way." He led Guy to a space behind the desk and showed him how to operate both machines. "If you require additional assistance, please let me know."

After thanking him, Guy went to work. First, he made a photocopy of the fragile writing, and next he faxed it to his son, Roman, with a message: "Son, we're in London and need your help. Please find someone to translate this and let me know what it says ASAP. It's important. Thanks, Dad." He added a P.S. instructing him to reply to the fax number indicated on the cover sheet—at the hospice—if he could reply within the hour. Otherwise, he should fax it to their home number. With luck on his side, Roman would be home to receive the transmission.

Guy informed the receptionist he might be receiving a fax within the hour, returned to the conference room with the original note, photocopy, and fax confirmation, and filled Claire and Mr. Penwright in on his activity. "Let's think positive," he said. "Maybe Roman will have this for us soon."

Sitting in the room, the threesome again studied the photos, the lepton, and the chain, and looked with anxiety at the morass of letters.

Fifteen minutes later, the receptionist interrupted them, rapping lightly on the door. "This just came in for you, Mr. Lombard."

Guy thanked him and accepted the sheet of paper. Roman had come through for them in record time. Guy read his response aloud.

> Dad:
>
> I'm assuming the case you guys are working on led you to London. Intriguing. Can't wait to hear all about it. Hope I got back to you fast enough! I'm at home with an Israeli friend of mine from class. Lucky for you, we're here reviewing materials for an exam tomorrow. Noah speaks fluent Hebrew and was able to give you the English equivalent of the faxed note. More about that strange coin again, huh? Hope it helps! Roman.
>
> P.S. Let me know when you'll be returning to Miami.
>
> P.P.S. The translation of the note follows:

==

> 14 February 1940
>
> Our Dearest Joseph,

> We are giving you this lepton coin we picked up when we traveled to Palestine in 1935. We are also giving one to your brother, David, as we are infinitely proud of the two of you, and so grateful to call you our sons. The Englishman who sold them to us engraved your initials on the back. We've put it on a chain. Keep it all your life in remembrance of us and our heritage. Wear it with pride. It came from the land of your ancestors. Always carry in your heart the knowledge that our love for you is eternal.
>
> Your loving parents,
>
> Saul and Sarah

Now they had written documentation that David Oved Posnick, alias David Crawford Post, had received a lepton coin on a neck chain from his parents—a coin and chain purchased long ago in the land now called Israel—an exact copy of the one Claire had held in her hands moments ago belonging to his brother, Joseph. And the note even confirmed their respective initials were etched onto the coins, differentiating the two pieces one from another.

They would also never know how these lepta and chains had survived the war and all these many years. It seemed to be yet another puzzle piece that would remain unanswered for all time. Although Guy had planned to ask Joseph about the lepton coin on the very day he died, sadly he was never given the chance. As both Guy and Claire knew from the outset, certain aspects of this case would never be established. But regardless of *how* the lepta had inexplicably survived—David wearing his around his neck, and Joseph keeping his safely tucked inside the claret box—they did survive. And the older and more recent photographs—they'd survived, too. And together, the coins, neck chains and pictures forever linked Joseph and David Posnick…as brothers.

Guy excused himself to send Roman a second fax—to thank him for the quick translation turnaround, and to inform him they'd be flying home to Florida the following day, after attending a memorial service. He also took the time to book return flights to the U.S. while he thought about it. Returning to the room, he updated Claire on the travel plans. "We'll leave for the airport just after the service tomorrow," he said.

"Let's attend the service together, Edmond, if you'd like," Claire said.

"Wild horses couldn't keep me away. I'll plan on picking the two of you up around 8:15 in the morning. Have your bag packed, and we'll load it into my car. That way, I can drop you straightaway at the airport after the service."

"That's a lot of trouble for you, Edmond. It's easy to grab a taxi," Guy said.

"Rubbish! I won't hear of it. I insist."

"That's very kind of you, Edmond," Claire said. "And it would make our lives that much easier. Thank you."

"Let's get that box packed up, Claire, and take it with us," Guy said. "We'll tape it up and check it as baggage tomorrow.

"There's one more thing in here," she said.

"What is it?" Mr. Penwright and Guy asked, simultaneously.

"Not sure. It's another envelope, but this one's much smaller."

"Open it," Mr. Penwright and Guy said, again speaking with one voice.

She pulled the letter-sized envelope from the bottom of the container and held it in her hands. This was something of grave importance. She could feel it in her bones.

"Open it," Guy repeated. "Let's see what's in there."

"There's only one way to find out," Mr. Penwright said.

Instinctively, she pulled a pair of evidence-handling gloves from her briefcase and slipped them on. Wanting to avoid any potential for mishap, she tugged gently at the seal and lifted the contents from its wrapper.

Anticipation built as Guy and Claire looked on with determined interest.

"It's two smaller yet sealed wrappings," she said. "One has the name '*David*' printed on it, and the other, '*Joseph*.'"

"What's inside them, Claire?" Mr. Penwright asked, wearing his excitement on his sleeve.

"We'll know in a minute," she said. Anxious to protect its contents from any harm, she slowly opened the packet marked "*David*," and looked inside. Her eyes moistened, and she felt a large lump in her throat.

29

"GARY? CLAIRE CASWELL calling." Since it was afternoon for her in London, it was morning for LuVasse in Miami, and she had fortunately caught him at his desk.

"Hey, how are you two coming with the case? I've been concerned. Haven't heard from you since I cleared your ticket to London at the beginning of the week, and now it's Friday. I started to think you and Guy had relocated to England and neglected to tell me. That must have been one helluva lead you followed."

"Well, it was. I apologize for not calling sooner, but we've had an intense few days over here, and with the time change and all, it's been difficult to find an opportunity to reach you."

"I understand. Actually I was kidding. It was my sorry attempt to interject some humor into a serious situation. What do you have?"

"Good news, or should I say, phenomenal news. We have identification on the skeleton, or at least we're ninety-nine percent sure. We're flying home tomorrow with a box of evidence and a hair and blood sample. We'll need McKay to run two final tests, and then, we'll be one-hundred-percent convinced."

"Sounds pretty solid to me right now, Claire. I don't know what to say. I'm astounded you two put a name on the victim."

"There's a story connected to the skeleton that you won't believe, but hold off on the praise for a short while."

"Give me the name of the victim, will you?"

"David Crawford Post. But that's an alias. Birth name was David Oved Posnick."

"Spell those for me."

Claire spelled out the names in full.

"I'm anxious to hear all about it. Be in my office at 8:00 Monday morning to fill me in, will you?"

"I'll be there."

"Can I release this name to the press?"

"Wait until McKay completes his final testing. It will be soon. I want to be absolutely sure."

"You got it. Now, I have startling news for you on the Lawden matter."

"You read my mind, Gary. What happened?"

"Tuesday of this week, at the break of dawn, Lawden and his consultant were seen pouring gasoline into the hole. The contractors had lifted the tank out the afternoon before, and planned to return to do the soil testing within the cavity at 8:00 a.m. Tuesday morning. I had one of our student interns go out there before daybreak, and stay out of sight, to watch, in case they did something illegal, and, wouldn't you know it, he caught them red-handed. They drove up in a red Lincoln Navigator. Our intern then observed Lawden walk directly to the shed, enter it, and exit holding the container of gasoline in his hand. Next the two of them—Lawden and McDonald—took turns dumping the gasoline into various spots within the basin. Our intern snapped pictures of everything with his digital camera, so the entire incident is fully documented."

"Unbelievable! It's what I always suspected they were doing. Catching them *red-handed*, now that's the tricky part."

"Always is."

"Let me guess," Claire said. "The soil testing done in the basin indicated extremely high levels of contamination as a result of the poured gasoline, and that, in turn, would have justified extensive remediation efforts, thereby allowing Lawden and McDonald to pad all invoices and apply for off-the-charts reimbursement monies. Doesn't take a rocket scientist to figure out that scam, does it? What it takes is sharp investigative work to catch the thieves in the act. When did the fraudulent requests for state reimbursement come in, that same day?"

LuVasse chuckled. "No, they waited until the *next* day. They filed it with our office on Wednesday. I'm sure they had the paperwork completed and ready to go. Just needed the manipulated test results to plug into the forms. They wasted no time."

"As far as we're concerned, they committed the fraud not when they poured gasoline into the hole on Lawden's property, but when they made application to the State to obtain reimbursement monies based upon their evil deeds," Claire said. "Lawden and McDonald just bought themselves a ticket to criminal prosecution."

"Precisely, although the act of intentionally pouring a petroleum product into the ground presents other big problems for them, too. I informed the Environmental Protection Agency of the incident and sent over copies of the intern's photos. Lawden and McDonald will have to deal with that agency, as well. So I would say it's a fair statement to make that those two will rue the day they chose to commit the crime."

"I hope the police arrested them on Wednesday, Gary."

"They did. I called Sergeant Massey and he got right on it. It made the news. Lawden and McDonald are sitting in jail, as we speak. But you know they'll be out on bail soon—awaiting trial."

"How did you know when they'd do it?"

"I figured that morning would be our best bet, and *early* in the morning—before the contractors arrived to do the soil sample testing. And my calculations proved to be correct."

"You deserve a feather in your cap, Gary. This will go a long way to send a strong message to the clean-up industry that fraud will not be tolerated—and that we're watching. I only regret not being there to see them hauled away."

"Claire, without your investigation and suspicions this would never have happened. You acted as the catalyst to nail them. Now get home safely and I'll see you on Monday. Again, I'm beyond impressed that the two of you determined the identity of the skeletal remains. Beyond impressed!"

"Thank you, Gary. See you on Monday."

Guy also called his office to report the nearly conclusive findings. Next he dialed Sergeant Massey to fill him in on the development, providing the unconfirmed name and alias of the victim. "Hold off, Sergeant, on letting the news people in on this," Guy said, "until we get home and obtain the final test results from McKay, will you?"

"Of course. No problem. Not bad work, I must admit. Kudos to you and Ms. Caswell." Sergeant Massey hung up and immediately punched in the number of the anonymous tip-line of a local television channel. Disguising his voice, he reported that the Miami-Dade Police Department was now aware of the identity of the skeletal remains found in Miami Shores. Reporters would flock to interview him once the word got out, and he'd provide the scoop and get all the publicity. It would be a good thing for his department, he told himself. Two tips in one week, both surrounding the skeletal find: first, the arrests of Lawden and McDonald on fraud charges, and now *this*—an identity on that morass of bones found at Lawden's dig site. Yes, it had been an opportune week—a red-letter week, indeed. The Sergeant lived by the motto, "The early bird gets the worm," and if someone was to receive the notoriety for a story, why not him? A self-satisfied, smug smile settled on his face, and he cracked his knuckles.

Saturday morning

GUY AND Claire packed their suitcase, and, with packing tape obtained from the inn's front desk, secured the box of evidence for travel. Then Guy took care of the lodging bill and met Claire in the dining room to eat their last fry-up breakfast. Sipping hot tea and enjoying the tasty morsels, conversation turned to the revelations of the day before—to the unexpected contents of Joseph's box.

"I would never have imagined we'd find a definitive piece of evidence to identify the skeleton when we first started this case," Claire said. "No one could have convinced me of that."

"Me either."

"I wonder if Joseph even remembered what the box contained?"

"We'll never know for sure, Claire. After being tucked away for so long, maybe not."

"What a shock when I opened the packet with David's name on it."

"Yeah. Who could have guessed it would hold a lock of his baby hair—a small curl of his *fair* hair?"

"It's much too much to fathom. It should make our case for identification indisputable, keeping in mind that we also have the blood sample from Joseph."

"Right. The hair should be the only real piece of evidence we need, though," Guy said.

"Yet we have so much more," Claire said. "The partial dental match, the lepton with two of David's initials on it, the note from the Posnick parents, Joseph's testimony confirming David Post lived in the Miami area, David's letters, the timing of his disappearance to the estimated length of time the skeleton has been in the ground, the shorter left leg on David and the skeleton, and on and on. We have *more than enough* evidence to prove a rock solid identification through and through. It's strange how, early on, we had *no* evidence, and thought we might not find any, and now we have much more than we need. Funny how things work, sometimes."

"I'll rest easier, though, when McKay tells us, with certainty, that the hair DNA matches the skeleton's DNA, and makes a positive match on the blood sample, too, if that's possible. In the meantime, Claire, let's hope those letters will give us some clues as to who murdered David."

"The employer sounds like a good place to start, based upon Joseph's testimony, if we can figure out who he is. Remember, David disappeared shortly after overhearing that phone conversation his boss had with another dealer. That's huge. Let's pray those letters provide a tip on the identity of David's employer at that time, and maybe even a clue as to who was on the other end of that phone call. We need to track those two down for questioning."

"Based upon what Joseph told us—about how careful David was never to give away any aspect of his life or exact whereabouts—I'd say that's wishful thinking on your part, my beautiful sleuth."

"We'll see. It's all we have to work with, Guy. When we get home, let's arrange the letters in chronological order—oldest to most recent—and then split up the reading."

"*All* of them? Sounds like the grunt work I detest."

"Come on. You know it's the meat of all investigations—the detail work. We'll have to read every last one of them. That's where the clues may be hiding out."

"If there are any," Guys said.

Hot teas refilled, they went to a long table to select mouth-watering desserts to sample.

Guy decided to change the subject. "I'm happy they arrested Lawden and that consultant of his, McDonald, Claire. Now, maybe the threats will stop."

"Maybe, maybe not. Only *if* they're the ones behind them, and the arrests scare them off."

"Point well taken."

"I imagine the two of them are out of jail as we speak—on bail. So no, I don't think I'd want to place a wager on the threats ending. Not yet, anyway. We'll see. Wish I knew who is behind them," she said. "We can't assume the same person is responsible for all the threats, either. It's safer to take nothing as a given."

"You're right, of course. But if I find out who made them, and who almost ran you off the road, I'll have that bastard arrested faster than a speeding bullet," Guy said, "on charges of making terroristic threats, and on attempted murder."

"I'll tell you this, honey. Lawden's leer, on the day I interviewed him after the discovery of the skeleton on his property, has haunted me. He had the smirk of a cobra."

MR. PENWRIGHT picked them up on schedule, and together they traveled to the hospice center to attend the memorial service for Joseph. A small number of people had gathered, mainly staffers from the hospice, and a respectful ceremony took place. The simple sermon stressed the point that *life is fleeting*. Afterwards, they stayed for tea and cake, and talked to Ms. Simpson.

"Thank you all for coming today," Ms. Simpson said. "I know it would mean the world to Joseph."

"We feel privileged to be here, Ms. Simpson," Mr. Penwright said. "And to have known him."

"Claire and I would like to thank you, Ms. Simpson, for all your help over these past few days," Guy said. "We're set to fly home this afternoon. And we'll be taking the box of Joseph's personal belongings back with us, hopefully to find the murderer of his brother, David, and to prosecute the culprit to the fullest extent of the law."

"Joseph would be indebted," she said. Then, so unexpectedly, she turned to face Mr. Penwright head on. "If you're ever in the neighborhood, sir, it would be lovely if you'd stop by to have a spot of tea with me." Seemingly uneasy with her spontaneous proposal, her gaze dropped to the floor.

"I would consider it an honor, Hilda," Mr. Penwright said. "Or, could I be so bold as to ask you out for dinner this very evening? Say, seven o'clock?" When she hesitated to answer, he immediately regretted asking the question. He was sure she thought him too forward.

But a moment later, Ms. Simpson smiled a demure smile, and nodded in agreement. "That would be brilliant, *Edmond*. I look forward to it."

Claire had not seen this coming. Nor had Guy. About the same age, Mr. Penwright and Ms. Simpson each lived a private, almost solitary existence—seemingly quite alone in the world. Ms. Simpson worked and lived at the hospice, and had no social life to speak of. Mr. Penwright, always a single man, got out very little himself. Now, maybe things would change for the two of them. What an unpredictably nice thing might be coming out of all of this, Claire thought. *The wheels of life keep turning!*

Goodbyes were exchanged with Ms. Simpson, and Mr. Penwright drove Claire and Guy to the airport. Upon their arrival, the three comrades expressed heartfelt farewells. Mr. Penwright had helped to make this part of the investigation so much more than tolerable and they genuinely appreciated his efforts.

"Keep me informed on the murder investigation," Mr. Penwright said. "Find the son-of-a-bitch who did this and lock him up. I don't care how old he is."

"That's the goal," Guy said. "We'll keep you posted. You have our numbers, as well, so don't be a stranger."

The men embraced quickly, but robustly.

Then Mr. Penwright embraced Claire. "I'll miss seeing the two of you. Things will not be the same around here." A mist of tears clouded his vision.

Claire was startled by the intense feelings he evinced. She had always thought the Brits very conscious of never showing too much emotion publicly. But today, Mr. Penwright proved that supposition false.

"Keep us posted on your life, Edmond," Claire said. "Remember, it's because of *us* that you met Hilda." She winked at him. "And thank you for all your help. Really. We couldn't have done it without you. We'll stay in touch."

She noted a look in Mr. Penwright's eyes she had not seen before.

Life seemed full of possibilities.

30

ONCE THE GIANT 747 lifted airborne, Claire let her mind wander. Maybe somewhere in David's voluminous writings a clue would surface to lead them to the killer. So much had happened since they had returned to Miami from Grand Cayman. Life had kicked into high gear and stuck. Three weeks had passed like one. She yearned to bring closure to the case for the sake of justice. Never in her wildest dreams could she have imagined where the trail would take them in this riveting investigation. She'd been selected to identify a dead man—a skeleton—and to find his murderer. Through Joseph's words, she'd received an unexpected glimpse into the life of the victim, into the kind of person he was, and into the family that raised him. And she'd seen photographs of the fatally injured man—as a child, and as an adult. She'd even held a glossy baby curl from his head of blonde hair in her hands.

An every-inch-extraordinary case of a lifetime had caught Claire and Guy in its web.

Guy reached over, grabbed her hand, and pulled it to his lap. He liked to fly that way—his hand holding hers. She turned her head toward him and devoted some time and attention to studying his face. He seemed so at ease. She smiled a contented smile. How she loved this man. Eyes closed, he would soon be asleep. Shutting her own, she leaned her head over and rested it on his shoulder. Before long, she, too, would be in the land of Nod.

Miami, Florida

THEY LEFT London on a Saturday afternoon flight, and arrived in Miami Saturday around dinnertime. It seemed odd—like they hadn't lost much time at all. Yet, due to jet lag, they required much sleep, and that's just what they did—they slept for hours. And when they couldn't sleep they did necessary chores around the condo. At one point Guy went out to grocery shop, while Claire stayed home to arrange David's letters in the sequence they had discussed. Later, they formulated a plan to share significant findings with each other, along the way, as they contemplated the voluminous writings. Monday they would hit it hard.

The remainder of the weekend proved uneventful until the doorman called late Sunday afternoon to announce the arrival of a visitor. Minutes later, there stood the handsome Roman at their door, suitcase in hand. "Surprise!" he said.

Stepping inside, Guy and Claire took turns hugging him. Then Guy stood back and looked his son over from head to toe. "You get better looking every time I see you, son. I mean it," he said. "Must be in your genes."

"In these old Levi's?" Roman looked dead serious before breaking into a broad, fixed grin that took over the lower half of his face. "Just playing with you. You have no idea how happy I am to be here. Especially after hours and hours in the air. Man, that's a long flight."

He walked in and glanced around. The three-bedroom condo in north Miami Beach looked just as he remembered. The impressive eighteenth-floor high-rise apartment offered magnificent panoramic balconies that allowed anyone standing on them to look down and view, firsthand, the glorious intra-coastal waterway. Roman walked over to the floor-to-ceiling windows and peered out—onto the procession of high-priced yachts, and other large and small boats, slowly making their way up or down the channel. This activity alone could provide endless hours of entertainment, he thought silently. Then he chuckled, more to himself than aloud. The full-bore sun heated up the recreation, and he could see passengers on several powered cruising yachts, each sipping from what appeared to be a flute of champagne—thoroughly enjoying the delightful day. "Ah, the life," he said, and turned back to Guy and Claire. "Place looks great."

"Make yourself comfortable, Rome," Claire said. She hugged him, again, and planted a kiss on both his cheeks. "I'm glad you're here. Did you sleep at all during the flight?"

"Are you kidding?" he said. "Not a wink. Each and every time I almost nodded off, a flight attendant brought another round of food, or beverages, or headphones, or made announcements. Sleep was not on the agenda. And the food.... I tried all of it, but none of it appealed to me, so I'm still hungry. *Very* hungry. But to tell you the truth, right now I'm even more tired than hungry, if possible."

"Then, please, get some sleep before we go out to dinner. The back, right room is waiting for you," Claire said.

"Into mind-reading again, are we?" A grin, similar to that of his father, spread across his face and deep dimples appeared from nowhere. "Just what I had in mind. But don't let me sleep too long or I won't be able to sleep tonight. An hour or so should do it. And don't forget to wake me for dinner. I'll be starved by then. Oh, and by the way, it's good to see you both." He disappeared into the bedroom reserved for his exhausted body.

Walking over to the bed, he turned and fell onto it with a thud, landing on top of the coverlet, too exhausted to crawl in between the freshly-laundered Egyptian cotton sheets in place for his arrival. Nor did he notice the crab-apple green vase, sitting proudly on the dresser, displaying a bouquet of extraordinarily fragrant stargazer lilies. For now, the need to rest took precedence over everything else, and life details, no matter how interesting, could not keep him from it. Before long, he entered the lively world of colorful dreaming.

Using the attached strap, Guy pulled Roman's suitcase to the bedroom, and quietly stepped in to place it near the end of the bed. He threw a lightweight comforter over Roman and paused briefly to gaze upon his son—who had already nodded off and was sleeping as soundly as a baby. Pictures of Roman, from babyhood to present, passed before him in his mind's eye, like a slide show set on fast. Where had the years gone? His eyes grew moist and he forced back tears. Life was moving along too quickly, and he didn't like that. Just yesterday, it seemed, Roman had been a youngster, needing his father to help him with everything, and Guy had felt so important in his life. Now, Roman had matured—becoming strong, self-sufficient, and so capable, no longer needing his dad in the same way he once had. Independence and strength of character were the very traits Guy had wished for his son to develop; yet, the reality of life's cycle yanked at Guy's heartstrings. Gently pulling the door shut behind him as he left the room, he felt an overwhelming sense of love for his *little boy*. He didn't remember growing older. When had Roman?

Flashing to Joseph and his life story, Guy felt keenly aware of the passage of time—*the wheels of life*—like never before. In the blink of an eye, Roman had grown up, and Guy had aged, too. Joseph had taught him to appreciate those he loved even more, as things could change so quickly and without warning. Lyrics from *Fiddler on the Roof* came out of nowhere and pounded loudly in Guy's head, as tears rolled down his face:

Sunrise, sunset
Sunrise, sunset
Swiftly flow the days
Seedlings turn overnight to sunflowers
Blossoming even as we gaze.

Sunrise, sunset
Sunrise, sunset
Swiftly fly the years
One season following another
Laden with happiness and tears.

Monday morning

THE ALARM sounded, signaling six in the morning, and Claire got up, showered, and prepared a special breakfast for Roman. She brewed a pot of hazelnut coffee, poured freshly-squeezed Florida orange juice into crystal glasses, scrambled eggs, toasted oatmeal bread, and placed a bowl of perfectly ripened sliced cantaloupe and strawberries on the table. She woke the men, and together they enjoyed the sumptuous fare.

"Wish you visited us more often, son. I *never* rate a breakfast like this!"

"He's right," Claire said. "Usually it's juice and dry rye toast."

While the conversation started out light, it quickly became more serious after they finished eating, when Claire began to fill Roman in on the details of their island vacation—including the amazing underground tunnel system they'd stumbled upon, and the discovery of the ancient relic hidden in a connecting cave. Roman listened in wonderment as she spoke.

"We've kept this entire incident very quiet, Rome, because we wanted to know more about the piece—both its history and value—before we discussed it with others. In fact, the only person we've showed it to so far is a longtime family friend of mine, an antiquities dealer in Miami—Robert Holden—a top expert in the field of rare artifacts. He's been in the business for close to fifty years and is someone we can trust. We asked him to do some research on it, confidentially, of course, and to give us his opinion. And while your dad and I believed with all certainty we'd discovered something of incredible magnitude, Robert Holden took it away for a short time, examined it thoroughly, and surprisingly concluded that what we'd found represented nothing more than a well-produced *replica* of a common artifact of Aztec worship, having little or no real value.

"You can imagine our disappointment at hearing that news. And I have struggled with why anyone would have gone to the trouble of concealing something of only nominal value in such a remote hiding place, where the chances seemed great no one would ever find it. It makes no sense to me."

"Maybe the person hiding it *thought* it was the real thing, too," Roman suggested. "But I have to admit, it does sound kind of odd. Where is this thing? Can I take a look at it?"

"We've been waiting to show it to you, son," Guy said. He walked to the den to retrieve it, and returned to the kitchen in no time, holding the statue—still wrapped in the flannel pillowcase—in his hands. Using extreme caution, he removed it from the soft, cloth covering and handed it to Roman, but only after first giving his son a stern warning about the bottom's razor edge. "I already gashed my thumb open on it, Roman, so be very careful when you handle it."

Roman gasped when he saw it. Holding on tightly, he rotated the mystifying piece in all directions as he examined it from every angle. "This is amazing! Simply magnificent! Who did you say appraised this for you?"

31

"WELCOME BACK, CLAIRE," LuVasse said.

"It's good being back. Believe me."

"Before we begin, I must tell you this. Someone leaked the name David Crawford Post to the press. It's all over the news."

"*What*?" She sighed in anger and disgust. "We told three people: You, the head of Guy's office, and Sergeant Massey. And I *know* you wouldn't have disclosed it. Maybe Massey's behind the leaks."

"Hard to say. It's big news and somebody talked. Even if Massey did divulge the information, despite being specifically asked not to, he'd be protected. Nothing would happen to him if we could finger him. You know that."

Claire shook her head in exasperation. "And if the information ends up being inaccurate by some strange twist, we will be blamed for it and left to pick up the pieces."

"Afraid you're right."

"It's frustrating when you have no control over a situation," she said. "By the way, Guy's over at McKay's office now, dropping off the evidence we brought home with us. We'll know, unconditionally, on the identification in a very short time."

"Good. Claire, tell me everything that happened. I want to hear it all."

GUY STOOD in front of McKay's office building tapping his foot, waiting impatiently for the Medical Examiner to arrive. When he did, Guy walked in behind him, shadowing each of his steps, and thrust the envelopes containing David's lock of hair and Joseph's blood sample toward McKay, hurriedly explaining that he needed each piece of evidence tested and compared to the skeleton.

"Slow down, counselor. *Slow down*. I just walked in. Mind if I set my briefcase and folders down on my desk first?" The tone in his voice was fraught with irritation.

"Sorry, McKay. Take your time." Guy took a breath and exhaled loudly, struggling for patience, looking at his wristwatch.

"Now, tell me again. These are *what*?"

"A twist of baby hair from David Oved Posnick, alias David Crawford Post—the name we are quite certain belongs to the skeleton. After you've completed DNA comparison testing, between the hair sample and the bones, we'll know for sure. And I'm also giving you a sample of blood from Post's brother. What can you do with that?"

"How did you get these?"

"Long story, McKay. I'll fill you in later. Can I count on you to do a rush job for me?"

"Calm down, counselor. I'll get at it first thing this morning, I promise. And I'll call you when the tests are completed."

"I'll be waiting, McKay."

"I'll call you."

"You'll hurry, right?

"I said I'll call you. Now get out of here." He ushered Guy to the front door.

"What about that blood sample?"

McKay did not answer him, but remained standing in the doorway as Guy left the premises. Walking away, Guy pointed to his Rolex watch as he glanced back at McKay. The medical examiner grimaced in annoyance. His magic wand was out of order today, so he'd be forced to run the tests the old-fashioned way—performing them one step at a time like other officials who investigate suspicious deaths—and he'd receive accurate and correct results that way. Some things could not be rushed, and the illustrious Gaston Lombard would just have to wait his turn, like anyone else. Since part of the work had already been completed, as the DNA from the bones had previously been tested and sat ready for comparison purposes, he could finish the work sooner than what would be typical, but there would be a certain amount of wait time nevertheless.

McKay walked back to his lab. Siblings of the same mother would share the same sequence of mitochondrial DNA. The blood sample obtained from David Post's brother would allow him to complete mitochondrial DNA sequencing, and then compare it to the sequencing already completed on the DNA extracted from the skeleton's bones. If the two had the same mother, he'd be able to conclude that fact with certainty. He slipped on gloves and looked over the lock of David Post's hair. It would have been better for testing purposes if it had been pulled out with the roots, but the possibility still existed to extract DNA from the curl. He went to work.

AFTER TALKING on the phone and agreeing to meet home at noon to commence the letter reading, Claire and Guy proceeded to weed through correspondence and phone messages that had piled up on their respective desks, checking for any situations that demanded immediate attention. In the meantime, chomping at the bit to hear back from McKay, they'd proceed as if it was a go.

Much to Claire's chagrin, another threatening letter appeared in her stack of mail. The envelope looked similar to the first—marked "confidential," no return address, her last name misspelled, incorrect title, and, again, some kind of discoloration evident on its backside.

But one difference became readily apparent. The message—*"Last chance bitch! Back off!"*—again computer generated, was underlined in wild scribbling with the use of a vivid red crayon. The red markings obviously symbolized blood. She got it.

The writer had gone a step further, and, for the first time, she felt a chill run up and down her spine. This person's persistence annoyed her greatly. And the red crayon bothered her in an unnerving kind of way. Could her time be running out? Were Lawden and McDonald behind it? Did the author of the threat merely plan to scare her off? Was the strategy to kill or maim her before she and Guy could figure out who committed the murder of David Post? Were the threats connected to either or both of these investigations? She wondered. The near car accident could have ended up much worse, she didn't deny that. Maybe they were closer to the perpetrator than they realized? That was a frightening thought. Something told her the noose was tightening, but around whose neck? Hers, or the murderer's? They needed to solve this crime and fast.

Claire picked up the phone, dialed Sergeant Massey, and filled him in on the latest threat. He agreed to send an officer over to retrieve the letter at once. Again he agreed to have it dusted for prints, but they both knew it would be a waste of time. The Sergeant congratulated her on putting an identity on the skeletal find. Since it had already hit the news, she merely said, "Thank you."

Next she called Guy and alerted him to the new threat. The sound of his voice instantly comforted her, but he was not happy. Thoughts that he would force her off the case for her own protection bombarded her, but he did not take that path. Rather, he talked about watching out for her more closely than ever—until the investigation was completed. She breathed a sigh of relief.

THE ARTIFACT baffled Roman. It looked and felt, weight-wise, like it might be comprised of solid gold. And he was certain that it qualified as a warrior idol from the Aztec civilization. He disagreed, wholeheartedly, with the assessment Claire's friend, Robert Holden, made. It would be extremely rare to find a relic of this age in *any* condition, let alone *mint* condition, and he believed without reservation the statue was, indeed, a priceless piece of antiquity. While not an expert on *Aztec* history, he did have a working knowledge of the area, and believed something definitely was not copasetic. The relic was not a reproduction, but the real thing. He was sure of it. On this he would bet a year's salary, if he had one to bet. But why on earth would Claire's friend have told them otherwise? He decided to conduct his own research.

Resting the relic face down atop the pillowcase on the couch, he vowed to learn as much as possible about the mysterious discovery during his visit. He walked to the den, settled into the desk chair, and opened the laptop. Logging in, he went to work. In total concentration, and with no distractions, the morning hours slipped away.

Guy arrived home around noon, and Claire followed close behind. Famished, Guy smiled to see Claire carrying two pizza boxes in her hands.

"Lunch is served," she said. "Grab Roman and I'll set the table." She made a lettuce salad, and poured tall glasses of lemonade.

"I'm so hungry, I could eat a horse," Roman said, appearing in the kitchen.

"Sorry, son, we only have pizza. Hope that works," Guy replied.

Everyone laughed, and then dove into the food like there was no tomorrow.

"I hope you found something to keep you busy this morning, Rome," Claire said.

"I've been working," Roman said.

"*Working*? On what? A school project?" Guy asked.

"No. On figuring out what the two of you really found in that cave."

"Oh? We're having trouble believing it's a worthless replica, too, just for the record," Guy said.

"I absolutely agree with you and plan to find out exactly what it is," Roman said. "I've sent out many e-mail messages. We'll see."

The food and drink disappeared within minutes. Claire refilled the lemonades and brought bowls of pistachio ice cream to the table.

"Back to work for me," Roman said, after devouring the dessert. "Mind if I continue to use the computer?"

"Not a bit. We have letter reading to get through for our case," Guy said. "Let us know if you need anything. And don't go missing. Pop your head out once in a while and say hi, will you?"

"Will do," he said. "Thanks for lunch. It hit the spot." He returned to the den and continued sending out e-mail messages to his fellow archeology students and professors at the University, in each case providing a detailed description of the artifact and asking for feedback. Next he inserted a CD into the computer, one he'd thankfully thrown into his suitcase at the last minute in case he needed it for any reason, containing a lengthy group list of e-mail addresses of both student and faculty members of the Archeological Society—a group of like-minded individuals that Roman held in high regard. He structured a similar e-mail addressed to this esteemed group, and clicked *send*.

Finally, he began logging onto various websites, seeking information regarding ancient artifacts and relics of history. Without much difficulty, he more than confirmed the piece to be Aztec in origin, as he'd suspected. But beyond that, he could not seem to glean anything specific about the exotic statue. He continued seeking answers.

Sitting at the kitchen table, Claire and Guy dove head first into the pool of letters. Each one of them took an inordinate length of time to read, and each one read like a novel—page, after page, after long page. Both wore reading glasses to clarify the writing, but in the end the task proved neither fast, nor easy.

Penned in the infinitesimal script of David Post, the writings set forth unbelievably scrupulous detail in their treatment of his everyday life—in the U.S.—in Miami, Florida. While certain words were difficult to make out, and some indecipherable altogether, most were quite clear. His grasp of the English language was impressive and he seemed to use the language with ease, although his tendency to be overly descriptive prolonged each sentence, and therefore every writing. Awed by his ability to articulate as clearly as he did, though, it did not surprise Claire that he could make the mundane seem interesting, and she thought to herself, as she disappeared into the world of David Post, that he could easily have built himself a career in writing—perhaps even creative writing.

The more she studied his *reports*, it became clear why they had provided a strong line of connection between the brothers. Yet necessarily, they could only be one-sided communications—David always writing to Joseph, but never the reverse. She sensed the ultimate frustration that must have saturated Joseph to his core. Without the letters, however, she wondered whether Joseph would have withered away—like a dying vine.

Father Time stole many hours, with Claire and Guy totally engrossed in their project and Roman holed up in the den. Late in the day, Guy's cell phone rang, breaking his concentration.

"Mr. Lombard," McKay said. "I've got those rush DNA comparison results for you."

"And…?" Guy asked.

32

"THE TESTS PROVE *beyond* a doubt that the skeleton found in Miami Shores is that of one David Crawford Post. And combined with the partial dental records match to boot, I'd say you've got your positive identification ten times over," McKay said. "And that's my final answer."

"Excellent, McKay! That's what we've been waiting for! The identification enigma is concluded. The remains are that of David Oved Posnick, also known as David Crawford Post. Thanks again, McKay, for a job well done."

"Of course. I know you'd expect nothing less from this office. And by the way, I'd like to hear all about what happened in London when you have the time."

"No problem. And thank you. You've never disappointed me, McKay."

Guy hung up, looked at Claire, and shouted, "We got it. It's final!" He grabbed her, pulled her close, and waltzed her merrily around the living room, lifting her feet off the floor, elated by the corroboration. At last, at long last, David Post could properly be laid to rest with a name on his headstone.

"I'm happy, but I'm sad," Claire said. "Poor David."

"I agree. But until those tests came back...you know the burden of proof we're under. At least we know the truth now."

"Yeah. We did the impossible."

Just then Roman emerged from hibernation. "What's all the commotion about?" he asked. "I could hear you all the way in the den."

"We just received absolute confirmation on the skeletal identification. That part of the case is over. On to part two."

"Hey, good work, guys. I'm proud of you." Roman walked to the refrigerator and grabbed a Coke.

Claire telephoned LuVasse to give him the news, and Guy phoned his office and Sergeant Jack Massey to spread the word—the final results of the DNA match came back *positive*!

"Maybe you can fill me in on why it took the two of you so long to put a name on that clump of bones. What was the holdup, Lombard?" Sergeant Massey asked. "Explain."

Guy was silent. Fully taken aback by the insensitive and stupid comment, he bit his lip while he considered the source. Guy had dealt too often with this despicable, hard-hearted man over the years, and knew firsthand his capability to sting viciously. Everyone who had had the displeasure of working with the man, in any capacity, recognized that he never complimented another's work—no matter how exemplary it might be. So why start now? Guy refused to let the repellent and contemptible human being offend him.

"I'm sorry. I didn't hear your answer, Lombard. And by the way, when should I be ready to arrest the perpetrator?"

"Any day now, Sergeant," Guy replied, civilly, stretching the truth until it no longer resembled reality. Acutely aware their work was cut out for them—to now place a name on the murderer—especially with no solid leads to follow at this juncture, he flatly refused to give the clueless and demanding man more bait with which to hook him, reel him in, and eat him up. It just wasn't that much fun.

The sergeant grunted a goodbye and slammed the receiver down.

"The nerve of that asshole!" Guy boomed. He filled Claire in on the conversation.

"The nerve!" she parroted.

Too late in London to notify Edmond Penwright and the Detective Chief Inspector at Scotland Yard, Guy made a mental note to call them both in the morning and alert them to the final test results. The missing person entry on David Crawford Post had to be pulled from the system—as David Crawford Post no longer could be classified amongst the missing, for he'd been found.

All attention turned to Roman, sitting patiently on the couch next to the artifact, waiting for a chance to talk.

"Dad, Claire, this is not going well—not yet, anyway. But I'm not giving up."

"What's happening?" Guy asked.

"Well, of course, I'm dealing with the time difference between here and Israel and other countries around the world, so many of the responses I'm waiting for will not come in until tomorrow, or even later. But I don't fly back to school until Thursday. So I'm hoping to have the information by then. Maybe even much sooner."

"We don't want you to spend your entire time off glued to that computer, doing research for us," Claire said. "I won't hear of it."

"I second that, son," Guy said.

"You don't seem to understand," Roman said. "I'm doing it as much for me, as the two of you. I need to know the truth about this crazy thing. It's hooked me."

"Yeah. I know what you mean," Claire said. "Those green eyes are mesmerizing, aren't they?" She sat next to Roman, pulled the artifact to her lap, and gazed into its eyes. For the first time, she noticed they looked different—different from how they had looked before Robert took it away. The eyes were the same, yet different. How could that be? Maybe she imagined it, but they seemed to have lost their brilliance. Perhaps her eyes were suffering from all the close reading she had done that afternoon? She looked away for several seconds, closing her eyes to give them a rest, and turned back to look at its eyes once again.

Just then the phone rang. She returned the relic to its flannel home and picked up the receiver. "Hello?"

"Hi Claire. It's your dad."

"Hi, Dad. Good to hear from you. Is everything okay?"

"Everything's good. But we haven't talked to you in a while and we're wondering how you're doing, and Guy?"

Claire told him a bit about the skeleton investigation, mentioning only information available to the public. She could not share other case information, even with her father, at this time. Not yet.

"So Robert was right. Your mother and I ran into Robert and Mae Holden out shopping the other day, and he mentioned that you and Guy are investigating a felony case."

"I am. We are. It's a long story, and I'll tell you all about it just as soon as I can. But speaking of Robert Holden, how is he?"

"Well, funny you should ask. We hadn't talked to Robert, or Mae, in many weeks—until we bumped into them recently. The last few times we've seen him, though, he hasn't seemed himself. Nothing was said, mind you, but we wonder sometimes if he feels well. It would be so difficult for Mae if anything happened to him. She relies on him so. By the way, honey, we want to have you and Guy over for dinner just as soon as you're done with this case."

"Can't wait, Dad. Miss you."

"I miss you too, my angel. Please, be careful. And tell that *guy* of yours—no pun intended—I want to challenge him to a game of *Trivial Pursuit*. Tell him, I'm waiting."

Claire laughed. "Consider the message delivered, and I promise we'll get together before long. Love you. Bye for now."

"I love you, too. Don't ever forget that."

Trivial Pursuit—the game Guy and Claire's father, Don, played whenever the opportunity arose, always guaranteed a tough match. Yet in the end, Don always pulled off the victory with the score tied. Don loved beating the celebrated Gaston Lombard at the game, and Guy felt humbled and even a little humiliated each time he lost.

Although never quite able to win against Don, Guy refused to give up trying, as it did not play well with his competitive nature to lose at anything—even a board game.

"That was my father, honey," Claire informed Guy. "They want us to come over for dinner after the case is resolved, and he challenges you to *the game*."

"I look forward to it. I mean that." An unpleasant, twisted expression appeared on his face as he contemplated the next challenge.

When Roman announced hunger pangs, they drove to the Rascal House on Collins Avenue for a quick dinner. That night, they went to bed early, drained by the day's events.

Roman tossed and turned throughout the turbulent night, unable to stop thinking about the warrior statue, its face haunting him relentlessly. He woke up too early, feeling exhausted, his sheet and comforter twisted into a tight ball at the end of the bed. Lying for close to an hour, eyes wide open, he was unable to move. At six a.m. he rolled out of bed, with effort, relieved that the nightmares had finally retreated.

He threw on cut-offs and a tee shirt, washed his face, brushed his teeth, and rushed to the den. Turning on the computer, he waited impatiently for it to boot up, anxious to see what the passing hours had produced. He smiled when he saw the dozens upon dozens of e-mail responses waiting to be read, including many from Israel. His queries, sent the day before, had specified the urgency of his need for information, and the recipients had come through for him. He opened and plowed through one message after another, each one hitting the target but none scoring a bull's-eye. Just as the few he'd received the day before, these responses were also too generic. He somehow needed to communicate even greater particulars about the piece. Clearly, the mere written description of the object, though highly detailed, was failing to produce the results he sought. A visual, that's what he needed. A *visual!*

Gazing absentmindedly around the room, deep in thought, his eyes fell upon the artifact, sitting in all its glory on the bookshelf. Guy had placed it there the previous evening before they went out for dinner. No longer in the protective covering, the statue seemed to be directing its menacing glare unswervingly at Roman. The word that came to mind? *Chilling!* Then Roman's eyes fell upon an object sitting next to the relic—a digital camera, still in its original box. He pulled it from the shelf. It looked brand new. Well-acquainted with this type of camera, he understood its capabilities, and knew at once it would serve his purpose perfectly.

Carefully retrieving the artifact, he set it gently on the desk, atop the white blotter pad, face up. Next he pulled the camera from its box, inserted the battery—it was charged, surprisingly—loaded the memory stick, and photographed the statue. Then he downloaded the digital image of the imposing relic to the computer, and, a second or two later, the clear picture appeared in living color on the screen, allowing him to e-mail it to all recipients of his initial queries. If this didn't do the trick, nothing would.

For the first time, Roman felt somewhat dispirited by the burden of the mission. He showered. A pot of brewing coffee filled the morning air with fragrant aroma and lured him to the kitchen. "I could use a cup of that," he said.

"You got it," Claire said. "Back at it early again this morning, weren't you? I heard you. How'd you sleep?" She gave him a hug.

"Not great, Claire. I'm afraid this statue of yours is getting the best of me. It seemed to taunt me all through the night."

"We've experienced the same thing. Have you learned anything about it, yet?"

"Well, my search hasn't been as productive as I would have liked to see by now, but I have a strong hunch I'll get what I'm looking for today.... In fact, I'm sure of it." He smiled a tight smile. "Or should I say, I have great hope."

Just then Guy strolled into the kitchen wearing yellow cowboy-print pajamas. His disheveled hair, half-opened eyes, and mighty yawn signaled his struggle to wake up. Roman held back a chuckle that, within seconds, turned into hysterical laughter building uncontrollably within him. He had never seen his father looking quite so silly, and witnessing his usually elegant and stately dad in this childhood-print getup called for more restraint than he could handle. Unable to hold back any longer, Roman bent over, holding his stomach, and exploded into out-of-control hysterics, taking minutes to contain himself, and triggering Claire to join in—until tears rolled down both of their cheeks.

"Something funny? Did I miss something?" Guy asked.

Neither Roman nor Claire could answer, and both struggled to bring the situation under control. It quickly became one of those moments in life when laughter triggers more laughter, and that laughter triggers even greater laughter.

Exasperated and feeling left out, Guy spoke loudly enough to be heard over the noise, and changed the subject. "I need a cup of that coffee I've been smelling. Works better than an alarm clock for me." He winked at Roman.

Roman and Claire dared not look at each other for fear of breaking into new and greater hysteria.

"Glad you're both having a good time," Guy said, oblivious to what had set them off. Sleepily, he walked over to Claire, kissed her on the cheek, and poured coffee into three cups. Then he looked at his son and grinned. "How goes the battle?"

Roman seemed to have sufficiently recovered from the moment. "Well, at sunup, I realized I needed to send a snapshot of the artifact to all recipients of my initial e-mail, so I broke out your digital camera and sent a downloaded photo of it to a few hundred of my closest friends. I'm waiting for a response from someone—from anyone—who's familiar with that piece."

"I knew that camera would come in handy one day," Guy said. "I've been meaning to read the manual and figure out how to use it myself, but I haven't taken the time. I got as far as charging the battery. Anyway, I'm happy we had it for your use, Roman. I actually saw how one of those works at the crime lab, not long ago, and I find the entire process incredible."

Back at the computer, Roman sat stiffly, reviewing countless new responses to his second e-mail as they began to trickle in. Now his routine, he scanned through them hurriedly, rushing the ritual, desperately wanting to learn more about the statue, determined to read every last one. The unproductive process continued for hours, until he opened and read a certain response that prematurely ended his task.

33

DEEPLY EMBEDDED IN the daunting task, Claire and Guy ingested one letter after another, swallowing and absorbing the information David Post had so poetically and powerfully set down in writing.

In one correspondence, he wrote of the short-term employment he'd endured after arriving in Miami: working at various restaurants, sometimes busing tables and other times as a short-order cook; apprentice work at a shoe repair shop; vending newspapers and magazines from a corner street stand; and clerking at a small luggage shop. Anything to exist—to put food on his table and a roof over his head, to cover the bare necessities until something better came along.

Other writings revealed the regular early evening walks he took around a nearby park, and on weekends his strolls along the beach, often stopping to drop a fishing line into the water, or sitting on a concrete bench to feed the birds. He so enjoyed watching children and couples cavorting nearby, the close proximity to other human beings temporarily seeming to sate the emptiness that lingered around and within him.

A voracious and indiscriminate reader, he shared the many books he read, summarizing each one for Joseph. Fiction, non-fiction, art, antiques, history, religion, cooking, world geography—you name it, he read it. He seemed to have an inexhaustible appetite for any and all kinds of learning.

David wrote, too, about a select few people he had met, describing each with astute cleverness, but never using names.

One letter in particular caught Claire's eye. In it, David informed Joseph he always wore the lepton around his neck, refusing to take it off, adding that it remained the only memento he still had to remind him of their beloved parents and family. He treasured it beyond measure, clinging to it like a drowning swimmer to a life preserver. In the same writing, he spoke of attending synagogues on a fairly regular basis, of studying and following the ways of Torah, including keeping the Sabbath. He tried, desperately, to live the Jewish way—the way of his ancestors—aggressively pursuing peace with his fellow man, and patterning his life to the best of his ability around the sacred teachings in the first five books of the Hebrew scriptures, at all times attempting to live a life pleasing to his Maker.

In another writing, David theorized why neither Joseph nor he had ever married, and why they seemed to avoid intimate relationships with the opposite sex. Being severely traumatized by the war and the savage murder of their parents, their lives had forever and permanently been scarred. Not returning to their family home when the war ended, but rather embarking down new paths and assuming new identities—*hiding out in life*—each secreted his heritage for fear of being again victimized, and that deception crippled them socially. He acknowledged they were in self-made prisons, neither able to fully reveal themselves in total honesty to another person, and he encouraged Joseph to find a way out—to pardon himself—to somehow forgive the past and move forward so that hatred no longer consumed him. And David said he was working with a therapist to learn ways of letting go of the anger and resentment that still dwelled within him. He had made significant progress.

In yet another correspondence, David mentioned meeting a woman about his same age, whose company he enjoyed, at first. But it turned out she had no understanding of the Holocaust and even questioned whether it had happened. Insulted beyond measure, he had refused to see or speak with her again. With sadness, and amidst nearly unbearable pangs of loneliness and yearnings to hold a woman in his arms, he concluded that no one would truly be able to understand the angst he carried with him at all times, and he accepted the inevitability of being alone for the remainder of his days.

More than anything else, however, he wrote of missing his adored brother, Joseph, and of how he dreamed of seeing him and spending time together some day. He saved any extra money he earned, and one day, when the time was right, he promised to fly him to the United States of America—to Miami, Florida—where they could grow old with each other. This, his single goal in life, became the fuel that kept his motor running. Only a pipe dream, perhaps, but it became the sole source of his inner drive and motivation.

As the dates on the letters progressed, David mentioned numerous times a good-hearted employer—a business owner—who had given him the responsible job of picking up and delivering prized pieces of art and antiques within the Miami area and its suburbs. But he was careful never to mention the name of his employer or the name of the business. David did say the man seemed to have a great respect for him and his surprising knowledge of antiques—knowledge the lord in London had instilled in him, as well as the many books he had read on the subject. He claimed the employer treated him *like a brother*.

We need a name, Claire thought. *The* name! Who was this employer?

The reading continued, uninterrupted, for several droning hours, with no clues emerging, until the energy level within both of them indicated *empty*. David had obviously written the letters being forever vigilant never to mention anything that would identify where he lived, the place he worked, or the name of his employer, operating under the belief that the correspondence could potentially bring harm his way if they fell into the wrong hands.

Guy suggested taking a break, and checking on Roman.

NEARLY COLLIDING in the hallway, Guy and Roman started talking simultaneously. Guy relented, and gave his son the floor.

"I've got something so big in my hands," Roman shouted, obviously exuberant. "*I have the truth.*" He danced along the passageway in a silly manner, waving sheets of paper in the air.

"What is it? What do you have?" Guy showed on-the-spot interest.

"Get Claire and go sit on the couch. You won't believe this!"

Guy called for Claire, and obediently they sat on the sofa, side by side, as Roman paced the floor.

"Dad, you've always said, *a picture's worth a thousand words*. Now I understand what that means. There are times when mere words don't cut it. But seeing something with your own two eyes, now that's a different story altogether. My incredibly detailed description of the relic in words alone did not produce the results I wanted, but when I photographed the piece and sent the image out to the same recipients, when they could actually *see* it, that's when the most remarkable thing happened."

Taking a seat on a chair across from them, Roman threw a startled look their way, and Claire followed by shooting a pensive glance toward Guy. Roman appeared spooked. Anxiety riddled Claire. What had he learned?

"Let me explain," Roman said. "Hundreds of responses appeared in my inbox—from the initial e-mail I sent out. They came in slowly at first, and then in a deluge. One after the other, I tore through them; yet, no one could identify this specific piece, other than to reaffirm that it sounded like an early object of idol worship, either Aztec or Mayan in origin—a fact we already knew. But when I sent the actual image out this morning, in a second follow-up e-mail to the same recipients, replies came in—several at a time and then so many all at once. I reviewed each of them as fast as I could; not one could identify your specific relic, until—"

"Until what? You're keeping us in suspense," Guy said. "Get to it. Until *what*?"

"You won't believe it," Roman said.

"Believe *what*?" Claire asked. "We need to know."

For the moment, Roman seemed to delight in keeping Claire and Guy hanging in suspense.

"Okay. Okay," he said. "The definitive answer came in, unexpectedly, from a Professor of Archeology at the University of Utah, Kenneth Darlington, a fellow member of my Archeological Society. According to the professor, the mysterious relic is indeed from the Aztec culture. Listen carefully as I read his response." Roman sat back in his chair, holding the sheets in front of him.

"An extraordinary tale comes along with this piece, an account of inconceivable theft and smuggling that went horribly awry. And when you read my response in its entirety, you will understand my utter amazement when I opened your e-mail.

"This particular relic is an extremely unusual version of an object of Aztec worship, said to have both supernatural powers and ancestry, a piece very rare even in its day, a statue made of stone and covered in gold. Remember, during this time in this culture, gold was not used in currency—as no metallic currency existed. Rather, gold was used for personal or ceremonial decoration only. While the Aztecs decorated many idols with gold ornaments, only a precious few were covered in gold. This was done using blow pipes to fuse gold to its surface. In fact, it's believed that fewer than a dozen of this exact piece were ever created. Large numbers of humans ended up sacrificed to these idols in their day, usually victims obtained during warfare. And while idols' eyes were commonly comprised of turquoise, the eyes on this piece were a precious jade."

Claire sat, mesmerized, as Roman continued to read the e-mail response.

"Miraculously, and over decades upon decades of digging, a total of three of these extremely rare pieces have been unearthed. One by one each of the three recovered pieces was dedicated, by the archeological dig team finding it, to the same museum of ancient Aztec history in Mexico City. These prized pieces are of inestimable value."

The words *inestimable value* resonated through Guy's head. The information Roman was about to read would stun him even more.

"Around forty years ago, the three artifacts mysteriously vanished from the Mexican museum. Nothing else was taken. The elaborate alarm system did not trip, and suspect fingerprints were not lifted from the crime scene. Police exhaustively questioned all employees, yet no arrest resulted. Although unable to determine who had committed the crime, law enforcement did conclude that it appeared to be an inside job. But the story gets even more interesting here."

Roman read on.

"About a year after the robbery, U.S. Customs officials in Miami, Florida, confiscated three crated boxes entering the United States—each separately marked "Fragile" and addressed to "Arts Associates, Inc." at a Miami address. Each of the crates separately indicated that an employee of the addressee would pick them up—due to the breakable nature of the contents. The customs forms, filled out by the sender, declared each container to hold an "antique art object," in the probable hopes of avoiding duty, and, therefore, closer scrutiny. But based upon an anonymous tip, officials seized the crates, opened them, and closely examined the contents."

A coldness shot through Claire.

"The results of the eye-opening inspection substantiated the tipster's warning. The seized antiques turned out to be *two* of the three stolen Aztec artifacts taken a year earlier from the museum. The thieves had stuffed the relics with raw, uncut emeralds, also presumably stolen. Even the jade eyes of the statues had been replaced with unusual cuts of the green stones before shipment. Customs officials, local police investigators, and the FBI worked diligently to identify the culprits behind the smuggling ring.

"Upon further examination, it was determined that a mastermind had concealed the raw emeralds inside of the relics after first carefully hollowing out each piece from the bottom. Once the stones had been securely packed within, the bottoms were skillfully refinished. It was an ingenious plan! No one would have suspected the smuggled objects to also be hiding precious jewels, even upon close inspection. Yet one thorough customs official thought he detected an ever so slight rattling when he shook one of the pieces, and that led to the second startling discovery.

"The officials also noted that the smugglers had apparently worked sharp, metal inserts into the bottoms of the relics. Authorities later concluded that action was most likely done to curtail thievery."

Guy and Claire's eyes seemed to be stuck wide open.

"But as I said, the customs agents seized and recovered only two of the *three* stolen artifacts—which were subsequently returned to the museum. The third confiscated crate contained nothing but worthless rock. Hence, the third stolen artifact was never recovered and remains somewhere out there even today. Rumor had it one of the smugglers took the real third piece during transit out of Mexico, and secreted it away somewhere en route to Florida, perhaps on a Caribbean island, presumably to be recovered at a later time and sold on the black market for a handsome sum of money. This was never proven, however, and the whereabouts of the third statue has remained a mystery to this very day.

"And you can imagine the total value of the rare artifact, together with the uncut emeralds, to the right buyer. At the time, I think I heard a figure of two million dollars being tossed around."

The third stolen artifact was never recovered.... The whereabouts of the third statue has remained a mystery until this very day.... These words burned into Claire and Guy with the intensity of a branding iron.

34

"THIEVES ROBBING THIEVES.... It's a prime example of the old adage: *There is no honor among thieves*," Roman said, and then continued on, reading the Professor's e-mail response.

"Ultimately law enforcement made no arrests in connection with the confiscation. Not surprisingly, the information identifying the shipper turned out to be bogus, as did the name and address of the recipient. No such business existed, and the address listed on the crates led investigators to a vacant lot, if I remember correctly. For a period of several months, the police and FBI monitored a sophisticated surveillance set-up at the customs pick-up counter. But in the end, no one ever came forward to collect the boxes.

"All in all, the whole thing seemed to be an atypical heist—as if the would-be recipient somehow caught wind of a problem and knew a trap had been set, a trap that would result in detainment, questioning, and arrest. And here, as unbelievable as it sounds, the case dead-ended."

Roman looked up. "There's a bit more."

Thunderstruck and numbed by the Professor's accounting, Claire and Guy sat motionless.

"Involved officials intentionally kept the story out of the newspapers for a considerable time, with the thought that maintaining a low profile might eventually encourage the smugglers to come forward to claim the confiscated crates once they believed the heat was off. However, no one did come forward, the trap was never sprung, and when the story finally appeared in newspapers a couple of years later—in detailed articles setting forth all facts surrounding the case—since it was no longer current news, it drew little or no interest. Ultimately, as I told you, authorities returned the two recovered artifacts to the Mexican museum, and, as far as I know, the uncut emeralds remain tagged as evidence to this day at the Office of the FBI. Officials were unable to determine who owned the emeralds as they were never reported missing.

"As you can surmise, a cloud of mystique still surrounds the entire matter. Because of the initial lack of press coverage on the story, I'm afraid this incredible tale of intrigue went virtually unnoticed, even by those of us who would be interested in it. So you are most fortunate I saw your e-mail today.

"Again, I apologize for the length of this response, but I thought a detailed elucidation was in order. If I can be of further help, please contact me. And know this with certainty, YOU HAVE GARNERED MY UNDIVIDED ATTENTION. I would suggest you contact the Miami police, or the FBI, without delay, if you know ANYTHING about the whereabouts of this third original piece. You have my e-mail address. I ask you to stay in contact."

Roman set the papers down on his lap. "He also left his mailing address at the University and a business and home telephone number. I already e-mailed him back a heartfelt thank you."

A hush blanketed the room.

"I'm reeling," Claire said, finally. "Looks like we stumbled onto the third stolen artifact, doesn't it?"

"Afraid so," Guy said.

"What I'm wondering is why on earth your friend, Robert Holden, a so-called *expert* in the field of ancient artifacts, so badly misled the two of you regarding the piece. It seems inconceivable he wouldn't have known," Roman said.

"Similar thoughts are crossing my mind, too," Claire said.

"Mine, three," Guy said. "Robert's permanently on my shit list."

Claire got up and walked slowly from the room, stopping in the den to retrieve the relic, and then continuing on to the bedroom she shared with Guy. After setting the amazing piece on a side table, she dropped face down onto the bed and laid there for a time—ruminating first about the true facts of the warrior statue, and then moving on to Robert and his false appraisal. Why would Robert Holden lie to them?

She simply could not understand it, and felt sorely betrayed by a person she would have trusted with her life.

Knowing Claire needed some solo time, Guy stayed in the living room and talked with Roman. "I'll have to turn the statue over to the FBI for safekeeping, until we know for sure about all of this," Guy said. "Who could have predicted…?" He put his arm around his son's shoulders. "Thanks."

Roman smiled a modest smile. "No big deal, Dad."

Somehow the thrill of the moment—of finally learning what they'd found in the Caribbean cave that stormy day—vanished for all of them, as the incredibly odd appraisal of Robert Holden took center stage. The pain was especially acute for Claire. This was a man she thought the world of, but now she had to question why his actions seemed duplicitous. Why would he have intentionally provided them with false and misleading information? It made no sense. But it also did not compute that he, as a lifelong expert in the field, would give them an opinion so askew. Even if he did not recognize this particular piece, he certainly had the knowledge to determine its authenticity, and not proclaim it to be a copy. Maybe he'd simply made a mistake. But this explanation made the least amount of sense.

Guy thought about his bright son, Roman. The timing of his visit could not have been more perfect. Whether they would have discovered this information on their own remained doubtful, and certainly it would have taken much longer not having the inner-circle contacts that Roman had.

Claire remained in the bedroom, sitting up now, holding the rare statue in her hands, her beautiful eyes nearly overflowing with tears. "Finally, we know all about you," she said. "And now, we'll have to turn you over to the authorities—to get you back to your rightful place in the museum." Suddenly, a strange feeling came over her as she stared into the artifact's eyes. She could not put her finger on it, but again she was struck by how different they looked. How utterly peculiar, she thought. Then, like a bolt from the blue, it hit her. Feeling as though she'd been kicked in the stomach, she gasped. How could she have missed it? The eyes. *The eyes!* She recalled the magnificent brilliance they had once exuded. That luminosity was gone, leaving behind only dullness and lifelessness. Their color, too, seemed strangely off from what she remembered—only slightly dissimilar, but dissimilar nonetheless—still green, but somehow not the same pure essence of green as when they'd found the piece. Also, the *magic* in them was no longer present. There was no doubt about it.

"Guy! Roman! Come in here, will you?" Claire yelled.

Seconds later, the two poked their heads into the room. "What it is? Is everything okay?" Guy asked, frantically.

"Come look at the artifact," she said. "Its eyes have been changed."

"*What*?" Guy asked.

"Look. Under the light. They're not the same. I'm sure of it!"

Guy surveyed the relic and had to admit that the eyes did not appear as he remembered either. Their earlier magnetism and sparkle seemed inexplicably absent.

"I had no idea the eyes looked different when you found this relic," Roman said. "I've only seen them the way they are now."

"Come to think of it, we really haven't looked at it closely since I picked it up in the flannel pillowcase at Robert's shop," Guy said.

"I did, once," Claire said. "And I hate to admit it now, but I thought then that the eyes appeared different than I remembered. I chalked it up to heavy letter reading that day, and never gave it a second thought, until now."

"Do you have a magnifying glass? A *good* one?" Roman asked.

"In the top desk drawer," Guy said.

"May I?" Roman turned to Claire and carefully took the piece of antiquity from her hands. Carrying it to the den, he placed it under the halogen desk lamp, retrieved the magnifying glass, and studied the area encircling the eyes. After some time, he returned to find Guy still sitting next to Claire on the bed, his arm around her shoulders.

"I've got the answer," Roman said. "I found minuscule, freshly made perforations around the eyes—almost indistinguishable without the enlarged perspective. There's no doubt it's recently been tampered with. I would guess *these* eyes are a green jade—*a precious jade*—consistent with what Professor Darlington said was originally used, if you'll remember. But he also said, the smugglers substituted *unusually-cut emeralds* for the jade eyes. The artifact you two found, tucked away in the cave, must have had the substituted emeralds for its eyes. That would explain this brilliance you keep talking about. Its bottom may also have been tampered with, but that's not as clear. I can't confirm it."

Claire looked at Guy, knowing he shared her thoughts. Silence ricocheted around the room. It certainly appeared that Robert had substituted the eyes when he took the relic away for appraisal purposes. Did that mean he'd also taken the emeralds tucked within? *Why, Robert? Why?* Claire wondered.

Guy questioned silently whether Robert needed big money for some reason. But neither he nor Claire dared to speak Robert's name at that moment—Claire, because she didn't want to believe it, and Guy, out of respect for Claire. There would be ample time to discuss it later, once they absorbed it all.

"Why don't the two of you go hit a bucket of balls at the range? It'll be light out a while longer. I'll stay back and throw something together for dinner," Claire said. At once it became clear that she needed more time to herself.

Guy gave Claire an extended kiss on the forehead. Then he gently touched her chin with his right hand and lifted her face upward, forcing her to look him squarely in the eyes. He kissed her lips, and contemplated the look on her face for a quiet second or two, his return expression telling her without words that he understood her dilemma. He kissed her again. "See you, honey," he said. "We need to decide how to handle this." He grabbed his regular set of golf clubs from the closet, together with a second, older set. "Come on, son. Let's get out of here for awhile."

"We'll be back before you miss us, Claire," Roman said. He smiled a concerned smile. "Please don't hate the messenger." He looked at her with kind eyes.

They left, and Claire went to the kitchen to start dinner, desperately trying to keep her mind from thoughts of Robert. All at once, an unexpected and heavy pounding on the door startled her. "Who's there?" she called out, wondering if the men had forgotten something. She heard no response. "Who's there?" she asked, again. Still, no answer. With the chain in place, she pulled the door open a crack. The hallway appeared empty. But as she started to close the door, her eyes fell upon something white laying on the doormat. She reached out, and pulled it in. It was a sheet of paper, folded in half. When she opened it, she contorted her face into a look of disgust.

Printed in bold red crayon, the message simply read: "*Start looking over your shoulder, Ms. Casewell. Time's up!*" Claire slammed the door shut, re-locked it, then checked the chain. She walked to the living room and shrunk into a deeply-cushioned wingback chair. Another threat! And this time the person, or a messenger, had walked inside their secure condominium complex to deliver it. Not listed in the phone book, it came from someone who *knew* where she lived or followed her home. And the predator had called her twice on their home unlisted number, as well. When she had been nearly sideswiped, she assumed the person had been following her, but maybe in actuality the person had laid in wait nearby, knowing exactly where she lived, waiting and watching for her to arrive home. This person seemed personally familiar with her, or at least was able to access her private information, and that narrowed the list of suspects in her mind.

Her last name was misspelled in the message, just as it had been on the envelopes containing the threatening letters sent to her office, so all of the written threats most likely originated from the same author. At least a reasonable person would assume so. Was her last name intentionally spelled incorrectly to make her think it came from someone who didn't know her well? She briefly pondered that thought.

Calling down to the doorman, she inquired whether an unfamiliar person had recently entered the building, explaining that an unidentified individual had just delivered something to her door. He informed her that he had not seen any stranger entering the building, but explained that the front doors had been propped open for a time to allow for luggage being carted from vehicles into the lobby, and someone could have wandered in, or out, without detection. He apologized profusely.

This time the message had been printed entirely in red crayon. Again, she got the intended drift. It was now time for blood. The last one, merely underlined in red, indicated the final warning. She dialed Guy's cell number.

When he answered and heard her voice, he knew. "What was it this time? Another call, Claire?"

"No. A loud pounding on our door, with no one there. Only a note left on our mat—a note telling me my time is up."

"We're on our way. Hang tight 'til we get there. Make sure the door's locked, and chained."

"It's *always* locked and chained when I'm alone. Guy, the person knows where we live and was able to bypass security. And has our unlisted number. Who *is* this?"

"Don't know, yet. But we will find out! Call Sergeant Massey and report this as soon as we hang up. If he's not in, leave a message. Ask him to pick up the note. This needs to stop. And don't cook dinner. We're going out. I want to get you away from there for a while."

Claire called the Sergeant, left him a detailed message, and remained seated in the chair, lost in thought. Hearing a knock on the door, she jumped, and froze in place, but when she heard Guy's reassuring voice calling out to her, she leaped to her feet and ran to the door, hurriedly removing the chain, and welcoming Guy and Roman back home. She collapsed in the comfort of Guy's strong arms for a time—until she was ready to pull away.

"I'm sorry you're going through this, Claire. Dad filled me in on the way back. I had no idea," Roman said.

"Thanks, Rome." She hugged him. "I can handle it, but I'll admit, it's a bit unnerving. It's not every day someone threatens to kill you."

"Any idea who this is?" Guy asked Claire.

"No, but it makes me think we're getting mighty close to finding the murderer. Someone's awfully scared of being exposed, wouldn't you agree? And that someone seems to have all of my personal information." She showed them both the note. "The person is targeting me alone, not you, Guy. That may be a clue."

"We need to get this solved," Guy thundered. "You're right. This person may feel we're closing in, and could do something desperate. You need to be more vigilant than ever. Remember that. Don't let your guard down for an instant, Claire."

"I checked with the doorman but he saw nothing unusual," she said.

"Figures," Guy said. "No help there."

Together, the threesome ate a quiet dinner at Tony Chan's Water Club. Always a favored spot, Guy thought a great Chinese dinner would be a good diversion for Claire. After all, she had held up remarkably well under the circumstances. He didn't know too many others who would stay as calm as she had after being subjected to numerous and ongoing threats. The evening turned into a grand escape, and before long Claire had forgotten about the latest threat—for the time being anyway.

Ah, yes, these are the times we remember, Guy thought to himself, staring across the table at Claire and Roman. He smiled a devoted smile. Thoughts of his two daughters popped into his mind—Eden and Lana. He loved Claire and his children so thoroughly and forever. Life had blessed him richly.

That night Guy cradled Claire in his arms as she slept. She felt safe. He, on the other hand, felt like the world's biggest coward. Tough in the courtroom, Guy went weak in the knees at the thought of Claire saying "no" to the question he'd been unable to ask. How would he ever find the courage? Or should he? Maybe he loved her too much to risk destroying what they had. He kissed her lightly on the cheek and lay awake for hours watching her sleep.

35

Wednesday morning

CLAIRE DAYDREAMED AS she sipped hot green tea on the balcony. The day had just begun, and Guy and Roman still slept soundly. After starting a pot of coffee and setting a plate of cinnamon rolls on the kitchen table, she needed time alone to think. Robert preoccupied her thoughts. Something didn't fit. A good and honorable man like Robert Holden would never engage in anything other than moral, upright conduct. Yet it appeared he had purposely tried to delude them. Why? This clashed with the grain of the man. It was a hitch in the giddy-up that threw everything else into a tailspin. He had always been a good man, and he'd been a lifelong friend of her family. He would never intentionally deceive her. This made no sense. None of it added up. The more she wavered back and forth with her reasoning, the more she kept coming back to the same conclusion. There must be some other explanation. Pure and simple. There would be plausible clarification for all of it. Robert would be able to explain and enlighten her. She remained sure of that.

Like a bolt from above, she recalled something from her training years ago. *When something doesn't make sense, look for the financial interest.* Could Robert be in trouble? Did he need money? But he had done so well for himself throughout his long career. Hadn't he?

Learning the truth about the artifact had opened her eyes, but Robert, being cast as a thief and liar, made the revelation bittersweet. And the threatening note left at their front door had had a profound impact on her. She wondered who crouched behind the threats. Someone who knew her well, it seemed. But who? Who would threaten to kill her? Her thoughts stopped short when Roman stepped onto the balcony, holding a cup of hot coffee in one hand and two cinnamon rolls in the other.

"Morning, Claire," he said. "How did you sleep?"

"Okay. But I woke up very early. How about you?"

"Like a rock."

"We owe you a huge thank you for doing all that research on the relic, Rome. It means so much to us to finally know its history."

"Actually, learning the truth made all my efforts worthwhile. What's on your agenda today? More of that letter reading?"

"Afraid so. We need to keep reading until we find something—anything—to follow up on. There's an unsolved murder out there, and we're committed to solving it. How about you?"

"Well, I thought about driving around to see my old haunts, if I could use one of your cars, and then I considered the thought of playing eighteen holes. You'll both be busy today, and I'd be back for dinner."

"Sure. Sounds like a plan. What do you feel like for dinner tonight?"

"Let's eat in. Maybe we'll be able to talk Dad into grilling some of his famous tuna steaks?"

"Great idea."

"Hey, Claire. What I said yesterday—I really meant it. I'm sorry you're being threatened. That has to frighten you a lot. Stay close to Dad until this is over, will you?"

Claire smiled at him. "Yes, of course." He was a lot like his father.

Just then, Guy poked his head onto the balcony. "I need coffee," he declared.

"Grab a cup and come join us," Claire said. "It's beautiful out here."

The temperature had already reached the mid-to-high 70s mark, and it was, in short, a perfect day—matchless, unparalleled, Utopian. The three of them visited for a brief time. Unfortunately, Roman would be leaving the following day to return to school. As always, his visit seemed all too short.

Roman showered and left to enjoy his time in Miami. Claire and Guy readied for the day, and then sat at the table to wade into the letters once again.

"We need to figure out how we want to handle this Robert thing, hon," Guy said.

"I know. I've been doing a lot of thinking about that. Let's give it a little time."

"Okay, Claire. I'll agree to let it ride for a short while, since this letter reading is crucial and our top priority, but that's it. He needs to be confronted. We'll have to question him."

"Of course, we will."

They fell into the familiar task before them, once again hypnotized by the world according to David Post. His style of expression, his emotional sensitivity, and his mode of communicating together captured their undivided attention. Hours passed.

"I need a clue, Claire. Give me a clue! Something to check out. I feel like we're spinning our wheels." Guy had reached a breaking point.

"Well, we are, at the moment. But that could always change. One of us will find something. Just watch and see. It's all about connecting the dots. If we find no dots, we can forget about locating the perpetrator. Stay with it. A dot will appear."

"Forever the optimist."

"Count on it." She flashed a winning smile.

So many more letters sat waiting to paint the picture, line by line, of David's staid life. By now, Claire had concluded that he led a private, almost reclusive existence—work and his letters to Joseph being his only outlets to the world. But he'd made his life interesting, he filled it with learning. Some of the writings had faded from age. Others had tattered, and she guessed those were the ones Joseph had probably read many times over. Her thoughts drifted to Joseph. She felt honored to have met the virtuous and unforgettable man. Suddenly, she remembered his last words to her. "Guy, we need to give David a proper burial."

"What?"

"Joseph asked us to give David a proper burial. We must do it."

"I'll let McKay know, and as soon as his remains are released, we'll take care of his burial. In fact, I'll call him now. And that reminds me. I think I'll phone Edmond and the Detective Chief Inspector, too. I need to fill them in on the positive identification and bring them up to speed on where the investigation is now."

As Claire continued reading, she realized that what seemed mundane to her had probably been like precious, life-sustaining *food* for Joseph. These two brothers only had each other, and life circumstances had cruelly separated them—not once, but twice.

At noon, Guy announced he would be taking the artifact to the local office of the FBI for safekeeping, but before he left he snapped several photos of it with a film-load camera. They would maintain the pictures as a lasting memory. As Claire gave the artifact a final look, she flashed back to the day in the cave and tunnel system, to the secret, underground labyrinth they had so accidentally stumbled upon during a dreadful Caribbean rainstorm, to the finding of the rare piece of antiquity hidden under the hollowed-out stone—a relic they now understood had been secreted away by a thief or thieves involved in a smuggling ring—and to the terrifying experience of being lost in the darkness that fateful day. In an odd sort of way, the statue had become an integral part of their lives, and now they had to surrender it to the authorities. She felt a tinge of sadness.

"I should be back within the hour," Guy said. "Lock and chain the door when I leave."

Claire locked up, and then made sandwiches, wrapped them, and put them in the refrigerator. They'd have a quick bite when Guy returned. She picked up another letter, but found she couldn't concentrate. She needed an interruption. Drawing a warm lavender bath, she let her body sink slowly down into the inviting water and closed her eyes. Bliss. Pure bliss. For a few minutes all tension melted away. She inhaled the glorious scent of lavender lingering in the air. Water always calmed her so. But all too soon, thoughts of Robert bombarded her momentary sense of peace and tranquility. She needed the truth. *The truth and nothing but the truth*. Reluctantly, she left the nurturing tub, cutting her time of relaxation short, and dressed. She called Guy on his cell phone to remind him to pick up tuna steaks for dinner, several ears of sweet corn, and a handful of limes.

"Okay, my beauty. See you shortly."

"Honey, before we hang up, how did it go with the FBI?"

"I briefed a lead agent on the story, and he agreed to keep the artifact locked up until we know what to do with it."

"That's good. See you soon." Claire returned to the letter she had set down before the all-too-short time out. The reading had become so tiresome—like reading the same story numerous times, with only a few minor changes in the plot or characters. It was not all that dissimilar from the endless scanning of the missing persons computer printouts that had consumed them days before. This part of an investigation was tedious, repetitive, monotonous, wearisome, dull, boring, irritating, annoying, exasperating and mind-numbing. But Claire knew all too well that, in the end, it remained the only thing that could produce results. Yet the task zapped her of energy.

Out of nowhere, her grandmother's words tumbled into her mind, "*If you keep seeking the truth, you will find it. It cannot hide forever. Nothing stays hidden forever*." The adage brought renewed strength to urge her forward. She believed a clue to the mystery lay buried within the letters. A hint, an inkling, or an out-and-out full-fledged clue had to be there somewhere. They just had to find it. Or see it. *Chin up, persevere, hammer away*, she told herself. There will be an end to this. So often things her grandmother had taught her came into her mind, when she most needed to hear them.

Guy returned, and they took a break to eat the turkey sandwiches Claire had prepared. Then, plodding onward, they grabbed one letter after another throughout the long afternoon hours. Guy yawned. "Let's take a nap before Roman gets home," he said. "I'm beat."

"Okay. I'm feeling drained, too."

Standing, he walked over to Claire. Lifting her up from the chair, he swept her into his arms in an overdramatic way. As they waltzed down the hallway, he kissed her face and neck, repeatedly and passionately. Reaching the bedroom, he laid her ever so gently onto the bed, as if she were a delicate and highly breakable glass doll. In no time at all, she realized that taking a nap did not include sleeping. Much too soon, Roman arrived home, and Guy forced himself to pull back on the reins in the middle of the run.

"Dad? Claire?" Roman called out.

"We'll be right out, son. Just waking up from our nap." Minutes later, they emerged from the bedroom—not a bit more rested.

Earlier in the afternoon, Guy had marinated the tuna steaks in his famous concoction of fresh lime juice and his secret ingredient. Now he proceeded to sear them on the balcony grill, while Claire boiled the sweet corn, made a mixed greens salad, and broiled garlic cheese toast in the oven. Roman set the table. Before they knew it, a mix of incredible aromas wafted through the air, signaling dinner was ready.

The food tasted great, and they laughed about Guy keeping the hidden marinade recipe from them for years now. Roman winked at Claire, and she returned the wink, as they both had known the undisclosed addition all along: Russian vodka, flavored with meadowland grasses, wild honey, and a hint of mint. But Guy so enjoyed the mystique of adding his *top secret ingredient* to the marinade, that they could never burst his bubble and tell him they knew what it was. So the historical and absurd pretense continued.

After cleaning up, they took a walk around the neighborhood to get some exercise. Roman's visit was winding down.

Thursday morning

ROMAN PACKED his suitcase in preparation for the evening flight. Not looking forward to the long trip back to Israel, he tried to put it out of his mind. If truth be told, he did not care for flying one bit. But he had realized, early on, that it provided the only reasonable way to see many places in the world—specifically, locations where he wanted to eventually lead archeological excavations. So he bit the bullet when he had to.

Today, until the time came to leave for the airport, he planned to lay by the pool, soak up some rays, and relax.

Claire and Guy returned to letter reading early. Reviewing the never-ending correspondence seemed to move at the pace of a *slow* tortoise, and in the worst way they wanted the task to end. But no shortcuts could be considered because they had a murder to solve. Reviewing the eternal listings of missing persons had produced the clue they'd needed to identify the skeleton, so they could not give up on the letter reading.

"What happens if we finish all of these and find no clue to follow?" Guy asked. "Then what?"

"Believe me, the thought has crept into my mind. I guess we cross that bridge if we get to it. In the meantime, I'm going to be of the opinion that a clue is in here somewhere."

Breaking only for a light lunch, they read into the afternoon until they reached the final four. And then, just two remained, and they each grabbed one.

As Claire began to look over the last correspondence she would read, she realized it was the longest one in the entire bunch. The postmark on the envelope had been cut out, like all the others, presumably to hide any evidence of where they'd come from. David couldn't have known this would be his last writing to Joseph. Her eyes begin to peruse the pages hungrily, craving a clue. Then Claire suddenly stopped reading.

"Guy, I've got something here. Listen to this."

36

GUY LOOKED UP, curiosity eating him alive. "Enlighten me."

"I've got a *name*," Claire said. "Hear me out…."

The ringing phone interrupted her, and Guy answered.

"Sergeant Massey here, Lombard. Calling to check on your progress in the skeleton case. Are we close to an arrest?"

"Close, yes," Guy said. "And you'll be our first call when it's time to pick up the perpetrator."

"Good. I keep telling the press a big story is materializing. Don't let me down, Lombard. Make it soon."

"Rest assured, Sergeant, there will be a startling story connected to this case. That, I promise you."

"I'll hold you to it—you and Claire Caswell, that is. Don't disappoint me. Get it done."

"Goodbye, Sergeant."

"I mean it, Lombard. Get it done!"

He hung up on the intolerable man. Maybe the Sergeant could do it quicker? He'd like to see him try. Guy's blood pressure rose, despite his attempt to ignore the words of the unmannerly Sergeant. Now they really had to deliver, and fast. A great and self-induced heaviness took a seat on his shoulders as he related the conversation to Claire. "I need a cigar. Hold your thoughts," he said.

Grabbing a stogie, he walked with purpose out onto the balcony. Lighting up the cylindrical roll of tobacco, he was mindful not to inhale too deeply. He puffed lightly on his *crutch*, until pressure within him begin to dissipate like released air from an over inflated balloon. Smoking cigars qualified as a disgusting habit to Guy, and he wanted in the worst way to break free from it. After they resolved this case, he'd quit, he promised himself, or try to, anyway.

His thoughts drifted to the impertinent Sergeant Massey. It seemed unfortunate that they, or anyone, had to put up with this rude human being, but they had no choice. As an officer of the law, and the Sergeant of the Miami-Dade Police Department, his position demanded respect, and he constituted a necessary cog in the system. But he was such a disrespectful man. He'd referred the investigation of the skeleton to Guy's office because his officers were overloaded with other important matters, he had said. In reality, the Sergeant probably didn't want his staff wasting valuable time on an age-old case that in all probability would never be solved. And now he had the unmitigated brazenness to lean on them for resolution. The *fucking* nerve! What a kick in the teeth. Guy took deep breaths to calm himself, and then puffed contentedly on the last of his cigar.

He stood up to look over the balcony railing, down onto the pool area, and without too much trouble spotted Roman, basking on a chaise lounge, enjoying the day. Soon his son would be sitting in a colossal metal bird winging its way back to Amsterdam, and then on to Jerusalem. He would miss him when he left. All at once, an onslaught of extreme dizziness gripped Guy—a sensation that often occurred when he smoked the dreaded cylindrical rolls—and he grabbed the railing to steady himself. These could not be good for him, he thought. He stepped inside to return to work.

"Now, where did we leave off, Claire?" he asked.

"I had just told you I found a name. I've gone over this, and finished the letter. Here we go. Listen."

Guy held a pen above his notepad. Claire was amazing. Her perseverance as an investigator both astonished him and put him to shame.

Claire began to paraphrase aloud as she studied the letter. "David's writing about the art and antiques dealer he worked for in Miami—a man about his age. He thought of him as such an upstanding person, but then one day he overheard him talking on the telephone to another collector or dealer, and they were discussing the smuggling of stolen goods into the United States. David overheard many of the details, and became frozen in fear. Thoughts that he may be implicated in illegal activities, merely because he worked for the man, devoured him. He didn't know what to do, but after careful consideration he determined that calling in a tip to alert the authorities—from a pay phone, of course, and without identifying himself—seemed the only appropriate course of action to take."

"Exactly what Joseph told us earlier," Guy said.

"Yes, but Joseph didn't mention the employer's name, and he also didn't recall some other specifics. Listen carefully. David decided to call in the anonymous tip regarding the nefarious scheme and warn them to watch for crates coming into the U.S., addressed to a Florida art dealer, declaring the contents to be 'antiques,' but in reality containing *priceless, stolen relics of history*. He decided to do the right thing, and immediately search for a new job, refusing involvement in any capacity with this kind of activity. High stakes abounded and he knew it. He wanted out. But first, he decided to confront his employer, James, tell him what he'd overheard and why he had to leave."

She looked up at Guy. "We have the name: *James!* And confronting *James* was David's fatal mistake. He promised to write again as soon as he found other employment. Sadly, it was his last letter."

"That's when he disappeared."

"Exactly. And now we have a motive for *James* to get rid of David. And am I going totally mad? We're dealing here with a *smuggling* case involving David Post and *crated, priceless relics*—just after hearing about the smuggling story connected to the artifact we found in the Caribbean. And Professor Darlington did say a tip had been called in to alert the authorities in that situation. What if the tipster was David Post? We're looking at an unusually large set of parallel circumstances, wouldn't you agree? The Miami connection, smugglers, crates indicating "antiques" that in reality held priceless relics, an anonymous tipster responsible for the bust.... In fact, the more I think about it...it could very easily be one and the same incident. Is that possible?"

"I would say no, Claire. They sound strikingly similar, I'll grant you that, but the *same* incident? Highly unlikely. Probably a lot of smuggling cases involve very similar circumstances. And if they were intertwined, that would connect David's death and the murder investigation to the very artifact we found in the Caribbean. How could that possibly be? I'd say, no way."

"You might be right...but I can't help but wonder. Think about this. Grand Cayman *is* only an hour's flight from Miami, and Mexico is close to both. Officials suspected the third stolen artifact was stashed away somewhere between Mexico and Miami, possibly on a Caribbean island. Both David's death, and the attempted smuggling of the two Aztec artifacts into Miami, as relayed to us by the Professor, happened around the same period of time—if you consider the estimated dates of death McKay gave us on David Post and the period of time Professor Darlington said the heist of the artifacts from the museum occurred. Maybe it's not so strange after all. Maybe destiny led us to that ancient statue to put this all together."

"Okay, now that's a stretch for me. But maybe you're not too far off the mark, after all. Let me think. Could this all tie together in some bizarre way? I guess stranger things have happened. Just when I'd told myself we'd hit a road block so high and so wide there would be no way over or around it...we found a name. And now this? It would seem inconceivable. And if we follow this to its natural end, are we to also conclude that Robert Holden recognized the idol, knew about the story of the foiled smuggling attempt, and failed to tell us so he could steal the gems packed inside, and the rare emerald eyes?"

Claire ignored the question. She was still trying to find a logical out for Robert's alleged actions. "Well, I heard you promise Massey a big story. Maybe, just maybe, we'll be able to deliver. Let's take this a step at a time, though, and first find out who this James character might be. Who knows? Sometimes coincidences are just that, and it will turn out there's no connection whatsoever. Let's call your office and ask them to put together a list of all the antiques and art dealers and collectors in the Miami area that fit the bill."

Guy picked up the phone, dialed, and asked to speak to Ann Hagersack, Senior Criminal Investigator. "Ann, I need a list of all art and/or antiques dealers, and collectors, in the greater Miami area, with the first name of James. I will almost guarantee the list will be lengthy… but it's a place to start."

"Pardon me. Put her on hold for a second," Claire said.

"What? Hold for a minute, Ms. Hagersack, will you? What, Claire?"

"Not so fast. I think we can narrow the list considerably. But first, I need to go back and find an earlier letter in my group. Bear with me. It might be relevant here…." Pulling out the first few letters she'd reviewed, she scanned them at a fast pace, knowing exactly what she was looking for. In a short time, she put her fingers on it.

"Here it is. I found it. Think outside the box. We know David's employer was *male* because he makes references to *him* several times. And in his last letter, he indicated his employer was about his same age. Now in the letter I'm holding, David tells Joseph he always addresses people using their *last* name. It's a respect thing with him. So I'm thinking, we want a list of men with the *last* name of James—not the *first* name of James. Also, the list should include those in the business currently, or previously. And only those who are eighty years of age or older—based upon David's date of birth and our learning that his employer was about his same age. That should cut the list dramatically."

"That *will* cut the list dramatically!" He looked at her in disbelief, pleased beyond measure with her keen investigative mind. Clicking back to Ms. Hagersack, he gave her the amended request.

Claire retrieved the Miami-Dade County White Pages from the kitchen cupboard and quickly thumbed through its pages until she came to the last name of "James." She looked up at Guy in surprise. "There are only three-and-a-half columns of people with the last name of James in this county. Not as many as I thought there'd be. Once we narrow the list to men only, eighty years and older, current or former major art or antiques collectors or dealers in this area, I imagine the list will be quite short."

"One would think so," Guy said.

"If it's the right lead, it may be the only one we'll need." Claire silently trusted that the list of names provided would give them the critical information they so desperately desired. Once David's Miami employer could be identified, and located, he would have to be questioned about the disappearance and murder of David Posnick, alias David Post, and about the smuggling of stolen goods into the United States—something so suspiciously close to the information Roman had learned about their mysterious artifact that it would not leave her mind. Mere coincidence? Maybe. But she usually didn't believe in coincidences when it came right down to it.

And Robert's apparent deception and tampering with their artifact continued to haunt and preoccupy her daily thoughts, as well. Was it really possible that he had stolen the rare emerald eyes and maybe even the emeralds hidden inside? That would mean he was a thief, and that he intentionally lied to her and Guy about the value of the piece so that he could commit a crime. Until they found David Post's murderer, she would leave the question of Robert's theft on the back burner. Stealing was one thing, murder was another. If they had to turn Robert in to the police at some point on theft charges, she would do it, but it was certainly nothing she looked forward to. In fact, it would overwhelm her.

Guy clutched his hand-held recorder and dictated an update regarding the discovery of the name, "James," as Post's employer. As usual, his office would transcribe his dictation and the typed version would be added to the investigative file. Meticulous in his record-keeping, he knew from past prosecutorial experiences that a very detailed paper trail could make the difference between winning or losing a case. He and Claire had dictated comprehensive notes throughout the investigation, and the file folder was now thick with those transcriptions and other information, including the tape recordings and transcriptions of Joseph's incredible statement—an invaluable part of the collective casework.

In addition to the written compilation of their combined efforts in the investigation, both Claire and Guy had called their respective offices on an irregular basis to check in, presenting updates and new findings to management along the way, and reviewing messages received—making return calls as necessary from home.

The waiting game resurrected its ugly head, once again, as they yearned to see the names Ms. Hagersack would come up with—information that could make or break the case. Like an uninvited guest, anxiety arrived and took a seat. The game of waiting held little interest for either of them. They waited with bated breath, ready to act upon the information they would soon receive.

Roman came in from his day at the pool and announced his voracious hunger. He'd consumed a burger, fries and a soft drink at the beach bar for lunch, but now he needed *real* food. Since the time for dinner was rapidly approaching, they decided to drive to Carpaccio in the Bal Harbour shops to get a good meal. Hopefully the maître d', a longtime friend, would fit them in without a reservation.

They arrived and were seated without delay. Just as they ordered, Guy's cell phone rang.

"It's Ann Hagersack, Mr. Lombard. I have that list for you."

37

Friday morning

"ONE POSSIBILITY. *ONE*," Guy said. "Do you believe out of three *maybes* only one fits the bill, Claire? Two are much younger than the parameters I gave Ms. Hagersack to search, and only one worked with all of the variables we know about this Mr. James—a man by the name of *George...George James*. But he died of a heart attack seven months ago. He made it eighty-four years, and then died a few months ago. So it ends here? We identify the skeleton, but are not able to prosecute his murderer? We walk away and no justice results for the brutal killing of Joseph's brother? For David Posnick...Post? We just chalk it up to bad timing? The skeleton didn't surface in time to allow us to find George James and bring him to trial? That's it?" These questions had spun around in Guy's head after Ms. Hagersack's call at the restaurant last evening—throughout the dinner with Claire and Roman, when they drove Roman to the airport later on, and throughout Guy's restless night.

"Whoa, slow down, counselor. Let's not *assume* anything here. I know you were chomping at the bit to prosecute this man, but we need to be smart and think this through. First of all, we don't *know* that George James acted as the killer. I agree with you that he *might* well have committed the murder, but we don't know that for sure. We know David's employer was talking to another dealer when he overheard the conversation about smuggling. But we don't know the identity of this other dealer. Maybe *he*, or *she*, killed David Post, or arranged for the murder? Right?"

"Go on."

"You let me know last night that Ms. Hagersack told you George James left behind a widow, Evelyn James, living near Biscayne and 90th and you said she gave you her street address and phone number. Did she say anything else about George or Evelyn James?"

"Yeah. She said they involved themselves deeply in charitable work—they were well-respected members of the community and all that. Apparently Evelyn still volunteers her time and money to worthy causes."

"What else?"

"She gave me the name of the business George James owned—Rare Relics, Incorporated. That's it."

"Guy, 90th and Biscayne is in Miami Shores—the same area where David's remains turned up. Interesting, don't you think? I say we drop in on Evelyn James, this morning. We need to talk to her."

Immediately his interest in finding the truth concerning the demise of David Post rekindled. They jumped into his car and drove to Miami Shores. With traffic, it took a good half hour to make their way to the fancy suburb. Using a laminated street map, they found the specific address easily, and pulled up in front of a stately house surrounded by well-maintained grounds—a site typical of that upscale, residential area of Miami.

They walked up to the front door, and using the heavy brass knocker, Guy rapped. Without delay, the door opened slightly and the face of the middle-aged woman peered out. Upon reviewing the identifications proffered, and satisfying herself of their legitimacy, she opened the door a crack further. At this point, they could observe her neatly pressed black-and-white uniform.

"Yes?" the housekeeper asked.

"We're here to see Evelyn James," Guy said.

"She's expecting you?"

"No. But we would like to see her. Now." His voice appeared stern.

"She may not be ready to receive guests."

Guy's patience waned with each passing second. "Tell her we're here, Miss. She'll see us. It's urgent." His tone made his request sound like an order and it appeared abundantly clear he would not take "no" for an answer. She seemed almost afraid to disobey. Hesitating but a brief moment, she opened the door fully, allowing the two entrance to the dwelling. The nervous housekeeper then led the way to the living room, instructing Claire and Guy to have a seat and wait. She scurried off to inform Mrs. James of her visitors.

Claire's eyes skillfully scanned the room. It was exquisitely furnished with rare seventeenth-century French and other European antiques. Pricey pieces, she thought. Her husband must have done well in his lifetime. Quite well. She wondered how much of his business had been legitimate.

Muffled shouting could be heard coming from the upstairs area—presumably between the housekeeper and Evelyn James. Shortly thereafter, the housekeeper returned. "I'm afraid she's unable to see you now. She said you'll have to call back and schedule an appointment."

"We're not going anywhere," Claire said. "Not until she talks to us."

"She was emphatic about it. She will not see you now. You're going to have to leave." The fearful housekeeper was jittery, frequently looking over her shoulder as she spoke.

"Well, tell her we will do this the *easy* way or the *hard* way," Guy said. "If she doesn't speak with us *now*, she should expect a subpoena in her hands yet today, and she'll be in my office at eight tomorrow morning."

"But she instructed me to…."

"Go give her that message," Guy said.

Frazzled and near tears, the housekeeper left the room, staying away for several minutes.

The next thing they knew, a noticeably perturbed elderly woman marched brusquely into the room, the humbled housekeeper at her heels. The woman turned, and in a sharp tone ordered the housekeeper out. Eyes seething, she next focused her attention on Guy and Claire.

"I am Evelyn James. What is this all about?"

By no stretch of the imagination could Evelyn be described as a shy woman, and although diminutive in stature, the descriptor words feisty, aggressive and bombastic instantly came into Claire's mind. Evelyn sat with *perfect* posture on the edge of an oyster-white velveteen chair and glared at them—first one and then the other. Claire thought Evelyn should have come with a warning label: *Handle at Your Own Risk*, as everything about her portrayed hostility and signaled readiness for battle.

Close to eighty in years, she, like her house, had been well-maintained, and a fair amount of plastic surgery had given her the appearance of a much younger woman. Dressed in a shell-pink Chanel silk suit, and low-heeled pumps of the same color, she wore a *perfectly*-matched single strand of South Sea pearls around her neck—a costly piece of jewelry that accented nicely her tightly *perfect* face. She looked as if she'd just stepped out of a fashion magazine or off a movie set. The television show *Dynasty* came to mind. Her chin-length hair had naturally grayed to a striking icy white, and she pulled it back and off her face with an extra-wide black velvet headband. She reeked of wealth and the attitude of many who have lived a charmed life. Claire imagined she probably had a *perfectly* lovely face, when she wasn't so angry—if ever such a time existed.

Guy quickly assessed Mrs. James as a vain, self-centered, extremely dominant, arrogant, pretentious and pompous individual who would do or say anything to protect herself and her self-opinionated ways.

Claire and Guy introduced themselves.

"Let's get started," Evelyn said. "My time is valuable."

Guy ignored his rapidly growing annoyance with the woman; Claire wondered whether the overconfident and overbearing manner of Evelyn James was genuine or merely a pretense. Claire watched her closely.

"I'm a busy woman," Evelyn said. "*Extremely* busy. Get on with it. What is it you want from me? What is so important that it couldn't have waited?"

"We've been investigating the death of a man named David Post that occurred several decades ago, Mrs. James. His skeleton surfaced recently—buried not far from here, in Miami Shores. Maybe you heard about it on the news? The Medical Examiner has labeled it a homicide," Guy said.

"Yes, I heard the news. Who didn't? And I, like the other residents of this fine neighborhood, shuddered to hear that such a thing happened around here. But what on earth does *that* have to do with *me*? You are wasting my time, my valuable time." Her enraged eyes flitted around the room.

"We believe Mr. Post worked for your husband, George, Mrs. James, for a period of time before his murder," Claire said.

This revelation did not seem to ruffle her in the slightest. "Go on," she ordered. Acting wholly disinterested, she looked out through the picture window, as if following something happening on her front lawn. Claire's eyes did not leave her. Evelyn began to lick her lips, repeatedly and nervously.

"Do you remember the name David Post, Mrs. James?" Claire asked.

"Am I supposed to recall the name of every employee my late husband hired?"

"That was not my question, Mrs. James," Claire said. "I asked you if you remember the specific name, *David Post*? Do you, or do you not?"

"I don't recall. My husband may or may not have had an employee by that name."

"Would you have documentation from your husband's business that would identify his employees?" Claire persisted.

Evelyn did not respond.

"We have reason to believe," Guy said, "that your husband may have been involved in a smuggling ring while he owned and operated Rare Relics, Incorporated."

That was the final straw. Evelyn turned abruptly to face Guy, and leveled her gaze at him, a look of defiance, even awkward glee, in her eyes. "What did you say?"

"Specifically, Mrs. James, we believe George, with the help of some other local dealer or collector, may have colluded to import stolen goods into the U.S. And Mr. Post may have stumbled onto their plans."

"That's it! I've heard enough." Stiff-necked, Evelyn stood and pointed to the front door. "Get out of my house now!"

"Mrs. James, calm down please," Claire said. "We need answers to some questions."

"My husband was a good and honest man, and would never have engaged in illegal activities of any kind, and I will not allow you to disparage his reputation and memory. Get out! Leave this house!" She again pointed to the door.

They ignored her command.

"Do you remember a Mr. Post?" Claire asked, unwilling to be put off.

"Absolutely not. Now, get out!"

Evelyn still pointed to the door as the housekeeper poked her head into the battlefield. "Is everything all right in here, Mrs. James?"

"Rosa, show these people out. They're leaving." Evelyn James marched to the doorway and walked out into the hallway.

Claire and Guy stood and followed her.

"One more thing, Mrs. James," Claire said. "Do you recall any names of dealers or collectors your husband may have worked with back in the early to mid-1960's?"

No response came from Evelyn. Her eyes darted downward, to the left, and then to the right. She licked her lips again.

Mrs. James, Guy and Claire reached the front door, held open by a shaking Rosa. Evelyn started to mount the large staircase near the entrance, holding on to the banister as she climbed.

Claire paused, and turned toward Evelyn, who for the first time looked worn-out and not as sure of herself as earlier.

Stopping dead in her tracks, she turned to face Claire. As their eyes met, she muttered something inaudible under her breath.

"Sorry. I missed that," Claire said.

"David Post. I guess I do recall a David Post…who worked for George. The name, anyway."

"What about dealers or collectors your husband did business with back then? Anyone special you remember?"

"He always worked alone. He never did business with other dealers…except for…there was one antiques dealer…he had some dealings with him. But I don't even recall his name."

"Please try. It's important."

"I don't remember…maybe it was Roger. Yes, it was Roger."

"Did you say Roger? Do you recall his last name?"

"No, I do not. And maybe it wasn't Roger, but…Robert. One or the other. I can't say for certain. And I don't recall his last name."

Evelyn again faced the stairs, and began to climb. With these disclosures, she hoped to set them on the trail of someone else, so they'd leave her alone. Maybe now, they'd go away and find this Roger person to question, instead of her. In any case, she had nothing to do with her husband's trade. *His* career had not involved *her*, and he rarely, if ever, discussed his business with her. The money had always been good and she'd never questioned any part of it, at least not openly. So she could be of no real help to these persistent enforcement people. And she never *knew* this David Post…but his name rang a distant bell. He had worked for her husband long ago.

As Guy stepped out the door, Claire pursued one final question. "Could Robert's last name have been…Holden?"

38

CLAIRE FOUGHT VALIANTLY to hold her own in the dark world of uncertainty in which she found herself. Stunned and haunted by the answer Evelyn James had given to her last question, she found herself fighting off the fierce combatants of suspicion and doubt, and, unprepared for battle, she was losing ground.

She hated herself for thinking of Robert as a villain. Things she had been absolutely certain about her entire life she was now questioning. She reached down deep within her core to keep focused and maintain a clear mind, to stay on track. With sinking thoughts tumbling all around her, she centered her energy directly on Robert and concentrated.

Robert was a friend, a "*family*" member, and someone who had always called her "*child*." He had spent a lifetime building and running a world-renowned antiques business. High ethics and morals defined him, and he was a man of honor and respect. The thought that he was anything less seemed incongruous. How could Robert not be the superhero she had always thought him to be? She swallowed hard, and warred against the conflicting emotions that built within her, trying desperately to bypass the flood of doubts seeking refuge in her mind.

How could Robert be involved in this murder investigation? Was it possible that Robert was a liar…a smuggler…a thief? A schemer…and potentially even a murderer? It did not compute. Something seemed categorically wrong. There was a malfunction in the circuit, a breakdown in the system, a snag in the scenario. Could she, and her father, too, have been so wrong about him all these years?

Evidence was mounting and pointing in his direction, and there seemed to be no way around it. Robert had unwaveringly told her the artifact had *nominal worth*, and was only a *replica* of an authentic Aztec idol. Yet Roman had proved it to be a *priceless* and *authentic* piece of Aztec history. And the artifact had been tampered with while in Robert's possession. No doubt about that. And now they discover that Robert did business with George James—David Post's employer. Evelyn James had clearly remembered, when asked the final question, and identified the man her husband had done business with as, "Robert Holden," and then she'd repeated his full name three times… "Robert Holden, Robert Holden, Robert Holden." George James had definitely been dirty. Was Robert, too? No, she argued with herself. Robert would not knowingly be involved in these things…there had to be another explanation…there simply had to be.

Continuing to fight her thoughts, she suddenly realized that if the murder of David Post and the artifact they found in the Caribbean cave were connected to the same incredible tale of smuggling and greed, and if Robert was involved with George James as a buyer of the stolen, smuggled artifacts, then Robert most certainly recognized the artifact immediately when he saw it at their condo, and he would have had intimate knowledge of the substituted emerald eyes and what lay concealed within the piece. That could explain his strange behavior that day.

Pulling into the underground parking space at their home, she spoke for the first time. "It's time to take a statement from Robert Holden."

"We have no other choice, sweetheart," Guy said. "It's not looking good for him." He said nothing more.

When they reached the door of their condo, Claire turned and looked at Guy. "You take the statement from Robert. It's best if I'm not there. And be gentle with him, please. He's an old man, and my parents mentioned he hasn't been looking well lately. Go easy during the questioning, if doable, and remember, we have no concrete evidence against him at this time—it's all circumstantial. There may well be plausible explanations for all of it." As she spoke, another possibility hit her squarely between the eyes. What if *no* legitimate answers cropped up to explain away the compiling issues seeming to finger Robert? She felt deeply saddened by what was unfolding.

"I'll do my best, but I have a job to do, or should I say, *we* have a job to do. Professional I will be, as always, and you have my word that I'll postpone the remainder of the statement anytime Robert indicates he's not feeling well. But one thing's for sure. Robert Holden needs to be questioned right away."

"I know this will work out in his favor, somehow, in the end. I refuse to believe he's involved in anything untoward. It's my job to read people and I read them like a book. Robert is not a criminal. He is not!"

Guy dropped Claire off at her office to catch up on other work, and drove straight to Robert's place of business. He preferred to talk with him at work, and not at his home, if possible, and as luck would have it, he found Robert chatting animatedly with a client when he entered the lobby. "Good morning, Robert," he stated.

"What a surprise," Robert said. Looking startled, he wondered what Gaston Lombard would be doing there during business hours—especially since the artifact had already been picked up. "Have a seat. I'm just finishing up with a customer and I'll be with you shortly."

"Take your time, Robert. I'm in no rush." Picking up the *Miami Herald* from a side table, he strolled over to an overstuffed red leather chair in the lobby and took a seat. Rarely did he enjoy the simple pleasure of reading the daily newspaper, and he took full advantage of the opportunity. About ten minutes later, the client meeting concluded, and Robert showed his customer to the door. He approached Guy with a puzzled look on his face and extended his hand to the counselor, giving him his full attention. "To what do I owe this unexpected pleasure?"

"I'm afraid it's not a pleasure call." He stood to face Robert. "I'm here today in my official capacity, to question you regarding the smuggling of stolen artifacts, and the murder of one David Crawford Post, around forty years ago."

Robert swallowed with difficulty, all color draining from his face. "What? Why? Who? Do I need a lawyer?"

"If you would prefer to have your attorney present during questioning, that is certainly your right. I'll wait here while you call him."

"I think it best under the circumstances."

Guy sat back down as Robert stepped into his office to make the call. Minutes later, Robert returned to the lobby and informed Guy his attorney had agreed to drive over, and had instructed him not to say another word until his arrival.

"There must be a terrible mistake here," Robert said, under his breath, as he walked over to the sign on the door and flipped it from "Open" to "Closed." Then he took a seat in the lobby, close to Guy, where together they sat in painfully awkward silence for the twenty-five minutes it took Grant Thompson to drive over and walk through the doorway. At one point, Robert turned to study Guy, as if waiting for him to burst into laughter and tell him it was all a big joke. Guy glanced over at Robert, too, from time to time, and noticed that color did not seem to be returning to his face, and, if anything, his complexion seemed to be turning an odd grayish color.

When Attorney Thompson arrived, he extended his hand, and he and Guy exchanged introductions and business cards.

"I presume you will be representing Mr. Holden in this matter, Mr. Thompson?"

"I represent him in all his business dealings, Mr. Lombard, so I would say, yes, at this point. But if it becomes apparent that he's in need of the assistance of a different kind of attorney, I'll so advise him at that time. Fair enough?" Mr. Thompson displayed a cool and self-important manner in his voice, signaling to Guy early on that the taking of Robert's statement may not be quick and easy. "We'll do this by the book."

"I would conduct it no other way, Mr. Thompson," Guy said. "Do you have a room, Mr. Holden, where the three of us can talk?" He referred to Robert as, "Mr. Holden," to send the immediate and unclouded signal to Mr. Thompson, and to Robert, that he meant business. From this point on, Guy's serious demeanor did not flinch, and Robert lost all hope that a charade was being carried out on him.

"Yes, of course, follow me. I'd like to get this cleared up as soon as possible, you understand," Robert said. He led them to a back conference room. Guy closed the door behind them, and took a seat at one end of the long table. Clearly a power move, it sent the unmistakable message that he was in charge. "Do you have any objection to my tape recording the statement, Mr. Thompson? Of course, a copy of the tape, or the written transcript—should we elect to transcribe it—will be provided to you upon request."

"No objection, Mr. Lombard. And I'm requesting a copy of the tape now, and expect one delivered to my office within two days of today's date. I am also requesting a copy of the transcript, now, should you opt to transcribe it."

"Very well, Mr. Thompson." Guy turned the recorder on, stated the date, time and place of the statement, indicated his name and position, and the reason for the statement. Next he asked both Mr. Thompson and Robert Holden to each, separately, identify himself for the record, swore Robert in, and read him his rights, including the Miranda Warning. He then asked Robert to state for the record whether he was giving the statement voluntarily, as opposed to being subpoenaed, and Robert answered in the affirmative. Next he obtained basic personal information from Robert Holden, including: home and business addresses, phone numbers for each location, date of birth, place of birth, education completed, and employment history. Once that was out of the way, the substantive questioning began.

Robert answered every question his attorney did not object to in a dignified manner, and even tried to answer the ones he did object to—despite Mr. Thompson's clarification, on the record, that he had instructed his client not to answer certain questions, but against his advice his client had elected to answer them anyway.

Guy conducted a detailed and meticulously thorough examination—an obvious pro, leaving no stone unturned. And Robert held up admirably, stating repeatedly, that he had "nothing to hide."

While he admitted, several times, that he and his firm had done a good amount of business with George James over the years, he vehemently denied any involvement in the smuggling of stolen goods, antiques, artifacts, or gemstones, and fiercely rejected the premise that he knew this Mr. Post had been murdered, and that he had had any involvement whatsoever in the killing. He admitted, upon further reflection, to remotely remembering an employee of James' by the name of David, from long ago, but it ended there. He claimed to recall nothing further about the man.

Sitting poised and unflustered throughout the statement, Robert added, for the record, "I feel utterly shocked, and saddened beyond belief, to be questioned in connection with this matter, as I've always held myself to the highest of standards and ethics throughout my lifetime—both in business and my personal life." And with respect to the artifact, Robert denied with vigor any tampering or theft of emeralds, repeating ad nauseam that he believed the item to be a "replica having only nominal value." He stuck to his story like glue and would not waver from his position.

Either Robert played a good game of bluff, skillful in circumventing all attempts to link him to any crime, or he told the truth. But for now, all eyes continued to focus on him, and all fingers continued to point in his direction.

Concluding the statement, Guy promised to get a copy of the tape to Mr. Thompson posthaste, and thanked them both for their time. "I'll get back to you, Mr. Thompson, in the very near future," Guy said. He then looked at Robert. "Until this case is resolved, I'm afraid I must ask you not to leave the state."

"I have no reason to run, Mr. Lombard. Where would I go?" He sat too still and too quiet—eerily like the eye of a hurricane. "This is all a misunderstanding, a grandiose mistake of some kind. Talk to Claire. She knows me as well as anyone. She *knows* I'd never do the things I'm being questioned about. Talk to her."

Driving home, Guy felt exasperated, but he could not identify why he felt the way he did. Something gnawed at him. He liked Robert, and hated putting him through this ordeal if he were innocent. Being questioned or suspected of wrongdoing could put an awful stress on a blameless person, and he would not want to be responsible for exacerbating any health concerns that Robert may be dealing with. On the other hand, he began to recall the apparent evidence stacking up against him, piece by piece, and his self-questioning began to dwindle. With Claire's help, he would get to the truth, remaining wholly unbiased and impartial throughout the investigation. Robert would be presumed innocent until proven guilty. That was a guarantee of his Constitutional rights. Yet something continued to bother Guy. What was he missing? What could it be?

NEXT ON the agenda would be a search of Robert's business and residence. Arriving home, Guy summarized the statement for Claire, and asked for her help in preparing the probable cause affidavit required to obtain a search warrant from the court. Together they walked to the den, and Guy situated himself in front of the computer. Claire pulled up a chair beside him and sat down.

They would need to present a comprehensive chronology of all of the information they had obtained, to date, and convince a judge to consent to the searches and sign the warrant. Some judges could be very persnickety when it came to signing search warrants, as Guy well knew. And the following morning, Saturday, it would be the luck of the draw as to which judge would be assigned to hear the matter.

If Guy could convince the sitting judge to sign, based upon the written documentation submitted and his oral argument, then he and his staff, assisted by the local police, and Claire, would search both

Robert's place of business and his residence—simultaneously, tomorrow afternoon, before incriminating evidence could be hidden, removed, destroyed or conveniently lost. Timing would be critical. Timing would be everything.

39

SECRETLY, GUY HOPED nothing would show up at either search to implicate Robert in criminal activity. But the evidence obtained, so far, clearly warranted the action, even though, admittedly, it appeared circumstantial in nature. Assuming the warrant would be issued, Guy would head the search of Robert's office, and Claire the search of Robert's homestead.

"I have trouble believing we've reached this point. It's a miserable time in my life," Claire said.

They worked long and hard on the affidavit, and each reviewed the end product for accuracy, content and clarity.

"It's all here, counselor, and it paints a pretty bleak picture for Robert, I'm afraid. We did an excellent job establishing probable cause of a crime being committed—but that's not the problem here. There must be something we're overlooking," she said.

"Convince me," Guy said.

Claire went out on the balcony, to think. Her burden was heavy, the feeling of tension palpable. They'd been on the case for close to a month now, and actually they had accomplished a lot—putting a name on the skeleton—something most thought an unattainable feat to accomplish—and, now, they seemed close to putting a name on the murderer. But she feared LuVasse would pull her off the case soon, and ask her to return to her regular caseload, because it seemed to be taking too long. She couldn't walk away. She wouldn't abandon the investigation. Not now. Not when it appeared they had come the closest ever to identifying the perpetrator. And moreover, Robert Holden—a man she called a friend—had startlingly surfaced as the prime suspect. How could this be happening? They needed to solve this brutal killing of David Post without delay. If Robert could be exonerated, they had to help him, and find the real murderer. Thoughts of how strangely Robert had acted the last time they saw him again occupied her mind, making her uneasy. What could possibly be happening in Robert's life that would otherwise explain his recent behavior? Was he ill? *If you seek the truth, you will find it!* From afar, the familiar words penetrated her being.

Bright and early the next morning, Guy showered and dressed in a double-breasted black suit, a heavily-starched white pima cotton shirt, a conservative black and burgundy striped tie, and black shoes—always black shoes. This was his customary look whenever he appeared in a courtroom setting. Today he appeared particularly debonair and in character for his performance in the court of justice. He picked up his briefcase containing the warrant affidavit, and kissed Claire goodbye. "I'm off. Wish me luck. I'll call to let you know what happened as soon as I step out of the courtroom."

Driving to the courthouse, Guy thought about Claire. He loved her to the depths of his being, and could see that this case was shaking her from her usual state of unfailing composure. First, the threats she had endured from the minute her name had been announced on the news broadcasts as being an investigator on the case, and, now, her lifetime friend Robert appeared to be the only live suspect involved in the felony murder investigation. Guy wanted to protect her, and to marry her. The investigation had been so all-encompassing and draining that the right time to ask her the question had simply not presented itself. What would her answer be? If she didn't want to commit, would it end their relationship? He wanted to legitimize the love they shared, and he hoped she felt the same way.

His thoughts turned to Robert. He wondered how this could possibly turn out well for him, for too much was pulling them in his direction. The artifact had definitely been altered while in his possession, for a purpose he thought obvious after hearing Professor Darlington's account—thievery; Robert had clearly lied about its value—something an antiquities dealer with any experience couldn't have missed, according to Roman; as of late, Robert seemed to be acting vastly different from his norm for some reason; he had associated with George James—the employer of David Post; and George James had colluded with another art or antiques dealer to smuggle stolen goods into the country. Also, David Post had overheard George James talking to this other dealer about the illegal activities of the smuggling ring, and David had disappeared shortly thereafter, never to be heard from again until his remains had recently come to light in Miami Shores—not far from the James' residence. The puzzle pieces seemed to fall neatly into place and paint a rather clear picture. Or did they? He needed more.

Things could begin to move quickly from this point forward, Guy's experience told him.

Regrettably for Guy, he did not luck out on the judge assignment that morning and ended up with Judge June Wicklund—a judge who had the reputation of rarely, if ever, consenting to searches. Confident that he and Claire had more than established probable cause in their written materials, Guy proceeded to orally argue the same facts before Judge Wicklund in an artful and eloquent manner, attempting desperately to convince her to affix her John Hancock on the warrant. He stressed that based upon a complete review of all of the information set forth in the affidavit, and in the courtroom that day, one could only conclude that a clear and convincing basis for probable cause of the existence of a crime involving Robert Holden did exist, and the warrant should be signed and executed immediately.

Judge Wicklund emerged duly impressed with his presentation, after reviewing the supporting affidavit, page by page, paragraph by paragraph, and line by line, as he spoke—asking probing questions, articulately formulated, as they came to her along the way. In the end, she announced that he had established probable cause to her satisfaction, and she signed the warrant without further ado. The judge had a final comment for Guy. "Mr. Lombard, I only wish all search warrant affidavits coming before me would be this well documented and presented. It would make my job much easier. I must compliment your exemplary work."

"Thank you, Your Honor."

Quite pleased she had signed the warrant, he appeared genuinely as impressed with her professional skills as she'd been with his. In all fairness, he thought her questions had demonstrated extreme competence, insight, and ability to rule from the bench, despite her reputation for being tough and at times unreasonable. He knew and she knew, from past experiences, that searching someone's home or place of business could be a traumatic and horribly disruptive event—for the target of the search, and others involved, and should be conducted only, and solely, in cases where strong evidence presented itself and warranted such dramatic measures.

Both searches would occur that afternoon. He'd make the necessary arrangements at once.

AVARICIOUSLY LOOKING over the emeralds, counting and recounting them one by one took time, especially with gloved hands. Returning the gemstones to their secure hiding place would keep them safe until this whole thing blew over. And once all the smoke had cleared, a move could be made to have the lovely green stones cut, polished and finally sold in lots. Oh, the money they would bring! To be rich at last—filthy rich! And to get away with it. A wicked smile appeared. Greed had destroyed a good soul.

GUY TELEPHONED Claire on the way to his office. "We got it, my beauty. The judge signed the warrant, and we're going in this afternoon. I'll arrange a meeting at my office at 11:30 this morning and I'll need you to be there."

"Congratulations are in order, I guess, but it's a thorny victory for both of us. I'll be there. I assume we'll be going over the logistics for the searches?"

"Yeah. I want to make sure everyone is on the same page and crystal clear on each particular role before we leave. It's extremely important. See you soon." He hung up and phoned the Miami-Dade Police Department. As it was the weekend, Sergeant Massey would not be there. Without delay, the dispatcher connected Guy to the supervising officer in charge. Guy identified himself, explained the situation, and requested several officers to assist in the afternoon searches, informing him he planned to hold a meeting at 11:30 sharp in the main conference room at his office to go over search procedures, and he wanted to see all assisting officers in attendance.

The supervisor handpicked eight of his best men and women to assist in the searches—four for each location—and sent them over to the State Attorney's Office for the meeting. The group gathered, and at precisely half-past eleven Guy started his presentation, making it clear from the outset that both sites must be searched at precisely the same time, thereby eliminating any chance of a "heads up" warning from one location to the other—the element of surprise then working to their benefit at both places. He'd also called in four staff members from his office to assist, in addition to him and Claire—for a total of fourteen people, or seven at each location.

Without delay, he summarized the case and briefed the group on what they sought, including, but not limited to: incriminating documentation involving the smuggling of pieces of art or antiquities or gemstones into the U.S.—Aztec artifacts, or other pieces—and any mention of David Post, or George James. He also stressed the need to look for the raw emeralds.

Next came the coordination and planning of the operation, and he divided the group into two sections—one to search the business, headed up by Guy, and the other to search the personal residence, directed by Claire. He then assigned one person from each group to record everyone present at the location searched, checking picture identifications and to take photographs; a second to assign a number to each area/item searched, such as desks, file cabinets, closets, and briefcases, and to record on a log sheet each item seized, indicating the location found.

He instructed the remaining four from each group to concentrate exclusively on searching the assigned location, from top to bottom, using a fine-tooth comb approach, being incisive and thorough in their efforts. Guy emphasized that either he or Claire would call the shots, and all questions should be addressed to whomever led their particular group. They would be in constant contact with each other on cell phones to cover any problems or issues arising that afternoon.

Guy repeated the procedure for the searches and emphasized that they must be carried out in the prescribed orderly fashion, with no exceptions: Individuals present identified, and names recorded; numbers assigned and posted throughout search areas; a floor plan sketched to indicate numbers assigned to each area and item; photographs taken of each room and area to be searched (making certain the assigned number would be visible in all photos); search conducted, with items seized placed in clear plastic evidence bags, clearly marked to identify exact location found; each seized item to be recorded on log sheets. No wavering from this regimen, on any point, would be acceptable.

He answered all questions posed by the searchers to the best of his ability, and made a special point to thank the participating police officers for contributing their vast experience to assist with the searches. "We never know, for sure, what we're going to walk into in any given situation," Guy said. "So we'll have to play some things by ear once we get there. But please, follow the direction of your leader at all times. Oh, and another thing, I included Robert Holden's vehicles in the search warrant, so we must also search his 2005 navy Volvo sedan, and his white Chevy panel truck. I'm assuming the delivery truck will be in the front business parking lot or back behind the building, but the Volvo could be at either location."

Next he turned his attention to the people from his office. "We'll need corrugated boxes with lids, masking tape, black markers, legal pads, pens, cameras and film, plastic evidence bags, staplers, Post-It notes, and anything else you can think of I'm forgetting to mention. You know the drill."

He glanced at this watch. "We'll leave at one o'clock sharp, utilizing two of our vans, half in one, and half in the other. Let's assemble downstairs in our garage a few minutes before one. I'd suggest you grab a quick sandwich across the street before we head out. Could be a long afternoon."

By five to one, the vans were loaded with all of the supplies, and at exactly one, the searchers piled into the vehicles, geared up to begin the work. Thirty minutes later, Guy and his team drove into the parking lot at Holden and Hartmann Antiques and Rare Collectibles and parked at the far end, where they waited for a call from Claire. Guy could see the navy Volvo parked out front and surmised Robert would be inside. Five minutes later, Claire called Guy and they confirmed to each other that they were in place and ready to enter the respective premises.

Simultaneously, Guy and his crew stormed through the front door of Robert's place of business, and Claire and her team entered Robert's personal residence, warrants in hand. Guy grabbed keys from Robert's desk and ordered two men to search the vehicles without delay.

Robert sat at a work table, consulting with a customer, when the searchers made their collaborative entrance. His entire body jolted, and stiffened, as the group barged in. "What on earth's going on here?" he roared.

"We have a search warrant signed by Judge June Wicklund, Mr. Holden," Guy said. He held up the document for Robert's perusal. "This gives us court authority to search your property now. We had no choice."

"*What*?" Robert asked. Visibly shaken, Robert asked his client to leave, promising he'd call her soon, and walked to his phone to dial his attorney. "Mr. Thompson, please.... I don't care if he's in a meeting. Interrupt him! It's an emergency."

Guy noted an anger he had not heard before in Robert's tone.

40

"MR. THOMPSON, MR. Lombard has returned with some other people to search my premises. Must I allow this?…Yes, they showed me a warrant…. I understand…. Yes, I understand…. Thank you." During the conversation, Robert's shocked and furious demeanor changed to quiet and morose. He hung the phone up, slowly, a pensive look on his bothered face. Instantly, the phone begin to ring. "Mind if I get this?" Robert asked.

"Go ahead," Guy said.

It was his wife, Mae, stammering through heavy tears. "Robert, Claire Caswell's here, and police are here, and some people from the State Attorney's office, and they have what they're calling a search warrant. They're looking everywhere, through everything in our home. What could they be looking for? What's going on? This is dreadful."

"I'll be right there, dear, and explain everything to you. I love you. We'll get through this. Make yourself a cup of tea, and sit down. Stay out of their way. I'll be home shortly. Don't worry about a thing."

Robert had summoned all the strength within him to sound calm and soothe his wife's concerns. Slumping into a chair, he held his head in his hands, rubbing his temples. Pulsing pain riveted through his head and it felt as if it might split apart. He reached into his pocket, pulled out a capsule, and swallowed it. Oh, how he longed to return to the peace and order of his once-simple life.

After a few minutes had passed, he composed himself sufficiently to approach Guy. "Mr. Lombard, I need to go home and be with my Mae. She's very upset and I'm terribly concerned about her. I'll be there, if you need me. I hope you understand. You continue with whatever you need to do here, and call me at home when you're finished. I'll drive back to lock up. And by the way, you won't find anything to implicate me in any wrongdoing, in either place." He shook Guy's hand, and looked at him with somber and defeated eyes. Guy did not respond. "Believe me. You'll find nothing inappropriate," Robert said. "We are honest people here."

DRIVING HOME, Robert's mind shifted into overdrive. If only he could find a way out of this nightmare. He had other things to take care of, and this presented a major inconvenience to say the least.

Arriving at his home, he immediately cornered Claire.

"Child, what's going on here? I'm in the middle of something I can't understand, or explain. It's like being thrown into a bad dream against my will, and I'm unable to wake up. Child, I never expected *you* to do this to me. I thought I could always count on you to support me. Please, tell me why."

"Robert, this is one of the hardest things I've ever had to do. I believe you when you say you're not guilty of the allegations. But the evidence…. Well, I'm hoping to help prove your innocence real soon. I'm sorry for this invasion of your privacy. We had no alternative."

A bullet would have been easier to take than the look he shot her way before turning his attention back to Mae. It ripped at Claire's insides.

The searches lasted most of the afternoon, and Robert's residence, and vehicles, failed to turn up any evidence of smuggling, the emeralds, or anything else incriminating. And not until close to the end of the search of his business did one of the State Attorney's office staff, Thomas McGinty, begin looking through the lobby area. When he unzipped the seat cushion of the overstuffed red leather chair, and began groping around on top of its foam insert, his fingers felt a small piece of fabric, and when he tugged at it, a small velveteen pouch appeared. When he poured out the contents of the small bag onto a sheet of white paper, he realized at once what he'd found.

Emeralds. Seven of them. Large-sized, uncut, green emeralds.

McGinty paused for a time, mesmerized by the moment. Feeling his way back atop the foam insert, he located a fairly long and deep slash in the foam, and delved inside. He pulled out three additional pouches—each containing exactly seven more uncut emeralds—for a total of twenty-eight, and a fifth pouch containing only two gemstones, apparently still emeralds, but very different in appearance from the others, these being flat-backed with smooth, curved tops.

Once the rough emeralds could be cut into highly-prized retail shapes, depending on the precise color, brilliance and size, McGinty knew they would command an enormous sum of money—either illegally in black market trade, or legally to legitimate jewelers, as there would be no way to detect the past of the stones.

"Mr. Lombard, I think you'd better come over here," McGinty called out, a sense of urgency present in his voice.

Guy approached McGinty to see him staring fixedly at the floor, at some piles of dark-greenish stones on sheets of paper—a pouch near each grouping.

"I found these hidden in the chair cushion, sir. Good hiding place, wouldn't you agree? I almost missed them."

"Superb work, McGinty. *Superb*. How many stones did you find?"

"Well, there are twenty-eight of the rough ones, and then two of these odd-shaped ones." He pointed them out to Guy.

Slipping on evidence-handling gloves, Guy turned the two *odd-shaped* gemstones over with his fingers. With a memory like a steel trap, he recalled the exact words of Professor Darlington, "*Remark-*

ably, even the eyes of the statues had been replaced with unusual cuts of the green stones." As Guy examined them closer, he had no doubt that they were the brilliant, magical eyes from the artifact he and Claire had discovered in the Caribbean tunnel system—the eyes that had so mysteriously changed after Robert examined the piece.

Instantly, Guy realized that Robert had also stolen the emeralds stuffed within the relic's cavity. Now, no question remained that Robert's deception was deliberate. He knew exactly what the relic was, and he was well aware of the value of its cabochon eyes and hidden contents, and he'd immediately planned to deceive them and grab the emeralds for his own purposes. He had motive to substitute the eyes with similar color stones, as well as take the raw emeralds stashed inside—sheer, unadulterated love of money—the root of all evil. And he had opportunity, as they had so innocently let him take the artifact away for *appraisal* purposes. He'd lied to them and duped them, all to satisfy his own selfish desire for extreme wealth.

"I know what these are," Guy said. "You didn't touch the emeralds with your bare hands, did you, McGinty?"

"No sir. Just poured them out onto the sheets of paper. And I'm wearing gloves, of course." He waved his gloved hands in the air for Guy to see.

"Good, McGinty. Photograph each grouping of stones beside the pouch it came out of, then return the gems to the appropriate pouch and put each one into a separate plastic evidence bag. Get a log number for each bag and make sure each one is entered on the log sheet correctly. When you've finished all that, bring them to me."

Once McGinty had completed the directives, he brought the bagged stones to Guy, who in turn asked the lead police officer to have the gemstones dusted for prints, appraised for value by a reputable jeweler—to be used at trial—and then delivered to the evidence locker at headquarters for safekeeping. He verified with the staffer doing the logging that she had properly charted the total number of raw emeralds seized, as well as the number of stones in each individual pouch.

The search of the business wound down with nothing further confiscated, except for several records confirming past business dealings with George James.

Guy hailed the remaining police officers. "As soon as we return to my office, I'd like two of you to go over to Mr. Robert Holden's residence and arrest him. Bring him in on a charge of possession of stolen property, for now. Other charges may be added later. And do this as easily as possible. No big scene. Do not be rough with him, and that's an order. Treat him with all the dignity you can muster." He provided them with the address.

That gnawing feeling, the same one he'd experienced before, started to eat away at his stomach, but he didn't know why. Punching Claire's number into his cell phone, he informed her of the staggering discovery.

WITHIN THE hour, a squad car pulled up to the residence of Robert Holden and the officers walked to his front door and rang the bell.

The search had ended at that location an hour and a half earlier, and a seemingly bewildered Robert and Mae sat huddled together on a swinging bench on the back porch. Robert had his arm centered squarely around Mae's shoulders, and he was squeezing her close to him and trying to reassure her that the worst was behind them, when they heard the sound of the doorbell. Robert got up to answer it, and Mae trailed behind.

At the door stood two uniformed police officers, and Robert and Mae could see the squad car with its red lights flashing parked on the street. Neighbors had already started to gather, craning their necks to see what excitement had found its way onto their lonely block—into their quiet neighborhood—a place where any event, no matter how insignificant, all too often became monumental news and fodder for the community gossip train. But by the looks of it, this incident seemed to actually *qualify* as legitimate, big news. It appeared to *truly* fit the grisly requirements of gossip worthy of spreading. It was disgraceful, dishonorable, humiliating and outrageous—and all in epic proportions, certainly providing the interfering and meddlesome people with much to chat about for months to come.

One officer asked, "Robert Holden?"

"Yes, that's me," Robert replied.

"You are under arrest on the charge of possession of stolen property. We have to take you in—to the stationhouse."

"No!" Robert said. "What *stolen* property? What are you talking about?"

"All that will be explained when you get there."

"Oh, Robert. No!" Mae said.

The second officer looked Robert in the eyes, and recited the Miranda Warning: "'You have the right to remain silent. Anything you say can and will be used against you in a court of law. You have the right to speak to an attorney, and to have an attorney present during any questioning. If you cannot afford a lawyer, one will be provided for you at government expense.' Do you understand the rights I have just read to you, Mr. Holden?"

"Yes, of course. But *stolen property*? I've never stolen anything in my life. You are wrong! Dead wrong!"

Spinning Robert around, each officer grabbed one of his arms to pull behind his back. Handcuffs were snapped firmly in place around his rather thin wrists and tightened until they were uncomfortable. Then the officers prodded the befuddled arrestee along the walkway toward the squad car, amidst his continual protests of innocence.

Peripheral vision allowed Robert to see the curious neighborhood children and their parents gawking at him from all vantage points, like he had suddenly become the leopard man at the circus. He felt great shame.

One cruel young boy yelled out to him. "Way to go, old man!" The mean-spirited comment triggered contagious laughter amongst the other youngsters, and the painful feeling of having done something disgraceful or improper cut through Robert like a knife. Looking backwards as they led him away, Robert saw his wife sobbing, an overwhelmingly heartbroken expression on her aging face, her body writhing. And this hurt him beyond measure—even more than the personal humiliation he felt at that moment, if possible.

"Mae, darling, I'll be home soon. I promise." Trying desperately to sound upbeat, he could not veil the quivering in his voice. "This will all get straightened out. It's just an error…a horrible mistake. Call my attorney and have him contact me at the jail. And call Harry."

As the police pushed him into the backseat of the car, Robert felt his heart beating violently and erratically within his chest cavity.

Mae watched Robert until he was gone from sight, and then, as fast as her legs would carry her, she ran back into the house to call Grant Thompson. Harnessing all inner strength, she forced her wails into whimpers, picked up the phone, and dialed his number. Her now raspy voice sounded weak, and her body trembled, but she would hold it together long enough to get through the call. She would be strong. When he came on the line, she blurted out that Robert had been arrested, and quickly filled him in on the details of the afternoon to the best of her ability, breaking down several times throughout the accounting, but each time pulling herself together in order to continue. She would help her husband through this crisis. He needed her now, more than ever.

"Go to the jail, Grant. See him. Talk to him. I beg you."

Strangely, when she finished her appeal, an unmistakable feeling of calm and sense of relief encompassed her being. She would be her husband's pillar of strength—his rock—as he'd always been for her. In this case, his life may depend on it. And whatever happened, they'd get through it together. Suddenly, she felt no fear at all.

"I'm on my way, Mae."

"Thank you, Grant. Something's wrong with all of this. We both *know* my Robert would never break the law. Please, help him. He's not feeling well these days, and this could be too much for him. We've got to get him out of there and bring him home…. He'll not last long locked up."

"I'll do everything within my power, Mae." He hung up and called Gaston Lombard to learn the details regarding the afternoon searches and the arrest of his client.

Next Mae dialed Robert's business partner, Harry Hartmann, to relay to him the events of the day and let him know that Robert was sitting in jail. He had not been present at the business during the search, and Robert had not been able to reach him when he'd tried throughout the afternoon, so she seriously doubted he was aware of any of it. Thankfully, he answered the phone, and listened intently as she filled him in on every detail.

His voice indicated no signs of nervousness, anger or any other emotion. He remained calm and serene. "Don't lose sleep over it, Mae. It will work out. Things have a way of working themselves out. Always do."

41

A THOUSAND THOUGHTS trickled through Mae's mind. Something did not add up. Her husband would not steal anything. It was out of the question. After fifty-four years of marriage, of this she remained solidly sure. She would stake her life on it. Getting down on her knees, she folded her hands, bowed her head, and prayed silently. Her unwavering faith had sustained her throughout her lifetime—in harrowing days and in regular days—and her all-powerful Maker would not forsake her now. Of this, she was also certain.

ROBERT WAS driven to the jailhouse, ordered to strip and put on an orange jumpsuit, photographed, fingerprinted, and led to a cell like a common criminal. He sat down on a cold concrete bench in one corner of the six-by-ten chamber, and wept. "You've all made a mistake. I'm *innocent*," he wailed. But his cries fell upon deaf ears. He'd never been arrested in his lifetime, and he ached with trepidation, whimpering softly, feeling painfully alone, wondering how he'd ended up in this ghastly plight. Just then, a sharp flash of pain lashed through his body. Not making a sound, he doubled over in agony, suffering severely.

A guard brought him a tray holding dinner, but he could not eat. He had no appetite. He asked for hot tea to stem his chills. Instead, they threw him a tattered blanket. Sitting slumped on the floor, the threadbare wool wrap around his shoulders, he envisioned the worst, and looked strangely pathetic. He'd heard stories of people being railroaded by the law, and now it seemed to be happening to him. Presumed guilty before a trial, the unbelievable appeared unstoppable. Teetering on the edge of his future, as weak as a kitten, treated with no respect or dignity, he realized in a grim and somber moment that he had no control whatsoever over what would happen next.

Fifty minutes passed before Attorney Thompson arrived to see him.

"My name is Grant Thompson," Robert's lawyer announced to the intake guard. "I represent Robert Holden, and I'd like to see my client, please."

"Do you have identification with you?" the guard asked, eyeing Mr. Thompson with alertness.

"Of course." He presented his lawyer's license and business card.

The guard photocopied both, logged him in as a visitor, asked him to sign in, and led him to Robert's cell. Another guard lingered nearby.

What Grant saw when he reached the locked space, enforced with iron bars, troubled him greatly. Crumbled into a pitiable ball in one corner of the barren place of confinement sat Robert, looking decidedly feeble. Quivering like crazy, the shabby blanket was insufficient to warm his fragile body, and his mien evidenced great anxiety and mental strain.

"Bring me some hot water, or coffee, whatever you have. *Now!* This man's in bad shape," Grant yelled.

A cup of steaming water arrived in a short time, and Grant helped Robert up and onto the bench and insisted he sip the warm beverage.

"Have you eaten anything, Robert?"

"Not hungry."

"You must eat to stay strong to fight this—for you, and for Mae. I promised her I'd take care of you." Grant again hailed the guard, this time demanding some hot soup and a sandwich.

"Kitchen's closed, but I'll see what I can find."

Ten minutes later, the guard returned, tray in hand. He had microwaved a bowl of overly-diluted tomato soup, and thrown a slice of cheese onto a piece of white bread. A cup of steaming instant coffee accompanied the meager morsels. Grant thanked him and sat next to Robert, forcing him to finish every bit of the unappetizing food.

"Now that's better, isn't it, my friend?" Grant asked. "You must keep up your strength. I'm here to talk with you and help you in any way I can."

"Thank you, Grant. I appreciate it more than you know," Robert mumbled, as if it took too much effort to speak audibly.

When Attorney Thompson looked at his client with considered interest, a monstrous wave of sympathy washed over him. Without question, Robert was in dire straits. "As your attorney, I must ask you if there's any truth whatsoever to the charge leveled against you. And before you answer, I will caution you to tell me the whole truth. I must know *everything* there is to know, if I'm to help you."

"Get me out of here. Mae needs me at home. She does not do well without me. I am innocent. Get me out. I must get home to Mae. I've done nothing wrong." Robert prattled on in a low monotone, panic evident in his demeanor, failing to mention that he did not feel at all well.

"I must ask you again, as my client. Is there any truth at all to the charge made against you? Please answer my question, Robert."

"No, there is not. I've said that all along. Why do you doubt me? Why do you ask me again?"

"I'm sorry, Robert. But I had to clear that up once and for all before we could proceed any further. I want you to think hard, my friend. What are we missing here? Do you know *anything* about this possession of stolen property charge that would be of help to the police? Anything at all?"

Robert shut his eyes and recoiled, exhaustion evident. "Nothing. Nothing, I tell you."

"They're talking about emeralds stolen from the Aztec artifact you recently appraised for Claire Caswell and Gaston Lombard. During the search of your business today, the green gems surfaced in the red leather chair in the lobby. And they're also talking about the brutal murder of a David Post approximately forty years ago. Serious stuff, Robert. I spoke with Mr. Lombard after Mae told me you'd been arrested, and, right now, it seems they're building a fairly good case against you. It sounds like the charges may be amended to include the importing of stolen antiquities and gemstones with the intent to distribute, and potentially, even *murder*. I want to help you, Robert, but you must think long and hard. I ask you, yet again, what do you know that will help clear this up for the police?"

"Nothing."

"Please be aware, right now all evidence seems to point only to you. There are no other suspects. You are the only one. I must advise you, too, if this is not cleared up quickly, you should retain the services of a *criminal* attorney to defend you. I no longer will be able to represent you in this matter, as I only practice civil law, and you will need the services of a very competent criminal lawyer if this continues."

"Don't you *know*, I've been preoccupied with thoughts of nothing else since Gaston Lombard walked into my office and announced his visit had to do with official business. I've not done what they're accusing me of doing. Make no mistake about it. I am innocent."

"Well, this certainly has become a dreadful situation, and I would strongly encourage you to continue to search your mind, to figure out why all roads seem to be leading to you. Who would want to frame you, if that's the case? And who would have the ability to do so? You'd better come up with some answers, my friend, some plausible explanations…and quickly. Please, Robert, the proverbial ball's in your court. Give me something to work with. Anything."

"I'll try…." He seemed to be searching his mind for something to provide a flicker of light and hope in the darkness, however faint.

"I must leave now, but call me anytime if you want to talk—night or day. I mean it. *Any time*. And I, too, will try to make some sense of it all. Goodnight, Robert. And try to get a good night's sleep, if possible, so you'll be able to fight this thing. Remember, Mae needs you. I'll call you in the morning."

He embraced Robert, called the guard to let him out, and began to walk away, but turned back. "If *anything* comes to mind, no matter how trivial it may seem to you, let me know at once. Your future may depend on it. Scroll through your memory bank and see what you come up with. There has to be something. And I'll phone Mae tonight and make sure she's okay."

"I'll do my best. Take care of my wife, Grant." He wore a dejected face.

"Are you feeling all right, Robert?"

"I'll be fine once I'm out of here. There's no place like home and that's where I should be." The look of utter discouragement, fixed on Robert's uncharacteristically pale and drawn face, stayed imprinted in Grant Thompson's mind all the way home.

Unbeknownst to Grant at that time, Claire had already taken care of Mae. She'd called her mother and asked her to go to be with Mrs. Holden. After hearing that Robert had been arrested, and Mae needed her, Abbey had asked no further questions. She'd driven directly to the Holden residence.

Robert had used his one allowable phone call to reach Claire, prior to the visit from his attorney, and she arrived at the jail just after Grant Thompson departed. Introducing herself to the guard on duty, she produced identification, and voiced her stated intention to visit Robert Holden. As Robert was permitted one visitor per day, in addition to counsel, she would be allowed a short time with him. After the proper procedures were followed, the guard led her to the cell.

Relieved to see her, Robert reached out and grasped her hands, holding on tightly, as if afraid to let go. He wanted to talk without his attorney being present, and the guard nodded affirmatively to Claire, acknowledging he had heard the request.

"Robert, Mom went over to stay with Mae. She's in good hands and you don't have to worry about her. How are *you* holding up?"

"Child. Child. I have not done the terrible things they say I have. You believe me, don't you? Help me." Marked hopelessness occupied his worn-out face.

Knowing time was of the essence, and would run out all too quickly, she talked fast, asking specific and key questions relating both to events many years ago, when David Post was still alive, and also to recent happenings. Sprinting through the questions with lightning speed, she listened carefully to each of his answers, observing from time to time that he seemed to pause, as if recalling.

"Life is full of surprises, isn't it, child? Sometimes you win…other times you lose. Perhaps this is my time to lose. I guess whatever will be, will be."

What a strange, unexpected and somewhat distasteful attitude sprang forth without warning in Robert. It seemed wholly inappropriate under the circumstances.

"Listen to me, Robert. Tell me, who else should we be looking at? I need an answer."

Suddenly and unpredictably, he leaped to his feet, a renewed energy seeming to take hold. He walked a few steps away from her, and then whirled around, wildly. "Harry Hartmann…. It must be Harry Hartmann…my business partner. It was staring me in the face the whole time. I just didn't see it. I *refused* to. Harry knew George James. They did business together years ago—often without my involvement. But since Harry and I always associated with each other, many people couldn't keep the two of us straight. Harry is the expert in Aztec artifacts, and he's the one who examined your piece and told me it had no real value. I never questioned his analysis, nor would I. He's been my right arm—my other half—in business for decades now, and has always been one of the most honorable people I know. I trust him completely. In fact, I would have trusted him with my life…or Mae's. But there's no other answer…."

His thoughts drifted, briefly, and then he continued, on course. "Yes. Yes. It must be Harry Hartmann. He had access to your artifact, and could have removed the emeralds and hidden them in our lobby chair. Oh. I've been so blind. So blind." He dropped onto the bench, emotionally spent.

As Claire watched him, he wrapped his arms around his torso and bent over, crippled with riveting pain.

"Robert. What is it? What's wrong? Let me call for a doctor."

"No! It's merely stress making sure I know it's there."

Attempting to fit all pieces back together in her mind while she comforted him, she knew they had to question Harry Hartmann immediately. For the first time, the sequence of events were starting to make more sense to her. Why had they all missed it? She looked kindly at Robert, and noticed the slightest sense of relief fighting boldly to surface and penetrate his tired and worn-down face. He hugged her tightly. With tears in his eyes, he looked childlike.

"I must leave. It is imperative you speak to Gaston at once. I'll call him." She motioned for the guard to let her out. "Hang in there, Robert. We'll figure this out."

Reaching the entranceway, she pulled out her cell phone and called Guy. "Honey, I'm at the jail and I just finished talking with Robert. This case has taken quite a turn and you'll want to get over here as quickly as you can."

"On my way. Sit tight." He asked no questions.

Claire waited anxiously for him to arrive, as Robert remained locked in his cell, contorted in physical pain. Twenty-five minutes later, Guy walked through the doorway.

"You'd better go in and talk to Robert," Claire said.

"What's going on?"

"I want him to tell you. Things are seldom as they seem."

42

GUY APPROACHED THE front desk and identified himself to the guard as Gaston Lombard, State Attorney prosecuting the Robert Holden case. He asked to spend a few minutes with Robert, and extended his business card.

"You need no introduction, Mr. Lombard. It's a pleasure to make your acquaintance. I do need your autograph here, though." He extended the visitor's book his way. "Mr. Holden's been a popular man tonight."

Responding with a courteous smile and nod of the head, Guy signed in and followed the guard to Robert's cell.

Robert perked up when he saw Guy Lombard, who explained he had the right to have his attorney present when they spoke, a right which Robert waived. Guy called the guard over to witness the waiver. Within minutes, Robert filled the state attorney in on all details he could remember concerning Harry Hartmann. Not long after Guy had entered the cell, he left it, and returned to the lobby.

"Come on, Claire. We've got some work to do. I'll meet you at home."

En route, Guy rapidly reviewed the case in his mind, concluding that Harry Hartmann needed to be questioned at once. He flipped open his cell phone and called the police captain on night duty at police headquarters.

"What can I do for you this evening, Mr. Lombard?" Captain Miller asked.

"We've got a potential break in the Holden case. I want you to pick up Harry Hartmann at his home and bring him in for questioning. As soon as you can. And give me a call when you have him, will you? He lives over on Collins Avenue in a condominium—57th and Collins, I believe. But you'll want to check on the exact address first. That's Harold Hartmann. Somewhere I think I've seen his middle name as Astor. Harold Astor Hartmann keeps sticking in my mind. Check it out."

"Consider it done, Mr. Lombard. How does he work into this Holden case?"

"I'm not certain, yet, but I may be able to tell you sooner as opposed to later. Get him as fast as you can, will you, captain?"

"Will do, Mr. Lombard. And I'll call you when we have him. Give me your cell number."

AT HOME, Guy paced back and forth on the balcony, a lighted cigar in his hand, waiting for the call-back. Claire watched him, and knew the pressure was building to a climax. She understood that chances were high a turnaround in the case was imminent. Yet her inner voice flashed a warning of trouble looming on the horizon. She didn't know the source.

Forty-five minutes later, Guy's cell phone rang.

"Mr. Lombard, Captain Miller here. We're out at the Hartmann residence, and I'm afraid it's not a pretty scene. We have an apparent suicide on our hands. Harold Hartmann killed himself with a .38 to the head. Lots of blood. Real ugly."

"I don't know what to say...none of us could have predicted...."

"Yeah. That's usually the case, isn't it? The place smells as if he guzzled a king's ransom in brandy before he pulled the trigger and dropped into a tarn of his own blood. So my guess would be he probably hit a pretty numb stage before he did it. But you'll want to hear this. He left a lengthy suicide note that looks like a full, signed confession of criminal activities. It's been bagged and marked as evidence, and I'll take it back to headquarters as soon as we photograph the scene, dust the place for prints, and get the body out of here. Medical Examiner's on his way. He'll do a prelim, and then he and his assistant will transport the body to his office for a full examination and report. You know the routine. Looks like he's been dead only an hour or two. Blood looks fresh. Definitely appears he acted alone on this. No real doubt about it. We had to break the front door down, chain and all, and the back door was also locked and chained. But as I said, we'll dust for other prints just the same."

"Thanks, captain. Your job cannot be an easy one tonight."

"No, sir. Sorry about the news, Mr. Lombard. These are never easy calls to make. And rest assured, we'll look around to make certain there's no evidence to indicate anyone else could be involved in this thing...but that doesn't seem to be the case. The note will be available for you to read in about an hour or so at my office."

"Thanks again, Captain Miller. Sorry you had to walk in on that. I had no idea...."

"Certainly understandable."

"Oh, and one more thing. Get *his* prints, will you, and a saliva swab for a DNA fingerprint? And captain, do you see a computer and printer around there?

"Both. There's a laptop sitting here on the desk."

"Bag it and bring it in, will you? And see if you can obtain a sample of the print from the printer. And what about a red crayon? See any of those laying around?"

"How did you know? There's one right here—in plain sight—near the laptop. I'll bag it and bring it along. Anything else?"

"Do you see a stack of business-sized envelopes anywhere?"

"As a matter of fact, I do. Right next to a stack of plain paper."

"Grab the envelopes, and paper, too. We'd like to look at them"

"No problem. They'll all be ready and waiting for you at the station house."

Guy hung up, flashed Claire a stunned look, and summarized the call.

Some people become very rich as the result of committing fraud, or theft, or even murder, she thought to herself, but almost always it comes with a high price tag in the end. The unanticipated and desperate act of Hartmann bore that out. Her mind flashed back to the cocktail holiday bash they'd attended at Harry's swanky condo on Collins Avenue, on Miami Beach, two years earlier. She again recalled the lavish and extravagant antiques furnishing his place—something that had always stood out in her mind thereafter, whenever she heard the name, Harry Hartmann. But being in the antiques business, it hadn't seemed *that* over the top. Now, she questioned just how much money George James and Harry Hartmann had together raked in illegally. Maybe his last note would provide answers to the niggling questions, and shed light on the big picture, as well as fill in the curious details.

A widower for more than a decade, Harry had no living relatives—Robert and Mae being the only real "family" he had. And now, after all Robert had been through, they'd have to tell him that Harry, the man so much like a brother to him, had confessed to being a criminal, and had taken his own life.

The evening was winding down. So much had changed in such a short time. How had they missed it? How had Harry Hartmann escaped scrutiny? Biding their time for an hour, they drove to the police station in great disquiet, unsure of what to expect from Harry's last script. Captain Miller greeted them, handed over the multi-paged note, and informed them he had dusted the pages for fingerprints, confirming that *only* Hartmann's prints were present. In fact, his prints alone covered the paper, envelopes, laptop, red crayon, brandy bottle, and the gun. Miller also confirmed they had been unable to lift

DNA from either envelope sent to Claire, as they had all suspected. He agreed, however, to deliver Hartmann's saliva sample to the Medical Examiner early Monday morning, in case that office needed Hartmann's DNA fingerprinting for any reason. Hartmann's printer sample matched the style and font size of the two threatening letters sent to Claire, and the paper and envelopes used to create the written threats matched those taken from Harry's condo. That meant Harry did not lick the envelopes to seal them, but rather used another method to wet the seals. Also, they had concluded he probably wore gloves when he prepared the threatening writings and put them into the envelopes, as none of his prints—even partial—could be lifted from those items, or from the note left at the condo door.

"I just realized Harry would have had access to our home address and unlisted phone number through Robert Holden's records—the Rolodex of friends and clients he kept at the office," Claire said. "That explains a lot."

"Of course," Guy said. "Captain Miller, do you have a room we can use? To read this?"

"I'd also like to look at the envelopes you brought back," Claire said.

"Sure, Ms. Caswell, but first let me tell you, we already analyzed the stains we found on the entire stack. It was the same substance we found on the envelopes sent to you. Turned out to be brandy."

"That's what caused the stains? Brandy?" Claire asked. "Makes sense, now."

"Yeah. Must have been his drink of choice. He had a lot of it stashed in his condo. The place reeked of it."

"You answered my question on the envelopes, captain," Claire said. "I no longer need to look at them."

He pointed to a statement room. "Go in there, if you'd like. I also made a copy of it to take with you. For whatever it's worth, I took a fast read through it before you got here. It's detailed, and I think it's going to answer a lot of your questions."

"Thank you, captain. You've certainly been a great help to us," Claire said.

He smiled at her. "Anything for Claire Caswell and Gaston Lombard. It's our pleasure."

Guy thanked him.

They walked to the room, pulled the door closed behind them, and sat down on the hard, wooden chairs. Guy removed the several pages from the evidence folder and read the written confession aloud, in its entirety. As Claire listened with fervent awareness, she realized Harry had answered many of the unanswered questions surrounding the case on those several sheets of paper. A half hour later, they emerged from the room, persuaded beyond a doubt that Harry Hartmann and George James, without the participation of Robert Holden, had together committed all of the crimes.

The confession, exhaustive and highly-detailed in nature, flawlessly depicted a series of events: his collusion with James to engage in a smuggler's dream—to import the priceless Aztec artifacts lifted from the Mexican museum (and stuffed with raw emeralds by the thieves prior to shipment); his agreement with James to split equally all profits from the sale of same to private collectors and unscrupulous jewelers on the black market or to unknowing legitimate jewelers; the irreversible *obstacle in the plan* that occurred when David Post, the *nosy* employee of George James, overheard a conversation James had with Hartmann concerning the smuggling arrangements, and their fear that he may blow the whistle and call an abrupt halt to their elaborately simple chance for incredible wealth plan—a plan that could have provided both James and Hartmann more money than either would have known what do with; how George had been forced to *take care of* the oh-so-proper Mr. Post before he could finger them or, worse yet, extort money in exchange for his silence; how Hartmann never knew the method of Mr. Post's demise, yet he became aware that Mr. Post had disappeared suddenly and permanently; and how Hartmann lived safely in his spinelessness, never mentioning the disappearance to anyone all these years.

And the note went on to clarify that Robert had, so innocently, asked him recently to appraise the artifact found in the Caribbean by Claire and Gaston, and had trusted his assessment so completely, so unquestioningly. Recognizing the piece immediately as the third missing Aztec idol, but never telling Robert what it was, Harry removed its hidden contents, and the cabochon emerald eyes, meticulously repairing the intrusions and replacing the fabulous moving eye stones with precious jade—like the originals—and then hid the gemstones in small pouches in the red leather chair in the lobby of the shop.

But once again fate had done him no favors, and this time his dearest friend, Robert Holden, had been arrested in his stead and he could not live with that. Only one option remained.

He'd concluded the note by saying he decided to leave this world as a coward, but by choice, knowing he could not change what he had done, nor could he survive life in prison. He left everything he owned to Robert and Mae Holden. He dated the confession, and signed it, "Harold Astor Hartmann."

A final notation, under his signature, indicated that he had sent the threatening letters, made the phone calls, left the note on the door mat, and even tried to scare Claire Caswell off the case by nearly side-swiping her car. Once he heard she'd been assigned to the case, he knew she would get to the bottom of it, eventually exposing his criminal past. He had heard Robert speak of her methodical and overly competent sleuthing abilities too many times. He apologized for terrorizing her, and admitted he never planned to actually hurt her, acknowledging the near-miss car collision as being a little too close for comfort.

"The question of whether this writing constitutes a legally-binding will becomes an issue for a court-of-law to decide," Guy said. "But for our purposes, it's a valid and signed suicide note confession, and it appears to let Robert Holden completely off the hook. I'm convinced."

"Yeah. It's ironic, isn't it, how the ancient artifact and the skeleton ended up entangled in the same mysterious web, after all. The odds must be a million to one...."

"Oh, I think it's safe to say, a *trillion* to one."

At that moment, Claire recalled Joseph talking about the "wheels of life" and saying how fate sometimes intervenes to steer things in a certain direction. She could almost hear his very voice.

NEXT ON the agenda came the release from incarceration of Robert Holden. And despite the clock striking half-past midnight, they decided he'd do better at home that night in his own bed. Never before had driving to a jail been joyous. Upon arriving, Claire and Guy identified themselves to the replacement guard.

"I'd like Mr. Holden released at once," Guy said. The charges are being dropped."

"Now? At this late hour? Or should I say *early* hour? Highly unusual, but whatever you say, Mr. Lombard. You're the boss. Please sign these release authorization forms and I'm off the hook. I'll have your Mr. Holden out of here in a flash—just as soon as I can rouse him and gather up his belongings."

Guy scribbled, "Attorney Gaston Lombard," on the forms.

"Seems like a decent old chap to me," the guard said. Five minutes later, he returned with an exhausted Robert Holden, now a free man. Robert walked sleepily toward Claire, clutching tightly a brown paper bag containing his personal effects. He looked befuddled.

"We're taking you home, Robert," Claire said. "We'll explain in the car."

As they walked Robert from the jailhouse, a nagging suspicion invaded Claire's thoughts, and remained there.

43

CLIMBING INTO GUY'S sedan, the threesome traveled the route to Robert's home. Along the way, Robert phoned his wife to let her know what had occurred, so she would not be startled or frightened when they arrived at the house. When he hung up, the floodgates opened and Robert wept. The past couple of days had been an emotional roller-coaster, and tonight, at last, the ride had come to a screeching halt, and he had jumped off, hopefully never to climb aboard again.

"Robert, there is no easy way to tell you this, and there couldn't be a worse time," Guy said. "When the police went to Harry's home this evening, to pick him up for questioning, they found him…dead. He took his own life, Robert. I'm sorry to be the bearer of that terrible news."

Initially, Robert could not respond. Words built up within him, but they would not come out, no matter how hard he tried to speak. He wept considerably more, and then murmurings sprang forth. "Thank you…for telling me…for letting me know. Bad news…this is *very* bad news."

"Things don't always turn out the way they should, or the way we think they will, Robert," Claire said. "Sometimes people do things you'd never imagine they're capable of." She turned in her seat and studied him.

"Such wisdom…from a child. Now I must thank you both for helping to free me from that hellish place, from the chill…. I didn't expect to make it through the night. Mae will be happy to have me back with her."

"If you'd like to rest your eyes until we get to your house, go ahead," Claire said. She could see the weariness on his face. "We'll wake you when we get there."

Within minutes, labored breathing could be heard emanating from the back seat, and they realized that sleep had already overtaken his compromised body. Pulling up to the Holden residence, Claire touched Robert gently on the arm to awaken him. He could barely open his eyes, so they each held one of his arms and guided him, steadily, up the walkway.

Abbey opened the front door, and Mae rushed past her, throwing her arms around the weakened Robert, pulling him close, holding on tightly, unwilling to let go. Together, Robert and Mae ambled inside, as if fused into one.

Robert looked at Claire through partially-opened eyes. "Thank you…thank you for your steadfast faith in me, child. I'll never forget it. I knew I could count on you." Kissing her softly on both cheeks, he then turned his attention to Guy. "And thank you, counselor, for everything." He shook Guy's hand, warmly. Next he hugged Abbey. "I owe you so much."

"Excuse us, please," Mae said, taking control. "I need to get this man to bed. He's been through the mill." She led the more-asleep-than-awake Robert from the crowded entryway down the hall to their awaiting bedroom, and helped him into his night clothes. He fell back on the bed, in silence, and Mae covered him with a mohair blanket before kissing his forehead tenderly. "Sleep well, my prince," she said. "You're home now, and you're not leaving again."

When she returned to the others, Guy informed her and Abbey of the evening's strange turn of events, including the suicide of Harry Hartmann.

Mae shook her head in disbelief. "Oh, no. I can't believe it!" She hung her head as memories of Harry rushed through her mind. What a bittersweet situation the evening had produced—a new beginning for Robert, but a heart-rending ending for their dear friend, Harry Hartmann.

They bid each other farewell, leaving Mae to be alone with Robert, and her sorrow. Everything Mae had counted on seemed to be in flux. The beautiful world she and Robert had shared for so long appeared to be unraveling before her eyes. She slipped out of her robe and slippers, turned off the lights, and slid in, unobtrusively, beside him, cupping within the form of his familiar body and scent. She laid in the darkness, content, listening to the slow and rhythmic breathing of the man she had loved more than fifty years, comforted in the safety of his closeness. "We are two of the lucky ones," she whispered. "We have each other."

She felt an almost undetectable squeeze around her middle, and with the starlight's illumination slipping through the blinds, she could see the slightest smile on Robert's sleeping face as she turned to look at him. Satisfied that the truth, at last, had come out, Mae rested effortlessly—relief embracing her total being and allowing for much-needed rest. It meant everything to her that Robert no longer would be the target of a criminal investigation. At last he, too, could sleep in absolute peace the remainder of that night and for the rest of his life, his adoring bride by his side—even though his life would soon be cut short.

Sadly, Robert was dying. Diagnosed with pancreatic cancer two months earlier, doctors had given him only a short time to live. Mae had shared the prognosis with Abbey that night and made her promise not to tell anyone, including Claire, as Robert wanted it that way. He wished for no sympathy—only to live life as normally as possible...to the end.

Claire thanked her mom for staying with Mae, and insisted she spend the night at their place because of the lateness of the hour.

Noticing Claire seemed unusually preoccupied, Guy watched her closely as they prepared for bed. "What is it, my beauty? I would think you'd feel great that Harry Hartmann ended up being the bad guy—and not Robert. So tell me, will you? What's bothering you? The cogs in that pretty head of yours are turning fast. I can feel it."

"I don't want to talk about it. Not now."

"Maybe we *should* talk about it."

"I have an unsettling feeling, but it's not definable in words—not yet, anyway. It might be nothing."

"You don't have doubts about Robert's part in all of this, do you, Claire? Because if you do, we should talk it out."

She didn't answer, and she slept uncomfortably that night, waking every hour or two, troubled by what she did not know.

LATER THAT morning, Robert awoke, and found Mae in the kitchen busily preparing a hot breakfast.

"My love, I have something to tell you," he said. "Please, sit down."

The seriousness in his tone frightened her. "What *is* it, Robert?"

He looked her squarely in the eyes. "Harry took the fall for *me*. To protect *us*. How do I live with that?"

"*What*?" Her mouth dropped open and she gaped at him, sickened by the revelation. "I don't understand."

"Harry was the one involved in the initial smuggling attempt with George James so many years ago. I knew about his plan, but never said a word to anyone. He always said he owed me—for going along with it and not exposing him. And George James arranged for or committed the murder of David Post. I also knew about that, and never said a word to anyone. I protected James—and, thereby, Harry. But *I* was the one who stole the emeralds from the artifact Claire and Guy found on the island, and I lied to them about its value. I, alone, did that. I recognized the piece immediately when they first showed it to me, and knew about the hidden contents deep within the magnificent piece, and of the great value of its mesmerizing eyes.

"I finally admitted to Harry what I'd done, after the fact, and told him where I'd hidden the green stones, and I promised to cut him in on the profits, once all the goods could be dumped for huge profits, that is. But things started to heat up. That's when Harry told me he'd take care of it for me—again, that he owed me. I had *no idea* what he planned to do. No idea, whatsoever. I only pointed the investigation in his direction for the sake of confusion—to throw some reasonable doubt into the pot, so they'd look to someone else besides me as a possible suspect—so I could get out of that hideous jail cell, where I most surely would have died. You understand what I had to do, don't you, Mae?"

"God, help us both." She looked upward, and then held Robert in her arms.

"I'm dying, Mae. I did it for you, so you'd never have to worry about money when I left this earth and could no longer care for you. I couldn't bear to leave you in need of anything. You understand, don't you? After careful thought, I decided I loved you more than I loved respect and a good name. But Harry. This all became very confusing. I never thought anyone would figure out that I removed the gemstones or substituted the eyes. I thought no one would be the wiser, and no one would get hurt. I never dreamed I'd be arrested. My plan went horribly awry. I pointed the finger at Harry to cause uncertainty with Claire and Gaston—to jumble up the investigation—to divert their attention from me. And then Harry killed himself to cover for me. Oh, Mae, he didn't know that I'm dying. I never told him." He hung his head. "My actions have caused a great wrong that's not reversible."

Mae thought quickly. "Hush now, Robert. Hush. It's over. There's nothing you can do to change what's happened. I never want you to repeat this nonsense to anyone. Understand? Those emeralds are with the police now, you're home with me, and that's where you're going to stay. Harry is gone, and you cannot bring him back. He made decisions of his own that you could not control. I don't want to hear another word about it."

Robert stared off into the distance. "I even fooled Claire."

"Hush, now. Just hush," she repeated. "Don't think any more about it. This will be our secret."

He nodded, reluctantly, as the face of Harry Hartmann, his longtime friend, haunted his conscience—as it would until his last day on earth.

CLAIRE AWOKE in a strange mood. Disconcerting thoughts regarding Robert's involvement and Harry's confession remained with her, weighing heavily on her mind and soul. The little voice within her—the one she paid close attention to—would remind her for a long time to come that the whole truth had not surfaced in this investigation. Robert had not come clean. She knew it. Whatever the secret, it would remain forever hidden, as no proof of his wrongdoing existed.

Abbey prepared breakfast and the three of them ate it out on the balcony, enjoying the balmy Florida air and watching the many boats in the channel. Then, after Claire and Guy promised to have dinner with her and Don one night soon, Guy drove Abbey to her car, parked in front of the Holden residence, and returned home to the condo.

Claire called LuVasse on his cell number to fill him in on the previous night's happenings, including the confession and suicide of Harry Hartmann, and to let him know the murder of David Post was solved. Sadly, no one remained alive to prosecute for his killing.

LuVasse was amazed and surprised by the resolution and thanked Claire, and Guy, for a "job well done." He said he looked forward to seeing her back at work the following morning, and agreed to call Sergeant Massey at his home to bring him up to speed on the unexpected and startling end to the mysterious case.

But first, LuVasse decided to call the press to beat Massey to the punch—for LuVasse had drawn his own conclusion that it was none other than the impertinent Sergeant who had leaked information and stories to the tip-lines all along. This time, Sergeant Massey would not steal the glory.

Guy phoned the head of his office, as well, to inform him of the unforeseen results of their investigation. Tomorrow, they'd call Edmond Penwright, Detective Chief Inspector Mollitt at Scotland Yard, and Roman, to share the staggering news.

That evening, the major news channels broke the story that the murderer of the skeletal victim—found buried at the dig site in Miami Shores—had been identified, promising the full and complete story on "tomorrow's news."

Claire felt unspeakable comfort that the threats against her would now stop.

Monday morning

THINGS MOVED fast, starting bright and early Monday morning. With all evidence combined, plus Harry Hartmann's fingerprints everywhere—including the signed confession note, and the .38 caliber suicide weapon registered to Harold Astor Hartmann, the police considered Harry Hartmann's death a confirmed suicide, and the murder of David Post and the recent theft of emeralds from the artifact solved, as well. With George James and Harry Hartman both deceased, the Miami-Dade State Attorney's Office had no one to prosecute in the matter, so the case would now, officially, be closed—after completing the lengthy, obligatory paperwork, of course. Hartmann's signed confession would be incorporated into the investigative file, together with the police and Medical Examiner's findings on his demise, expert fingerprinting comparisons, and Claire and Guy's final, in-depth summation of the case, copious in every detail.

Resolving the age-old mystery had predictably triggered the immediate interest of the media and other entities. Claire and Guy's work phones began to ring off the hook with requests for their stories and personal interviews. The police held a press conference to curb the appetites of the intensely eager reporters from local and national news channels, prime-time networks, and newspapers and magazines. The story captured the public's attention for days to come.

The astonishing outcome of the investigation made headlines in London, too, where Edmond Penwright agreed to countless interviews regarding his participation in the age-old investigation. CNN and FOX News networks covered the case as a "feature news item," and *60 Minutes* came forward expressing interest in doing an upcoming segment on this *case-of-a-lifetime*, interviewing the investigators that brought it to closure.

When a well-known and respected journalist called, promising a factual accounting for all to read—a book that would expose the truth concerning the lives of Joseph and David Posnick—Claire and Guy signed the contract. Claire's last words to Joseph constituted a promise—"we will be your witnesses"—to keep his story alive, and she intended to do just that, insisting, up-front, that all proceeds earned from the sale of the biography would be donated to a charity for Holocaust survivors.

Voracious interest in the case, on the part of the public, would be insatiable for a time, and then, as always, it would wane once another breaking story hit the news. This established pattern proved the cycle of life, time and again. That in mind, Guy and Claire committed to numerous interviews, always with reputable correspondents, to get the remarkable story out while it remained hot, as it needed to be heard.

The local FBI office agreed to transfer the artifact back to the museum it had been taken from, where it would hold its rightful place on a shelf next to the other two, and the Miami-Dade Police Department and the FBI agreed to cooperate fully with the Mexican authorities, should they desire to re-open the case. Now a very old theft, however, it remained doubtful that any interest would be generated. And since the emeralds had never been reported stolen, an assumption could be made that their owner had been a co-conspirator in the botched smuggling plot, and, therefore, would never come forward to claim the lovely green stones. In all likelihood, those parts of the story would always remain a mystery. Eventually, the enforcement agencies would mutually decide on the disposition of the precious emeralds.

Claire and Guy's respective offices, duly impressed that the two of them had cracked the cold case, now openly admitted the wagers that had been placed.

Guy made a date with Claire, and over lunch they discussed an important loose end to tie up—the proper burial of David Posnick's remains. They agreed to place a call to Edmond and with his help arrange to have David Post's remains flown to London, where he would be laid to rest beside his brother, Joseph.

"You did a remarkable job on this case," Guy said, looking at Claire with that strange look she had not seen in quite a while.

"Why, thank you, counselor, for the compliment. But I must make a correction…. *We* did a remarkable job, *together*, on this case."

"All I know is that your work highly impressed me, my beauty. And we can't forget about the trials of Lawden and McDonald. They're coming up soon. You helped nab them, too."

ROBERT ASKED Mae to close her eyes and open her hand. She did as he asked, and he dropped a single, green, uncut stone in her palm.

"That's for you, Mae. I kept one separate from the rest, and I can't turn it over to the authorities now."

44

THAT EVENING, GUY surprised Claire by taking her to her absolute favorite place for dinner—the famous Joe's Stone Crab Restaurant in South Beach. They had important things to discuss, so he picked a special place.

Over the delightful dinner, the two of them talked about their island vacation in the Caribbean, the adventure of finding the hidden relic, and its seemingly implausible connection to the mysterious murder investigation they had found themselves pulled into in Miami.

"Do you think it's safe to assume the intruder who ransacked the condo probably saw us go in and out of the cave and followed us home? And then waited until we left that evening to break in and look around for whatever we may have found and taken with us?" Guy asked.

"I think there could be no other plausible explanation. Especially since nothing was missing."

"That's my reasoning, too."

"What about the bald-headed man with the handlebar mustache, the one you saw staring at us from across the way on New Year's Eve? Will we ever figure that one out?" Claire chuckled.

"Doggone it! I forgot to tell you. I had a copy of the *Cayman Compass* in my briefcase, one I had taken back with us to read on the plane, and never got to, and I pulled it out at the office one of the days I went in to do catch-up work. You won't believe this, but when I opened it to the second page, I saw a photo of him, attached to an article talking about how the island's Minister of Tourism watches tourists at all the local restaurants—along Seven Mile Beach and elsewhere—to make sure they're having a good time on the island. That's all it was, Claire. The Tourism Minister wanted to make sure we were enjoying ourselves on his island."

"Unbelievable!" She laughed. "Now it makes sense why the police officer—the one who wrote up the ransacking report, held back a smile when you described the man. He *knew* immediately that you were describing the Tourism Minister. He just didn't tell us."

Together, they broke into heartfelt laughter. Another mystery solved.

"And the coins we found with the artifact?" Claire asked. "I've been thinking about those, too. I make a motion we send them back to the island, to be displayed at the Cayman Islands National Museum in Georgetown."

"Or we could keep them as a souvenir of our great adventure," he said. "We'll have to find out if they have any value. If they do, we'll turn them over to the museum."

"I've wondered, also," she said, "why the smuggler never returned for the artifact he so carefully concealed in that cave. Maybe he died before he could get back to it."

"It's also quite possible he couldn't find the right cave if he did return. It's a convoluted configuration down there."

"Don't remind me. I shudder just thinking about it," she said. "I guess we'll never know for sure why the smuggler didn't return for it. But without that relic, chances are good we'd never have put it all together. So it was a good thing. Maybe, destiny."

"I've thought of another option. Perhaps the pirate ghosts got him," Guy said, a serious look appearing on his face. When Claire looked at him as if he'd lost it, he began to chuckle. "Just kidding! I thought a little pirate humor might be in order."

Conversation then turned to work.

Each had been assigned new cases for investigation that morning; yet they knew regular cases would somehow seem mundane compared to the one they'd just closed. With several extraordinary breaks, and clever detective work, they'd managed to solve a virtually unsolvable case. And now they were itching for a change.

"My beauty, why don't we open the private investigation firm we've dreamed about? Soon," Guy said.

"Funny, I thought about suggesting the very same thing to you tonight over dinner."

"Great minds think alike! Then it's a deal. To us, and our future." He lifted his glass of wine to meet hers in a toast, and they smiled warmly at each other, thrilled at the prospect. They agreed to give one-month termination notices at their respective places of employment the following day. It was time to strike out on their own, and they'd work out of their home until a suitable office location could be secured.

"Let's call our new firm *Lombard and Caswell, Private Investigations*," Guy suggested.

"Or *Caswell and Lombard, Private Investigations*," Claire suggested.

Renewed courage surged through Guy. There would never be a more perfect moment.

"Why not *Lombard and Lombard, Private Investigations*?" Guy proposed. He pulled the ring from his pocket and held it in his hand, awaiting her answer.

"What?" Claire's heart leapt into her throat.

His gaze was intense. "How does *Lombard and Lombard* sound to you?"

Claire blinked. He'd done it. With his usual flair, he'd just asked her the question she'd been afraid to hear. Now she had to answer.

As for man, his days *are* as grass: as a flower of the field, so he flourisheth.

For the wind passeth over it, and it is gone; and the place thereof shall know it no more.

Psalm 103:15,16